THE
SARACEN
STORM

A NOVEL OF THE MOORISH INVASION OF SPAIN

J.M. NUNEZ

Author's Note

Though based on historical figures and events, The Saracen
Storm is a work of fiction. Most of the characters and events
are the products of the author's imagination and are by no
means to be considered or relied upon as historical fact.

ISBN/ISMN 978-1-9992197-0-3

For my sister, Carmen.

Death is the inevitable close of every man's life, however much he tries to save it by skulking in some obscure corners; but the truly brave should not hesitate to draw the sword on all honourable occasions, armed with fair hopes of success, and, whatever may be the results, to bear with resignation the will of Providence.

—Dionysius

PROLOGUE

IT IS THE close of the seventh century, some three hundred years after the fall of the Roman Empire. Much of Western Europe has slid into the Dark Ages. The centralized systems that once defined Roman order, such as trade and commerce, art and literature, systematic record keeping, and more importantly, the rule of law, have all but disappeared.

Brutality has become ingrained in the very fabric of society. Human life holds little value. The punishment for killing a man is oftentimes less than that meted out for stealing a cow. In Gaul, the term 'Carolingian divorce' refers to the act of a lord sending his wife on an errand to the kitchen, only to have her throat slit by the castle's butcher.

Centered in Damascus, the Rashidun and Umayyad Caliphates have conquered the Arabian Peninsula, Persia, Syria, Egypt and all the territories in North Africa that had once been part of the Roman Empire. Driven by religious fervor, their armies are now casting their eyes north, to the underbelly of Europe. Hispania stands in their way.

There, an aging monarch, King Witiza, rules with an iron fist over a system of fiefdoms, presided by a cadre of dukes and barons. And in a rural villa in the northern province of Asturias, in the year 693, a young boy named Pelayo has just lost his mother to illness.

CHAPTER 1

NIGHT WAS FALLING as the two mounted men-at-arms led the eight-year-old boy through the main gates and into the city of Gijón. The storm clouds that had been chasing them since early evening finally caught up to them and rain began spattering down. Pulling up the hoods of their riding cloaks over their heads, the three steered their mounts down one of the alleyways leading toward the heart of the Asturian capital.

As darkness closed in, the glow of oil lamps began spilling out from the shuttered windows. The rain had driven everyone indoors and only a handful of people were walking about. Occasionally the threesome would ride by an alehouse or an inn and the murmur of voices or a peal of laughter would spill out onto the street.

At first Pelayo was wide-eyed as he took in the unfamiliar sights, sounds and smells of the city. But after a time his attention waned, and the long journey began to take its toll on him. Struggling to keep his eyes open, he made a game of trying to guess the nature of the establishments along the road by attempting to interpret the painted signs hanging over their doors. Some, such as those depicting a fish or scissors or a common boot, were easy to figure out. Others, like those portraying a dragon wrapped around a tower or crossed swords over a helmet, left him mystified.

Riding slightly ahead of him, the soldiers turned into a dirt road and headed up a steep hill toward a formidable-looking castle that was barely visible in the gloom. As they approached, a guard up on the watchtower exchanged greetings with the two soldiers, Lucio and Octavio, then ordered the men below him to unbolt the gates.

After riding through the narrow passageway of the gatehouse, Pelayo emerged into a large courtyard now turned into a muddy pond by the rain. Against the wall on his left, between the two circular, crenellated towers, stood several ramshackle sheds and thatched-roofed lean-tos. Abutting the other two walls, incorporating one of the towers, was a large, three-story stone building.

As the soldiers drew their horses to a stop by the building, the light rain turned into a steady downpour.

"We're here," Lucio announced, his voice cutting through the sound of the pelting rain.

Soaked and feeling miserable, Pelayo grabbed his pack and dismounted onto the thick mud. After tying the reins of his mount to a hitching ring on the wall, he followed Lucio and Octavio up the stone steps leading to the main entrance of the building. Lucio held one of the oaken doors open for him and he stepped inside into a large hall lined with stone pillars rising to a vaulted ceiling. Though lit by a row of torches set in iron sconces, most of the cavernous interior lay in shadows.

The soldiers set off at a brisk pace down the hall, the sound of their hobnail sandals echoing through the silence. Pelayo followed them, cowed by the castle's forbidding interior, finding its darkened alcoves alien and vaguely menacing. He had spent his entire life in a villa, surrounded by gardens and sun-drenched terraces overlooking a bay. The prospect of living in this gloomy, foul-smelling place made his heart sink.

At last, the soldiers came to a stop by a door at the far end of the hall. Just as Lucio was raising his fist to knock, an imperious, female voice called out from behind them.

"The Duke is not to be disturbed."

Pelayo turned and saw a woman wearing an embroidered, maroon tunic walking toward them. Her straw-colored hair was bound in two thick braids coiled on each side of her head. She appeared to be a few years older than his mother had been. Despite the woman's elegant attire and striking beauty, her eyes were cold and the gaze she fixed upon him made him feel uncomfortable.

"You may leave the boy with me," the woman told the soldiers.

"Begging your pardon, Doña Izaskun, I have orders to hand the boy over to the Duke himself," Lucio said.

Frown lines appeared on the lady's face. "Did you not understand what I said?"

"Of course, I…forgive me, my lady."

The other soldier, Octavio, tugged on his arm. "Our business here is done," he muttered. "Let's go."

Once the soldiers had left, the woman turned her gaze toward Pelayo and stared at him without speaking.

Pelayo did his best to meet her eyes.

"So," she said slowly. "You're Pelayo."

"Yes, my lady."

"Wherever did you get such a strange name?"

"It's ancient Roman," he said. "It comes from the name Pelagius."

"I see," she said, studying him. "I'm Doña Izaskun, Duke Fáfila's wife."

A hollow feeling spread in the pit of Pelayo's stomach. His mother had never explained to him why it was that his father didn't live with them, but now he understood. Aware of the lady's eyes on him, he did his best to quell his turmoil and bowed as he had been taught. "It is a pleasure to make your acquaintance."

The corners of Izaskun's lips twitched upward in a smile that did not quite reach her eyes. "Was it your mother who taught you such good manners?"

"Yes."

"I must say I'm impressed. I was expecting to meet a little savage."

Pelayo gazed up at her, trying to figure out whether or not her words were meant as a compliment.

"Well," she said. "Heaven knows why my husband has taken it into his head to have you come and live with us, but I suppose we'll have to make the best of it, won't we?"

Pelayo nodded, not knowing what to say.

"We have prepared a room for you in the west tower. No doubt there will be many an eyebrow raised at your sudden appearance. Unfortunately, there doesn't seem to be any way of avoiding this unpleasant situation."

Pelayo said nothing, gazing down at his feet.

Doña Izaskun's brow furrowed as her eyes fixed on the gold medallion peeking out from the open collar of the boy's riding shirt. "Did my husband give you that?" she asked, an edge in her voice.

Pelayo shook his head. "It was my mother's. She gave it to me before she died."

The sound of approaching footsteps diverted Doña Izaskun's attention and she turned to look behind her.

Following her gaze, Pelayo saw a boy with light-colored hair, several years older than himself, walking across the hall toward them.

"Julian dearest, you're just in time to meet…" Doña Izaskun hesitated. "Your half-brother."

The youth's lips curled up in a mirthless smile. "You mean Father's bastard, don't you, Mother?"

Pelayo flushed with shame, the words cutting into him like a knife. He suddenly wished he was back at the villa with Magda and the other servants. He didn't like this woman or her son.

"Come now, Julian, no need to be rude," Doña Izaskun chided him.

"I don't know why the little snot has to come and live with us," Julian said.

Looking pained, Doña Izaskun sighed. "Really, Julian, it's the mother who's to blame, not the boy."

"I don't care. He's here and the whore is not."

Pelayo felt his cheeks grow warm. There was a raven-haired woman in the village that the boys used to whisper about, and he knew the meaning of the word whore. A wave of anger began surging through him, sweeping away his discomfort. His eyes fastened on the older boy, no longer conscious of the forbidding woman or of the intimidating surroundings. Letting his pack drop to the floor, he launched himself at the youth. Crossing the distance separating them in the blink of an eye, he drove his fist into the boy's face.

Julian let out a cry, then staggered back, trying to protect himself as Pelayo kept pummeling him, not giving him a chance to recover.

The attack on her son had been so swift and unexpected that Izaskun had frozen in surprise. Recovering from her shock, she grabbed Pelayo by the back of his collar and pulled him roughly away.

"Stop it, you little demon!" she cried, shaking him, her face red with fury. "How dare you strike my son in our home?"

Pelayo flailed about for a moment, then stopped as he realized that he was firmly caught in the woman's grip.

A few feet away, the wooden door that Pelayo and the soldiers had been heading toward suddenly swung open and banged against the wall.

In the door frame stood his father, his burly figure silhouetted against the brightly lit chamber behind him.

"What the devil is going on here?" his father bellowed.

"Look what your wretched child has done to Julian!" Izaskun cried out, holding on to Pelayo's collar.

His father glanced at Julian, who was trying to staunch his bleeding nose with the hem of his tunic, then turned back to his wife. "I know the boy; he's a gentle lad. He would not have struck Julian unless provoked."

Izaskun was visibly seething with anger. "I want this child out of here!"

His father turned toward Julian. "What did you do to him?"

"Nothing," Julian said sullenly, not meeting his father's eyes.

"Did you hear what I said?" Izaskun cried out.

His father turned back toward her. "Let the boy go."

Izaskun held his gaze for a moment, then released her grip on Pelayo.

His father shot him a stern look. "Come here."

Pelayo felt suddenly wary of the man standing before him. Physically, he looked the same as the person who had visited him and his mother every few months throughout his life:

tall, with a trimmed beard and dark brown hair falling to his shoulders. But this was a side of his father he had never seen before. As he took a step forward, he felt as if he was approaching a stranger.

"Why did you strike Julian?" his father asked him.

Feeling shame, Pelayo hung his head and said nothing.

"Go on," his father snapped. "Answer me, boy."

"He called Mama a whore," Pelayo said softly.

His father's face hardened with anger as he turned his gaze toward Izaskun and Julian. "I suppose it was too much to hope that the two of you would show the boy some compassion on his first day here."

"Are you so deluded that you expect your wife and son to embrace your bastard with open arms?" Izaskun asked, her voice full of scorn.

"What I had hoped for was some measure of understanding from you both," his father said. "You may as well know now that I plan to adopt the boy. The sooner you get used to his presence here the better."

"It'll be a cold day in hell before that happens," Izaskun shot back.

His father and Izaskun stared at each other, their gazes as implacable and hostile as two crossed swords.

Izaskun finally turned toward her son. "Come Julian, let's get you cleaned up."

Julian dutifully followed his mother for several paces, then turned back and shot Pelayo a look of venom, conveying that it was not over between them.

Once the two had left, his father turned toward him. "Well, that wasn't quite the homecoming I had in mind for you."

"I'm sorry," Pelayo said, certain that his father must be having second thoughts about taking him in.

"You have nothing to be sorry for. My difficulties with my wife started long before you were born."

"Maybe you should have left me with Magda."

"No," his father answered firmly. "Your place is here with me now."

Pelayo said nothing, but he felt reassured that at least one person wanted him there.

"Things will get better, you'll see," his father said, as if reading his mind.

Remembering Lady Izaskun's fury and the menacing look her son had given him, Pelayo wasn't at all certain that this father was right. He hesitated for a moment then ventured tentatively, "I didn't know you had another family."

His father seemed surprised. "Your mother never spoke to you about...our arrangement?"

"No."

"I suppose she must have wanted to wait until you were a little older to tell you."

A feeling of sadness washed over Pelayo. After a moment he asked his father: "Why didn't you come to visit us when Mama got sick?"

"I was away at a King's Council. When I returned, I found two letters waiting for me. One was from your mother telling me that she was ill; the other from your village priest, informing me that she had passed away. If I had been here when your mother's letter arrived, nothing in this world would have prevented me from going to her side."

His father's answer satisfied him. He still had many questions he wanted to ask, but his eyes were closing with exhaustion. When he let out a yawn, his father put a hand on his shoulder.

"Come, let's get you into a warm bed. We'll talk again in the morning."

After entrusting his son to a servant, Fáfila retired to his bedchamber for the night. His manservant had lit all the oil lamps in the room. A flickering glow washed over the frescoed walls as he walked to the window, opened it wide, then gazed out into the night. He stood there for a time, savoring the sound of the rain and the feel of the cool, moist breeze on his face. The conversation with Pelayo had stirred up his emotions, leaving him filled with longing and regret.

Memories of that fateful winter day when he had met Pelayo's mother for the first time came drifting back. It had been at the end of a long and ultimately fruitless campaign against some Basque raiders who had been preying on Asturian settlements along their eastern border. He had been leading a small party of soldiers down a mountain pass, when a fierce blizzard had lashed into them. Caught out in the open, a half-day's ride from the nearest town, he and his men would have probably frozen to death had they not stumbled upon a mountain fortress belonging to a local Basque warlord.

As the frigid winter winds had howled around him, he had banged on the door and asked for shelter. Fortunately, as the Basque people had no great love for Asturians, the warlord had taken pity on them and had offered them sanctuary.

Later, while he and his men were warming themselves by the fire in the great hall, the Basque warlord had introduced him to his wife, his son and his daughter, Edurne. With flowing red hair, blue eyes and white skin dusted with freckles, the warlord's daughter had enchanted him at first sight. Giving him a beguiling smile, she had extended her hand for him to kiss, stealing his heart in that one moment.

He and his men had ended up staying at the fortress for two weeks. He had told the warlord that he would pay in gold for the feeding and sheltering of his party, and it was that offer that no doubt accounted for the warlord's forbearance at allowing them to stay far longer than was necessary. Though he had never admitted it to anyone, the truth was that he had been unable to tear himself away from Edurne. Once the snow had melted away however, he had run out of excuses to stay. So, one morning, with great reluctance, he had bid farewell to Edurne and her family and had set off for home with his men.

Once back in Gijón he had done his best to again pick up the threads of his life. Yet something inside him had changed. He had found that he could no longer tolerate his loveless marriage to Izaskun.

As the days passed, he came to understand what should have been obvious to him from the start. He had fallen in love with Edurne. From then on, he began trying to find a way to return to the Basque stronghold. Months later, under the pretext of having to hunt down another raiding party, he took a company of soldiers and headed north, determined to see Edurne again.

He and his men reached the warlord's mountain fortress on a summer afternoon. After dismounting, he walked alone to the stockade and banged on the gate, expecting the same cordial welcome he had received on his first visit. Instead, the warlord greeted him with a stone face, told him that Edurne no longer live there, then asked him to leave and to never trouble his family again.

Surprised and confused by the warlord's coldness, he got back on his horse and, not knowing what else to do, led his men away. As the road circled around a bend, Edurne's old nursemaid, Magda, came running out of the woods. Panting from exertion, she revealed to him that shortly after he had left the previous spring, Edurne had discovered that she was with child. When she had begun to show, her father learned of her condition. Enraged by what she had done, spoiling his plan to marry her off to a neighboring warlord's son, he had sent her to a convent.

It took him three days to find the Carmelite retreat. Surrounded by several acres of cultivated fields, the abbey's stone buildings all faced inward, giving it the stark and defensive appearance of a fortress. After pounding on the sole entrance door to the compound, a small, viewing portal opened up, and the stern face of an elderly woman peered out at him. After identifying herself as the abbess, she demanded to know what it was he wanted.

He told her that he had come for one of her charges, Edurne, and he asked that she and her infant be brought out to him forthwith.

The abbess at first refused his request, but then thought better of her decision, when he threatened to torch the abbey's fields and granaries.

The sight of Edurne walking out of the convent toward him, holding their infant in her arms, was a sight he would never forget.

The realization that Edurne was gone now and that he would never see her again, struck him anew, like the reopening of a painful wound. Turning away from the window, he clung to the one thought that offered him any solace. Edurne was not lost to him, at least not completely. Part of her still lived on in Pelayo. He had risked his wife's ire by bringing the boy to Gijón, but it was a price he was willing to pay. In her letter, Edurne had asked him to care for their son and nothing in the world would prevent him from honoring her dying wish.

CHAPTER 2

MAKING SLOW PROGRESS along the old Via Augusta, Theodosius came to a stop in the shade, under one of the elms bordering the road. Leaning on his staff, he surveyed the fruit groves and farmsteads spreading out around him. In the distance lay his destination, the city of Gijón, whose ochre-colored walls he could see rising over the plain. As he stood there, a farmer pushing a handcart shot him a sideways glance as he hurried by, carefully avoiding eye contact.

Theodosius figured the farmer must have taken him for a beggar and had probably feared he would be asked for alms. Theodosius could forgive the man for making such an assumption. Bearded, wild-haired and clothed in little more than filthy rags, he knew he certainly looked the part. Despite the humility to which he aspired, however, the disdain so clearly written on the farmer's face had stung him more deeply than he cared to admit. Truth be told, he still thought of himself as the man he had once been, a monk, honored for his intellect and renowned for his scholarly knowledge.

It had been two years now since he had left the monastery at the age of twenty-seven. Filled at the time with youthful optimism, it had been a rude awakening to discover just how little the world outside the cloister valued his abilities. Unfortunately, as he possessed no other skills, at least none that were deemed useful, he had been forced to take on a variety of menial jobs, and even those had been difficult to find. Certainly, they had not been enough to pay for his food, clothing and shelter and his descent into hunger and deprivation had been shockingly swift.

After taking a measured sip from his waterskin, he considered the choices before him. He still had many hours of walking ahead of him before he reached the city. Unfortunately, he was already feeling lightheaded with hunger. He considered stopping at one of the nearby farmsteads to offer to work for food, but the day was wearing on and the city gates would be closing at sunset. Uncertain of what to do next, he turned and looked back along the stretch of road that he had just walked.

In the distance, he could see a horse-drawn hay wagon slowly making its way toward him. He waited for it patiently by the side of the road, then hailed the farmer sitting atop the wagon bench as he approached. "Good day to you, sir," he called out, respectfully doffing his cap.

The farmer eyed Theodosius warily as he drew his horse to a stop.

"Are you by chance heading to Gijón?" Theodosius asked with a friendly smile.

The farmer hesitated, then nodded. "I have to turn off a little ways before, but you can ride in the back of my wagon till then if you wish."

"That would do nicely, thank you."

The farmer nodded. "Hop on."

Theodosius clambered up onto the wagon, unslung the pouch containing his meager belongings, then settled down in the sweet-smelling hay. He found it comfortable enough, and as the wagon continued along the bumpy road, the motion rocked him to sleep.

Some time later, the farmer called out that he was about to turn off onto another road. After stirring to life, Theodosius thanked the man, jumped off the wagon and set off on foot once again.

He reached Gijón by late afternoon and entered through the town's main gates. A gaggle of honking geese waddled by, forcing him to step back against a wall. He passed by a shop owner sweeping his entrance, then made his way down a series of narrow, crowded streets toward the citadel. As was the case in most fortified towns of any significance, the ruling lord's castle sat on the highest hill, dominating the landscape. As he trudged toward it, he got a better view of its roughhewn stone walls and towers.

Once he got closer, he spotted two uniformed soldiers standing outside the open gates, the butt end of their spears planted firmly on the ground. One of the two was eyeing his progress with a less than friendly expression. He gave the man his most disarming smile, but before he could open his mouth to utter a single word, the guard waved him off.

"Go away," the man called out. "There's no begging allowed here."

Behind the two guards, through the open gates, Theodosius could see several boys and girls playing in the courtyard. The sight of the children raised his hopes of finding employment there.

"I'm sorry to be a bother," Theodosius said diffidently. "I'm looking for work. Might your lord perchance have need of a tutor for his children?"

The guard ran his gaze up and down Theodosius, his

expression revealing what he thought of the gaunt, filthy figure standing before him.

"You...a tutor?" The guard snorted. "You take me for a fool? Get the hell away before I kick your arse out of here."

Head bowed, Theodosius stood as if rooted to the ground. It wasn't defiance; that fire had long ago been extinguished in him. It was just that the combination of hunger and disappointment had brought on a wave of dizziness.

The guard handed his spear to his companion. "All right, don't say I didn't warn you," he said ominously, advancing toward Theodosius.

In a bewildering jumble of sensations and images, Theodosius felt rough hands taking hold of him. Adding to his woes, his vision began going dark around the edges. The guard spun him around, then shoved him hard from behind, propelling him back down the road.

Theodosius went stumbling forward, his arms flailing about. He tried to remain on his feet, but after a few steps, he lost his struggle and fell down in a heap. He lay on the ground, half-stunned, then, with a sinking feeling, he realized his humiliation was not yet over.

The guard grabbed him by the back of his tunic, then dragged him away from the gates, as if he were nothing more than a sack of grain.

Suddenly, from somewhere behind him, a youthful voice call out, "Stop, let him go!"

After a moment's hesitation the guard released Theodosius and he collapsed face down in the dirt.

Blinking away his dizziness and trying to gather his wits, Theodosius took a deep breath, then propped himself up on his hands and knees. Looking up, he found himself staring into a pair of light gray eyes, set in the tanned face of a boy of around ten or eleven years old.

"Are you all right?" the boy asked, helping him to his feet.

Theodosius licked his dry lips. "I'm fine," he said faintly.

The guard shot him a warning glance, then returned to his post at the gates.

"You don't look well," the boy said. "Are you sick?"

Theodosius shook his head. "I haven't eaten in days. The effects are about the same, I suppose."

"Is that why you're here, to beg for food?" the boy asked.

"No," Theodosius said, dusting off his clothing. "I'm looking for employment."

"In the kitchen or in the stable? I can inquire for you, if you'd like."

"That's most generous of you, but I'm actually seeking work as a tutor." The dizziness had subsided, though he still felt somewhat light-headed.

The boy gazed dubiously at him. "You don't look like a tutor."

"Nonetheless, that is what I am," Theodosius answered with quiet dignity. "I can speak and write both Greek and Latin. I have studied the history of the ancient world. I can teach anyone willing to learn the mystery of numbers."

The boy shrugged, clearly unimpressed. "Wait here. I'll go fetch you some food from the kitchen."

Before Theodosius could answer, the boy had run off, leaving him under the menacing glare of the guards. Trying to put some distance between himself and the soldiers, he edged away toward a nearby tree, then sat down in the shade. It seemed that for today at least, he would not have to worry about finding his next meal.

Some time later, the boy reappeared, carrying half a loaf of bread, a link of dried sausage and two small onions.

Theodosius carefully divided the food, then put half of it inside his pack for later. "May I know the name of my generous benefactor?"

The boy looked at him blankly.

"What's your name, lad?"

"Pelayo."

"Well, Pelayo, thank you for the food." Theodosius took a bite of the sausage. As he chewed hungrily, his glance happened to stray over the boy's shoulder. One of the children from the courtyard, a pretty girl of about eight or nine, came running toward them.

"Pelayo, come quickly!" the girl cried out.

"I'll be there in a moment," the boy yelled back. He turned toward Theodosius. "That's Valentina. She likes to order everybody around," he said with a good-natured smile.

"Is she your sister?" Theodosius asked.

Pelayo shook his head. "No. She's the daughter of Baron Ernesto of Cantabria. They're guests of my father."

Theodosius raised an eyebrow. "And your father is…?"

"Duke Fáfila."

The young girl came to a stop several paces away, then stamped her foot impatiently. "I told you to come. Yxtaverra called Julian a cheat and Julian hit him in the face."

Pelayo's smile faded. "I guess I'd better go," he said to Theodosius.

As Pelayo was walking away, Theodosius overheard the young girl telling him, "I don't know why Julian always has to barge in on our games and spoil everything. I hate him. I hope he gets the pox and dies."

Theodosius realized that the moment was slipping away and

that he might not have a second chance to speak with the boy. "Could you ask your father if he needs a tutor?" he called out, then added, "If not, maybe there's other work I could do here."

Pelayo turned back toward Theodosius. "It may be a while before I can talk to him; he's a very busy man. But I'll try," he shouted over his shoulder as he set off again.

Remarkably mature for someone so young, Theodosius thought to himself, watching Pelayo and the young girl disappear into the courtyard. Knowing he'd probably have a long wait ahead of him, he leaned back against the tree and continued to munch on the food the boy had brought him.

As the afternoon wore on, Theodosius began to wonder if the boy had forgotten about him. When dusk fell, he grew convinced that Pelayo was not going to show up. Just as he was mustering the courage to get up and leave, the lad sauntered through the gates. As he neared, Theodosius saw a purple swelling around the boy's right eye.

"What happened to your face?" Theodosius asked.

"I got into a fight," Pelayo answered. "It's nothing."

"Did you have a chance to speak to your father?" Theodosius said, unable to mask his anxiety.

Pelayo nodded. "He told me he's open to the idea of replacing our tutor. He said he's willing to meet with you tomorrow."

"He is?" Theodosius brightened. "That's wonderful!"

"I thought you'd be pleased."

"Why is your father thinking of replacing your tutor? Did he do something wrong?"

"No. I think it's just that Father Franciscus is getting old. Half the time he falls asleep in the middle of our lesson. Last month, we caught a bat and put it under his cassock while he was snoring away," Pelayo said with a grin.

The boy's good humor was infectious, and Theodosius found himself smiling back.

"He made us kneel in penance for a long time, but it was worth it," the boy added.

Though the possibility of being hired had lifted Theodosius' spirits, he was careful not to allow himself to become overly hopeful. In the past, other good prospects had fallen through in the end. Still, the boy had gone out of his way to help him and whatever the outcome, he was grateful for the lad's help. "Thank you," he said warmly. "For asking your father, I mean."

The boy cocked his head and eyed Theodosius' shabby clothing. "I don't suppose you have anything else you could wear for tomorrow?"

Theodosius' shoulders slumped. "I'm afraid not."

"I'll just have to find something for you then."

Pelayo sprung up and was about to dash off when he stopped. "I have a better idea. Come with me. I'll show you a place where you can wash up. Maybe you can sleep inside too. This way you'll be clean for tomorrow when you meet with my father."

Theodosius liked the idea but doubted the guards would allow him to enter the castle, and he said as much to the boy.

"Just wait here." Pelayo turned and sauntered off to speak to the guards. A moment later he waved to Theodosius to come.

As Theodosius followed Pelayo past the two soldiers and through the gates, he whispered to the boy, "I'm surprised they're letting me in. What did you tell them?"

Pelayo waited until they were in the courtyard and well out of earshot of the guards to answer. "I told them my father has given his permission for you to sleep in the kitchen."

Theodosius looked at Pelayo in surprise. "Did your father really say that?"

"He would have, had I asked him."

Theodosius frowned. "You shouldn't have lied."

"Why, what's the harm? You're not planning to make off with our pots and pans, are you?"

"That's not the point," Theodosius said. "You have betrayed the trust of the guards."

The words did not seem to have much effect on the boy. Theodosius shook his head. If he had the good fortune to be hired as his tutor, he would have some serious work ahead of him to teach the boy the value of truth and honor.

Theodosius followed Pelayo through a small doorway tucked under the portico of one of the buildings and stepped into a noisy, smoke-filled kitchen with a high vaulted ceiling. A dozen or so servants were bustling about in a controlled frenzy, busily preparing the evening meal. Pelayo tugged at Theodosius' sleeve, then led him toward another door. Before they reached it, a loud voice erupted from the other side of the kitchen.

"Hey you! What are you doing here?"

Theodosius turned and saw an apron-clad man pointing at him with a chopping knife. The man's face was set in a scowl as he pushed his way through the servants toward him. As he came closer, his gaze fell on Pelayo, who was standing at Theodosius' side.

"He's with me," Pelayo said in a tone full of assured authority.

The cook hesitated, then shrugged and walked away.

Theodosius breathed a sigh of relief as he followed Pelayo into a small courtyard. In the center stood an old marble fountain adorned with a bronze spout in the shape of a fish.

"You can wash up here while I go find you some clean clothing," Pelayo said.

Theodosius glanced about nervously. "I'm not sure it's a good idea for you to leave me here alone."

"Don't worry, I won't be long."

After the boy had run off, Theodosius took out a washcloth from his pack, stripped down to his waist, then began scrubbing away the weeks of accumulated dirt. Once he had finished, he sat down on the edge of the fountain and let the evening breeze dry him off.

It wasn't long before Pelayo returned with a bundle under one arm. In the fading light, Theodosius watched as the boy unrolled what appeared to be a tunic of russet-colored wool.

"I hope it fits," Pelayo said handing it to Theodosius.

Theodosius eyed the garment but did not reach for it. The tunic looked much finer than anything he had ever owned. "Where did you get this?"

"At the bottom of one of my father's chests."

Theodosius' eyes widened in alarm. "Have you taken leave of your senses? You expect me to wear your father's tunic when I see him tomorrow?"

"My father has many tunics. I'm sure he won't recognize this one."

"Of course he will!"

"If you had ten tunics, would you remember them all?"

Theodosius gazed wordlessly at Pelayo. Seemingly sensing his weakening resolve, the lad pressed on. "Unless you look presentable tomorrow, you'll have no chance of becoming my tutor."

Theodosius let out an exasperated breath. "You have the honeyed tongue of the devil himself, boy. If I listen to you, I'll end up with nothing but a good flogging."

"No, you won't." The youthful gray eyes stared calmly back at him. "I know my father; he's never going to notice the tunic."

"That's easy for you to say; it's not your skin that'll get

flayed, is it?" Theodosius muttered darkly, taking the garment from the boy.

"I've spoken to the head cook in the kitchen," Pelayo said, adroitly changing the subject. "He's given his permission for you to sleep there tonight. You can also eat with the other servants after the tables are cleared."

Theodosius' mood lightened somewhat.

"Am I a good benefactorum?" the boy asked with a smile.

"Benefactor, not benefactorum," Theodosius said, chuckling despite himself. The boy obviously had a fine mind. With the proper education and guidance, he might just turn out to be an exceptional young man.

That night, Theodosius slept fitfully. He had waited until all the servants had chosen their usual places on the floor, then he had found a vacant spot for himself in one of the alcoves off the main hall. After piling up a bed of rushes and using his pack as a pillow, he had wrapped himself up in his cloak, then had settled down to sleep. He had been comfortable enough, but he wasn't used to sleeping with so many people around him and the snoring, coughing and wheezing had kept him awake half the night.

Shortly before dawn, at the first crowing of the roosters, the servants began to rise. Grumbling and yawning, they soon ambled off in various directions.

Theodosius found a quiet corner and changed into his new tunic. He fished out a wooden comb from his pack, then made his way to the fountain where he had washed up the previous evening. Splashing water over his head, he did his best to tease the knots out of his hair and his beard. Afterward he found a jagged stone and used it to scrape the dried mud off the soles of his sandals. Once he felt he had done all he could to look presentable, he sat down on the edge of the fountain and waited for Pelayo to come for him.

Time passed agonizingly slowly. The more Theodosius thought about his upcoming audience with the duke, the more apprehensive he became. His imagination conjured up all sorts of unpleasant scenarios, the best of which was that he simply got thrown out of the castle for stealing the duke's tunic.

Pelayo finally showed up and inquired politely whether Theodosius had slept well.

Theodosius muttered a curt answer, which didn't seem to faze the boy's cheerful demeanor in the least.

"I suppose we should go then," Pelayo said. "Follow me."

Pelayo led Theodosius back to the courtyard, now teeming with tradesmen and servants, then continued toward the main building. The boy skipped up the stone steps leading to the entrance, pulled on the iron studded door, and held it open for Theodosius to enter.

After stepping inside, Theodosius stopped and glanced about nervously.

"It's this way," Pelayo said, heading down the large hall toward a door at the far end.

As Theodosius and Pelayo drew near, the door opened, and a striking-looking woman came walking out. After closing the door behind her, her glance fell on Theodosius.

"Who is this?" she demanded of Pelayo.

"Father is waiting to see him," Pelayo answered.

"That's not what I asked you, is it?" the woman said, turning her icy gaze on the boy.

Seemingly impervious to the hostility radiating from the woman, Pelayo stared back at her.

After an uncomfortable silence, Theodosius interjected nervously, "I am seeking a position as a tutor, my lady."

The woman studied Theodosius for a moment, then with a shake of her head that spoke volumes about what she thought of him, walked off without saying a word

Theodosius stared after her. "Who was that?" he asked Pelayo in a hushed voice.

"My father's wife," Pelayo answered. "Forget about her," he said dismissively. "Are you ready?"

Theodosius drew a deep breath, then let it out slowly. "As ready as I'll ever be, I guess."

Not bothering to knock, Pelayo opened the door to his father's study, popped his head inside, then turned back toward Theodosius. "He's alone; you can go in."

Theodosius did his best to steady his nerves, then stepped inside the chamber. At the far end, sitting behind a marble-topped table, a distinguished-looking man, obviously Duke Fáfila, was scribbling away on a parchment.

Theodosius approached the desk, then waited in silence. After a moment, the duke put down his quill and looked up at him.

"My son told me your name, but I'm afraid I've forgotten it," Duke Fáfila said.

"It's Theodosius, sire." Despite the coolness of the morning hours, he found himself sweating.

"Ah yes, that's right. He said you were looking for work as a tutor."

"I am indeed, sire."

"What experience do you have?"

"I was a monk for fifteen years, four of which I spent teaching novices how to read and write."

"When did you leave the monastery?"

"It's been some two years now, sire."

"And what have you done since then?"

Theodosius hesitated. "Nothing of relevance to the position I am seeking, I'm afraid," he admitted.

Duke Fáfila continued to probe him with questions about his days at the monastery, his facility with languages, his knowledge of the scriptures. Theodosius was impressed by the intelligence behind the duke's questions, designed to peel back the layers of his past and get to the true nature of his character.

He did not try to exaggerate his skills nor his accomplishments and answered all the questions posed to him truthfully.

Finally, the duke sat back. "I'm curious as to why you left the order."

"It's complicated, sire. I…"

Seemingly sensing his reluctance, the duke cut in, "The truth now, there are ways for me to find out."

Theodosius cleared his throat. "I had a disagreement with the abbot."

"About what?"

"The answer is rather complicated, I'm afraid." Theodosius said, stalling before answering, while he tried to think of a way to explain what had happened in the best possible light.

"I have time; go ahead," Duke Fáfila said.

Theodosius collected his thoughts, then said, "I suppose it all began when I was nineteen and the prior at the monastery discovered that I had an aptitude for illustration. One day, he assigned me to work in the library, embellishing the copies of the ancient Greek and Latin tomes we were transcribing. As the years passed, I became increasingly interested in the ideas they contained. As a result, I began spending more and more of my time in the library, reading everything I could find. The abbot learned of my interest and encouraged me in my pursuit of knowledge. Unfortunately, one day he fell ill and died."

"A new abbot was appointed and from that day on, life

in the monastery changed completely. This abbot considered the study of the ancient works to be a waste of time. Once a center of learning, the monastery turned into a place of physical labor, of prayer and of contemplation. I grew unhappy at having to spend my days toiling in the fields and I suppose I was too outspoken in voicing my frustration. One day things came to a head. The abbot told me I was being disruptive and that I was setting a bad example for the younger monks. He then said that he thought I would be happier if I moved on."

"So, he threw you out," Duke Fáfila said dryly.

"I agreed that it was time for me to leave."

Duke Fáfila leaned back and studied Theodosius for a moment. "I appreciate your honesty, though not enough to overlook your obvious lack of piety and obedience. I don't see how you can mold my sons into honorable men without instilling in them the virtues you are so clearly lacking."

Theodosius had no answer for that.

"I'm sorry," the duke said. "I think it is best if I look elsewhere for a tutor, another priest perhaps."

Theodosius' hopes were dashed. It had seemed to him that this time his luck was going to change, that he was going to be able to pull himself out of his miserable existence. But no, it had all been another colossal waste of time. As he contemplated the bleak future stretching out before him, a sense of desperation drove him to boldness.

"If I may point out, my lord," Theodosius said, "a priest will no doubt be able to teach your sons to read and write, but will he know the military strategies of Julius Caesar, or the horoscopic astrology of Ptolemy? Or be able to teach them Greek, the lingua franca of the world outside our borders? If I was a mighty lord such as yourself, I would require a better education for my sons than that which a common priest can provide."

Duke Fáfila frowned. "My own tutor was a priest. Are you suggesting that I had a poor education?"

Theodosius felt stricken. "Forgive me sire, I did not mean any disrespect. It's just—"

The duke waived his hand, silencing him. "Perhaps you're right. It is true that these are changing times. It may well be that my sons will have need of new skills."

Theodosius held his breath, not daring to utter a word.

The duke drummed his fingers on the table, his gaze fixed on Theodosius. "Very well, I suppose there's no harm in giving you a try for a month. Be warned, however, that I shall be watching you closely."

A sense of immense relief swept over Theodosius. "Thank you, my lord," he said, the words coming out in a rush. "I promise you will not regret your decision."

"We shall see, won't we?" Duke Fáfila said. "To begin with, your pay will be two silver reales a month."

Theodosius broke out in a delighted smile. "That will be quite acceptable." *To say the least!*

"There is one other matter," the duke said, looking at Theodosius.

Theodosius suddenly felt wary of the change in the duke's tone.

"The cost of my tunic, which you are wearing with such impudence, will be taken out from your wages."

Theodosius blushed with mortification. He had forgotten all about the damn tunic. "I… I wasn't going to keep it, sire, I swear," he said miserably.

"I understand you are not responsible for taking it, at least not directly. If I suspected you were, the punishment would be swift and severe," the duke said sternly. "No, I have a fair idea of how you came by the tunic." He shook his head slowly.

"I'm afraid his mother, may God bless her soul, was much too lenient with the boy."

Despite the dire words, Theodosius was surprised to see a gleam of amusement in the duke's eyes.

"You will start tomorrow," Duke Fáfila said. "I shall see to it that you are listed as part of the household staff and given accommodation fitting your position." He then waived Theodosius away, ending the meeting.

Theodosius turned to leave the chamber, trying to contain the emotions battering him. He had reached the door when the duke called out, "Theodosius."

Theodosius turned, his heart beating with trepidation. "Yes, my lord?"

"The tunic; consider it a gift," the duke said gruffly.

Theodosius was speechless for a moment. Recovering his composure, he bowed deeply from the waist. "Thank you, my lord. I can see where your son gets his generous spirit."

After getting a nod from the duke, Theodosius retreated and closed the door behind him.

Theodosius spent the rest of the morning exploring the grounds and the buildings of the castle. In the main courtyard, next to the stable, he found a barber plying his trade under a reed canopy. Explaining to the man that he had just been hired by the duke as a tutor, he managed to talk him into letting him borrow an old pair of scissors and a bronze mirror. He took the items to an area that afforded him some privacy, then, propping up the mirror on a rock, he began trimming his beard and cutting his hair. As the locks fell away, a gaunt, hollow-cheeked face he hardly recognized stared back at him from the mirror.

He had just returned the borrowed items to the barber when a bell began clanging in the distance. Moments later men and women came trickling out into the courtyard. It was time for the noonday meal. As he was now part of the duke's retinue, he joined the people heading toward the great hall. He wondered how many of those around him appreciated having food served to them each and every day.

It took a moment for his eyes to adjust to the dim interior of the castle. He had been too nervous to pay much attention to his surroundings earlier, when he had gone to meet with the duke. Now, however, he studied every detail of the great hall with interest: the lancet windows that let in narrow, vertical shafts of light; the animal hunting trophies displayed on the walls, looking down with sightless eyes; the rows of torches set in iron sconces, their flames dancing in the drafty air; the oily plumes of smoke swirling upward toward the beamed ceiling. In contrast to the silence of that morning, the great hall now rang with voices, laughter, the clatter of metal dishes and the scraping of wooden benches. A score of servants scuttled about, unloading platters of food onto the trestle tables.

There were over three dozen people, mostly men, sitting on the benches by the dining tables. Judging by their clothing and appearance, Theodosius figured they were clerics, scribes, craftsmen, administrators, counselors and others belonging to the skilled professions needed to run a large estate. The duke was sitting at a table on a raised platform at the far side of the hall.

Sitting on the duke's left was his wife, the ill-humored woman that Theodosius had encountered that morning. Beside her was a fair-headed boy, and next to him, a bishop and a cleric. On the duke's right side sat a distinguished-looking couple as well as the young girl he had seen the previous day playing in the courtyard.

Theodosius found it odd that Pelayo was not sitting at his father's table. As he walked through the packed dining hall, the smell of food was making his stomach rumble. He caught sight of Pelayo sitting at a nearby table, all but hidden by the people towering around him. There was space next to the boy that he thought he could squeeze into, and he hurried toward it before someone else beat him to it.

"Is it all right if I sit with you?" Theodosius asked when he was at the boy's side.

"Of course," Pelayo said, sliding over, making more room for him on the bench.

Theodosius squeezed himself down between Pelayo and a portly, middle-aged man. "Why aren't you sitting at your father's table?"

"It's a little crowded up there today," Pelayo said. "How did it go with my father this morning?" he asked, changing the subject.

"Rather well, I would say."

As Theodosius began piling food on his plate, he told Pelayo that his father had offered him the position of tutor on a trial basis.

Pelayo's face lit up. "That's great news. No more Father Franciscus for us, I guess."

Theodosius glanced sideways at Pelayo. "Your father noticed that I was wearing his tunic."

"Oh." The boy's smile wavered. "What did he say?"

Theodosius chuckled. As he peeled a boiled egg, he told Pelayo what had happened. He had just finished his story when Duke Fáfila rose to his feet and held up both arms in an appeal to the diners for silence.

The servants stopped in mid-stride and all conversation around the tables abruptly ceased.

When silence took hold, Duke Fáfila let his arms fall to his side and addressed everyone in the hall in a deep, sonorous voice.

"It gives me great pleasure to announce the betrothal of my son, Julian, to Valentina, the daughter of my good friend and closest ally, Baron Ernesto of Girona, and his wife, Doña Katerina."

Murmurs of surprise rippled through the hall.

Smiling, the duke lifted his goblet in the air. "Would you all join me in a toast to celebrate this happy occasion?"

The sound of benches scraping the floor filled the air as everyone rose to their feet. Lifting their cups, they toasted the betrothed and wished them well. After tossing back their wine, they all erupted into a cheer.

Later, when everyone had sat down again and conversations resumed, Theodosius noticed that Pelayo had gone strangely quiet. "Well," he said tentatively. "The betrothal sounds like a fine match, don't you think?"

"It won't seem that way to Valentina," Pelayo said. "She hates Julian."

"She's just a child," Theodosius replied. "Give her a few years; I'm sure she'll get over her distaste for him."

His words did nothing to change Pelayo's long face.

Theodosius suddenly remembered the lad's smile the previous day when Valentina had come running up to them. In a flash of insight, he suddenly understood Pelayo's change of mood. "The world is filled with pretty girls, my boy. One day your father will find you a nobleman's daughter every bit as captivating as Valentina."

The man on his right snorted, then muttered loud enough for Theodosius to hear, "As if that's bloody likely."

Theodosius turned and found himself staring into the eyes of his dining companion, a stout man in his forties who had the look of a tradesman about him.

"You shouldn't fill the boy's head with dreams," the man said in a low voice.

Theodosius blinked at him. "What on earth do you mean?"

The man leaned closer. "Everybody knows the boy is the duke's bastard. No lord of any importance is ever going to allow his daughter to marry him."

Theodosius turned back to Pelayo and noticed that the boy's eyes were rigidly fixed on the dish before him. He was suddenly certain that Pelayo had overheard the man's remark. Despite his feeling of sympathy for the lad, he could not think of a single thing to say to him.

Shortly after, Pelayo rose to his feet. "When are you planning to hold our first lesson?"

"I hadn't thought about it," Theodosius answered. "I suppose we could start tomorrow morning."

"I'll go tell everyone."

"All right, my boy," Theodosius said.

"Until tomorrow, then."

Theodosius watched Pelayo walk away. *What an extraordinary situation I've stumbled into,* he thought to himself. *It must be difficult for the lad to live with the stigma of being the duke's illegitimate son. Well,* he reflected philosophically, *some children prosper against adversity, while others are destroyed by it.* As he finished his cup of watered-down wine, he wondered which of the two destinies lay in store for the boy.

CHAPTER 3

A LOUD AND annoying thumping reverberated through the bedchamber. "Are you up, Master Pelayo?" a man's voice called out from outside the door.

Pelayo stirred in his bed, a wine-induced headache beginning to throb behind his eyes. His slight movement precipitated a variety of aches throughout his body, making him wonder if perhaps he had fallen down a flight of stairs. As the cobwebs of sleep dissipated, jumbled images of flying fists, broken crockery and upturned tables came flashing back.

"Your father wishes to see you," the voice called out.

Good news travels fast, Pelayo thought sourly. "All right, I heard you."

"He's in his study. I wouldn't keep him waiting if I were you."

Pelayo could not muster the energy to answer. Mercifully, silence returned. Fully intending to get up, he made the mistake of closing his eyes for what he thought would only be a moment.

When he next awoke, the morning coolness in his bedchamber had been replaced by the torpid heat of a summer afternoon. Shifting his legs over the edge of the bed, he rose to his feet, wincing as a needle of pain lanced into his right knee. *Perfect,* he thought morosely, as he limped across the floor littered with his discarded clothing.

Reaching the window, he threw open the shutters and gazed out into the courtyard below. Servants were scurrying about, hauling wicker baskets filled with freshly baked bread from the outdoor ovens. It was well past midday. His father would not be pleased that he had ignored his summons.

After relieving himself into a chamber pot, he made his way to a washing table, poured some water from a pitcher into a tin basin, then dunked his head into it. The pain behind his eyes receded a little. As he dried himself with a cloth, he noticed the water in the basin had turned a rosy pink. He lifted an exploratory hand to his face and discovered that his right cheek was swollen. As his fingers continued probing, he found another tender area around his left jaw. Unfazed, he shrugged off his injuries. He had suffered worse in the past.

Feeling almost human again, he went to the clothes chest at the foot of his bed and picked out a clean tunic. After dressing, he left his chamber and made his way down the stone staircase to the ground floor of the castle. Normally, at this time of day, he would be starving. But now, the smell of cooking wafting in from the kitchen made his stomach lurch.

He was halfway across the hall when he ran into Theodosius. His former tutor bore little resemblance to the half-starved creature who had shown up at the gates of the castle some eight years earlier. Now elegantly attired and impeccably groomed, Theodosius looked every inch the part of the powerful and influential chief steward he had become. "Morning, Theo," he called out.

Theodosius looked at him with concern. "Good Lord, my boy, what happened to you?"

"It's nothing. Got into a bit of a squabble at an inn last night."

Theodosius frowned. "That's getting to be something of a habit with you, isn't it?"

"It wasn't my fault. Trouble has a way of finding me these days, Theo."

"Yes, that must be it," Theodosius said dryly.

"I'm looking for Father. Any idea where he might be?"

"The last time I saw him he was heading toward the armory. He had a sword merchant from Toledo with him."

After taking his leave of Theodosius, Pelayo made his way to the north tower. The door to the armory had been left ajar, and he stepped inside.

The armory, occupying the entire ground floor of the castle, was a circular chamber with a high-vaulted ceiling and narrow, barred windows that kept the interior in perennial twilight. An array of spears, pikes and lances bristled from stands lining the wall. A dusty collection of breastplates and coats of chainmail hung from hooks affixed to wooden beams in the ceiling.

His father and the chief armorer were at the center of the armory, both hunched over an open crate. Off to one side, a heavy-set man who he guessed was the arms merchant stood beside four other wooden crates.

His father ignored his entrance and continued inspecting the swords in the crate. When he was done, he stood up and turned toward the merchant. "They're not quite up to the standards one expects of swords from Toledo."

The merchant seemed to have his answer ready. "They may not be of the finest quality, Don Fáfila, but my price more than reflects that."

His father turned toward his chief armorer. "What do you think?"

Known to be a man of few words, the armorer sampled several of the swords, first wiping each blade clean of its packing grease, then swinging it through the air, testing its feel. When he was done, he turned and made his pronouncement. "The swords feel somewhat unbalanced, sire. They're also on the light side. But the blades seem to be well-tempered. I don't know though how they'll hold up in sustained combat."

The arms merchant cut in. "They'll be fine, you have my word on that, Don Fáfila,"

His father studied the swords in the crate, clearly undecided.

The merchant fidgeted about anxiously. "You won't find a better value for two dozen swords anywhere in the kingdom, I can assure you."

His father nodded. "That's probably right, I suppose. Very well, I'll take the lot off your hands."

The merchant looked relieved. "Thank you, Don Fáfila."

His father turned toward the armorer. "Bring him upstairs and ask Theodosius to settle accounts with him."

Pelayo waited for the merchant and the armorer to leave before approaching his father. "You wanted to speak to me?"

His father wiped the grease off his hands with a cloth. "The innkeeper of the Three Sirens came to see me this morning."

"Did he?" Pelayo said carefully.

"He wanted ten silver reales for the damage you and your friends inflicted on his establishment last night."

"Ten reales? For a few broken tables and chairs? That's absurd. Besides, I don't see why I'm the only one he's holding responsible. Everyone at the inn was fighting."

"And as usual you were probably right in the thick of it, weren't you?"

"You can't expect me to bolt for the door every time someone in a tavern throws a punch," Pelayo said.

"Of course not, that would be too sensible, wouldn't it?"

"More like craven, I'd say," Pelayo shot back, recalling the previous evening's events.

He had been sitting at a table with two of his friends, talking to a serving maid, when a group of bargemen had come through the front door. As they had walked by him, a coarse looking lout, his arms roped with muscles, had bumped into him, making him spill some of his wine on himself. He would have readily accepted an apology, even an insincere one, but the look in the brute's eyes had told him that he wasn't going to get one.

The bargeman had stared down at him with dead eyes, daring him to start something. Wishing to avoid trouble, he had swallowed his pride and turned back to his friends. No doubt encouraged by his timid response, the bargeman had bumped into him again before strutting away. That had done it. Seeing red, he had sprung to his feet, grabbed the man by the shoulder and spun him around. Then, putting every ounce of muscle into it, he had hammered his fist into the brute's face. The bargeman had dropped to the floor like a sack of stones.

Unfortunately, his companions had put up a more spirited fight.

"I don't know what's gotten into you lately," his father said, shaking his head. "I can only think it's those low-born ruffians you surround yourself with these days. Why can't you associate with young men of your own station for a change?"

Pelayo's head was throbbing again. The last thing he needed was a dressing down from his father. "And what station would that be exactly?"

"You know damn well," his father said. "You're the son of a duke; you're a nobleman."

"Thank you for reminding me. I sometimes forget."

"You live a life of privilege here," his father said, raising his voice. "If you feel you're not being treated with the respect you deserve, it's because of all your whoring and drunken brawls."

"I could be a saint and it wouldn't make the slightest difference."

"What the devil is that supposed to mean?"

"Julian will be the duke one day," Pelayo answered. "No one who hopes to curry favor with him can afford to be seen in my company, much less be openly civil to me."

His father considered his words for a moment, then said, "I realize there were times when you were treated unfairly. I suspect Izaskun's hand in that. But you should have tried to rise above the situation."

"I did; I learned not to care what anyone here thought about me."

"And that's worked wonders for you, I suppose," his father said, irritation creeping back into his voice.

Pelayo thought of all the abuse he had had to endure over the years, until he had become old enough and strong enough to fight back. "Yes. Actually, it has," he said.

His father's expression hardened. "Really? Because as I see it, all you've done is taint our family's good name with one scandal after another."

"I'm sorry I'm such a disappointment to you," Pelayo said, biting off his words.

"You're not sorry at all; I can see it in your eyes," his father said.

Pelayo and his father stood gazing at each other in hostile silence.

The pealing of church bells sounded in the distance. As if reminded of the time, his father turned on his heel and walked away.

Pelayo stood there alone in the armory, his chest tight with resentment. It occurred to him that the time may have come to leave Gijon. Perhaps he could buy a ship and start a trading venture. He would like that, he thought; a blue ocean and an endless horizon to greet him each morning. And no one to look down his or her nose at him or to scold him as if he were a child for getting into a minor altercation. His father would advance him the funds, he thought, if for no other reason than to see the back of him.

Over the next few day, Pelayo did his best to avoid being anywhere near his father. The charge that he had sullied the family's good name had wounded him deeply.

At the end of the week, an officer approached him while he was having supper and informed him that General Olivar, the field commander of the Asturian legion, had assigned him the temporary command of a cohort.

The announcement, seemingly coming out of the blue, caught Pelayo by surprise. But after a moment's reflection, he began warming to the idea. Though he had considered pursuing a trading venture, a life in the legion seemed more to his liking. After all, what did he really know about navigating by the stars or reading the winds, or steering a ship through a storm? The more he thought about it, the more he found the idea of becoming a cohort commander appealing. He was disappointed, however, that his father, obviously behind the appointment, had not chosen to give him the news himself.

That evening Pelayo saddled up his horse and left for the officers' barracks situated outside the city. He didn't bother saying goodbye to anyone.

He had arrived in Gijon as a stranger one rainy night, some ten years earlier. Now, as he rode through the gates and out of the city, he felt nothing had changed. He was, and always would be, the unwelcome outsider.

CHAPTER 4

SITTING ON HIS horse atop a hill, General Olivar, Field Commander of the Third Legion, watched the two cohorts march into position from opposite ends of the field below him. Shielding his eyes from the rising sun with his hand, he turned and studied the throng of people sitting on the surrounding slopes.

Normally only a county fair or a hanging would compel this many of Gijón's citizens to leave their homes on a Sunday morning. But the occasion was actually a military exercise, one of the most important of the year. Today marked the final and decisive competition, a culmination of eleven months of matches that had pitted the Northern Legion's best two squadrons against each other.

General Olivar knew the news that Duke Fáfila's two sons would be leading the opposing cohorts battling it out for victory had attracted the larger than usual crowd that had turned out to watch the mock battle this year.

After the two cohorts, each comprised of four hundred soldiers, came to a stop below him, Olivar nudged his horse down the hill, eliciting a ragged cheer from the crowd.

Everyone there that morning, save perhaps for the youngest children, understood the simple rules of the competition they were about to witness. One cohort had to defend and hold a small hill at one end of the field. The hill didn't look like much, just a grassy mound rising some forty or fifty feet in the air. The objective of the opposing cohort was to wrest away control of the hill in a certain span of time. The entire exercise would be conducted on foot, without cavalry support. Any man who was knocked to the ground would be considered mortally wounded and would have to withdraw from the field.

Even from a distance, it was not difficult to tell the cohorts apart. The *Principes* carried distinctive red and black shields. Their commander, Lord Julian, the duke's eldest son, was wearing a black, silver embroidered cloak over his thigh length, chainmail shirt.

Their opponents, the *Aguilas,* carrying blue and white shields, were positioned some thirty paces away. Slightly ahead of the formation, accompanied by a single staff officer, stood a tall, broad-shouldered figure wearing the blue cloak of a cohort commander. Most everyone in the crowd knew that the man was Lord Pelayo, the duke's youngest son, who today was replacing the regular commander who had suffered a broken arm in the run-up competition.

Although strategy and well-executed maneuvers were preferred over brute force, injuries were not uncommon in these mock battles. To minimize risk, every soldier had to wear a special quilted garment stuffed with hay beneath his armor. Despite this protection, the wooden staves used as substitutes for swords, could still inflict a painful bruise or even break a bone. The chance of injury to the officers was even greater, as putting them out of commission was the surest way for the opposing side to gain the advantage.

General Olivar reined in his horse some twenty feet away from the two cohorts, now arrayed in formations five men deep.

"You all know the rules," he called out, his booming voice carrying to every soldier on the field. "Anyone caught striking a blow above the collarbone will forfeit a week's pay. So keep your wits about you, even when your blood is up. I don't want anyone losing an eye or a mouthful of teeth today." He paused for a moment to let his words sink in. "Good luck to you all. May the best cohort win!"

A hush descended over the crowd. This was the second time in as many years that they would be watching Lord Julian in the final round of the competition. Today however, was their first opportunity to see the duke's youngest son in action. For years they had heard stories about his drunken bouts and sexual escapades, and their curiosity about him was understandable. Tall, handsome and encased in bronze breastplates, he certainly looked the part of a young warrior prince. But his scandal-plagued reputation had them wondering whether he had the mettle to lead his cohort to victory.

Down on the field, Pelayo felt the eyes of the crowd upon him as he tied the thongs of his helmet under his chin. The layer of padding he was wearing was already making the sweat trickle down his back. He knew it would get worse as the morning wore on. While waiting for events to unfold, he let his gaze stray over the crowd. Most of the people were seated, but there were still a few milling around the makeshift betting stands.

"What do you reckon our odds are of winning today?" Pelayo asked his adjutant who was standing at his side.

The earnest, square-jawed young officer kept his eyes straight ahead of him. "I don't really know, commander."

"If you had to guess," Pelayo pressed him.

The adjutant hesitated, then answered, "About three to one against us. At least those were the odds yesterday."

"That bad, huh?" Pelayo said with a faint smile.

"No offense, commander, but the oddsmakers probably think Lord Julian's experience gives him the edge."

"Think they're right?"

"I couldn't say," the adjutant said stiffly.

"Lighten up, man. It's just an exercise."

The adjutant turned and gave Pelayo a level look. "This means a lot more to us than that, commander. The *Aguilas* have sweated blood all year to get here."

Pelayo nodded, knowing his adjutant's rebuke was a fair one. To him the competition was just some meaningless, military game and the truth was he didn't really care all that much who won or lost. But it was clear that he would need to pretend otherwise.

General Olivar's voice sounded in the distance. "Cohort commanders! To me, if you please."

As Pelayo set out at a brisk march toward General Olivar, he noticed his adjutant had fallen in step beside him. Stopping, he frowned at his aide. "Where do you think you're going? The general asked to see the cohort commanders," he said, stressing the last two words.

"Adjutants are expected to accompany their commanding officers when they march out. It is protocol."

Pelayo heard the note of condescension in his adjutant's voice. To the officer, he was just another spoiled, young noble, wet behind the ears, who had to be tolerated until properly broken in. Not far from the truth, he supposed.

"All right then, let's go," Pelayo said, resuming his march toward General Olivar who was speaking to his aide-de-camp.

A moment later, he caught sight of Julian and his adjutant approaching from the other side.

As were most of the men in the Witiza clan, Julian was tall, fair-skinned and broad-chested. With his aquiline nose, thin-lipped mouth and habitual, unblinking stare, Julian always reminded Pelayo of an unhooded falcon about to be released into the air to hunt for prey.

A look of distaste flitted across Julian's face as he caught sight of Pelayo striding toward him. He still hadn't gotten over the fact that General Olivar had chosen his half-brother to lead the *Aguilas* against him. *What glory is there in beating an inexperienced novice? Olivar should have appointed one of the other commanders, Maricone perhaps, or even Xocobo. Now that would have given the crowd a reason to get on their feet and cheer.*

Getting bored from all the waiting, Julian's eyes swept over the surrounding slopes, searching for his father. Strangely, there was no sign of him yet. *I wonder who he'll be favoring this year? The bastard, no doubt,* he thought, his rancor chaffing him like an open sore.

Pelayo's arrival at the castle years ago had marked the beginning of a gradual estrangement between him and his father. It had also caused a rift between his mother and father, who now hardly ever spoke to each other. Like a blight upon the family, Pelayo had ruined their happy existence and Julian would always hate him for it.

Now Julian's gaze tracked Pelayo as he came to a halt a few paces away from him.

"Well, well," Julian called out. "Look who's shown up on time for a change. I would have wagered a fat purse that we'd have to search the bedchambers of every whore in town to find you this morning."

Pelayo smiled back at him, looking unfazed by the taunt. "I don't pay for women, Julian. Unlike you, they come to my bed willingly."

Standing just behind Julian, his adjutant suppressed a grin as he looked on. It was common knowledge that the Duke's youngest son had a penchant for wine and women. The latest scandal making the rounds was that Pelayo and his friends had gotten into a drunken brawl over a serving maid at an inn down by the waterfront. The fight had left one man with a broken jaw, three others lying senseless on the floor and the establishment in shambles.

Still and all, the adjutant reflected, if given the choice to serve under one of the Duke's two sons, he would pick the unruly but amiable youth over his older half-brother any bloody day. The reason being that most officers with even a modicum of common sense learned that they needed to find a balance between demanding obedience and maintaining the morale of their men. The problem with Julian was that he didn't seem to place any value on finding that middle ground. Perhaps he thought it was enough to be feared. Whatever the reason, Julian was the worst kind of commanding officer one could encounter. Though the *Principes* ranked as one of the top cohorts, they were also one of the most god-cursed, joyless bunch in the legion and he rued the day he had been transferred into the unit.

Pelayo's brow furrowed as he studied Julian's adjutant. "You look familiar. Have we met before?"

The young officer dipped his head in acknowledgement. "We have indeed." he said, his eyes crinkling with humor.

Of course, Pelayo thought, the timbre of the adjutant's voice invoking a youthful face. The man was the son of his father's quaestor. "It's that new beard of yours that threw me. Good to see you again, Yxtaverra," he said, extending his hand.

"Likewise," Yxtaverra replied, clasping Pelayo's wrist.

"I had no idea you had joined the Third," Pelayo said. "Where have you been hiding all this time?"

"I just got back from a two-year stint in Punta Vedra," Yxtaverra said, referring to the garrison town situated a few hundred leagues to the northeast of the city, just shy of the Basque border.

"No wonder I haven't seen you around," Pelayo said. "What's it like up there?"

"About what you'd expect from a northern settlement; cold barracks, bad food and women as dour as they are plain."

"Sounds pretty dismal."

"It wasn't so bad, I guess," Yxtaverra said with a shrug. "We were hardly ever there. Most of the time we were out on patrol, making sure the Basques didn't stray over the borders."

Julian cut in, "Bloody waste of time that, if you ask me. Instead of sending out patrols, we should just root out the bastards' nests once and for all."

"We've been trying to do that for years," Yxtaverra replied. "Trouble is there are too many mountains and valleys up there in which to hide."

Julian snorted. "That's the excuse we always use. When I become duke, I'll stamp them out like the vermin that they are."

Yxtaverra nodded politely. "I hope you do, sire."

General Olivar, who had been in discussion with his aide-de-camp, turned toward the four men waiting for him. "All right. Time to begin." His gaze fixed on Pelayo. "Since this is your first time, I'll give you the choice, defend or attack?"

Pelayo had been mulling over that question for days now.

He had only been drilling with his cohort for less than a week and he felt he didn't have their measure yet. This made it difficult to lead an effective attack. On the other hand, though defending the hill was in many ways the simpler task, it wasn't a choice he found appealing. He instinctively disliked the passive nature of trying to hold on to a patch of barren ground.

Julian stirred impatiently. "Well, you going to pick a side or not?"

Pelayo held Julian's eyes for a moment. He might as well have been staring into the face of a basilisk for all the warmth he saw in them. "I'll defend the hill."

"Good," Julian said, regaining his humor. "Just like old times, eh?" he said to Pelayo, referring to the games of war they used to play as boys.

"Not quite, Julian," Pelayo replied. "This time we'll be evenly matched."

Julian's smile faded, and his eyes turned flat. "I'll still grind your face into the dirt."

"That's enough!" General Olivar cut in. "This is a military exercise, not an excuse for one of your cockfights." He glared at Julian and Pelayo, daring them to say something. "All right, get back to your cohorts."

General Olivar waited for Pelayo and his men to take position around the hill, then raised his arm.

Three trumpet blasts rang through the air.

Standing at the head of his cohort, Julian pointed ahead with his stave. "Forward, double march!"

Behind him, the *Principes,* divided into three phalanxes, began moving across the field.

The crowd grew quiet. The rhythmic pounding of feet filled the silence.

Julian bellowed another order, "Draw to center!"

The two flanking phalanxes behind Julian veered sharply, then merged into the center one. There was a moment of confusion, then a single, wedge-shaped formation began to form.

"Stow shields!" Julian shouted once more.

Every soldier except for those on the outside slung their shields across their backs. The formation compacted. Squad leaders ran up and down, firming the lines until the perimeter of the wedge formed an unbroken and impregnable wall of shields. Finally, with the tip of the wedge aimed at the center of the hill ahead of them, Julian bellowed another order, "Slow run!"

Some distance away, standing with his adjutant on a hillock, Pelayo watched the *Principes* bear down on him and his cohort. He had foreseen the change in Julian's formation. Even if they had had long spears, the phalanx was not known to be effective in breaking through an entrenched position. But the wedge-shaped configuration that Julian had settled on had come as a complete surprise. He had expected something a little more elaborate from Julian than a blunt, frontal attack.

"They're coming straight for us," his adjutant said tersely. "They're going to try to punch their way through."

"Yes, it looks like it," Pelayo said. He had positioned his men in four concentric rows around the hill in a classic defense formation to prevent them from being outflanked. It seemed that he had guessed wrong.

"They're closing in fast, commander. We should reposition all the men to the front."

"I agree. Let's do it."

Julian's *Principes* broke into a run over the last two or three dozen paces as they closed in. Shouting at the top of their lungs, they smashed with the force of a mailed fist into Pelayo's *Aguilas*. From one instant to the next, the eastern base of the hill turned into a writhing press of bodies. Hoarse cries and the sound of staves hammering on shields filled the air with a constant din.

Within moments, the center of Pelayo's first line of defense began to buckle inwards.

Julian exhorted his men to greater effort, "Push on! Hit them hard!"

Julian's soldiers responded with renewed zeal, pounding away at their opponents, opening up a gap in the *Aguilas'* first line of defense. They pressed on, fighting their way through the gap, widening it, flattening dozens of Pelayo's men in the process.

Trying to avoid being trampled, the fallen men picked themselves up, then to the jeers of the crowd, began limping off the field.

Pelayo's second defensive line, arrayed in a semi-circle higher up on the hill, now came under direct attack. It fared no better than the first. Julian's men broke through with minimum effort.

The crowd let out a roar of appreciation as the *Principes* swarmed up the hill toward the *Aguilas'* third defensive line.

Watching from the hilltop, General Olivar shook his head in dismay. For the life of him he couldn't remember any other defending side buckling under quite so quickly. He now regretted having let Fáfila talk him into giving Pelayo command of Tertius' cohort.

He was so absorbed in the scene playing out below him

that he didn't notice his horse's ears twitching at the sound of a rider approaching him from behind.

"Greetings, Olivar," a familiar voice called out.

Olivar turned to see Duke Fáfila guiding his horse up the hill toward him. The morning light accentuated the grooves of age on the duke's face, making him appear careworn and aged beyond his years. It was obvious that the demands of office were taking a heavy toll on his old friend. "Good morning, Don Fáfila. I was beginning to wonder if I'd see you today."

"The council meeting took up more of my time than usual," Fáfila said, drawing his horse to a halt alongside Olivar's. "So, how goes the battle?"

Olivar turned and studied the clash in the distance. "I expect it'll be over soon."

Fáfila looked at Olivar in surprise. "What, already?"

"All that's left is for Pelayo to realize he's beaten."

"Maybe I should have waited a year or two before asking you to give him command of a cohort," Fáfila said.

"I'm not sure waiting longer would have made any difference. The lad's impetuous. He likes to take chances. Those are difficult traits to temper."

"Yes, I suppose they are," Fáfila said quietly.

On the field below them, Pelayo's third and fourth defensive lines were standing firm. But Julian's men now had the bit between their teeth and were pounding away at the *Aguilas,* pressing them back with well-drilled efficiency.

Olivar's attention turned to the other side of the embattled hill, where some unusual activity seemed to be taking place. It looked as though the remnants of the *Aguilas'* first and second lines were regrouping into two wings. A moment later they began harrying the sides of Julian's wedge formation, striking, then disengaging, mimicking a cavalry's disruptive attacks.

Figuring that the contest would go on for a while longer, the crowd cheered and whistled in appreciation.

Julian's men fought off the running attack on their sides, all the while continuing to press forward, trying to smash their way through Pelayo's third defensive line. Just when it appeared Julian's men were going to break through, reinforcements from their opponents began to arrive, shoring up the *Aguilas'* beleaguered line.

Julian's advance ground to a halt.

Watching from the hill, General Olivar smiled faintly. Perhaps he had been too rash in predicting a quick end to the contest. "So, what kept you so long at the council meeting this morning, Don Fáfila?"

"We were discussing a dispatch I received yesterday from Don Ernesto."

Olivar's first thought was that the dispatch had something to do with the upcoming wedding of the baron's daughter Valentina to Julian.

"Anything of importance that I should be aware of?"

"It seems the Saracens are raiding the Catalonian coast again."

Olivar's expression darkened. "That's the second attack they've launched against us in less than a year."

"I know. I was hoping we'd seen the last of them, at least for a while."

"Maybe there's more to these raids than meets the eye."

"What do you mean, Olivar?"

"That stretch of coast is sparsely populated. Except for Barcinona, which is unlikely to be their target, there are only two or three small towns in the area as well as a few dozen churches and monasteries, and those are situated well inland."

"So?"

"Why would the Saracens sail all the way here just to pillage a handful of settlements and religious centers? Perhaps the first time they didn't know any better, but to strike the same stretch of coast again? It just doesn't make sense to me."

"So why do you think they've returned?" Fáfila asked.

"Isn't it obvious? They're testing our defenses."

"You think they're planning an all-out invasion?"

"I don't see what else it could be, Don Fáfila. The Saracens have swept across the northern coast of Afriqiyah like locusts. There's nowhere for them to head now but north."

Fáfila let out his breath tiredly. "I hope you're wrong, Olivar. We're far from being ready for war."

"I sense it's coming," Olivar said. "You should advise the King to prepare the kingdom."

"The Saracens aren't the kind of enemy we are used to fighting. They're fanatics. They believe dying in battle brings them untold rewards in the afterworld. We rejoice in life. They glorify death. How do we battle a foe that has no fear of dying?"

"I don't have an answer for you, Don Fáfila. All I know is that we have to prepare for war, otherwise the Saracens are going to overrun us."

Fáfila nodded glumly. The stories of the Saracens' propensity for war and destruction had for years sent shivers down the spine of everyone in Christendom. The thought of them landing on their shores was so disturbing, that everything in him wanted to dismiss it as fevered imaginings. But, over the years, he had learned to trust Olivar's instincts. If the old warrior said that war was coming, he would be wise to heed the warning. "How much time do you think we have?"

"That depends on what the Saracens learn from these incursions. If they conclude that we are weak and that our kingdom can be easily toppled, they'll come for us sooner rather than later."

Fáfila's spirits plummeted even further.

Back on the field below, Olivar noticed that the *Principes'* charge up the hill had stalled. Even more worrisome for Julian and his men, was the fact that they seemed to be losing their compact formation. Indeed, they appeared to be falling more and more into disarray. Pelayo's harrying attacks were proving to be quite effective.

Olivar had witnessed similar situations in the past. If Julian couldn't hold firm in the next few moments, he would need to order a strategic retreat. To buy time for his men to pull back in an orderly fashion, Julian would have to abandon at least a quarter of his men, which would leave him critically undermanned for his next assault. And that would spell the beginning of the end. The contest was turning out to be a little more balanced than he had first thought. "Was there anything else in Don Ernesto's dispatch?"

"He wants us to send him a cohort to fight off the Saracens," Fáfila answered.

Olivar cocked an eyebrow. "Shouldn't that request be addressed to the King?"

"There's a rumor that King Witiza is gravely ill. If that's truly the case, Ernesto thinks it'll be impossible to find someone in Toledo with the authority to respond to his request."

"There's bound to be someone who has taken over the day-to-day affairs of the kingdom," Olivar said.

"I don't share your confidence, Olivar. Witiza has grown increasingly distrustful in his old age. He'll not want to relinquish his authority to anyone, not while he's got a breath left in his body. In any case, Ernesto believes the situation is too critical to chance a delay. From my experience with the King and his court, I'm inclined to agree with him."

"Sounds like you've made up your mind on this."

"I don't see that I have a choice, Olivar," Fáfila said.

"You don't have the authority to use the legion without the express consent of the King, Don Fáfila, you know that."

"If it turns out that Witiza is in good health, and if at some point he learns what I've done, I'll just have to weather his displeasure," Fáfila answered.

"That's all very well for you to say, but with all due respect, I don't have the advantage of being married to the King's niece. If I go along with you, I'll be accused, and rightly so, of abusing my command."

"And what exactly would the King reproach you for?" Fáfila asked with a guileless look on his face. "Providing an escort to bring my son's betrothed from her home in Girona?"

Olivar snorted. "You really think that excuse will wash with the King?"

"Why not? Every word of it is true. Or could be."

"Four hundred men? For an escort?"

Fáfila smiled innocently. "Protection from the Saracens."

Olivar shook his head and turned his attention back to the battle.

Kept back as reserves, Pelayo's fifth squadron, comprised mostly of young recruits wearing brown cloaks, sprinted down the hill to join the fray. Olivar couldn't see how the move was going to have any significant effect. Pitching green recruits against soldiers used to facing real swords instead of staves was, in his opinion, a losing strategy.

"Do we know the size of the Saracen raiding party?" Olivar asked, his gaze still fixed on the scene below him.

"Baron Ernesto reckons the number could be as high as five or six hundred, but he doesn't know for certain."

"Does he know where the Saracen ships have landed?" Olivar asked.

"I don't think he does, no."

"He doesn't know much then, does he?" Olivar said testily.

"You can't blame Ernesto for that, Olivar," Duke Fáfila said mildly. "Most of the Catalonian coastline is wild and unpopulated."

General Olivar stared into the distance, lost in thought, then came to a decision. "Very well, Don Fáfila, I'll do as you ask. I'll provision a cohort and set off for the coast before the week is out."

"You needn't go yourself, Olivar. Why don't you send out one of your commanders?"

"This is too important a mission to entrust to any of my officers. It's not going to be enough to beat back the Saracens this time. We've got to crush them under our heels. That's the message the heathens have to take home with them."

A roar from the crowd brought Fáfila's and Olivar's attention back to the field below them.

Julian's wedge formation was grinding forward toward the crest of the hill, pushing through the line of desperate *Aguilas* defenders. Victory again seemed to be within Julian's grasp.

Olivar's gaze shifted to the far side of the hill, where a maneuver of some kind seemed to be unfolding. Pelayo, recognizable by his blue cloak, was leading a company of some one hundred soldiers around the base of the hill. Breaking into a run, they circled to the back of Julian's cohort, then began attacking it from the rear.

It took a while for Julian's men to realize they were being attacked from behind. Erupting in alarm, they put up a frenzied attempt to counter the threat. In the ensuing confusion, Pelayo's adjutant led the remaining troops of the *Aguilas* in what seemed like an all-out countercharge.

Attacked from both the front and the back, Julian's formation began to disintegrate. Pelayo's forces pressed their advantage, egged on by the cheering crowd.

The fighting continued for some time, even after the outcome was no longer in doubt.

At last, with only a few dozen of his men still standing around him, Julian raised his stave in the air and gave the command to surrender.

Pelayo's men broke into ragged cheers. Those of his soldiers who had been put out of commission ran from the sidelines and joined in the celebration. Around them, the townspeople erupted to their feet, applauding and cheering.

Atop the hill, Fáfila turned toward General Olivar, an amused gleam in his eyes. "So, what were you saying about Pelayo's impetuousness?"

Olivar chuckled ruefully. "Not much surprises me these days Don Fáfila, but I must admit that son of yours has managed to do that today."

"Yes, Pelayo does have a knack for doing the unexpected," Fáfila said, his mood lifting. He smiled as he watched the soldiers hoisting Pelayo onto their shoulders.

"Shall we go down and award the *Aguilas* the victory standard?" Olivar asked.

"In a moment; there's something I'd like to ask you first."

"Of course."

"Would you take Pelayo with you when you go to Catalonia?"

The request puzzled Olivar. Given the choice between the Duke's two sons, he would have preferred to take Julian, who was older and had years of command experience. But it wasn't his place to question the Duke's judgment, he reminded himself. "Very well, if that's your wish."

"I'd like you keep an eye on him for me," Fáfila said. "The boy has a reckless streak in him, as you've correctly pointed out."

Olivar frowned. "We're not going to a fair, Don Fáfila. If you want Pelayo safe, I suggest you keep him here with you."

"No, there's no question of that. He needs to leave this place."

Olivar gave Fáfila an inquiring glance.

"I'm seeing a change in Pelayo these days, Olivar," Fáfila said quietly. "He always seemed capable of dealing with any unpleasantness directed his way, but that's no longer the case. He's full of resentment now, quick to anger. He has no respect for anyone, no loyalty save to himself. Oh, he still has a kind heart, but there are too many grievances eating at him now. I fear if he stays here, that bitterness will turn into something darker."

"I understand, Don Fáfila."

"So, will you do it; will you keep an eye on Pelayo for me?"

Olivar hesitated then nodded. "Of course, Don Fáfila, I'll do what I can to keep him out of harm's way."

"That's all I ask, Olivar."

Four days later, in the quiet of an early morning, Pelayo slung his travel pack over his shoulder, then left his bedchamber. When he descended the staircase, he found his father waiting for him in the hall. They greeted each other quietly, then walked together toward the main door.

Pelayo had arrived at the castle the previous evening, hoping to clear the air with his father before setting out with General Olivar. Unfortunately, his father had been playing host to some members of the King's Council and the opportunity to speak with him in private had not presented itself.

Pelayo followed his father out the door and into the courtyard. The eastern sky was filled with red and purple colored streaks and the air smelled of wood smoke and freshly baked bread. A young groom standing outside the stable spotted him and began leading his horse toward him. A silence, heavy with an awkwardness that had never existed before, settled between Pelayo and his father as he dropped his pack on the ground.

The groom murmured a greeting, then picked up Pelayo's pack and began tying it to the saddle of the stallion he had led out.

"I have something for you," his father said to Pelayo, reaching into his pocket and pulling out a small leather purse. "Here."

Pelayo heard the clinking of coins as he took the purse from his father. By its weight he knew his father had been very generous. "Thank you."

"I want you to be careful out there," his father said. "The Saracens have had fifty years of war to hone their fighting skills. They'll be as fierce an enemy as any you'll ever face."

"I won't take them lightly, I promise."

From the distance came the sound of voices, then the guard on the watchtower hollered to the men below him to open the gates. A moment later a party of soldiers came trotting into the courtyard, then headed straight toward Pelayo and his father.

The lead rider called out as he neared, "Greetings, my lords!"

"Good morning to you," Fáfila answered. "What brings you here at this hour?"

"General Olivar asked us to escort your son to our camp, Don Fáfila."

Standing at his father's side, Pelayo snorted. "We both know he sent you to fetch me, not escort me."

The squad leader smiled as he brought his horse to a stop. "Perhaps that was the general's intention, sire. I believe he hopes to set off as soon as possible."

"Very well," Pelayo said. "Give me a moment to say good-bye to my father."

"Of course; we'll wait for you by the gate, sire."

Once the horsemen had ridden away, Fáfila turned toward Pelayo. "I'm sorry we had words the other day in the armory. I may have spoken to you a little more harshly than I intended to."

"That's all right," Pelayo said, pleased that his father had brought up the subject himself. "You had good reason to be angry with me."

"I was more upset than angry. It's been difficult watching the way you've been acting this past year."

"I'll try to behave better when I get back," Pelayo said. "No more scandals, I promise."

"I'm going to hold you to that," his father said gruffly, enfolding Pelayo in an embrace. "God speed, my son."

"Goodbye, Father," Pelayo said, feeling a tug at his heart. "I'll be back before you know it."

Pelayo gathered the reins of his horse, then swung up onto the saddle.

Before he could ride off, his father called out to him, "What do you say when you get back, we take the hawks and go hunting in the mountains like we used to do?"

"There's nothing I'd like better," Pelayo said.

"Good. Stay safe," his father said, raising his hand in farewell.

CHAPTER 5

SITTING AT HIS desk in his study, Fáfila looked at the King's quaestor slouched in a chair across from him and sighed in exasperation. He had spent the greater part of the morning holed up with the insufferable idiot and his patience was wearing thin. As was usually the case when discussing how to apportion the annual costs of maintaining the Third Legion, the quaestor was refusing to listen to reason.

"I've told you," Fafila told the man. "I can't afford to make up the difference."

The quaestor, a tall, thin man wearing a medallion of office over his tunic, shrugged off Fáfila's protest. "Then you will have to raise the taxes," he replied in an unruffled manner.

They'd been going around in circles on the issue and Fáfila felt his temper fraying. "I'm already taxing my people to the limit of what they can afford to pay. If I demand more from them, they'll go hungry this winter."

"You had bountiful crops last year. I'm sure your farmers can afford to pay a small increase."

"This is the fourth demand from the King in as many years. I'll have an uprising on my hands if I raise the taxes again."

"It's either that or you'll have to cut your own expenses to make up the difference."

Fáfila was about to retort, when the door to his chamber cracked open and a servant stuck his head inside.

"Pardon the intrusion, sire. Baron Porfiro and a party of men have just ridden in."

Fáfila nodded to the servant, then turned back toward the quaestor. "It seems I have some unexpected guests I need to attend to. We'll have to postpone our discussion until later."

A look of irritation flitted across the quaestor's face, then his expression smoothed. "As you wish, Don Fáfila." he said, rising from his seat.

Glad for the excuse to end his talk with the quaestor, Fáfila strode out the door and made his way to the courtyard outside. It had been raining since early that morning and as usual the ground had turned into mud. Several men, satchels slung over their shoulders, were standing by the doors of the stable, waiting for the grooms to lead their horses inside. In their midst stood his friend, Porfiro, who had a cloaked stranger at his side. The rest of the newcomers were men-at-arms.

It had been some eighteen months since Fáfila had last seen Porfiro and the sight of his old friend brought a smile to his lips.

The two had first met at a King's council in Tarragona some fifteen years earlier. They had been on opposite sides of a contentious argument that had split the council into two factions. Fáfila had initially taken a dislike to the portly Baron of Cuenca, pegging him as a loud, overbearing oaf. As the days had passed, however, he had found himself warming to Porfiro's intelligence and his irreverent sense of humor. Eventually, the two of them had put aside their differences and had come to see eye to eye on the issue. They had visited each other countless times since that occasion, and Fáfila now considered Porfiro to be not only a trusted ally, but also a steadfast friend.

"Fáfila!" Porfiro called out in a jovial voice. "How can you Asturians stand this god-cursed weather of yours?"

"I'd like to say that we get used to it, but then I'd be a bloody liar. How are you, my friend?"

"Fine, just fine," Porfiro said, beaming.

Porfiro's waistline seemed to have expanded somewhat since Fáfila had last seen him. His face was rounder too, his chin disappearing into folds of fat around his neck. Perched atop his head was a peaked leather hat with a brim that was channeling rainwater down a thumb's length away from his nose.

After engulfing Fáfila in a bear hug, Porfiro stepped back and studied his friend with a critical eye. "You're looking well, Fáfila, a little thin maybe."

"Not many people accuse me of that these days, Porfiro," Fáfila said with a chuckle, patting his paunch.

The distinguished looking stranger, wearing an oiled leather cloak slick with rain, walked over and joined them.

Porfiro put his hand on the stranger's shoulder. "This is Lord Roderic, the new Military Governor of Baetica."

Fáfila studied the man before him with interest. He appeared to be in his late thirties, with broad shoulders and a stocky frame. He had a trimmed brown beard, intelligent looking eyes, and a bearing that exuded confidence.

"I heard of your appointment," Fáfila said to him. "You're Duke Felipe's eldest son, I believe."

Roderic inclined his head. "I have that honor," he said, his voice deep and measured.

"I got to know your father well at the Council over the years. I was sorry to hear of his passing. He was a good man."

"He was, indeed, Don Fáfila. Not a day goes by that I don't miss him."

A clap of thunder sounded alarmingly close. The wind suddenly picked up and the rain turned into a torrential downpour. "Come, let's go talk inside," Fáfila called out, shepherding everyone quickly toward the castle.

After finding refuge in the great hall, Fáfila ordered a servant to take Porfiro's men-at-arms to the kitchen and have the cooks prepare some food for them. Once everyone had left, he turned toward Porfiro and Roderic. "So, what business brings you here?"

Porfiro raised an eyebrow. "Do I need an excuse to visit an old friend?"

"You know you're always welcome, Porfiro, but I'm guessing you're not here on a social visit. If you were, I expect you'd have brought along Leonora and the children."

"You're right, Fáfila," Porfiro admitted. "We've come on a serious matter."

"You have my attention. Out with it."

Porfiro's expression turned somber. "King Witiza is dead."

Fáfila's eyes widened. "Good Lord," he muttered. *The King's only heir, Olmund, had just turned eight; much too young to take over the reins of power. All hell will break loose now*, he thought in dismay. "When did it happen?"

"Two weeks ago," Roderic answered. "And before you ask, there was no foul play; the King died of natural causes."

"Someone's done an excellent job of suppressing the news," Fáfila said. "I've not heard a whisper about it."

"Some members of the Council, and that includes me, thought it wise to keep the news secret for the time being."

"I don't understand," Fáfila said. "Why the secrecy?"

"To buy us time," Porfiro said. "We thought it would be

best to announce the King's death and his successor at the same time."

Fáfila thought about it, then nodded. "There's some sense to that, I suppose."

Fáfila led his two guests toward a table by the fire in the great hall. As he lowered himself onto a bench, Porfiro and Roderic removed their sodden hats and riding cloaks, handed them off to a servant, then sat down on the opposite side of the table.

"So," Fáfila said, gazing at the men before him. "I have a feeling the two of you haven't ridden all this way just to bring me news of the King's death."

"You're right," Porfiro said. "There's something of grave importance we need to discuss with you. The succession of the throne."

Fáfila was instantly on his guard. "What is there to discuss? The King has a male heir. All the Council has to do is appoint a regent until the boy comes of age."

"And who do you think the Council will appoint?" Porfiro asked.

"The most obvious choice would be the King's brother, Baron Siberto."

"That's right. Can you imagine what it will be like to have that miscreant as regent? He'll suck the country drier that an old whore's tit."

Fáfila frowned. "The man you're speaking of happens to be my wife's uncle."

"I don't have time to soothe your ruffled feathers, Fáfila," Porfiro said curtly. "Siberto is an unscrupulous leech and you know it. Think what it would be like to have him ruling the country for the next ten years."

Fáfila stared wordlessly at Porfiro. King Witiza had been

no saint, but he had been a passable ruler who had kept his excesses at a tolerable level. The same could not be said of his brother, Siberto, who had run his once prosperous estate into the ground through a mixture of incompetence and greed. Having him as regent would sentence the kingdom to years of ineptitude and unbridled corruption. "All right, I'm listening. What exactly are you proposing?"

Though there was no one within hearing distance, Porfiro lowered his voice and said, "I intend to offer up a new claimant to the throne at the next High Council."

Fáfila had suspected something of the sort but having Porfiro lay out his intention so bluntly still unsettled him. "That's a dangerous game you're playing, my friend."

Roderic spoke out, "We wouldn't be doing this if we didn't believe the situation merited drastic measures, Don Fáfila."

The three men fell silent as a servant approached and placed a tray with three goblets of wine on the table. After the servant left, Porfiro gazed across at Fáfila. "Aren't you going to ask me who I plan to nominate?"

"I don't need to," Fáfila replied, looking squarely at Roderic.

Roderic dipped his head in acknowledgement.

"He'll make a fine king, Fáfila," Porfiro said.

"I know a dozen men who, given the chance, would govern decently," Fáfila answered in a flat tone.

"And how many of them would have the balls to step forward and declare himself a contender?" Porfiro asked.

"Not many," Fáfila admitted. The consequences of being on the losing side of a struggle for the throne were too harrowing for most men to stomach.

Porfiro said, "I wish I could give you the time to think things over for a day or two, Fáfila, but the Council is set to meet next month and there are other members we need to speak to. I need to know right now where you stand. When the time comes, can we count on your support?"

Fáfila held Porfiro's gaze. "Are you really asking me to back a challenger over my wife's blood relation?"

"There are more important things at stake here than blind loyalty to one's family, Fáfila," Porfiro said.

Fáfila let out his breath tiredly. "Look, even if I felt free to cast my vote for whomever I please, I would never do so for someone I know nothing about."

"Don Fáfila," Roderic cut in, putting down his goblet on the table. "It is true that I'm a stranger to you, but you knew my father. Perhaps you could put your trust in me and give me the benefit of the doubt."

"I'm sorry, that is more than I care to give," Fáfila answered evenly.

Porfiro's shoulders slumped. "I thought you would be the first to be on our side, Fáfila. Are you really going to cast your lot for that fool, Siberto?"

Fáfila felt cornered. As he had feared, the issue of the succession was going to pit them all against each other. The burning question was, could he stand apart and not take sides?

"You can't hide behind the walls of Gijón forever, Fáfila," Porfiro said, as if reading his mind.

Fáfila gazed at the two men across from him, "What sort of support do you have in the Council?"

Porfiro thought for a moment, then answered, "Seven have given us their commitment."

"Out of eighteen? That's not exactly a ringing endorsement."

Roderic spoke up, "We should be able to win a few more to our side by the time the Council reconvenes next month."

"Perhaps you will and perhaps you won't," Fáfila said.

"That is why we need your help," Porfiro said. "To sway those who are undecided."

"What of Augusto, Arañales and Cassano?" Fáfila asked.

"They usually vote the same way. Have you contacted them yet?"

"They're next on our list," Porfiro said.

"So, who on the Council has said no to you?" Fáfila asked.

"The Witiza's usual allies: Lucio, Juvenal, Maximiliano and Llorenç." Porfiro said. "Quentinus and Gaona both told us they need more time to think before they give us their final decision."

"They'll sit on the fence and wait to see which way the wind blows," Fáfila said.

"I know," Porfiro fell silent, looking uncharacteristically subdued.

"What of the legions?" Fáfila asked. "Where do they stand?"

"The Fourth will follow me," Roderic said. "The First and Second will back the King's heir. I expect the Third will line up behind you."

"So that leaves the First and Second to worry about," Fáfila said, gazing at Roderic. "How do you plan to deal with them?"

"Two weeks before the Council meets, I'll call up the Fourth to Toledo. The First should still be camped out in Valentia and the Second in Cáceres. Even if Siberto summons them, it will take them several weeks to mobilize and reach Toledo. By then, I should be firmly in control of the city. Once the First and Second learn that I've been proclaimed King, they should fall in line with the others and offer me their allegiance."

"It's a good plan," Fáfila said. "It just might work."

"I can't take credit for it; it's Porfiro's idea."

Fáfila eyed his friend. "You've become quite the master schemer, Porfiro."

"Mock me if you wish, Fáfila, but these are dangerous times

for the country. To survive we need a strong king, not a snot-nosed boy."

Fáfila remembered Olivar's warning that war with the Saracens was imminent. With such a formidable foe lying in wait, could he, in good faith, entrust the fate of the kingdom to an incompetent hothead like Siberto? The more he thought about it, the more he grew convinced that he really had no choice at all, not if he wanted to sleep soundly at night. "I think I know of a way we can get Augusto and Llorenç to change their minds."

Porfiro arched an eyebrow. "We?"

Fáfila nodded. "I'm casting my lot with the two of you."

Porfiro broke into a wide smile. "I knew you wouldn't let us down, Fáfila. All that nonsense you were spouting." He shook his head. "You didn't fool me for a moment."

At his side, Roderic cleared his throat. "I realize this was not an easy decision for you to make, Don Fáfila. Win or lose, know that I shall forever be in your debt."

"If we lose, you won't have to worry about repaying me for anything," Fáfila said. "Siberto will hang us all for treason."

CHAPTER 6

BROTHER BONIFACIO WAS attending evening prayers in the chapel when a large band of Saracen warriors burst through the doors like wolves tearing into a henhouse. With his heart hammering in his chest, he bolted through a side door, then fled down a corridor, the sounds of screaming goading him into a fear-crazed run. Gripped by panic, his mind blanketed by terror, Bonifacio followed some other monks fleeing toward the refectory.

Like fish swimming into a net, they ran into a band of Saracen warriors who had been lying there in wait. With nowhere to go, Bonifacio cowered back against a wall, and watched in horror as the heathens began slaughtering his fellow monks.

After what seemed like an eternity, a shouted command cut through the screams of pain and cries for mercy, bringing an end to the killing.

Some of the warriors grabbed hold of Bonifacio and three other monks, the only ones left standing, and dragged them outside into the courtyard.

There Bonifacio found a scene of devastation. All the

monastery's buildings and sheds were burning, spewing smoke and orange flames into the evening sky. Turning his face away from the heat, he caught sight of the mangled bodies of his brethren scattered across the courtyard. Tears sprang to his eyes as he took in the terrible fate that had befallen their peaceful refuge.

A tall, bearded figure made his way through the ring of warriors toward Bonifacio and his fellow monks. Clad in black leather and a knee-length chainmail shirt, the man told them in heavily accented Iberian that he would spare their lives in exchange for information about the roads and towns in the area.

Bonifacio and his three brethren looked at each other, knowing full well that revealing that information would lead to the death or enslavement of the people in the settlements they identified.

The cellarer, a frail, elderly man with wispy white hair, spoke for them all. "I shall not tell you anything. Nor will anyone else here."

Nodding, as if he had expected the cellarer's answer, the leather-clad man turned and addressed his men in their tongue.

Two warriors immediately sprang forward and seized the sacrist who had been standing at the cellarer's side. They grabbed one of his arms, pulled it straight out, then a third man hacked off the limb at the elbow.

The sacrist let out a tortured cry, the likes of which Bonificio had never heard before coming from a human being. The gorge rose at the back of his throat as he stared at the blood spurting from the stump of the man's arm. Mercifully, the sacrist's eyes rolled back in his head and he collapsed senseless to the ground.

The Saracen chieftain turned toward another monk, a young initiate who worked in the kitchen. Now the subject of the Saracen's attention, the youth visibly blanched. To his eternal credit, though his lips were trembling with fear, he shook his head.

The chieftain swung his sword in a swift and lethal arc. With the dull thunk of a butcher's cleaver, the curved blade bit through bone and sinew, lopping off the young monk's head.

Though sickened by the wanton brutality, Bonificio could not wrench his gaze away from the headless figure on the ground.

The Saracen chieftain turned his brooding eyes to the cellarer. No doubt seeing the resolution written on the old man's face, he turned away and addressed his men.

Several warriors seized the cellarer, then bound his hands and feet with rope. Grabbing him under the armpits and by the feet, they carried him off to one of the burning buildings. The cellarer struggled desperately but in vain as the warriors heaved him into the blazing inferno.

Bonifacio averted his gaze, not wanting to witness what was going to happen. But at the first blood-curdling scream, his willpower crumbled. The image of the old man engulfed in flames seared into his eyes.

With the stench of smoke and burning flesh permeating the air, the chieftain's pitiless gaze fixed on Bonifacio. "You are the one who will tell me what I want to know," he said in an assured voice.

Trembling, as if in the grip of a high fever, Bonifacio bowed his head, tears trailing down his cheeks. "Yes," he whispered.

How had that spawn from hell seen into his soul and known that he was the weakest of them all; that he would betray everyone and everything to save his own worthless skin?

He wondered how many innocent people he was about to condemn to rape, enslavement and death. *"Oh God, please forgive me."*

CHAPTER 7

IT WAS LATE afternoon when General Olivar's cohort reached the coastal town of Benidum. It had been raining since they had crossed into the province of Catalonia two days earlier, and the prospect of staying in the town's barracks and having a solid roof over their heads had lifted everyone's spirits. After weeks of eating plain food and sleeping on cold, hard ground, all the men were looking forward to enjoying the comforts of civilized life again.

Commander Cayo was yearning to take a good, long soak in the town's famed Roman baths. Commander Xocobo had his heart set on finding a tavern with a few comely girls and a succulent pig roasting on a spit. Pelayo just wanted to stay off his damned horse for a few days.

As the column drew closer to Benidum, Pelayo began to sense that something was not quite right. There was no sign of life, either on the road or in the surrounding countryside. No farmers, no sheep, no cows, no barking dogs. Nothing but an empty landscape.

An uneasy silence settled over everyone as the column rode up to the gates. The massive doors were open and unguarded, a sign that something untoward had happened. The sickening smell of rotting flesh wafted over them as they caught their first glimpse of the burned-out buildings inside the walls.

General Olivar called a halt, then picked a squad consisting of Pelayo, Commander Xocobo and a dozen soldiers. Leaving the rest of the cohort to wait outside the walls, Olivar led his party through the gates and into the town.

No one spoke as they gazed at the devastation around them. The once prosperous town had been reduced to a wasteland of debris-littered streets, collapsed buildings and half-burnt timbers poking out like ribs from a blackened carcass.

Pelayo thought the destruction appeared too thorough to have been caused by a fire that had gotten out of control. It looked like Benidum had been deliberately torched.

General Olivar led the party toward the town's center. After several turns, they emerged into a square dominated by a church with a partially collapsed roof. Despite its sorry-looking appearance, the church seemed to be the only building in Benidum still standing.

Having seen no sign of life, they were about to turn back when an old man, holding on to the shoulder of a young boy for support, came walking out from the ruined church. Clad in little more than rags, the two appeared dirty and malnourished. As if some signal had been given, other bedraggled figures began emerging from inside the church.

The old man and the boy came to a stop, some half-dozen paces away from General Olivar and the mounted party. Raising a skeletal arm, the old man pointed an accusing finger at them. "You've come too late," he cried out bitterly. "What use are you and your soldiers to us now?"

Before General Olivar could answer, a tall, broad-shouldered man in his thirties pushed his way through the crowd toward the front. "Forgive the old man's insolence, sire," he called out. "He's lost his entire family save for his one grandson."

General Olivar studied the bearded, dark-haired man who had spoken. "What is your name?"

"Bartolomeo, sire."

"What happened here?"

The old man with the young boy cut in, "Hell opened up and the devil descended upon us."

Bartolomeo placed a hand on the old man's shoulder, silencing him. "We were attacked by heathens, sire. Four days ago. They came just before sunrise, when most of us were sleeping in our beds."

"Did the guards at the gates sound a warning?" General Olivar asked.

"If they did, we didn't hear it. Most of us only learned of the attack from the shouting in the streets."

"How large was the force that attacked you?" General Olivar asked.

"I couldn't say, sire. My only thought was to try to get my family to safety."

A middle-aged man in the crowd called out, "I got a good view of them as they came through the gates. There had to have been at least a couple of hundred."

Others in the crowd voiced slightly different numbers.

"Go on with your story," General Olivar told Bartolomeo. "What happened then?"

"The heathens stormed through the streets, killing everyone who crossed their path. That was no great feat, as none of us had any weapons, other than a cleaver or a hammer. Then they started torching our houses, giving us the choice to either burn alive, or come out and get hacked down."

"How is it that you all managed to escape then?" General Olivar asked, gesturing with his hand to encompass the crowd.

"Most of us here had the good fortune of living on the other side of town," Bartolomeo answered. "We managed to flee through an old southern portal into the forest."

"So you people are the only ones left alive?" General Olivar asked

"Yes, sire. The Saracens slaughtered everyone, even babes in their mothers' arms. The only ones they spared were the young women. The pretty ones."

General Olivar addressed the bedraggled group of survivors before him. "Did any of you happen to see in which direction the Saracens headed when they left here?"

"I did," a woman at the front of the crowd called out. "Most of them took the old road east. A smaller group went off down the coastal road, heading south."

"They split in two?" Olivar asked.

"It's what I saw," the woman answered. "The ones heading down the coastal road had our girls with them."

"How is it you know this?" Olivar asked the woman, obviously trying to determine whether he could rely on her information.

"I'm a midwife. I'd been up all night delivering a baby at a nearby farm. I was making my way home, when I saw our town burning in the distance. When I got closer, I saw two groups of horsemen head off in different directions."

Pelayo saw Olivar frown. The news the Saracens had managed to steal enough horses to mount all their warriors was a worrying development. It meant they could extend their range and strike settlements further inland.

A middle-aged woman wearing a tattered headscarf cried

out, "The Saracens took my two daughters. They're only fourteen and sixteen. You must find them for me, sire, I beg you."

A chorus of voices erupted as other people began calling out similar pleas.

General Olivar's eyes swept over the crowd. "We'll do what we can."

Pelayo caught Olivar's eye as they were turning their horses to leave. "These people look like they're starving, general. Could we share some of our supplies with them?"

Olivar hesitated then nodded. "I suppose we can spare some salted meat and a couple of sacks of flour. Why don't you take care of it?"

"I'd be happy to, general," Pelayo answered. The plight of the villagers brought home the seriousness of their mission. This wasn't just some exotic adventure or a meaningless pursuit like that of the Legion's mock battle. The Saracen raid posed a serious threat to the country. People's lives and liberty were at risk. It was a sobering thought that put everything in a different perspective.

The cohort spent the night encamped outside Benidum. At dawn the next morning, General Olivar met with his three senior officers, Pelayo, Xocobo and Cayo, outside his tent.

Kneeling on the ground and unrolling a vellum map, General Olivar told them, "I've decided on a change of plan. "I'm going to split the cohort into two companies."

Pelayo peered over the general's shoulders at the map, guessing what was coming.

General Olivar continued, "I'll take one company and go after the band of Saracens heading east," he said, tapping his finger at a point on the map. "Xocobo, you'll take command of the other company and hunt down the Saracen band heading south with the women. Your objective is to find their landing site and destroy their ships. Once we've accomplished our respective missions, we'll meet up in Girona. Any questions?"

If Commander Xocobo felt surprised at suddenly being thrust into a command position, he hid it well. "None that I can think of general."

"What about the captured women?" Pelayo asked.

"As I said, your prime objective is to destroy the enemy ships," General Olivar said. "Freeing the women is secondary. If you can save them without jeopardizing the mission, do so by all means."

Pelayo wasn't entirely satisfied with the answer, but he nodded his agreement.

General Olivar studied Pelayo for a moment. "I'm appointing you as Xocobo's second-in-command. You'll be going after the smaller Saracen band, so it'll be less dangerous. Your father will have my hide if anything happens to you, so when you engage with the enemy, keep your head about you and don't do anything foolish."

"Rest easy, general," Pelayo said. "I don't plan to get myself killed on my first sortie."

"Good. That's what I wanted to hear."

When the last of General Olivar's horsemen had disappeared down the road, Xocobo gave his saddle strap a final tug.

"Our turn, let's go," Xocobo told Pelayo as he swung himself up on his horse. Once mounted, he gave the signal to the men behind him to head out.

For the next two days, Pelayo and Xocobo led the column of two hundred soldiers and a dozen pack mules down a well-traveled, dirt road. The weather remained stormy, with bouts of rain that seeped through the gaps in the men's collars, soaking them to the bone. Finally, on the third day, the cloudy weather broke, and the sun came out.

Two days later, they found the first unmistakable tracks of the Saracens' horses imprinted on the hardening mud. After several leagues, the tracks angled away from the road toward a narrow trail that branched off into the woods. The trail then led to a large clearing pockmarked with the burnt-out remains of a dozen campfires. Judging from the ashes that appeared undisturbed by rain, Pelayo figured that the campsite had been used as recently as the previous day. There could be no doubt now that they were closing in on the Saracens.

The tracks re-appeared on the other side of the campsite and Pelayo and Xocobo followed them to a mountain pass that opened up into a broad valley. There, in the distance, stood a cluster of stone buildings surrounded by cultivated fields.

Pelayo and Xocobo consulted a map and concluded that they were looking at the monastery of Santo Tomas. It was the first sign of human habitation they had come across since leaving Benidum. Given the balmy weather, there should have been monks toiling in the fields and in the vineyards. But the entire area seemed deserted. Remembering what had happened in Benidum, a sense of foreboding began stealing over Pelayo.

Pelayo and Xocobo led the column down a rutted road that curved through fields toward the monastery. As they neared, they saw that the main gate had been ripped off its hinges. A slight breeze carried the unmistakable stench of rotting flesh.

With their men trailing behind them, Xocobo and Pelayo rode into the monastery's courtyard, setting off a cloud of ravens that took to the air in a flurry of beating wings.

Pelayo tried to take shallow breaths as he gazed at the fly-covered corpses scattered around. All the wooden structures, what must have been the stable, the stockrooms and sheds, had burned to the ground, leaving behind heaps of charred timber.

The soldiers that had followed Pelayo and Xocobo into the courtyard began crossing themselves.

Xocobo gazed around him as he dismounted. "Looks like these poor wretches have been dead for a while. At least a week, I'd say."

Pelayo slid down off his horse. "That means the Saracens struck the monastery before heading off to Benidum."

Xocobo nodded. "It seems they're doubling back along the route they took from the coast."

At the far end of the courtyard, a vanguard of ravens, began touching down amongst the corpses again. One particularly daring bird landed close to Pelayo and Xocobo and started pecking at the eye socket of one of the bodies near them.

"I doubt we'll find any survivors this time," Xocobo said quietly.

Pelayo nodded, finding the stench increasingly oppressive.

"We'll set up camp outside the walls tonight," Xocobo said. "We can use the remaining daylight hours to bury these bodies."

Pelayo's stomach lurched at the thought of having to man-handle the corpses.

"There's another storm heading our way," Xocobo said, pointing to a line of dark clouds in the distance.

"They're still some ways off," Pelayo said. "If we work quickly, we should have time to dig the graves, then put up the tents before the storm hits us."

"That's not what I'm concerned about," Xocobo said. "Sooner or later the Saracens are going to turn off the road and cut through the forest toward their landing site on the coast. If we wait until tomorrow, the rain could wash away their tracks, leaving us with no idea as to which way they've headed."

"Why don't we send out a couple of men to keep tracking them."

"Exactly what I was thinking," Xocobo said. "I'll send out
Rubio, he's the best tracker we've got."

"I don't think I know the man."

"He's one of the archers." Xocobo studied Pelayo. "I have a
feeling you're not going to be much use to me here. Why don't
you go along with him?"

"I'd like to, if you think you can spare me," Pelayo said
quickly, trying to mask his relief.

"I think I'll manage," Xocobo said dryly. "But the moment
you find the spot where the Saracens have left the road, you
turn around and report back to me here, understand?"

"Of course," Pelayo said. He would have promised Xocobo
the moon, if the man had asked for it. "Just make sure the sentries don't riddle us with arrows if we happen to wander back
in the middle of the night."

"I'll think about it," Xocobo said. "All right, let's go find
Rubio. You two have a race to run with those storm clouds
over there."

CHAPTER 8

"CAPTAIN DIEGO!" A female voice called out, cutting through the sound of horses clopping along the forest road.

On point position at the head of the riding party, Diego, captain of Baron Ernesto's house guards, turned in the saddle and peered at the four civilians riding midway down the column. A look of irritation flitted across his weather-beaten face, as he pulled off to the side of the road and waited for the column to pass by him. Eventually Valentina and her party, consisting of her guardian Rosaria, her cousin Benito, and her companion Carmela, came riding toward him. With a nudge of his heels, he steered his horse alongside Valentina's chestnut mare. "What is it, my lady?"

"Is there a reason why we're riding at such a breakneck pace, captain?" she asked.

Diego weighed his answer. He did indeed have a reason, but sharing it with her would just worry her, and he didn't see the point of doing that. Truth was he'd been feeling uneasy ever since he had received word that morning that Benidum had been sacked. Though the town was a considerable distance away, he had nonetheless found himself setting an ever-quickening pace as the day wore on.

"Well captain?" Valentina said, an impatient note in her voice.

"We need to take shelter for the night at the monastery of Santo Tomas. I want to make sure we get there before sunset."

"We've made this journey half a dozen times. There's plenty of time left. I don't see why we have to lather the horses just to get there early."

"I've only picked up our pace a little, my lady," Diego protested.

Valentina's hazel eyes fixed on Diego. "Have you ever ridden side-saddle, captain?"

"Can't say that I have."

"Perhaps you should try it sometime and see how it feels."

"I'll certainly add it to my list of things to do. Is there anything else, my lady?"

Valentina stared at him with a stony expression, then shook her head curtly.

God Almighty, Diego thought with an inward sigh, as he made his way back to the head of the column. *Two more days of locking horns with her... It's going to be one hell of a long journey.*

As Diego steered his horse down the road, he thought about Valentina, wondering what made her so quarrelsome, so different from the other well-mannered ladies of good family. The blame, he decided, had to be laid squarely at the feet of Doña Katerina and Baron Ernesto. Like many parents blessed with children late in their lives, the two had doted on Valentina from the moment of her birth.

In all fairness, Diego could understand why. Valentina had been a delightful child, with a sunny disposition that warmed the heart of anyone who came in contact with her. That was the trouble, he thought. The winsome child had grown up to become a spoiled young woman, used to weaving her spell and getting her way with everyone. *Except with me;* Diego thought. *I'm not going to let her wrap me around her little finger, that's for damn sure.*

Diego and his men had arrived the previous day at the estate of Baron Ernesto's brother, with orders to escort Valentina and her companions back to Girona. Valentina had pleaded with him to delay their departure for a few days, so she could attend a banquet being thrown in her honor by her aunt. Diego had tried to explain to her that her father was concerned about the Saracen raids and had instructed him to bring her home immediately. As usual their discussion had degenerated into an argument that had lasted far longer than it should have. In the end, however, no doubt fearing her father's displeasure, Valentina had reluctantly agreed to leave. It had been a rare victory for him.

That morning, Diego and his party had gathered in the courtyard of the estate shortly after daybreak. Before her aunt and uncle had bidden Valentina goodbye, they had secured a promise from her that she would keep a close eye on their eight-year-old son, Benito, whom they were allowing to travel to Girona with her for a family visit. As the sun had risen over the rolling hills that made up much of the southwestern corner of Catalonia, Captain Diego had led his party of twenty-four soldiers, three women and a young boy, on the first of several back roads that would eventually bring them home to Girona.

Valentina's laughter roused her guardian, Rosaria, riding just ahead of her, from the sleepy daze that she had been lulled into by the warm September sun. Blinking owlishly, she turned in the saddle and fixed her gaze on Valentina, riding between Benito and Carmela. "What is it you find so amusing?"

Valentina tried to keep a straight face, but the corners of her lips kept twitching with suppressed laughter. "I'm just telling them the story about Julian, when he came to visit us in Girona."

Rosaria eyed Valentina. "I didn't think you had found Julian all that amusing."

"You're right," Valentina said. "I thought he was an ill-mannered boor."

"Really, Valentina," Rosaria said with a disapproving frown. "You shouldn't speak so disparagingly about your betrothed."

"I'm sorry, I found him disagreeable and arrogant and I don't care who hears me say it."

Rosaria shook her head. "I don't understand why you hold him in such low regard. You couldn't ask for a more handsome and strapping young man. And he'll be a duke one day. You should count yourself lucky."

"He's got another side to him, Rosaria; you don't know him like I do."

"That may be so, but I know a little more about the world than you do, my dear. Young men such as Julian can sometimes appear rough around the edges."

"He certainly seems more at ease with his hounds than he does with me. I'd be quite happy leaving him to their company forever."

"Oh, hush now, child." Rosaria said, looking around her. "You always exaggerate and make a situation seem worse than it really is."

Valentina's high spirits deserted her. *Only four more months until my eighteenth birthday, then my freedom comes to an end.*

She had spent many a night lying awake wondering what

her life would be like as Julian's wife. She would probably have to simper at his every glance, smile at his crude comments and lie meekly beneath him as they coupled, pretending to enjoy it. She shuddered in disgust. *I'd rather be a nun than have to spend the rest of my life with him.*

It was midafternoon when the riding party left the cultivated farmlands behind them and entered a forest. The air took on a rich, loamy smell. Above their heads, dappled light flickered through the canopy of branches arching over the road.

They had made good time and Diego was feeling calm as he steered his horse up a steep hill. At the top, an expansive view of the surrounding countryside opened up before him. Suddenly, in the distance, some half-a-league way, he caught sight of a flock of birds taking flight. His sense of peace suddenly vanished as he became aware of the unnatural stillness in the forest.

"Pass on the word to the men to stay alert," Diego told his second-in-command riding at his side. "Do it quietly, without alarming the civilians."

His second acknowledged the order, then turned his horse and trotted away.

Riding alongside Valentina, young Benito seemed to sense a change in the mood of the soldiers. "Why has everyone suddenly gone so quiet?" he asked, glancing about him.

"Oh, heaven knows," Valentina said. "Captain Diego is like an old hen. He's always worried about something or other."

"Maybe he's afraid of encountering witches," Benito said in a hushed voice. "They live in forests like this one, you know."

Valentina smiled. "I've traveled through these woods many

times, Benito. I've never encountered anything more unusual than a fox chasing a rabbit."

Riding on point, Diego froze as he caught sight of movement on the road ahead. Raising his arm in a signal to the column, he brought his horse to a halt. Squinting his eyes, he peered into the distance.

Some three hundred paces up the road, darkly clad riders began to pour over the crest of a hill. The sight sent a chill of fear running down his spine.

The horsemen in the distance seemed as surprised as Diego, and they too brought their horses to a stop, blocking those coming behind them and swelling their ranks.

Diego swore a steady stream of oaths under his breath, cursing his luck. His worst fear had come to pass. They had stumbled upon a Saracen raiding party, probably the same one that had sacked Benidum.

As more and more horsemen crested the hill, it dawned on Diego that if they didn't turn around and beat a hasty retreat immediately, they'd all be captured or killed. The realization focused his mind. He was about to issue the command to turn and flee when a sudden thought stopped him cold. Valentina and her companions were all riding mares, specifically chosen for their placid nature. Their horses would never be able to outrun the Saracens.

Diego sat on his horse, frozen with indecision, losing precious moments that he knew could mean the difference between life and death. At last, with great reluctance, he settled on the one solution that he had striven to avoid. The only way of ensuring the safety of his charges was to make a stand and buy them time to get away. Doing so would probably doom him and his men to certain death, but as captain of the house guards, it was his duty to protect Valentina, no matter the consequences. With the path before him now clear, a preternatural calm descended over him.

Turning in the saddle, he bellowed to his men, "Break out your shields and prepare for battle! We're going to hold off the Saracens until the civilians get away!"

Chaos instantly erupted down the length of the column.

"Valentina!" Diego shouted again, his voice cutting through the din. "Take your companions and head back to your uncle's. Don't stop until you get there."

"All right, captain," she shouted back.

Valentina struggled to tamp down her terror. She glanced at Carmela, Benito and Rosaria and saw her fear mirrored in their faces.

As she tore her gaze away from them and looked behind her, she saw that they were in the middle of the column, and that the road behind them was clogged with soldiers who were untying their shields and drawing out their swords.

"Stay close to me!" Valentina shouted to Carmela, Benito and Rosaria. "As soon as the road clears behind us, we'll make a run for it!"

At the front of the column, Diego's gaze remained locked on the distant rise where about a dozen or so Saracen archers were running down the road toward him and his men. He knew that once the archers came within range, they would lay down a barrage of arrows to provide cover for the forty or so horsemen gathering for a charge on the summit of the hill. By the speed and efficiency of the Saracens' deployment, he knew that he and his men were facing battle-hardened troops.

The Saracen archers released their first volley just as Diego had slid off his horse. A swarm of arrows began whizzing around him. Frantically he reached for his shield tied to the saddle, his finger plucking at the thongs. A feathered shaft hissed by him and punched into the thigh of a nearby soldier running for cover. Another arrow struck a horse in the withers. Suddenly the air filled with frantic shouts and cries of pain.

"Get off the road! Take cover!" Diego hollered, grabbing the reins of his horse and sprinting toward the relative safety of the forest.

After what seemed like an eternity to Valentina, the last of Captain Diego's men melted away. With the road behind her open now, Rosaria, who was first in line, shot off at a gallop. Then it was Valentina's turn. Before she could urge her horse forward, a shrill whinny erupted from behind her. Casting a glance over her shoulder, she saw Benito's horse rearing up, its front hooves beating high in the air. Fighting desperately to stay on the saddle, Benito had his arms wrapped around the neck of his horse.

"Hold on, I'm coming!" Valentina shouted, turning and urging her horse forward. Timing her move to avoid the thrashing hooves, she reached across and grabbed the bridle of Benito's horse. The animal fought her, but she held on, pulling its head down, forcing it onto all fours.

Valentina thought she had succeeded in her task, when Benito suddenly let out a tortured cry. Arching his back, his face contorted in agony. His hands clawed at his back, trying to reach an area between his shoulder blades.

Before Valentina could get to him, he slumped over his horse and slid to the ground. It was then she saw the wooden shaft protruding from his back. "Benito!" the cry tore out of her.

Carmela put her hand to her mouth. "Oh my God! He's hit!"

Feeling sick to her stomach, Valentina jumped off her horse and knelt at her young cousin's side. She was vaguely aware of Carmela joining her. *This can't be happening,* she told herself feverishly.

Benito looked up at her with frightened eyes. "It hurts, Valentina," he whispered.

"It's going to be all right," Valentina said, fighting back tears. Careful of the arrow protruding from his back, she raised him off the ground then cradled him in her arms, his head pressed against her breasts.

Benito's lips moved as if he was trying to tell her something. Then from the corner of his mouth, a trickle of blood began running down his chin. His eyelids fluttered, then a long breath escaped his lips.

Valentina stared in horror at the still face of her young cousin, his eyes half-closed, gazing into the distance. Though she had never seen anyone die before, she knew with certainty that Benito was gone. An unbearable pain lanced like a dagger into her heart. Holding his body tight against her chest, her cheek on his forehead, she rocked him back and forth, unaware of the moaning sound she was making.

Once deep in the woods, Diego slapped his horse on the rump and sent it scampering away. Gripping his sword in one hand, his shield secured on his left arm, he took cover behind a large oak. He waited for the pounding in his chest to slow a little, then peered around the trunk of the tree. The road, the portion he could see of it anyway, now lay deserted. It seemed most of his men had managed to take shelter in the forest.

The unnatural silence stretched on and on. Then finally, a

strange ululating cry rose in the air, making the hairs on the back of his neck stand on end.

"God preserve us," a soldier said from somewhere behind Diego.

"Steady now!" Diego shouted, furious at the soldier who had spoken, knowing that fear was contagious and could spread as easily as a fire racing through dry grass. "Wait for the Saracens to come to us!"

Some hundred paces away, Carmela, her eyes wide with barely contained panic, cried out to Valentina, "Our horses! They're running away! We have to go after them!"

"I can't leave Benito," Valentina said, tears streaming down her face. "I gave my word to my aunt and uncle that I'd watch over him."

"He's dead Valentina! There's nothing more you can do for him. Let's go!"

The drumming of galloping horses and those high-pitched, wavering howls grew steadily louder. Turning, Valentina saw dozens of Saracen horsemen swarming down the hill. The sight penetrated the fog of grief engulfing her. Forcing herself to lay Benito down, she whispered to him, "I'll be back for you, cousin, I promise."

With Carmela urging her on, Valentina allowed herself to be drawn to her feet. A glance around her revealed that the horses were long gone.

"Come this way!" Carmela cried, grabbing Valentina by the hand and pulling her along. "We'll hide in the forest!"

CHAPTER 9

STANDING WITH HIS hands on his hips, General Al Qama surveyed their newly erected camp, his experienced eye missing nothing. The circular white tents were all up in neat rows, the dun-colored canvas stretched taut by the guy ropes. To his right, at one end of the clearing, a half-dozen men were standing guard outside the perimeter of the roped-off area holding the women. The cooks and their assistants had started preparing the evening meal and the breeze carried the smell of smoke. At the far end of the grounds, by the wagons and tethered horses, an elite cadre of soldiers trained in the healing arts were stitching up the wounded.

This last sight brought a frown to his lips. Suffering casualties in battle was normal, but it galled him that an enemy they had so greatly outnumbered had exacted such a heavy toll on his men. He had always thought of Iberian soldiers as an ill-trained lot, lacking the stomach for combat. But the enemy he had encountered this day had shown courage and discipline. He dared not think what would have happened had they been more evenly matched.

Al Qama's attention strayed to a squad of horsemen that was

slowly cutting a path across the grounds toward him. Trailing behind them on foot were two women, their wrists bound in front of them. When the squad was within hailing distance, he called out to the lead horseman, a pockmarked troop leader called Umar. "Where did you find them?"

"I saw them running into the forest when we attacked," Umar answered, dismounting. "It took us until now to flush them out."

"You did well," Al Qama said, studying the women as Umar and his men began untying their wrists. Both were young and pleasing to the eye. They would undoubtedly fetch a good price in the slave markets.

When the ropes fell away, Umar grabbed the arm of one of the captives, a pretty girl of about seventeen or eighteen. "This one fought like a tigress when we cornered her," he said with a grin, revealing yellowing teeth.

The girl shook off Umar's hand. Annoyed, he reached out and grabbed her by the hair. Instead of submitting, the girl whirled about and raked his pockmarked face with her fingernails.

Uttering a curse, Umar slapped the girl hard across the face, the force of the blow snapping her head to one side.

"What's the matter, she too much for you?" Al Qama taunted Umar.

The men who had gathered around them sniggered.

Eager to make amends for his lapse, Umar seized one of the girl's wrists and twisted her arm behind her back, bringing her under control.

Al Qama circled the girl, who stared defiantly back at him. Though pale skinned and foreign looking, he found her attractive. His gaze strayed down the length of her body, wondering if the rest of her was as delectable. "Disrobe her."

The girl squirmed and struggled against Umar's grip as two men pulled off her tunic, leaving her naked.

Al Qama's eyes feasted on the girl's perfectly shaped body, her firm young breasts and white skin. Desire began stirring inside him. All the other women he had bedded over the last few weeks had been fearful, teary-eyed creatures, as unsatisfying as a meal eaten without spice. But he could tell this one would fight him with a fiery passion. An image of her naked writhing body, pinned under him, formed in his mind.

An unwelcome thought intruded into his fantasy. *The girl's too fine a prize to waste on a single night's pleasure.*

By now, Al Qama's blood was up, and he did not immediately yield to his better judgment. Yet the seed of reason had been planted, and the idea took hold that the girl's value as a gift to either the Governor or to the Caliph himself far outweighed her use as a momentary balm to his itch. With a sigh of regret, he turned toward his men.

"This one is not to be touched, understand?" Al Qama's eyes swept over the faces before him, daring anyone to protest, but his words were greeted with silence.

Al Qama turned toward the second young woman, who seemed to wither under his gaze. *This one does not possess her companion's spirit,* he thought with disappointment. As he had done with the first girl, he ordered his men to disrobe her. A moment later she too stood naked before him. She was of slighter built than her companion with small, shapely breasts that made her seem younger than she had first appeared. The girl began to tremble with fear.

He turned toward the horsemen who had brought him the two women and said, "You did well. You can each have a turn with this one after I'm done."

CHAPTER 10

PELAYO AND HIS tracker, Rubio, had ridden at a steady pace ever since leaving the monastery, stopping only once to water the horses by a mountain stream. Though they had been on the lookout for any sort of sign as to where the Saracen party may have veered off the road, they had so far found nothing. They were riding through a stretch of road deep in a forest, when a rumble of thunder erupted from behind them.

Turning in the saddle, Pelayo noticed that the storm clouds were rapidly closing in on them. "We'll have to pick up our pace a little," he called out to Rubio, hoping they could cover a few more leagues before the rain came down and washed the ground clean.

Rubio gave him a nod and they rode on in silence, scanning the shoulders along the road for signs of disturbance. The two were so engrossed in their task that it took a while before they raised their heads and noticed vultures circling overhead. Shortly afterward they rounded a bend and came across the object of the birds' attention: the body of young boy lying on the road, a feathered shaft protruding from his back. It appeared the birds had been feasting on his remains for some time.

Pelayo and Rubio looked around, searching the forest on both sides of the road and immediately spotted other bodies lying between the trees. These too had attracted the vultures.

Rubio dug his heels into his horse's flanks and charged the scavenging birds pecking away at the child's corpse, sending them flapping away. He then steered his mount into the trees and disappeared from sight.

Pelayo dismounted and knelt at the boy's side. Swatting away the flies, he winced at the ravaged face of the youth before him.

From somewhere to his right, Rubio called out, "Commander! I've found someone alive."

Pulling his horse along by the reins, Pelayo found Rubio a dozen paces inside the forest, kneeling at the side of a soldier who was slumped against a tree trunk, an arrow protruding from his chest. The stricken man had his head down, chin on his chest, and his eyes were closed.

"He's lucky the vultures didn't get to him," Rubio said over his shoulder.

"I don't believe it was luck; I think he fought them off, at least until he passed out," Pelayo said. He looped the reins of his horse around a sapling, then crouched down beside the wounded soldier. Judging by the embroidered fret border on his tunic, he figured the man was an officer.

"Should we pull out the arrow?" Pelayo asked Rubio. "I have a spare tunic in my saddlebag that we can cut up and use as bandages."

"You just can't pull out an arrow from a man's body, commander," Rubio said. "He'll bleed to death. It's got to be carefully cut out and the wound stitched closed immediately.

We should wait for Commander Xocobo to come to us tomorrow and let one of our physicians deal with it."

"This man may not make it until tomorrow," Pelayo said.

"At least he'll have a chance. It's more than we can offer him now."

Pelayo was wondering what to do when the wounded man stirred to life.

"Water…" the man whispered.

Pelayo went to fetch his waterskin from his saddle pack, then knelt down and held the spout to the man's lips. The water seemed to revive the officer and a moment later he opened his eyes and blinked slowly, his gaze unfocused.

"You're in safe company; I'm Commander Pelayo of the Third Legion."

The wounded man licked his cracked lips and looked up at him. "What day is it?" he asked in a hoarse whisper.

"Sunday."

Suddenly agitated, the officer tried to sit up.

"Easy now," Pelayo said, gently pushing him back. "You're going to bleed out."

The man quieted.

"What's your name?" Pelayo asked.

"Diego," came a raspy whisper. "Captain Diego."

"What happened here?" Pelayo asked.

"We ran into a band of Saracens," the captain said, his voice barely audible. "We were escorting Baron Ernesto's daughter to Girona."

Pelayo gave a start. "You mean Lady Valentina?"

"Yes," the captain whispered. "I heard women screaming in the distance. I think the Saracens may have taken her and her companions captive."

Pelayo could hardly believe his ears. Though he hadn't seen

Valentina in years, he remembered her fondly, and the thought that she may have fallen into Saracen hands left him fearful for her. His mission to save the women taken by the Saracens took on a more urgent note. "Do you have any idea how far we are from the coast?"

Captain Diego's chest heaved up and down for a moment. "A day's ride, maybe," he said softly.

Pelayo turned toward Rubio, who was kneeling at his side. "There are still a few hours of daylight left; I'm going to keep going and see how far I can get before the rain comes. You stay here with the captain and wait for Commander Xocobo to come up the road tomorrow."

"With all due respect, sire, I'm considered the best tracker in the cohort," Rubio said. "You should be the one staying with the captain."

"This is a personal matter to me now, Rubio. The woman we are speaking of is my half-brother's betrothed."

"Commander Xocobo gave us orders to stay together."

"And I am countermanding those orders," Pelayo said. "Do you have a problem with that?"

Rubio stared into Pelayo's eyes for a moment. "No, commander."

Pelayo rose to his feet, untied his horse then mounted, anxious to set out. "Can you lend me your bow and quiver?" he asked Rubio.

Rubio hesitated, then rose to his feet, walked to his horse and returned a moment later. "You know how to use one of these?" he asked, handing his bow to Pelayo.

"I can hit a calabash at twenty paces." *At least I used to be able to, once upon a time,* Pelayo thought to himself.

"Not bad," Rubio said, handing Pelayo his quiver.

"Thank you, Rubio. I know how much a bow means to an archer."

Rubio shrugged. "We have spare bows in the supply carts back at the camp. Good luck to you, commander," he said, touching the rim of his helmet.

CHAPTER 11

A HUM OF voices echoed off the stone walls as Izaskun and Julian made their way across the great hall. After taking their seats at the head table, a manservant appeared at their elbows and poured them each a cup of mulled wine from a silver ewer.

Izaskun glanced at the vacant chair next to her on her right. *Fáfila is still away in Toledo,* she thought to herself, noting the fact without any particular interest or concern.

Turning her attention to the salvers of food spread out before her, Izaskun took her time serving herself. Silence settled over the hall as everyone waited for her to take her first bite, then the murmur of voices resumed, this time accompanied by the clinking of drinking cups and the scraping sound of knives against metal plates.

Izaskun was halfway through her meal when a guard made his way toward her.

"Begging your pardon, Doña Izaskun," the guard said discreetly. "Your uncle, Bishop Oppas, has just ridden in."

Izaskun stared blankly at the soldier for a moment. *How odd,* she thought. *I can't remember him ever arriving at the castle so late in the day.* "Ask him to join me here."

"He says he wishes to speak to you in private, my lady."

"Oh, very well," Izaskun said, putting down her knife, annoyed at having to interrupt her meal.

Julian stopped eating long enough to give her an inquiring glance.

"Oppas has just arrived," she explained, rising to her feet. "I'm going out to greet him."

Julian nodded and went back to his food.

Two torches set in iron sconces lit the stone steps leading down to the courtyard. A few paces away from the bottom landing, a stable hand was helping her uncle untie his travel bag from the saddle of his horse. Next to them stood a black-robed acolyte. Despite the cowl that partially hid his face, she could see that the cleric was young and handsome.

"What an unexpected surprise, Uncle," she called out as she descended the steps.

"Unexpected, but welcome, I hope," Oppas called out heartily.

"Why of course," Izaskun answered. As was often the case when she hadn't seen her uncle for an extended period of time, she was struck by how much he resembled his brother, King Witiza, whose death six weeks earlier had rocked the kingdom. The two had the same thick lips, broad face, coarse features and stout build. Luckily, she herself had taken after her father, Siberto, the third and youngest sibling, who had managed to remain slim and handsome despite his advancing years.

Oppas handed the reins of his horse to a stable boy, then gave Izaskun a perfunctory embrace. "You're looking well, my dear."

"Thank you, Uncle. What brings you here? We didn't expect to see you until Candlemas."

Oppas glanced pointedly at the stable hands around them. "Can we find somewhere private to talk?"

Izaskun nodded, her curiosity piqued even further. "We can go up to my quarters, if you wish."

"Yes, that will do nicely."

Izaskun suggested to the young cleric that he go to the great hall to have some dinner. She then led her uncle to her bedchamber in the south-east tower of the castle and ushered him inside.

A servant had lit the oil lamps, allowing Oppas to study Izaskun's quarters, which he was seeing for the first time. Two narrow windows along the outer wall faced a darkened courtyard. A wooden canopied bed dominated the chamber, its headboard abutting a wall that was painted in the traditional whitewash of slaked lime and chalk. An intricately carved oaken chest squatted at the foot of her bed. Expensive-looking tapestries of outdoor scenes covered the left wall. Between the windows were two chairs and a table bearing a pitcher of water, several goblets and a tin basin

"Shall I order a servant to bring you some wine, Uncle?" Izaskun asked.

"No, don't bother; water is fine."

Izaskun walked over to the table, filled a goblet, then came back and handed it to him. "So, tell me, what brings you here?"

"I'm afraid I have some bad news."

Izaskun shot him a worried look. "Has something happened to my father?"

"No, no, your father is fine."

"What is it then?"

"The Council of Barons has rejected Olmund's claim to the throne."

Izaskun drew a sharp breath. "How can that be? Are you certain?"

Oppas nodded. "I got a first-hand account from Siberto."

Izaskun stared at her uncle in dismay, the news hitting her like a bolt out of the blue. It had never occurred to her that the council might bypass Witiza's son and elect someone else. Granted Olmund was only eight years old, but he was the legitimate heir and by all rights, he should have been made king. "So, who did the council elect?"

"Roderic," Oppas spat out in disgust. "Baron of Baetica."

Izaskun sank into a chair. "This bodes ill for us."

"It certainly does," Oppas said, his expression somber.

Izaskun understood that the council's decision meant that the power the family had wielded for some twenty years was about to slip away from their grasp. Not only would their influence be greatly diminished, but the vast tracts of land which her uncle Witiza had seized and given to various members of the family would, in all likelihood, have to be given back. Like everyone else, they would be at the mercy of the new king. Worse still, the upstart would undoubtedly regard the entire Witiza clan with suspicion.

"How many council members voted against us?" Izaskun asked.

"Save for Siberto..." Oppas paused dramatically. "Every damned one of them."

It took a moment for her uncle's words to sink in. "Llorenç, Umberto, Fáfila..." She stopped. "Surely they couldn't have..."

"Roderic's supporters were very clever. They voted first. When the rest of the council saw they had the majority, they cast their lots for Roderic as well."

Izaskun's eyes narrowed in anger. "How could you and Father have allowed this to happen?"

"We never suspected there was another contender until the night of the vote."

"So, the upstart outmaneuvered you both," Izaskun said, her voice dripping with scorn.

Oppas dragged a chair in front of Izaskun, then sat down facing her. "We were caught flat-footed all right, but not by Roderic."

"What do you mean?"

"Think about it," Oppas said. "Baetica is a backwater province. Roderic is new to the council, with no real influence. He could never have waged a successful campaign for the throne on his own, and certainly not without some word of it leaking out."

"What are you trying to say?" Izaskun asked.

"Roderic had the support of two council members; men we trusted, men we thought were on our side."

Something in her uncle's tone made Izaskun feel uneasy. "Who are these men you speak of?"

"Baron Ernesto."

Izaskun's throat tightened. "And the other?"

"Your husband."

Izaskun felt shaken to her very core. Fáfila had no love for her, but they were still husband and wife and this betrayal hurt her deeply. As she struggled to recover from her turmoil, she caught her uncle watching her with an odd, calculating look in his eyes. She suddenly understood that he hadn't come all the way from Toledo simply to bring her the news. "Why are you here? What do you want from me?"

Oppas studied her through hooded eyes. "I want to know where your loyalty lies."

"What kind of question is that?" she asked.

Oppas leaned forward in his chair, his eyes glistening with

intensity. "We're not going to slink away with our tails between our legs. It will take Roderic months to consolidate his hold on the kingdom. We still have our old allies. We'll raise an army and crush him before he's ready."

"Have you gone mad? Your so-called allies just deserted you."

Oppas sat back, studying her. "Llorenç and Umberto have already agreed to join us. Conditionally, of course."

"Conditionally?"

"On having the Asturian legion on our side."

Izaskun gazed incredulously at her uncle. "You want me to persuade Fáfila to change his mind and support Olmund? You're a fool if you think he'll listen to me."

Oppas eyes bored into hers. "I'm not talking about persuasion, Izaskun. It's too late for that." He let the silence stretch for a moment. "It's time for Julian to take his father's place as Duke of Asturias."

"Stop!" Izaskun cried. "I will not have you speak another word of this."

Oppas' expression hardened. "I'm afraid I must, my dear."

"You have no right to involve me in your machinations!" Izaskun blazed. "You've wasted your time coming here."

"Have I?" Oppas reached into the pouch on his belt, withdrew a folded parchment then held it out to her without comment.

Izaskun eyed the parchment warily. "What is that?"

"A letter. From Fáfila to Baron Porfiro."

"How did you come by it?" she asked suspiciously.

"Porfiro's chamberlain is a distant cousin of a priest I know," Oppas said blandly. "Go on, read it."

Izaskun reached out for the folded parchment. The handwriting appeared to be Fáfila's. The message was brief, just a few lines.

My dear Porfiro,
You are a wise old fox, my friend. I just met with Roderic and
as you predicted, he offered me a boon for my support. He's given me
his word that if he's elected king, he will make Pelayo my sole heir.
I shall now set in motion the course of action we agreed upon. Rest
assured that I shall not lag in my efforts to persuade the council to
elect Roderic. May God be with us and grant us success.

The letter was signed: '*F*'.

Izaskun felt sick to her stomach. The revelation that Fáfila could have conceived such a despicable plot was too much for her to bear, and for a moment she could scarcely breathe. She rose to her feet, went to the table and with a trembling hand poured herself some water. "I never thought Fáfila was capable of such guile," she said, her back to her uncle.

Oppas, his face in shadows, said nothing.

Izaskun drank the water from her goblet, buying herself time to regain her composure. The silence stretched on until at last, she turned to face her uncle. "What exactly do you want from me?" she asked, her tone as flat as her expression.

Only the glint in Oppas' eyes revealed his sense of triumph. He had correctly figured what would be the one key that would unlock Izaskun's heart. The letter, a rather clumsy forgery based on the documents that Fáfila had written to him over the years, seemed to have been good enough to fool Izaskun. With Llorenç and Umberto on his side, and Izaskun ready to do their bidding, he and Siberto could now move ahead with their plans.

CHAPTER 12

A GUST OF wind swept along the beach, buffeting Valentina with a stinging spray of sand. She closed her eyes and felt the warmth of the rising sun on her face. The roar of waves crashing on the shore all but drowned out the sound of women weeping, allowing her to forget for a moment where she was. When the wind died down, she opened her eyes and was thrust back once more into her harsh reality: the sea stretching out to the horizon, the women clustered around her, their faces etched with despair. All her fellow captives were young and straight of limb, with unblemished skin and good teeth. Despite their cheap linen tunics, and their wild and unkempt appearance, they were all comely, the flowers of Iberian womanhood in the full bloom of youth. Each one was a prized specimen that would fetch a premium in the slave markets of Afriqiyah.

Behind her, the Saracen camp was teeming with activity. There were men everywhere, dismantling tents and lugging casks and sacks down to the waterline. To her left, a group of bare-chested men were wading into the shallows, hauling on a thick rope, pulling the last of the beached sailing vessels toward the sea.

She watched the ship as it inched down the sandy slope, picked up speed, then slid into the surf. Immersed in its natural element, the craft glided gracefully through the water toward the other three ships anchored one hundred and fifty feet from the shore. After coming to a stop, the vessel bobbed gently in the swells.

Using the ropes dangling over the side of the ship, the bare-chested men clambered onboard and threw an anchor over the side. They then manhandled the mast into a sleeve-like fitting at the mid-section of the ship. As they worked, the wind began nudging the vessel about, turning it parallel to the shoreline in a position ideal for loading.

It wouldn't be long now before the ships were ready to take on their human cargo. Valentina had clung to the belief that her father and his soldiers would eventually find the Saracen camp and rescue them. But it was clear to her now that the windswept cove, tucked away in the wild, northeastern coast of Hispania, had in the end, eluded them all. Her fate, and that of her fellow captives, was all but sealed.

Looking over her shoulder, she caught sight of the loath-some, Saracen chieftain to whom she and Carmela had been brought when they had first been captured. Clad in black leather, he cut an imposing figure as he strode purposefully along the beach, shouting out what seemed to be orders.

Scores of men waded into the sea and began forming a human chain that stretched from the beach to one of the ships in the water. When the line firmed, the men began passing down, hand to hand, the casks and burlap sacks that had been piled up on the beach.

At Valentina's side, Carmela stood gazing sightlessly into the distance, her hair a bird's nest of straw and bits of leaves. The bruise under her right eye had faded to a light, purple hue.

"Hungry?" Valentina asked, touching Carmela's arm to get her attention.

Carmela glanced down at the leaf-wrapped packet that Valentina was holding out to her. "Not really."

"It's quite tasty; it's some sort of dried fruit."

Carmela turned away. "Maybe later."

"You didn't touch your food last night; you need to eat."

"Why, so I can be a heathy slave?"

"So you can keep up your strength and get through this nightmare," Valentina said.

For the first time in days, a crack appeared in Carmela's eerily passive demeanor as emotion sparked in her eyes. "There's no waking up from this, Valentina. Once we get aboard those ships, we'll never set foot on these shores again."

"You mustn't lose hope. We'll find a way back."

"You may be able to lie to yourself, but I can't. I know what awaits us."

"Whatever it is, we'll get through it."

"Will we? Do you know what it's like to have one man after another force himself upon you, taking you against your will?"

Valentina stayed silent, glad that Carmela was finally speaking to her about the terrible ordeal she had endured four days earlier.

"No, of course you don't," Carmela said bitterly. "They didn't lay a hand on you, did they? Well I know, and I won't let that happen to me ever again."

Valentina put her arm around her friend's shoulders. "I'm so sorry Carmela; I can't begin to imagine the horror you went through."

The fire that had flared inside Carmela disappeared as quickly as it had come. "God has abandoned us," she said dully.

"I just hope that when the time comes, I have the courage to jump overboard and end it all."

"Don't say that. Killing yourself is not the answer."

"Then what is? Tell me."

Valentina searched for something to say that would offer her friend a measure of solace. An idea began to form in her mind. The plan was wildly improbable and fraught with danger, but at least it offered them a possible path to freedom.

"You're right," Valentina said. "Once we sail away, there'll be no way for us to come back. We have to try to escape before we get on those ships."

"How? We're surrounded by guards," Carmela said. "They'll catch us before we've gone twenty paces down the beach."

"We're not going to make a run for it; we'll swim away."

Carmela stared at Valentina as if she'd lost her mind. "And just how are we supposed to do that?"

"Once we wade into the water and head toward the ships, the guards will have a difficult time keeping track of all of us. The last thing they'll expect is for the two of us to swim away."

"There's nothing but an empty sea out there. To where are we supposed to swim?"

"To the other side of the cove."

Carmela gazed at the far end of the crescent-shaped beach then turned and eyed the crashing waves battering the shore. "I've never swum in the open sea before. You know I'm not as good a swimmer as you."

"For God's sakes, Carmela, a moment ago you were saying you wanted to drown yourself."

Carmela looked into Valentina's eyes. "Do you really think we have a chance?"

"Look at it this way; what do we have to lose?"

Carmela hesitated then nodded. "All right, let's give it a try."

After all the items had been cleared from the beach, a man standing on the deck of the second vessel cupped his hands around his mouth and shouted something. At once the guards on the beach began separating the women around Valentina into two groups.

It seemed the Saracens were going to take them in different ships. One of the guards pulled Carmela toward the dozen or so women being herded toward the water. When Valentina tried to follow, another guard blocked her way.

Carmela continued walking, looking back over her shoulder at Valentina, her eyes wide with desperation.

Valentina backed away from the guard, feigning disinterest. The moment the guard turned his attention elsewhere, she darted forward, going around him, then broke into a run toward Carmela.

The guard lunged at Valentina and managed to grab the back of her tunic. With her heart pounding in her chest, she dug her heels into the sand and pulled free. Suddenly released from the guard's grip, she stumbled forward. Recovering her footing, she sprinted toward Carmela, now standing at the water's edge.

Only after she had caught up with Carmela did Valentina dare to turn and look behind her. As she had hoped, the guard who had tried to stop her seemed to have decided that it wasn't worth expending his energy to chase her down.

Prodded onward into the water by the other guards, Valentina took Carmela's hand and waded into the surf. A large wave swept in, enveloping them both in water up to their waists. After it receded, a smaller wave surged and ebbed around their knees, leaving them shivering with cold.

By the time they reached the ship, the water was up to Valentina's chest. Most of the other women in their group were already there, holding on to the ropes that were dangling over the side of the vessel. The men onboard were leaning over the side, extending their hands and plucking the women out of the water.

"Let's go," Carmela whispered, her face glistening with saltwater.

"No, not yet," Valentina said, keeping her voice down.

"What are you waiting for?"

"I'm not sure...A distraction of some sort."

To her right, a pretty, dark-haired girl from Benidum was being pulled up the side of the ship, her wet tunic clinging revealingly to her body. Valentina lost sight of her once she was hauled on board, but a moment later she heard the girl cry out, drawing raucous, male laughter.

Valentina figured the men had been unable to resist groping the girl. *This is our chance*, she realized. "It's time," she whispered to Carmela. "Ready?"

Carmela's teeth were chattering, but she managed a nod.

Valentina took a deep breath, then sank beneath the water. Sound dimmed, turning into a dull muffle. A heartbeat later, Carmela's face appeared an arm's length away, her hair undulating like Medusa's snakes around her head.

Doubling over, Valentina knifed down to the bottom. The tide had stirred up the sea into a murky soup, but she could just make out the ship's hull curving downward in an arc that flattened some two feet above the sea floor. The ship sat lower in the water than she had expected, and she wondered if there was enough space under the hull for her and Carmela to squeeze through to the other side. After a moment's hesitation, she decided there was only one way to find out.

Kicking hard with her legs and stroking with her arms, Valentina angled toward the gap beneath the ship. As she swam under the hull, she felt the barnacle encrusted boards scraping her back. Grasping some rocks poking up from the seabed, she pulled herself along. When the hull began to curve upward, she kicked away again, propelling herself to the other side of the ship.

Valentina surfaced, gasping for air, facing the open sea. The water was deeper on this side of the ship and she couldn't touch the bottom. As she treaded water, Carmela popped up beside her, spluttering and gasping for air. For a moment they stared at each other, blinking away the sea water from their eyes, their ears pricked up for any shout announcing that their attempt to escape had been discovered. But there was only the sound of the waves slapping against the ship's hull.

Valentina knew that she and Carmela had to keep moving while the Saracens' attention was centered on bringing the women on board. Looking at Carmela, she pointed toward the tip of the cove in the distance, then pushed quietly away from the ship.

Slowly, with only the top of their heads showing above the water, Valentina and Carmela began opening some distance between themselves and the ship. There were no waves of significance to contend with, only swells that raised and lowered them in steady repetition. When they were far enough away from the ship, they began veering in an arc, trying to skirt the last vessel that lay between them and the end of the cove.

As Valentina swam by the last ship, she cast a glance behind her, expecting to see Carmela. But there was only an endless expanse of water. Fearful for her friend, Valentina scanned the sea around her and after an anxious moment, caught sight of Carmella floundering about in the water some thirty feet away.

Valentina swam quickly toward her. As she got within a

few feet, she heard Carmela call out to her, "Can't… swim … too tired…"

"Turn over on your back," Valentina told her, trying to pitch her voice low so it wouldn't carry to the ships. "I'll pull you."

Carmela was too exhausted to answer, but she managed to roll over.

Valentina grabbed the collar of Carmela's tunic, then began to kick away. At once she discovered how difficult it was to drag a dead weight through the heaving sea. *Just keep swimming*, she told herself.

After a dismayingly short amount of time, Valentina felt the strength ebbing out of her limbs. With no choice but to continue swimming, she began angling away from the last ship. Everything faded from her mind, everything save for one solitary and all-encompassing thought: keep swimming or drown.

After some time, sensing Valentina was tiring, Carmela turned over and began to swim on her own again.

But the measure came too late for Valentina. Now numb with exhaustion, she only managed a few more feeble strokes before her legs seemed to turn to stone. *Keep going, just a little longer,* she urged herself desperately. But her limbs refused to obey.

She just had time to take one last breath of air, then dragged down by the weight of her waterlogged tunic, she began to sink into the sea. She tried to hold her breath as the water closed in above her head. In her state of exhaustion, her lungs started to burn. With mounting horror, she realized that she wouldn't be able to keep herself from opening her mouth and breathing in water. As her body cried out for air, her right foot brushed against something hard and unyielding.

It was the sea floor.

Hope flared inside her. The surface was less than an arm's length above her head. There was no way she was going to drown in seven or eight feet of water, she told herself, tamping down her panic. Using her hands, she made herself sink further. Then, bracing herself on the sea floor, she unfolded her legs and thrust herself upward.

Her head shot above the surface. She took a quick breath, filling her lungs. All too soon she sank into the sea again. This time, however, her terror did not consume her. She knew now what she had to do, repeat the crouching and upward thrusting motion to propel herself in the general direction of the shore.

She surfaced a second time, and then a third, allowing her to fill her lungs with air. On her fourth attempt, a large swell lifted her up and nudged her toward the shore. As the frothing waters receded, Valentina found herself standing chest high in the water.

Exhausted, her chest heaving, she stood for a moment, recovering. Raking her hair back off her face with her hand, she scanned the sea around her. Her heart leapt with joy when she caught sight of Carmela's head poking out of the water a short distance away. They gazed at each other, looking like half-drowned creatures, afraid to wave or to call out, as some one hundred paces away, the beach was crawling with Saracen warriors.

The rocky spur marking the end of the cove now lay tantalizingly close. If they could reach it without being discovered, she and Carmela would be able to use the outcrop as cover and steal into the woods unseen. Filled with renewed determination, her strength returning, Valentina gestured to Carmela to keep going. When Carmela nodded back, she set off through the water, half-trudging, half-swimming.

Their progress was achingly slow, but finally she and

Carmela reached the outcrop at the end of the cove. Water sluicing off their garments, they clambered up onto the sloping ledge of a boulder-size rock. Pausing only to catch their breath, they kept going, bent over low so as to present as small a silhouette as possible. Scrambling and jumping from boulder to boulder, they reached the crescent shaped beach on the other side of the cove. As soon as they were out of sight from the Saracen camp, the two of them collapsed on the sand.

"I thought we'd never make it," Carmela said, lying on her back, her chest heaving.

"We're too exposed here," Valentina said. "We have to get out of the open."

Carmela didn't answer, but after a moment she rolled onto her stomach and pushed herself to her feet.

With Carmela trailing, Valentina made her way across the strip of beach toward the tree line. Just before reaching the woods, she heard a sound coming from behind her. Turning, she caught sight of two Saracen horsemen splashing through the shoals toward them. Her blood turned to ice. Had the horsemen seen them?

"Come on," Valentina whispered, taking Carmela's hand and breaking into a run.

Fear fueling their tired legs, they bolted into the forest. Afraid of what they might see, they ran without looking back, the trees whipping by them, the sound of the surf slowly fading away.

Their pell-mell run took them to the edge of a ravine. Without breaking stride, they plunged down the scrubby slope. At once, Valentina realized the foolishness of running down a steep incline at full tilt.

Unable to get her legs moving fast enough, Carmela's feet flew from under her. Valentina was more successful at keeping her balance and tried to hold on to Carmela's hand. But her friend slipped from her grasp.

Her arms flailing about, Carmela went sliding down to the bottom of the ravine. Valentina skittered down the slope after her, somehow managing to control her descent. After reaching the bottom safely, she went to Carmela who had come to rest by the bank of a creek that ran through the clearing.

"Are you all right?" Valentina called out to her softly.

Looking dazed, Carmela sat up slowly, her face smudged with dirt. Wincing in pain, she grabbed her right foot. "I think I've twisted my ankle," she said, a catch in her voice.

Valentina's heart sank. "Do you think you can walk?"

"I don't know."

"You have to try. Here, take my hand."

Carmela pulled herself up. Favoring her right foot, she held on to Valentina then took a tentative step forward.

Carmela grimaced. "Ow...It hurts."

"We have to keep moving."

Carmela's face crumpled. "I don't think I can," she said, fighting back tears.

From somewhere above, beyond the ridge, came the sound of breaking twigs.

Valentina and Carmela both froze.

"We have to get to the other side of the clearing and hide," Valentina whispered, her heart pounding in her chest. "Hold on to me."

Carmela put her arm around Valentina, then, trying not to put any weight on her injured foot, took a step. Biting her lip, obviously in pain, she hobbled across the clearing.

The whicker of a horse sounded from somewhere close by.

Valentina glanced over her shoulder. On the ridge of the ravine, the two Saracen riders she had seen splashing through the shoals earlier were gazing down at her and Carmela. The nose guards of their iron helmets partially hid their faces, leaving only their eyes and bearded chins visible. Wrapped in dark cloaks, they looked like two menacing birds of prey about to swoop down and tear them both apart. A soul-crushing dread spread through her as she figured that their one chance to escape had failed.

The two horsemen urged their mounts down the slope. A trickle of stones and dirt cascaded down after them. One of the men said something, bringing forth a grunt from the other man.

Valentina put her arm around Carmela, who was trembling, and held her tight. A dark despair stole over her.

The two horsemen reached the bottom of the ravine. After riding to opposite ends of the clearing, they began closing in on Valentina and Carmela from two sides, like shepherd dogs herding stray sheep.

Suddenly, a third helmeted rider appeared atop the ridge, his black cloak wrapped around his shoulders. After seeming to appraise the situation for a moment, he urged his mount forward. As his horse picked its way down the slope, the other two Saracen horsemen became aware of him and called out what sounded like a question.

The newcomer remained silent, as his horse skittered down to the bottom of the ravine. The question or statement directed at him was sharply repeated.

In a sudden burst of motion, the lone horseman threw back his cloak, drew out his sword, then dug his heels into his horse's flanks. As if catapulted, his mount shot forward.

The other two riders froze in surprise, seemingly confused by the sight of one of their comrades charging them with obvious hostile intent.

Closing in at a gallop, the newcomer swung his sword at the closest horseman, striking the man in the chest. The force of the blow toppled the warrior off his horse. The newcomer yanked at his reins, steering his mount toward the second warrior, now scrambling to draw out his sword.

The newcomer drew within range of his quarry, then unleashed a scything blow at his opponent's head. The horseman under attack pulled back reflexively, catching the blow on the side of his helmet. The stricken warrior reeled in the saddle for a moment, before seemingly managing to shake off the effect.

The newcomer's charge took him to the end of the clearing. With a tug on the reins, he slowed his horse and circled around. For a moment, the two horsemen sized each other up from opposite ends of the grassy clearing. Then, almost simultaneously, they both dug their heels into their horses' flanks and flew at each other.

Valentina's ears rang with the sound of clashing steel. For the life of her, she couldn't make sense of what she was seeing. Why was the third warrior attacking his comrades? Were they fighting over her and Carmela like slavering dogs over a bone? She knew that, as young women, the two of them were valuable spoils of war, but the barbarity of it all sickened her.

As the two Saracen horsemen continued to pound on each other, trying to break through the other's defenses, Valentina knew that she and Carmela had to seize the moment and try to get away. Before she could act on the thought, she caught sight of a sword lying by the outstretched body of the first horseman. She hesitated for a moment, wondering if she should waste valuable time going after the sword. But having a weapon and using it against a tired or wounded man might make the difference between being recaptured or escaping to freedom.

Deciding on the second option, she set off at a run across the clearing toward the sword.

The two horsemen, oblivious to anything save trying to kill each other, ignored Valentina as she skirted around them. Reaching the sword, she scooped it off the ground, then headed back toward Carmela. As she circled by the rearing horses again, she saw the newcomer duck under the sweeping blade heading his way, then thrust his sword into his opponent's midriff.

The stricken man let out a grunt of pain as the sword bit into him. Though much of his face was hidden by his helmet and nose guard, he seemed stunned with shock as he stared at the blade sprouting from the lower part of his chest.

The newcomer pulled out his sword, unpinning his opponent. The mortally wounded man swayed in the saddle for a moment, then fell to the ground in a heap of arms and legs.

The fight had ended so quickly that Valentina hadn't gotten the chance to slip away with Carmela. She now rued the missed opportunity, as the victorious Saracen warrior slid off his horse. Though his helmet and nose guard cast a shadow over his eyes, she could feel his gaze on her, sending a shiver of fear running down her spine.

She felt better having a sword in her hand, but she had witnessed the man's speed and skill and she had no illusions about her chances of fending him off successfully. Her only hope lay in the fact that his recent skirmish might have taken a toll on him. Perhaps that was all the edge she needed to catch him off guard.

Valentina tensed as the Saracen warrior began walking toward her and Carmela. She knew she would only have one chance to catch him by surprise and kill him. As he stepped into range, she tightened her grip on the hilt of her sword. Planting her feet firmly, she swung the curved blade at his neck, pivoting her upper body to give herself added speed and strength.

The Saracen warrior stepped back nimbly, avoiding the sword's cutting path with a good foot or so to spare.

The sword was heavy, and Valentina's all-or-nothing effort threw her off balance. She stumbled forward a step before catching herself. As she whirled around to face the warrior again, it occurred to her that he could have easily knocked her sword away, or worse. But he just stood there, his arms hanging loosely at his side.

"You need not fear me," the warrior said in perfect, unaccented Iberian. "I mean you no harm."

Valentina's brow furrowed as she studied the cloaked and helmeted figure standing before her. "Who are you?" she asked.

"A friend," he said. Reaching up, he untied his helmet, then took it off, keeping his movements slow, so as not to alarm her.

Valentina's first impression of the warrior was that he was young, her age perhaps, and didn't look like any of the Saracens she'd seen in the camp. He had light skin, a trimmed brown beard and regular features in a face she found handsome.

As if sensing her wariness, the warrior drew back his cloak, pulled up his chainmail shirt, revealing the gray, military tunic that he was wearing underneath.

Valentina's eyes widened as she stared at the stylized griffins embroidered along the border of the warrior's tunic. *Good Lord... He's an Asturian commander!*

Her heart raced as she lifted her gaze and met his eyes. A thought burst through her like the warm glow of a summer sunrise: *We're safe!*

She turned toward Carmela and saw the same stunned expression that she suspected was on her own face as well. In a flash of understanding, she understood that her perception of everything that she had just witnessed had been wrong. A wave of relief washed over her, leaving her lightheaded.

The Asturian officer stepped forward and held Valentina by the arm, steadying her. "Are you all right?" he said, his voice filled with concern.

"I am now," Valentina said breathlessly.

The officer let go of Valentina and eyed the sword in her hand, "You're not going to try to run me through again, are you?"

"No, of course not."

"Good," he said, the corners of his lips turning up in a smile. "I've had enough of people trying to kill me for one day."

Valentina gathered herself. "Thank you for coming to our aid, commander," she said, realizing how inadequate her words must sound.

Carmella, her voice thick with emotion, chimed in, "You've saved us from a life of slavery, commander. We're forever in your debt."

The Asturian officer turned toward Carmela. "Knowing that you and Valentina are safe is reward enough for me, my lady."

Valentina gave the Asturian officer a puzzled look. "How is it you know my name?"

"We knew each other as children."

Valentina gazed into the officer's pale, gray eyes. Suddenly, a memory of a tousle-haired boy surfaced in her mind. "Yes, of course," she said, her expression clearing. "You're Pelayo, aren't you?"

Pelayo inclined his head. "I've been wondering if you'd remember me. It's been a long time since those days in my father's courtyard."

"What are you doing here?" Valentina asked.

"I'm part of a cohort sent to help your father fight off the Saracens," he said. "My men and I have been on their trail since they attacked the town of Benidum."

"Your soldiers had better get here soon," Carmela interjected. "The Saracens are about to set sail."

"I know. I've been watching them all morning," Pelayo said to her. "I noticed you're nursing your foot. Are you all right?"

Carmela made a face. "I sprained my ankle falling down the ravine."

"Bad luck. What is your name?"

"Carmela."

"All right Carmela, wait here. I'll get you a horse. We need to get out of here before another Saracen party stumbles upon us."

The ravine formed a natural pen that had prevented the Saracen horses from wandering off too far. Calling out softly to gain their trust, Pelayo rounded up the horses, then led them back to the center of the clearing.

Choosing a white Arabian for Carmella, he helped her up onto its saddle. When he turned toward Valentina, intending to help her as well, she grabbed the saddle of the second horse and hoisted herself up with lithe grace, settling herself astride her mount as would a man.

Sensing his gaze upon her, Valentina pulled down the hem of her wet tunic and arranged it chastely around her upper thighs.

Pelayo mounted his horse, then led the two women out of the ravine. Reaching level ground, he picked out a path through the trees, heading away from the beach. Aware of the Saracen threat, everyone remained silent.

After several leagues, they came upon a woodland trail that Pelayo took, heading west.

"Where are we going?" Valentina asked him in a hushed voice.

Pelayo slowed his horse until he was riding beside Valentina. The narrow width of the trail forced them so close together that their knees were nearly touching.

"This path should lead us to the main road," he said. "Hopefully we'll run into my men there."

"How far do you think they are?" Valentina asked.

"I don't know," Pelayo answered. "I think they may have missed the sign I left to mark the spot where I turned off. If that's the case, God knows where they might be now."

They rode side by side in silence, Carmela trailing slightly behind them. "I still can't believe what just happened," Valentina said, shaking her head in wonder. "What an incredible stroke of luck that you stumbled upon us when you did."

"It wasn't luck. The captain of the guard who was escorting your party told me that you'd been taken captive. I was watching every move you and Carmela made on the beach this morning."

Valentina felt a surge of joy. "Diego's alive?"

"He was badly wounded, but I think he'll mend."

"I pray to God he does," Valentina said fervently. "What about the rest of his men?"

"I'm afraid he was the only survivor we found," Pelayo answered. He told Valentina that he had left the captain of the guard in the care of one of his men and had gone ahead on his own, following the tracks the Saracens had left. After finding their landing site, he had kept watch from a spot in the woods, waiting for his column to arrive. It was pure chance that he had caught a glimpse of her and Carmella clambering up onto the outcrop at the end of the cove.

Valentina held his gaze. "Thank you for coming for Carmela and I on your own. And for risking your life to save us."

"I couldn't very well leave my brother's betrothed in the hands of the Saracens, now could I?"

"No, I suppose not," Valentina answered quietly, disappointed that it seemed it was simply familial duty that had driven Pelayo to come to her rescue.

By mid-afternoon, Pelayo, Valentina and Carmela reached the main road. The strip of cloth that Pelayo had tied around the branch of a tree to mark the spot where he had veered off the road was still there. It would have been impossible for Xocobo to have missed it, and again Pelayo wondered what was keeping him. After a moment's hesitation, he decided to head in the direction of the monastery.

Some time later, figuring the horses needed a rest, Pelayo led Valentina and Carmela toward a nearby brook that he had spotted from the road.

After everyone dismounted, Pelayo brought the horses downstream to drink, then secured them to a tree to prevent them from wandering off. Rummaging through the saddle-bags on the backs of the Saracens' horses, he found several leaf-wrapped packets that he thought contained food. He unwrapped one and sniffed it. It had a spicy smell that he found strange, and he bit into it gingerly. It turned out to be some sort of paste made of ground legumes that was quite tasty. As he walked back, he called out to the two women, "Anyone hungry?"

Valentina, sitting alongside Carmella on the bank of the stream, unwrapped one of the leaf-wrapped packets Pelayo had given her and began eating. "What will you do once you meet up with your men?" she asked Pelayo between mouthfuls.

"We'll take you and Carmela back to your father in Girona, then I guess we'll head for home."

"I have a favor to ask of you. Would you mind if I come with you to Gijón?"

Her question seemed to take him by surprise. "I would have thought that after what you've experienced you'd want go home and be with your family."

"I'd rather go with you and take advantage of having a safe escort to Gijon," Valentina said. She'd been worrying about her upcoming marriage to Julian for months now and this seemed to be the perfect opportunity to spend time with him and figure out once and for all if she could stand to be his wife. If she waited much longer, the plans for their wedding would be finalized, making it impossible for her to back out of the marriage.

"It's fine with me," Pelayo answered, "if your father agrees to it."

"My father won't mind me going with you," she said, stretching the truth a little. In actual fact she had not the slightest idea what he'd say. "We can head straight to Gijon and save a week of travel time."

Pelayo turned toward Carmela. "What about you? What do you want to do?"

"I'll go wherever Valentina goes," Carmela said. "It would be improper for her to travel without a female escort."

Pelayo turned back to Valentina. "Are you sure your father won't object to you going with us?"

"I'm certain of it," Valentina said as convincingly as she could. "All you need to do is send one of your men to inform him of my decision."

"I can do that, I suppose. Any other requests?" he asked with a smile.

Before Valentina could answer, she caught sight of a column of Asturian troops heading toward them in the distance. For the first time in days she felt truly safe. Only one thing troubled her now, the uncertainty of what awaited her in Gijón.

CHAPTER 13

THEODOSIUS HAD ONCE taught Pelayo a Greek theorem which establishes that the shortest distance between two points is a straight line. When the ancient Romans began building a system of roadways to stitch together their vast empire, this concept had been used as a guiding principle in their construction efforts. In the mountainous regions of northern Hispania, however, building straight, Roman-style roads had proven to be too costly and difficult a challenge and the area had been left to languish.

In the centuries following the collapse of the Roman Empire, when commerce between nations began taking root again, some of the lords in the northern regions decided they too needed to link their towns to the existing trade routes that connected the major cities to the ports. However, lacking the skill and knowledge of the ancient Roman engineers, the local builders had left a legacy of shoddily built roads that had quickly become overrun with vegetation and pitted with potholes large enough to break the axle of a wagon. Had it not been for these poor road conditions, Xocobo and a wagon he had commandeered to transport the wounded Captain Diego, would have most likely arrived in time to save the captive women and prevent the Saracens from sailing away with them.

All in all, Pelayo thought, the campaign against the Saracens had ended in dismal failure.

It had been a week now since Pelayo and Xocobo had parted company. Xocobo had taken the wounded Captain Diego, as well as most of the soldiers and had headed off to Girona to try to reunite with general Olivar and the rest of the cohort. Pelayo had requested and been given a contingent of thirty men to escort Valentina and Carmela to Gijón.

That morning, after eight days of trekking northward, Pelayo had caught his first glimpse of the slate-gray waters of the Atlantic shimmering in the distance. A half-day's ride through rolling hills and verdant plains led them to a small, sandy cove on the coast. Though it was only mid-afternoon and there was still plenty of daylight left, Pelayo called a halt and gave everyone a well-deserved rest.

They set up camp on a windswept stretch of beach. As had become their routine, they put up the women's tent at the far end of the camp. The weather was warm and pleasant for a change, and after the work was finished, everyone whiled away the remaining daylight hours drinking wine and playing dice.

Pelayo had recently replenished their food supplies in one of the larger towns they had ridden through, and when night fell, everyone feasted on a stew of salted pork and lentils, freshly baked bread and strong cider.

After he finished eating, Pelayo wandered through the camp, occasionally stopping to speak with some of his men. Once night had fallen, he decided to check on the sentries stationed around the periphery of the camp. As he strolled by the women's tent, he caught sight of Carmela, sitting on a log, facing a small fire. Next to her was one his men, a young squad leader who seemed to have taken a liking to her, and she to him, judging by the animated look on her face. Nothing would come of it, of course, Pelayo thought, as there was a gulf of class between the two. However, he supposed there was no harm in letting them enjoy each other's company for the duration of the journey.

As he continued walking, he spotted a solitary figure on the beach. Drawing closer, he recognized Valentina. She was sitting on the sand, her legs outstretched in front of her, staring off into the distance. It was rare to see her on her own without Carmela. Giving in to an impulse, he headed toward her. "You seem lost in thought," he called out quietly, not wanting to startle her.

Valentina turned her head and looked over her shoulder. "Oh it's you," she said. "I'm just watching the sunset. The sky looks like it's on fire this evening."

"I know, it's beautiful, isn't it?" Pelayo said, sitting down on the sand beside her. For a moment they sat in silence, gazing at the vermillion streaked horizon, listening to the sound of the waves rushing toward the shore.

"How much longer before we reach Gijón?" Valentina asked.

"About a week, I figure. Anxious to get back to civilization?"

"Of course; it's going to be wonderful to sleep on a soft bed again." she said. "How about you? Are you looking forward to returning home?"

"I suppose so."

Valentina looked at him curiously. "You don't sound too enthusiastic about it."

"My life there is rather complicated at the moment."

"Matters of the heart?"

Pelayo shook his head. "It's not that."

"Really, no young lady pining for you back home?" she said with a teasing smile.

"None I care for in particular."

Valentina arched an eyebrow. "In all of Gijon, there's not a single girl you've taken a fancy to?"

"There was someone, the daughter of a magistrate. Her father learned that we were spending time in each other's company and told me that my attention was unwelcome."

"Why?"

"He didn't say. He probably thought I wasn't good enough for her."

"Oh."

"We kept seeing each other, though, until one day he caught us together. He made quite the scene. It set tongues wagging for a month."

"That must have been unpleasant," Valentina said, her tone sympathetic.

A silence settled between them as the rosy glow of the sunset faded away, leaving a full moon to fend off the encroaching darkness.

"How long are you planning to stay in Gijón?" Pelayo asked Valentina.

"I'm not sure; a few weeks perhaps."

"Why such a short visit?"

"I've been away from home for most of the last two years, serving as one of the Queen's companions in Toledo. I'd like to get back to Girona and spend some time with my family before I have to leave them for good."

"That's understandable," Pelayo said. "How did you find life at court?"

"It was tedious. Not what I expected at all. There were days I wanted to scream."

"Why?"

"I had to attend to the Queen's every whim, and there was

nothing to do except gossip about everything and everyone. I was glad when my time there came to an end."

"I would have thought that a provincial girl like you would have found life in the King's court exciting," he said with a smile.

"Well, I didn't find it so in the least," she said. "Anyway, tell me about your father; how is he?"

"We're on rocky ground these days," Pelayo said. He told her about an argument they had had before he left.

"What was it about?"

"I was involved in a fight at a local inn. It turned into a bit of a brawl."

"Did you start the fight?"

"No, but I wasn't totally blameless either. In any case my father was really upset with me. He accused me of tarnishing his good name."

The stars came out as they continued speaking, their topics wide raging, their conversation filled with banter and easy laughter.

By the time they returned to the camp, the fire outside Valentina's tent had burnt down to embers and there was no sign of Carmela.

Pelayo stood by Valentina's tent with her for a few moments, feeling strangely reluctant to part with her company.

"I suppose we should get some sleep," Valentina said.

Pelayo nodded and wished Valentina goodnight.

CHAPTER 14

DUKE FÁFILA WRAPPED his cloak a little tighter around his shoulders, then went to put another log on the fire. His study felt cold and damp that evening and he stood close to the flames, warming his hands, listening to the wind howling outside the shuttered window. He was lost in thought when the door opened and Izaskun entered, carefully balancing a tray bearing a silver ewer and two goblets.

"I've brought us some mulled wine," she said.

"Good, just what I was in the mood for," Fáfila answered.

After placing the tray on the desk, Izaskun turned toward him. Her fur trimmed cloak was folded back, exposing the swell of her breasts above the low-cut neckline of her tunic. As usual, she seemed oblivious to the chill in the air that had him shivering like an old man. "So, what is it you wanted to speak to me about?" he said.

Izaskun arched her eyebrows. "You could ask me how I am, Fáfila, or do you not have time for pleasantries anymore?"

"It's late, Izaskun; I'm tired."

"Very well, I'll get to the point," she said. "I'd like to discuss the arrangements for Candlemas with you."

"Candlemas? For God's sake woman, that's more than two months away. Could this not have waited until morning?"

"Must I wait my turn with the other servants to speak with you?"

"Of course not. Its just that, well, I find it strange."

"Why?

"I can't remember the last time you sought me out in the evening to speak about anything."

"I know," Izaskun said. She stared at him with a wistful expression. "Tell me Fáfila, do you ever feel disappointment about the way things have turned out between us?"

Fáfila blinked in surprise. "What do you mean?"

"How we live separate lives. Have you found it as lonely as I have?"

Fáfila studied her for a moment. *What the devil is she up to now?* he asked himself. A draft swept through the room, a remnant from the blast of wind that had rattled the shutters. Unable to read her expression, he gave up the effort. "It's too late for reconciliation, Izaskun, if that's what you're hoping for."

"It's never too late, Fáfila."

"I'm afraid it is, my dear. Any affection there might have been between us withered away long ago.

Izaskun's eyes filled with resentment. "And who's to blame for that? First you betrayed my trust with that harlot of yours, then you had the gall to bring your bastard son to live with us in our home, flaunting your infidelity in my face."

"I'm sorry, it was never my intention to hurt you."

"How could it not? Do you think I'm made of stone? You destroyed any hope we ever had for happiness."

Fáfila shook his head wearily. "There was never a chance of that between us, Izaskun. We're different creatures you and I.

You were never able to fulfill my desires anymore than I could satisfy yours."

Izaskun's lips tightened into a thin, hard line. "And the whore you took to your bed could, I suppose."

Fáfila bowed his head, overwhelmed by the weight of regret. He wished that Izaskun would just go away and leave him in peace.

A change seemed to come over Izaskun and the look of anger faded from her face. "I'm sorry, Fáfila, I didn't come here tonight to argue with you."

Fáfila stared at her, surprised at the sudden change in her tone.

Izaskun picked up the ewer from the desk and filled the two goblets with wine. Her hand shook a little, spilling some of the liquid on the floor as she handed him one of the goblets. "Let's have a toast to happier times, then I'll take my leave."

Fáfila took the goblet, clinked cups with her, then quaffed down his wine. It took him a moment to register the bitter taste it had left on his tongue. Grimacing, he peered at the empty goblet in his hand. "Where in God's name did you get this wine? It's bloody awful."

Izaskun avoided his eyes, a strange expression coming over her face. "It's from Galicia."

Fáfila noticed that she hadn't yet touched her wine. "It's gone sour," he said placing the goblet down on the desk. "I've told you before, you should never buy a wine before tasting it."

"I can have a servant bring us another ewer, if you'd like."

"No, don't bother. It's late and I'm holding council tomorrow morning," Fáfila said.

"In that case I'll bid you goodnight," Izaskun said. "We can talk about Candlemas some other time."

A pain, vague and unfocused, blossomed in Fáfila's gut.

Like fire it spread swiftly, and he held on to the edge of his desk for support.

Izaskun looked at him with concern. "Why don't you go to your room and rest."

Fáfila winced as another stab of pain lanced through him. "Yes, perhaps I should."

Izaskun took the tray with the ewer and goblets. "I'll bring this back to the kitchen and check on the rest of the wine. Are you going to be alright?" she asked solicitously.

Fáfila took a deep breath and nodded. "Probably just a little indigestion."

After Izaskun closed the door behind her, the pain in Fáfila's stomach intensified, becoming sharper, more insistent. It felt like hot knives twisting in his gut. He bit his lip, trying not to cry out, shocked by how strong the pain was becoming. He was suddenly worried that he might not be able to make it to his bedchamber. Bent over, clutching his stomach, he staggered across the room toward the door.

CHAPTER 15

A LINE OF storm clouds had blown in from the west, bring-ing in a steady downpour that had turned the day's hunt into a sodden, dismal affair. By late morning, despite their boiled wool cloaks, Julian and his three companions were soaked to the bone. Deciding they'd had enough, they turned back and headed for home.

It was well past noon when Julian and his friends got back to the castle. As they rode into the courtyard, a guard informed Julian that his mother had requested that, upon his arrival, he proceed immediately to his father's bedchamber.

Julian had been looking forward to changing into dry clothes and he felt aggrieved by his mother's order. "Did she say why?"

"It's your father, sire. He's…" The guard's words trailed off. "I think it's best you go and find out for yourself."

A sense of foreboding stole over Julian as he dismounted and handed the reins of his horse to the guard. Without another word, he turned and strode across the courtyard, leaving his companions trailing behind him. After entering the castle, he quickened his pace, loped across the hall, then took the stairs up two at a time to his father's quarters. Reaching the landing, he saw a throng of people milling outside the door of his father's bedchamber. Guards, servants and advisors, many with tears glistening in their eyes, grew silent when they caught sight of him. Slowly they parted and let him through.

Julian's heart was thumping in chest as he walked into the chamber. His gaze was immediately drawn to the bed. A blanket lay over his father's body, leaving only his head exposed. His eyes were closed, but there was no mistaking his repose for sleep.

Julian turned his gaze to his mother, who was speaking quietly with a handful of somber looking men who had gathered around her. Amongst them were his great-uncle Oppas, Spyros, the family's physician, Theodosius, his father's chief steward, and Aurelio, the temporary commander of the Third Legion in General Olivar's absence.

Julian felt a sense of otherworldliness as he approached the bed. He and his father had grown estranged over the last few years and the sight of the still figure, now transformed by death, shook him, though perhaps not as deeply as it once might have. Still, as the dull ache in his chest proved, he had loved his father as much as he could love anyone.

Aware that his every move was being closely watched, he bent over the bed and kissed his father's brow, already grown cold. As he straightened, a startling thought occurred to him: his father's death meant that he was now the Duke of Asturias. A heady feeling of power surged through him, eclipsing all other thoughts and emotions. Hitching his shoulders, he walked across the chamber toward his mother and the group of men around her.

"What happened?" Julian asked, a newfound timbre of authority in his voice.

"Your father's heart gave out," his great-uncle Oppas said, his voice carrying to the people standing outside in the corridor, peering in through the open door.

Julian's brow furrowed. "His heart?"

"Yes," his mother said. "He was complaining of pain in his chest last night."

Julian looked at her in puzzlement. "Was he?" He had dined with his father the previous evening and he couldn't recall his father mentioning that he was feeling ill.

"I should have sent someone yesterday to fetch Spyros," his mother said, sniffing and dabbing her eyes with a handkerchief.

Julian glanced at Spyros, the physician, and for a brief moment he thought he saw something other than grief lurking in the man's eyes. His attention was diverted by his great-uncle, Oppas, who placed a hand on his shoulder.

"I'm sorry for your loss, Julian," Oppas said. "Your father was a great man. Everyone in Asturias will mourn his passing."

A murmur of agreement went around the chamber. A wave of sadness washed over Julian.

Three days later, Julian awoke in the middle of the night with a burning itch in his crotch. After tossing and turning and feeling that he was slowly going mad with frustration, he threw back his covers and padded across the floor of his bedchamber toward the brazier in the corner of the room. Stirring the ashes with a poker, he uncovered a glowing ember. He picked it up with tongs, blew into it until it turned an incandescent crimson, then used it to light a taper. Squatting on the cold flagstone floor, he held the flame up close and examined himself. Even in the weak light, he could see the rash of minute sores that had spread over his pubic area.

"That goddamned whore," he muttered under his breath,

certain it was the new kitchen girl who had given him the rash. He felt like finding the bitch and slapping her senseless. His anger gradually gave way to anxiety. Had he caught something serious? No matter, he tried to reassure himself, Spyros would know how to cure it.

Cupping the lit taper with his hand, Julian made his way down a series of dark corridors to the Greek physician's quarters in the west tower. There, he rapped on the door and called out, "Spyros, wake up! I need to see you."

There was no response and Julian banged on the door again. "Come on, man, open the damn door!"

Again nothing. Julian reached for the latch, and to his surprise, discovered that the door was unlocked. He pushed it open with his foot and stepped inside the dark chamber.

Holding the taper above his head, Julian glanced around. All of Spyros' chests were gone. So were the vials of medicines and potions that had once crowded the shelves along the walls. Except for a single cot, stripped of its mattress and blanket, the chamber was empty.

Spyros had been their family physician for years and his sudden disappearance struck Julian as odd. He made a mental note to ask his mother about it, but for now, there was nothing he could do but return to his quarters and wait until morning.

Once back in his chamber, Julian lay down on his bed and tried without much success to ignore his itch and go to sleep.

Finally, when the sun rose over the horizon, he gave up the effort and rose to his feet. After dressing, he left his room and wandered aimlessly through the castle, trying to distract himself. He was heading up the main staircase when he saw his mother descending toward him. She was giving instructions to a servant girl who was following one or two steps behind her.

His mother looked surprised when she caught sight of him. "What are you doing up this early?" she asked.

Julian ignored her question. "What's happened to Spyros? His chamber is empty."

"Why do you ask? Are you feeling unwell?"

Julian's hand moved unconsciously to his crotch. "I just need to see him."

Izaskun dismissed the servant girl and waited until she was out of earshot before addressing Julian. "Spyros left yesterday. He received a letter from his family asking him to return home at once. Apparently it was a matter of great urgency."

Julian frowned. "Why wasn't I told about this?"

"It slipped my mind. I'm sorry, dear. He left in the middle of the night. He said he had to reach the port by sunrise to catch a ship to Hellas."

"Damn him to hell," he said with feeling. "He should have given us notice."

"It's not the end of the world," his mother said mildly as she passed by him. "It shouldn't take us long to find a replacement."

Julian watched with a sour expression as his mother kept going down the staircase. It was easy for her to say it wasn't the end of the world, but the truth was he didn't see how he could live with his itch for another day. He considered going into town to look for a physician, then dismissed the idea. Everyone knew the so-called healers in town were nothing more than butchers and charlatans.

As he walked down the stairs, it occurred to him that the cooks in the kitchen regularly suffered burns. Perhaps one of them had an ointment that he could use on his rash.

It turned out that one of the cooks in the kitchen claimed to have a concoction that worked wonders on burns. After he went off to fetch it, Julian settled himself on a stool and called out to one of the passing servants to bring him some wine.

The manservant returned a moment later with a goblet in his hand. "My sympathies for your loss, Don Julian," he said, handing Julian the wine.

Julian nodded absently, not wanting to encourage the man to blather on.

Seemingly oblivious to Julian's reluctance to engage him, the manservant continued, "Not many people know this, but I helped your father to his room the night he died."

Julian turned and eyed the servant, a slightly built man with a trimmed, gray beard and sorrowful eyes. The man's name came to him after a moment: Osorio. "I thought my father died suddenly in his sleep."

"Oh no, Don Julian. Your father was in his study when he started getting sick."

"How do you know that?"

"I saw him coming out of his study, clutching his stomach. He was in such pain that he could hardly walk."

"What time of day was that?"

"It was late evening."

Julian studied Osorio a little more closely. "What were you doing outside my father's study at that time of night?"

"I was in the great hall checking on the torches. It's part of my duties to replace them when they burn out."

"I see. Were you at my father's side when he died?"

"No, Don Julian. Once I helped your father to his bed-chamber, I left him in the care of his manservant, Grammaticus. After that I returned to my duties."

Julian gazed thoughtfully at the servant. "Thank you for coming to my father's aid."

"No thanks are necessary, Don Julian. I held your father

in great esteem. Like everyone here, I would have laid down my life for him."

Julian nodded.

As the manservant was walking away, Julian called out to him, "Are you sure my father was clutching his stomach, not his chest?"

Osorio turned. "Oh yes, I'm quite certain, Don Julian. It was his stomach. He told me he thought it was the wine he had drunk. He said it had tasted bitter."

Julian eyed the goblet in his hand, "Did you think to check on the wine kegs in the kitchen?"

"That's the first thing I did. There was only one cask open. I took a sip from it and it tasted fine. But I asked the steward for permission to get rid of it anyway, just to be on the safe side."

The man who had left to fetch the ointment returned and handed Julian a small clay pot with a lid. "Here you are, Don Julian. I hope this helps"

CHAPTER 16

AFTER FOLLOWING THE coastal road for several days, Pelayo led his riding party into Castro Urdiales, a small, seaside town of a few hundred inhabitants. The town had once been a trading center of some importance, but now the deserted streets and crumbling buildings revealed its decline into a backwater, fishing village. There didn't seem to be much of interest in the town center, and Pelayo decided to ride on through.

On the outskirts of the town, they came across a small crescent beach where several overturned fishing boats lay basking in the sun. Nearby, a group of fishermen were sorting their catch. Pelayo hailed them and after some bargaining, he bought several basketfuls of fish.

The rest of the afternoon's journey proved uneventful. As the sun crept lower in the sky, Pelayo began searching for a suitable location to set up camp. He soon spotted a flat stretch of land by the water's edge that looked large enough to accommodate their horses and tents. More importantly, the site had a nearby stream that would provide them with fresh water for drinking and cooking.

With dusk falling, the cook and his two assistants set about preparing the evening meal. Soon the aroma of grilled fish began wafting through the air, drawing the men to gather around the cooking fires. Once the skin of the fish started to char, the cook declared the supper ready and the assistants began handing out dishes of food to the men lined up before them.

Just as everyone settled around the campfires and began to eat, the wind picked up and ominous looking clouds moved in. Midway through the meal, with a suddenness that caught everyone by surprise, rain began pouring down. The men all grabbed their dishes and ran for cover.

Valentina was about to dash off after Carmela when Pelayo grabbed her by the arm and shouted over the sound of the wind and the pelting rain, "Why don't you come to my tent. It's closer."

Valentina hesitated, then realized that her food would turn to a sodden mush if she tried to reach her own tent. "All right, lead the way."

Pelayo hurried toward his tent that was a few dozen paces away. After unhooking the tent flap, he held it open for Valentina to enter, then followed her in. It was dark inside, and he left the tent flap slightly open to allow in some light.

He retrieved his fire-starting kit from his travel bag, put a small amount of wood shavings into a bronze dish, then struck a flint against an iron rasp a few times, sending sparks flying. When the wood shavings began to smolder, he blew on them carefully until they caught aflame. He then used a sliver of wood to light an oil lamp, and soon, the gloom gave way to a flickering, reddish glow.

Valentina put her dish down, then took off her damp cloak. She ran her fingers through her wet hair, raking it back from her face. Noticing Pelayo's eyes on her, she gave him a self-conscious smile. "I must look like a drowned cat."

"Not to me," he said with a smile as he closed the tent flap. "I think you look lovely."

Valentina made a face at him. "Liar." Over the past few weeks, she had spent a lot of time in Pelayo's company, regaining some of the easy familiarity the two of them had shared as children.

She glanced around the tent, then sat down on the canvas floor and watched Pelayo as he knelt by his travel pack again and rummaged through its contents. "It must be nice not to have to share your tent with anyone." she said to him.

"Privileges of rank. I don't have to listen to someone snoring all night."

Valentina picked up her dish and continued to eat. "Speaking of rank, is it true that you're being groomed to take command of the legion from General Olivar?"

"Who told you that?" Pelayo said over his shoulder.

"I overheard some of the soldiers speaking about it the other day."

"It's just a rumor," Pelayo said. He came back with a wineskin and two cups, then sat down facing Valentina.

"I don't know," Valentina said. "Commander of the Northern Legion has a nice ring to it. It's just the sort of title a father might want to confer on a second son."

Pelayo poured some wine into a cup, then handed it to her. "There's no chance of that happening."

Valentina noticed the edge that had crept into his voice. "What makes you so certain?"

"My father knows that Julian would revoke my command the moment he inherits the title."

"You really think Julian would do that to you, his own half-brother?"

Pelayo snorted. "Julian would cast me out to the dogs if he had half the chance."

"There's never been any love lost between the two of you, has there?" she said, remembering Julian and Pelayo as children.

"We've hated each other from the moment we first met," Pelayo said.

"What a shame the two of you never got along. He's your only blood relation besides your father, isn't he?"

"I may have some family on my mother's side, but I don't really know much about them."

"Your father must have known your mother's family. Have you ever asked him about them?"

"All I need to know is that they packed my mother off to a convent when they found out she was with child," Pelayo said.

"Oh, I see."

A silence settled between them for a moment.

"You must have been very young when your mother died," Valentina ventured. "Do you remember anything about her?"

"Just that she had red hair and was very beautiful, at least until she got sick." Reaching under the collar of his tunic, Pelayo pulled out the medallion he was wearing around his neck. "This belonged to her."

Valentina leaned in and studied the gold disk in the dim light. "I've never seen anything like it." Her brow furrowed as she squinted. "I can't quite make out the inscription. What does it say?"

"I wish I knew. Even Theodosius, who's the smartest man I know, couldn't decipher the words."

"He was your tutor wasn't he? Is he still in Gijón?"

Pelayo nodded. "He's now my father's chief steward," he said, slipping the medallion back under his tunic.

"I remember when he first arrived at your father's castle. You had a fight with Julian that day."

"I'm surprised you remember that," Pelayo said.

"I should. It was because of me the two of you got into the fight."

"That's right, I'd forgotten that you disliked him as much as I did."

"Disliked? Loathed is a better word. I cried myself to sleep the night your father announced my betrothal to him."

Pelayo seemed surprise. "I had no idea the announcement had upset you so much."

"I never got the chance to tell you. You and I never really spoke after that day."

"Really?"

"You know very well we didn't," she said with a good-natured smile. "Every time I came back for a visit and caught sight of you, you pretended not see me. For the longest time I couldn't understand why you were avoiding me. Then one day I figured it out. You thought I was a pest and you wanted nothing to do with me."

"That's not true."

"It's all right, you needn't deny it," she said with an easy laugh. "I know I must have been an insufferable brat."

Pelayo finished his wine then filled their cups again. "How do you feel about marrying Julian now?"

The laugher went out of her eyes. "Like I've been sentenced to the dungeons."

"Have you discussed it with your father?"

Valentina nodded. "He says that I'll find him quite acceptable once I get to know him a little better. That's the main reason I'm going to Gijón. To see if my father is right."

"And if he isn't?"

There was no hesitation in Valentina's reply. "I don't intend to spend the rest of my life with someone I despise."

"Julian will not take the annulment of your betrothal lightly, if that's what you end up deciding."

"He'll just have to learn to live with his disappointment."

"Suffering with grace is not in Julian's character. He'll do everything in his power to get you to change your mind."

"Why would he care?" Valentina asked. "We're practically strangers; he has no feelings for me."

"Julian will see it as a humiliation."

"I don't care. Anyway, there's nothing he'll be able to do about it."

"You're wrong about that; there's plenty he could do."

"Like what?"

"He could ask his great-uncle, King Witiza, for his help in dealing with the issue."

"By dealing with the issue, you mean forcing me to marry Julian against my will?" she asked, an ironic edge in her voice.

"It would no doubt be couched in more flowery words, but that would be the essence of it."

"You paint a grim picture of my prospects," she said.

"I'm afraid that's how I see it. I'm sorry."

"No, don't apologize; you're probably right," Valentina said, feeling uncharacteristically subdued.

"I have an idea. Why don't I speak to my father on your behalf? Perhaps I can persuade him to quietly annul the betrothal, so that it doesn't become a public matter."

"You really think your father would do that?"

Pelayo nodded. "He knows full well the consequences of a loveless marriage. I could be mistaken, but I think he'll see there's nothing to be gained by forcing you to marry Julian."

Valentina thought about it for a moment. "It's worth a try, I suppose."

The discussion seemed to have cast a pall over them both and they finished their food in silence.

After her second cup of wine, the dreary topic of her betrothal to Julian faded from Valentina's mind. Feeling the effects of the long day's journey, she yawned, arching her back, stretching her arms above her head.

A gust of wind shook the tent. The lamplight flickered, casting shadows around them. The keening of the wind and the murmur of the surf lapping on the beach filled the silence.

The storm had brought in a damp cold and Valentina began to shiver, wrapping her arms around herself for warmth.

Pelayo rose to his feet and fetched his sleeping blanket from his pack. After unfolding it, he draped it over Valentina. His arms lingered around her shoulders for a moment.

Valentina turned and gazed up at him. His face was so close that she could see the glint of the lamplight in his eyes. Before she could react, he leaned down and kissed her.

She did not resist, nor did she respond. When he drew away, she gazed up at him coldly. "You shouldn't have done that," she said, her tone flat.

"I'm sorry, I thought you wouldn't mind."

"I'm spoken for."

"Does it matter, out here, in the middle of nowhere?"

"Of course it does, and had you drunk less wine, you'd realize that."

Valentina rose to her feet, the blanket slipping off her shoulders. "I think I'd better go."

"Wait," Pelayo called out, rising to his feet as well.

She had reached the entrance of the tent when Pelayo caught up to her and grabbed her wrist, preventing her from leaving. "Let go of me," she said tightly.

"Just tell me you feel nothing for me."

"It doesn't matter what I feel. It doesn't change anything."

Pelayo let go of her wrist. "Do you want to know why I avoided you every time you came to visit us in Gijón?"

Valentina grew still.

"It was because I couldn't bear to be reminded that one day you would be marrying Julian instead of me."

Valentina let out her breath, her pent-up tension fading away. She knew that she was on dangerous ground, and one misstep now could lead them both to ruin. But the emotions stirring inside her were too strong to resist. As if sensing her weakening resolve, Pelayo reached out for her. Feeling as though she was falling into an abyss, she let him sweep her into his arms.

With his body pressing against hers, Pelayo kissed her, first softly, then with mounting urgency. Around her, the tent dissolved and for a timeless moment nothing existed, nothing save for the yielding softness of his lips against hers.

Locked in an embrace, they tumbled in a swirl to the ground, wrapped in each other's arms.

There was just a hint of light in the sky when Valentina returned to her tent. As she laid down on her reed mat, she heard Carmela's voice emerging from the darkness.

"Where have you been?" Carmela asked in a drowsy voice.

"I'll tell you later. Go back to sleep,"

"You've been with Pelayo all night, haven't you?"

"There's nothing for you to worry about."

"Just tell me you haven't done something foolish."

"I haven't," she lied. "We'll talk about it in the morning."

After Carmela fell back asleep, Valentina lay on her mat, staring up into the darkness, struggling with her conflicting emotions.

CHAPTER 17

THREE DAYS AFTER Spyros' sudden departure, the new physician knocked on the door of Julian's bedchamber and introduced himself. The two exchanged the usual pleasantries, then the portly, middle-aged man asked Julian to remove his clothing and go stand by the light of the window.

When Julian complied, the physician crouched down and examined the area around Julian's groin.

"What have you put on here?" the man asked, wrinkling his nose.

"It's an ointment I got from one of the cooks in the kitchen."

"It smells like rancid fat. Did it help?"

Julian shrugged. "I'm not sure. A little, perhaps."

"Well," the physician said, straightening. "It's nothing serious; I see this sort of thing all the time."

"What do I have?"

"An imbalance of humors. An excess of phlegm."

"It itches like the devil. Is there a cure for it?"

"I'm pleased to say there is, Don Julian. First, you must wash off that vile ointment, then I'll apply a proper poultice. Afterwards, you'll need to cover the affected area with a satin cloth. You'll also need to add a mix of fenugreek, juniper berries and milk thistle to your food for a month to rebalance your humors."

Julian expelled the breath that he'd been unconsciously holding. "Thank you," he said with feeling. It was a relief to have a proper physician in the household again.

When Julian awoke the next morning, he found his itch had gotten significantly better. Cheered by the thought that the poultice was starting to work, he rose from his bed and began to dress. He was planning his day when he suddenly remembered the talk he had had in the kitchen with the servant, Osorio, about his father.

Something about their conversation was nagging at him. As he laced up his sandals, it came to him. Osorio had told him that his father had complained that the wine he had drunk had tasted bitter. Yet later, when Osorio had sampled the open keg, he said he had found that the wine tasted fine.

Julian could think of only one possible explanation for that. As he replayed the conversation again in his mind, he remembered that Osorio had mentioned that he had handed his father over to the care of his manservant, Grammaticus. Perhaps the man would be able to shed some light on the final moments of his father's life, and either confirm his suspicion or dismiss it as a figment of an overwrought imagination.

What he discovered next surprised him. No one had seen Grammaticus since the day his father died. He found that not only odd but troubling. After trying to figure out what to do next, he went looking for Osorio, the one man left in the castle who had spoken with his father on the night of his death.

Julian found him sitting alone at one of the long tables in the kitchen, polishing a stack of silver platters.

Catching sight of Julian, Osorio scrambled to his feet, "Good morning, sire."

"I have a question for you, Osorio. It's about the night of my father's death. You told me you were checking on the torches in the hall. While you were there, did you happen to notice anyone going in or coming out of my father's study?"

Osorio knitted his brow as he thought back. "Why yes. Your mother came out just before your father."

Julian's blood ran cold. Without saying another word, he turned and left the kitchen.

He went looking for his mother, first in the chapel, then in the storeroom, and then in the stable. Finally he went to her bedchamber and knocked on the door.

"Who is it?" his mother called out from inside.

"It's me, Julian. I need to talk to you."

There was a momentary silence, then the door opened a crack. His mother peered at him. "I was about to change to go riding. Can this wait until I get back?"

"No. I need to talk to you now."

His mother gave him an annoyed look, but then opened the door for him.

Entering the chamber, Julian glanced at the neatly laid out clothing on the bed, then turned to face his mother. "I thought you'd want to know that one of the servants has gone missing."

"Oh? Which one?"

"Grammaticus," Julian answered. "No one has seen him since the night Father died."

"That's the first I've heard of it," his mother answered.

"You're in charge of the household. How could you not know?"

"Servants come and go all the time. I'm certain there's a perfectly reasonable explanation for Grammaticus' absence."

"He would have had to ask you for permission to leave, if that had been the case, would he not?"

"Since when do you care about the comings and goings of the servants?"

Julian ignored his mother's question. "Don't you find it peculiar that the two men who were at father's bedside the night he died have both gone missing?

"What are you implying?"

"One of the servants told me that he saw you coming out of Father's study the night he died. He said that when Father came out a moment later, he appeared to be in such pain that he could hardly walk."

"It's no secret that your father wasn't feeling well that night."

"Yes, but you said Father was complaining of pain in his chest. According to the servant, Father was clutching his stomach, right after drinking wine that he said had tasted sour."

"It's possible I might have been mistaken. Is it that important? Really Julian, what's gotten into you tonight?"

Julian's expression hardened. "Father's heart didn't give out. Someone put something in his wine, something that killed him."

"That's absurd! Who put that ridiculous notion in your head?"

"It's the only explanation that fits the facts."

"I see." A calculating look crept into in his mother's eyes, as if she had just realized that it would take more than bluster to pacify her son.

"You were the last person in the room with Father," he told her. "At the very least you must have witnessed his distress. Yet instead of calling for a physician, you left him alone to die."

There was no reaction from his mother this time, not even the batting of an eyelash. Considering the accusation he had just leveled at her, she seemed strangely calm and composed. "Well? Do you deny it?"

His mother held his gaze. "No."

The world lurched beneath his feet and he suddenly felt sick to stomach. Despite all the indications of her guilt, he had nursed the hope his mother would be able to offer him an explanation that would absolve her of any involvement in his father's death. But now he had to confront the reality that his own mother had murdered his father. "How could you do that?" he asked hoarsely. "How could you poison your own husband?"

Julian saw a shadow flit across his mother's face, but then it was gone, her composure intact again.

"I did what I had to," she answered. "Your father was planning to make Pelayo his sole heir. He was going to cheat you out of your inheritance."

Julian felt the blood rushing to his face. "That's a damn lie! Father would never have done that."

His mother held his gaze. "Your father always did exactly what he pleased, no matter what pain he caused anyone. He had a relationship with another woman behind my back, then brought his bastard child to live here with us, rubbing his infidelity in my face. Do you really think your father wasn't capable of betraying your trust as he did mine?"

"Even if Father had wanted to, he could not have made Pelayo his heir. Our laws forbid it."

"The king can override any law he wishes. That was the price your father asked of Roderic for supporting his bid to the throne."

"You expect me to believe that?"

"There's proof. Uncle Oppas intercepted a letter your father wrote to Baron Ernesto. You can ask him for it and read it for yourself."

Julian studied his mother. He could tell she wasn't lying.

A numbing weariness began stealing over him. In the space of a single day he had learned that his mother had poisoned her own husband and that his father had schemed to deprive him of his birthright. *Quite a day*, he thought bitterly. He now wished Osorio hadn't said a damn word to him and that he'd been left in blissful ignorance. As he gazed at his mother, he knew that he would never again feel the same way toward her. No matter how many years passed, he would always look upon her with revulsion. Though she had acted on his behalf and he had her to thank for inheriting the title, he would never be able to forgive her for the cold-blooded murder of his father.

He let out a long breath, a weary acceptance settling over him. *What's done is done*, he told himself. All he felt now was an overwhelming desire to find a dark corner somewhere and drink himself senseless. Before leaving, however, he realized that there was one final item he needed to share with his mother. "The manservant who helped Father to his room the night he died; his name is Osorio."

His mother absorbed the information without a change of expression. "I'll take care of it."

"I don't want him killed. Just lock him away somewhere for a few years."

"Very well."

Julian turned and walked out of his mother's chamber, intending to find his friends and drink himself senseless.

CHAPTER 18

SOME THREE MONTHS after setting out from Gijon with General Olivar, Pelayo led his riding party across the bridge spanning the Deva River, whose waters marked the eastern boundary between Cantabria and Asturias. The verdant hills and the coastline dotted with coves and golden beaches had for days taken on the familiar look of home. As they left the bridge behind them, Pelayo caught sight of a band of horsemen heading down the road in their direction. When they neared he saw they were uniformed men-at-arms.

The leading horseman hailed him from afar, "Good morning; welcome back, Commander Pelayo."

"Thank you," Pelayo called back. "It's good to be home again."

The squad leader reined in his horse in front of Pelayo, then nodded in greeting to Valentina and Carmela.

"Where are you heading today?" Pelayo asked the officer whose face looked vaguely familiar.

"Girona, sire. Lady Izaskun has charged us with delivering a message to Baron Ernesto. Actually, the message is of concern to you as well."

"You've got me curious," Pelayo said. "What is it?"

"It's about your father, sire." The squad leader paused for a moment. "I'm afraid he's dead."

Pelayo's breath caught in his throat. *Dead? How can that be?* "What happened?"

"I was told his heart gave out. I'm sorry to be the bearer of such terrible news, sire."

The moment took on an air of unreality for Pelayo. A single thought broke through the maelstrom of his emotions: the memory of saying goodbye to his father, promising him they'd go hunting together when he returned. As sense of loss and grief suddenly overwhelmed him. He was dimly aware of Valentina leading her horse to his side and placing a comforting hand on his shoulder.

Pelayo and his party took four more days to reach Gijón. When they were within sight of the city, he parted company with his men, who then headed off on their own to the legion's campgrounds.

It was well past noon when Pelayo, Valentina and Carmela entered the city through the southern gates. The sight of the whitewashed houses topped with red tile roofs and of bustling narrow streets would normally have lifted Pelayo's spirits, but the realization that his father would not be there to greet him robbed his homecoming of any sense of pleasure.

As they had agreed earlier, Pelayo and Valentina dropped Carmela off at her sister's house near the city center, then continued on their way toward to the castle by themselves.

When they reached the gates, a guard by the name of Thiago hailed Pelayo and asked him how he and General Olivar had fared against the Saracen raiders. Glossing over the fact that their quarry had sailed away with their numbers intact, Pelayo replied that the campaign had gone well enough.

After entering the courtyard, Pelayo and Valentina steered their horses toward the stable.

Pelayo sensed his father's presence everywhere. When they had parted company a few months earlier, he could not have imagined that he would never see his father again. A feeling of overwhelming loss welled up inside him again.

After leaving their horses at the stable, Pelayo and Valentina walked across the courtyard, then up the steps and into the castle. As they entered the great hall, they caught sight of Theodosius hurrying toward them.

"Welcome home, my boy," Theodosius called out.

"Thank you, Theo. It's good to be home."

"This place hasn't been the same without you," Theodosius said, embracing him. He next turned toward Valentina and gave her a bow. "Greetings, my lady. What a pleasure to see you again. It's been so many years."

"It has indeed," Valentina answered, smiling. "It's good to see you too, Theo."

After exchanging pleasantries with Valentina for a moment, Theodosius turned back toward Pelayo, his expression turning grave. "Have you heard the news about your father?"

Pelayo nodded. "We ran into some soldiers a few days ago. It was the last thing I expected to hear."

"It caught us by surprise as well," Theodosius said. "One day your father was fit and hale, the next he was gone. It was a terrible shock to all of us."

"I still can't believe it, Theo. I wish I could have been with him in his final hours."

"I know, my boy."

"I didn't get much of an explanation from the soldiers about how he died. Do you know what happened?"

Theodosius hesitated. "Why don't we talk later? You and Valentina should go and pay your respects to Doña Izaskun."

"You're right, I suppose we should," Pelayo said without much enthusiasm.

"She's in your father's study. I'll wait for you out here," Theodosius said.

Izaskun put down the document she had been reading and looked across at Pelayo from behind his father's old desk. "So, you're back," she said tonelessly. Her cold expression thawed an instant later when she saw Valentina entering the room behind Pelayo.

"Valentina! What a pleasant surprise," Izaskun said, rising from her chair and walking around the desk to greet her.

"Good day, Doña Izaskun," Valentina replied.

"We weren't expecting you until next summer."

"I made a spur of the moment decision to come, Doña Izaskun. I hope I am not imposing on you by arriving unannounced like this."

"No, of course not; it will be a pleasure to have you stay with us." Izaskun took Valentina's hand and looked her up and down. "What a ravaging beauty you've become, my dear."

"You're too kind," Valentina said.

"How are your father and mother?"

"They're both in good health. And you, Doña Izaskun?"

The two women chatted politely, ignoring Pelayo. When their conversation began to lag, Izaskun excused herself and called over a female servant who was hurrying by.

"This is Lady Valentina," Izaskun told the girl. "She's going to be staying with us. Show her to the south facing chamber next to the stairs. Make sure there's fresh bedding for her."

The girl bobbed her head in assent. "At once, Doña Izaskun."

Izaskun turned back toward Valentina. "I need to speak to Pelayo in private for a moment. Why don't you go and settle into your room and join us later for supper?"

"Yes, of course," Valentina answered.

"I'll send a servant to fetch you when everything is ready."

"That sounds fine. Thank you again for your hospitality, Doña Izaskun."

"You're most welcome, my dear."

Once Valentina had walked away, Izaskun turned toward Pelayo, the cordial expression fading from her face. "So, how did the campaign go against the Saracens?"

"Not well. They sailed off before we could engage them."

"That's a shame."

"Yes."

Izaskun walked around the desk and sat down on her chair again. "I assume you've been informed of your father's death."

"I have. Is that what you wanted to speak to me about?"

"Not exactly. I'd like to discuss your father's will."

"Very well," Pelayo said curtly, annoyed that Izaskun was bringing up the subject so soon after his arrival. *She could have had the good grace to wait for another time.*

Izaskun gazed across at him. "The king's magistrate came to Gijón two weeks ago and read out your father's last testament in the presence of the assembly, as the law requires. Your father was very generous to you."

Pelayo nodded and waited for her to go on.

"He left you several townships, including Pola del Mar, as well as fifty gold escudos."

Pelayo looked at her in surprise. Usually all the lands passed to the male heir next in line. "That's more than I expected."

"The gold is yours to keep, but I'm afraid the townships must remain as part of our family's estate."

Pelayo's brow furrowed. "I don't understand."

"I thought I was being clear; you cannot have the townships."

"You have no right to deny me my inheritance," he said, remembering Theodosius' lessons in common law.

"Oh, but I do have the right. Your father was getting on in years. Clearly his judgment was impaired. There is no other explanation for why he would overlook the fact that the revenues from the townships are needed to cover the expenses of running our household."

Pelayo felt his anger stirring. "There was nothing wrong with Father's judgment and you know it."

"I can call upon a dozen witnesses who will swear otherwise," Izaskun said blandly.

"Yes, I'm sure you can," Pelayo said, biting off his words. "With bribes and threats. You've always been good at that."

Izaskun stiffened. "I'd watch my tongue if I were you. Your father is no longer here to protect you."

"I thought I had your measure, Izaskun, but you're a more contemptible creature than I ever imagined."

Izaskun erupted to her feet. "I've had enough of your insolence! You're no longer welcome under this roof."

"I never was, at least by you."

"Theodosius will give you your father's money. I want you gone by sunset."

Pelayo fought the urge to wrap his hands around Izaskun's neck and throttle her until her eyes bulged out. "That's what you've always wanted, isn't it?"

"I could deny it, but I'd be lying," she said, her tone cold.

Pelayo felt his cheeks burn. It took all his willpower to turn and walk away before he did something rash. In truth he had never expected to inherit anything of significance from his father, therefore the loss of the townships did not trouble him greatly. What made his blood boil was the contemptuous manner in which Izaskun had dealt with him.

He was so consumed by his thoughts that he didn't notice Theodosius approaching him.

"So," Theodosius called out. "How did it go with Lady Arachne?"

Despite his dark mood, Pelayo smiled at Theodosius' use of their name for Izaskun. The title had always seemed fitting for her, but today it seemed even more relevant. "She just told me to get my things and clear out."

Theodosius' face fell. "Oh dear. What happened?"

Pelayo told him of his conversation with Izaskun.

When he finished, Theodosius shook his head. "It looks like she's finally gotten her revenge on you. I'm sorry, my boy."

Pelayo shrugged. "She mentioned my father left me some funds."

"He did indeed; two fat purses. Shall I fetch them for you from the chamberlain?"

"In a moment. First tell me about my father's death."

"There's not much to tell. It seems Bishop Oppas went into your father's room and found him dead in his bed."

"I was told that his heart gave out," Pelayo said.

"That is the general assumption," Theodosius said. "Izaskun said your father had been complaining about a pain in his chest the night he died."

"There was nothing Spyros could do for him, I suppose," Pelayo said.

"I don't know, I never got the chance to ask him about

anything. He left in the middle of the night, the day after your father's death. It seems he didn't say goodbye to anyone."

"He didn't give notice that he was leaving?"

"Apparently not."

Pelayo stared at Theodosius, lost in thought. He found it strange that Spyros would have left without first taking his leave from the people he'd known for years. "Have you spoken to Father's manservant, Grammaticus? He would know whether Spyros had been summoned to Father's bedside."

"That's the other curious thing. Grammaticus has not been seen since the night your father died."

"Has anyone questioned his wife?"

"First thing I did when I heard he had vanished. The poor woman was frantic with worry. She still has no idea what has happened to her husband." Theodosius paused, cast a furtive look around the hall, then lowered his voice. "There's more. Another member of the household staff went missing a week ago."

"Who was it?"

"A servant called Osorio."

Pelayo mulled over the information. It strained credulity to think that the disappearance of three men within days of his father's death was simply a coincidence. "Have you spoken to Julian or Izaskun about this?"

"No. I didn't think it was wise to raise the subject with them."

"Why not?"

"Izaskun told everyone that Spyros' family had sent for him," Theodosius said.

"So?"

"Spyros once told me he had no family."

Pelayo felt a chill run through him. "You are telling me Izaskun had something to do with Spyros' disappearance?"

Theodosius took a moment to answer. "I don't know what to think." He let out a long breath. "I'm sorry to have brought all this up now. I should have waited for a more opportune moment to speak with you."

"No, I'm glad you've told me," Pelayo said. "Look, I have to go find Valentina and let her know what's happened. Then I'm planning to take a room at the inn by the riverside. Can you meet me there tomorrow and bring me the gold my father left me? We can talk some more then."

"Of course, my boy. I'll meet you at the inn tomorrow."

Pelayo said goodbye to Theodosius, then set off to find Valentina. She wasn't in the bedchamber where he had expected to find her, nor was she in the great hall, nor in the kitchen. As he stepped out into the courtyard to continue his search, he spotted two men in clerical robes standing by the fountain. One was a stranger, but the other he knew only all too well. There was no mistaking the bloated figure for anyone but Bishop Oppas.

Pelayo recalled Theodosius mentioning that Oppas had been the first person to discover his father's body. Giving in to an impulse, he set off toward the two men.

Oppas had stripped to his leggings and was kneeling by the side of the fountain, leaning over the rim of the basin. His companion was pouring water over his head using a long-handled metal dipper.

After washing himself, Bishop Oppas rose to his feet and wiped the water off his face with his hands. A look of irritation flitted across his face when he caught sight of Pelayo walking toward him. Oppas turned and muttered something to his acolyte, who immediately stepped in front of Pelayo, blocking his way.

"Can't you see the bishop is busy?" the cleric said. "Come back later,"

"I need to speak to him now," Pelayo said, attempting to step around the man.

The cleric reached out and grabbed Pelayo's arm. "You deaf? Did you not hear what I said?"

Pelayo yanked his arm free, then put his hand on the cleric's chest and shoved him away. Stumbling back, the man hit the edge of the stone basin with the back of his knees, then fell over backwards into the water.

Oppas' face flushed red. "You arrogant, young whelp!" he said, his voice quavering with indignation. "How dare you lay your hands on a man of the cloth?"

Though Pelayo knew he should keep a civil tongue when speaking to Bishop Oppas, he was still angry about how Izaskun had treated him and his blood was up. "Call me a whelp again and you'll find yourself in that fountain with your friend."

Oppas clenched his jaw and glowered at Pelayo. "What the devil do you want?"

"Is it true you were the first to discover my father's body?"

"Yes," Oppas bit off. "What of it?"

Stepping out of the fountain dripping wet, the young cleric made his way purposefully toward Pelayo.

Oppas glanced at the cleric and gestured for him to stay put.

"Did you notice anything unusual about my father when you found him?" Pelayo asked Oppas.

"He was dead. Is that unusual enough for you?"

"Was there any sign of a wound, or bruising of any kind?"

"There was nothing like that. Your father died of natu-ral causes."

"Did the physician, Spyros, tell you that?"

Oppas studied Pelayo for a moment, then turned toward the young cleric. "Leave us."

The cleric seemed surprised at being so summarily dismissed, but then he shrugged and walked away.

Once the cleric was out of earshot, Oppas addressed Pelayo, "All right, what's this all about?"

"I want to know about my father's death. It seems everyone who was at his side the night he died has disappeared."

"I was there, and I'm still here."

"Father's physician and his manservant are both gone. That's rather peculiar, don't you think?"

Oppas reached down for his robe, then slipped it over his head. "Your father died of a bad heart, a common affliction that strikes men of a certain age. As for the disappearance of the men you mentioned, I'm certain it has nothing to do with your father's death."

"My instincts tell me differently," Pelayo said.

"Instincts are often wrong. You'd be better off relying on reason."

"I'll bear that in mind," Pelayo said, turning and walking away.

"What are you planning to do?" Oppas called out.

"I'm going to find out what happened to my father in the final hours of his life," Pelayo said over his shoulder.

After Pelayo disappeared, Bishop Oppas sat down on the ledge of the fountain and stared into space. He had thought that he and Izaskun had covered their tracks and that the entire Fáfila affair had been laid to rest, but now he realized there was a chance that Pelayo, through either luck or persistence, might stumble upon something linking them to Fáfila's death.

His brother Siberto had hired the men who had taken care of Izaskun's physician and the servants. But they were scum, the dregs of the earth, and Oppas was concerned about the possibility that one of them might, in some drunken moment, let something slip out one day. As he dried himself off in the sun, he considered his predicament. In the end, he decided that something would have to be done about Pelayo. There was simply too much at stake to let him run around loose, asking question about his father's death.

Izaskun was sitting behind her desk when her uncle Oppas barged into her study. Annoyed at the interruption, she looked across the room at him, not bothering to conceal her irritation. "I'm busy at the moment, Uncle. Can you come back later?"

"I'm afraid this can't wait," Oppas said striding into the chamber as if it was his own.

Izaskun put down the document she had been reading. "Very well, what is it?"

"I've just had an interesting conversation with your stepson," Oppas said.

"Let me guess, about his inheritance?"

"No. He's found out that Spyros and Grammaticus have gone missing."

"That's not exactly a secret, is it?" Izaskun said.

"He suspects the disappearances are linked to Fáfila's death."

"Oh, I see," Izaskun said, settling back in her chair.

"Look, I know it's unlikely, but if Pelayo discovers what we've done, he might go to the King with the story."

"You're worrying for nothing," Izaskun said. "We can trust Siberto's men to stay silent; it's their heads that will roll if anything leaks out."

"Are you willing to stake our lives on that?"

Izaskun didn't answer.

Oppas continued, "King Roderic is a clever man. If he learns that you and I were involved in Fáfila's death, he might just figure out what we're up to."

A shadow seemed to flit across Izaskun's face. It was not the first time that she wondered about the wisdom of getting herself enmeshed in her uncle's schemes.

"It's too late to back away now, Izaskun," her uncle said, as if reading her mind. "We're up to our necks in this."

Izaskun stared warily at him. "What do you suggest we do?"

"We make Pelayo vanish, like we did with the others."

"You never cease to amaze me. You are a bishop, a man of the cloth. How can you justify all the blood on your hands?"

"One must sometimes wield a sword to fight for a just cause. I believe that's what God expects from us."

"Do you really believe that God wishes you to murder Pelayo?"

Oppas raised an eyebrow. "Who said anything about murder? The last thing we need now is for someone to find the body of Duke Fáfila's youngest son floating in the river or to have to explain yet another mysterious disappearance. And this time it wouldn't be a servant of no significance. No, this time we have to act openly."

"And how do you propose we do that?"

"We charge Pelayo with a crime, then throw him in the dungeons. After a few months, everyone will have forgotten about him."

Izaskun felt as if she had been backed into another corner by her uncle. After a moment's reflection, however, she realized they had no choice but to continue on the path she had set for herself. "The offense will have to be serious. Tongues will wag unless there are witnesses to support the charge."

"That shouldn't be a problem for you, should it?" Oppas said.

Pelayo found Valentina outside the chapel, talking to a priest that Pelayo did not recognize. After chatting politely with the two of them for a moment, he excused himself and led Valentina away.

"Is there something wrong?" Valentina asked, sensing Pelayo's tension.

"Izaskun has ordered me to leave the castle."

Valentina looked at him with dismay. "What happened?"

Pelayo recounted his conversation with Izaskun, including her avowed intention to keep the townships his father had bequeathed to him.

Valentina stopped walking and turned to face him. "Can she do that, ignore your father's last testament?"

"She's saying my father was old and addled," he said. "It's a lie, of course. His mind was as sharp as yours or mine."

Valentina let out an exasperated breath. "I can't believe she would do that. What a horrid woman. You should go to the King and plead your case to him."

"That would just be a waste of time. The King won't want to involve himself in a family dispute over an inheritance, especially when the claimant is a second son."

"You have to do something," Valentina said. "You can't let Izaskun get away with stealing your inheritance."

"I don't intend to. I'm going to stay in town for a few days and try to figure out what to do next."

"Will you let me know where you're staying, so I can come and see you?"

"I'm not sure that's wise Valentina."

"I don't care if it's wise; I'm not ready to say goodbye to you yet," she said.

"We shouldn't be seen in each other's company anymore, you're Julian's betrothed."

"Not for very much longer."

"What do you mean?"

"I'm not going to marry Julian."

Pelayo raised an eyebrow. "When did you decide that?"

"Just now, when you told me you were leaving."

Pelayo took a moment to answer. "I am not a good prospect, Valentina. I have neither title nor land."

"I'm not some peasant girl you need to provide for. My father is the Baron of Catalonia. When I tell him how much I care for you, he'll welcome you with open arms. We'll never lack for anything. You can—" Valentina suddenly stopped and searched his face, her certainty suddenly deserting her. "Am I being too bold?"

"No," Pelayo said, reaching for her hand. "There's nothing I'd like better than to spend the rest of my life with you, but—"

Suddenly, from somewhere behind him came the sound of footsteps crunching on stony ground.

Pelayo let go of Valentina's hand and turned to look. A squad of men-at-arms was making its way toward him and Valentina. Leading the men was the new commander of the guard, Aurelio, obviously sent by Izaskun to cast him out of the castle.

"Greetings, my lady, Don Pelayo," Commander Aurelio said as he came to a stop. His men positioned themselves at his flanks.

"I just need a little more time to settle my affairs, Aurelio," Pelayo said. "Then I'll leave the castle, you have my word on it."

"I'm afraid you won't be going anywhere, sire. I have orders to place you in confinement."

Pelayo's brow furrowed. "Confinement? What am I being charged with?"

For a moment Commander Aurelio looked troubled, then as if a curtain had been drawn, his eyes went flat and hard. "Treason. For plotting to overthrow Lord Julian." He gestured to his men. "Seize him."

As the soldiers advanced, Valentina stepped in front of Pelayo. "Wait! You can't do this. The charge is absurd!"

"I'm sure he'll have the opportunity to defend himself," Commander Aurelio said, grabbing Valentina by the arm and pulling her out of the way.

"It's all right, Valentina," Pelayo told her, injecting a note of confidence in his voice that he did not feel. "I'll be fine."

Valentina looked at him, her eyes filled with anguish. "I'll go find Julian. I'm certain this is all a big mistake."

Pelayo didn't have the chance to answer her as the soldiers marched him away.

CHAPTER 19

JULIAN LIFTED HIS goblet to his lips and took a long swig of wine. Wiping his mouth with the back of his hand, he gazed at the three leather-clad men sitting with him at the table. It was late afternoon and they had the great hall all to themselves.

Casimiro, a thick-necked man with curly black hair, was staring at his friend on his right. "I still can't believe you missed the bloody stag," he said, with a scornful shake of his head.

Usebius, the sharp-featured man addressed, focused his wine-glazed eyes on Casimiro. "How many times do I got to tell you? A gust of wind got hold of my arrow."

"In a pig's eye," Casimiro shot back. "Your aim's gotten so bad you couldn't hit a cow if it was standing right in front of you."

Joaquin, the youngest of Julian's companions, sniggered as he propped up his mud encrusted sandals on the table.

A silence fell over the group when a servant came over to top up their goblets. Despite the predominance of female servants, only the men ever ventured out from the kitchen to serve Julian and his companions when they were drinking. And these bouts, capping the end of a day's hunt, had become a more frequent occurrence in recent weeks. On this particular day, however, circumstances had prevented Julian from joining his companions on the hunt, thus accounting for his dark mood.

In fact, the day had been a trying one for Julian. In the morning he had met with the quaestor in an attempt to sort out the affairs of state which, following his father's death had been allowed to languish more or less unattended. Every new idea he had proposed to the quaestor had been met with an observation or a question. When he had told the quaestor that he wished to shore up the castle's defenses, the man had replied that it was an excellent idea, but then had inquired where the gold to pay for the improvements would come from. It was then that Julian had learned that the state coffers were nearly empty. Alarmed by the news, he had instructed the quaestor to raise taxes immediately. The old man had agreed, but then had observed that the previous harvest had been a poor one and that the peasants would have little to eat over the winter months if they were obliged to give away any more of their grain.

Julian had told the quaestor that he had no intention of coddling the peasants like his father had done, and that raising the taxes would make them work harder the following year. The old man had nodded, seemingly in agreement, but then mentioned that several of the farmers had abandoned their land in the last few months and that an increase in taxes would undoubtedly drive more of them away.

All his life Julian had observed his father as he had carried out his official duties. It had all looked so simple, but now he was coming to understand what an irksome and thankless task they really were.

In the afternoon things had gone from bad to worse. He had met with Theodosius to discuss the various legal claims for which he had to render a judgment the following day in open court. Theodosius had argued against most of his opinions, pointing out how they went against his father's precedents or violated either secular or ecclesiastical laws. It was at some point during their discussion that Julian had decided to rid himself of his supercilious ex-tutor at the first opportunity. But first he would have to become familiar with the laws of the land as well as with the inner workings of the court.

Joaquin was in the middle of recounting a bawdy tale involving a priest and a nun when a servant placed a platter of roast pork in the middle of the table. Another servant brought them a stack of wooden plates. Joaquin's tale was quickly forgotten, as everyone drew out their knives and began spearing slices of pork onto their plates. The smell of food brought in the hounds. One skulked by Casimiro's bench and he tossed it a chunk of meat. Another hound darted in and a fight broke out. Cutting through their snarling, the sound of footsteps came echoing down the hall.

Facing outward, Casimiro was the first to spot a female figure walking toward their table. Noticing Casimiro's stare, Joaquin turned to look over his shoulder.

"Don't think I've seen her around here before," Joaquin muttered.

"Neither have I," Casimiro replied. "Toothsome little morsel, isn't she?"

"That she is," Joaquin said in agreement. "I'd sure like to nibble on her toes."

"That's not the part I'd choose," Usebius said with a smirk.

Julian's indulgent smile faded as he suddenly recognized Valentina. "Shut your pox-ridden mouths, all of you. That's my future wife you're speaking about."

Valentina sensed a strange tension in the air as she approached Julian. She cast a cursory glance at the three rough-looking men sitting at the table, dismissed them all as louts, then turned her attention to Julian. She was anxious to bring up the subject of Pelayo, but she knew she had to observe the social niceties first. "Good evening, Julian. Forgive me for intruding on you like this."

"What a surprise to see you here, Valentina," Julian said, rising to his feet. "I had no idea you were coming."

"I made my decision to come rather suddenly," Valentina said. "I'm sorry I didn't have a chance to give you advance notice,"

"No matter," Julian said.

Julian seemed a little older than the last time she had seen him. With his striking blue eyes and neatly trimmed beard, there was no arguing that he was a handsome man.

"When did you arrive?" Julian said, slurring his words a little. It was obvious that he was trying to gather his wine-sodden wits.

"This morning. I'm surprised no one told you."

"I've been tied up all day with matters of state," Julian said.

"It must be burdensome to have all those responsibilities on your shoulders now."

"It's a bloody bore, I can tell you that."

"Yes, I can imagine," Valentina murmured.

"Well," Julian said. "I suppose I should go and greet your father and mother."

"They're not here. They didn't come with me this time."

Julian's eyebrows arched. "You came without them? Was that wise?"

"I was in good hands. Pelayo and two dozen of his soldiers escorted me here."

Julian's expression changed. "So, Pelayo is back, is he?"

"Yes."

"I trust you had a chaperone."

Valentina nodded. "Carmela was kind enough to accompany me."

"Good, I don't want anyone spreading gossip about you."

Valentina glanced at the three men at the table who seemed to be watching her with avid interest. "Do you think we could continue our conversation in private, Julian?"

Julian's companions stirred and began to rise, but Julian waved them back down.

"You can speak freely here," Julian told Valentina. "These men are my friends."

Father was wrong, Valentina thought to herself. *Julian will never change. He'll always be a churlish boor.* "As you wish," she said.

Putting the three men out of her mind, Valentina addressed Julian directly, "I've come to ask you why you've accused Pelayo of treason."

"Treason?" Julian said, appearing genuinely surprised. "That's the first I've heard of it."

Valentina gave Julian a skeptical look. "You are the lord here. How could you not know what is taking place under your roof, especially about something as important as this?"

Valentina saw Julian frown. It was obvious that he did not like being spoken to in that manner by anyone, especially by a woman and doubly so in front of his friends.

"Maybe it was my mother who gave the order," Julian said. "If she did, I'm certain she had a good reason for doing so."

"The charge is ridiculous. Pelayo doesn't have a treacherous bone in his body."

"You seem to hold him in higher regard than I do," Julian said.

"Apparently so."

"Why are you meddling in this matter anyway?" Julian said, irritation creeping into his voice. "It doesn't concern you."

Valentina saw that she was getting nowhere with Julian. "I'm sorry I interrupted your gathering. I'll go find your mother and leave you to your friends."

"If you're going to speak to her about Pelayo, I'd advise you to watch your tongue. She won't be as tolerant of your hectoring tone as I am."

"Thank you for your advice," Valentina said coldly. "Perhaps I should just return home and tell my father that you've thrown his friend's youngest son into the dungeons under a made-up charge, the same son, by the way, who just saved my life at great risk to himself. I have no doubt my father will want to pursue this matter with the King."

Her words seemed to penetrate Julian's wine clouded head. By the smile he forced on his lips, she knew that Julian had just come to realize that he had not handled the situation with his bride-to-be as tactfully as he should have.

"Look," Julian said. "Perhaps I could speak to my mother and sort out the situation with Pelayo. I'm certain it's just a simple misunderstanding."

Valentina searched his face. "Are you really willing to do that?"

"Of course. Pelayo and I may have had our differences, but our father's blood runs through both our veins."

Valentina wanted desperately to believe Julian, but his capitulation had come a little too quickly for her liking. "May I come with you when you speak to your mother?"

"I think it's better if I see her alone."

Valentina hesitated. All her instincts were telling her that Julian was just trying to placate her. Yet what choice did she have? "Very well, I'll wait to hear from you."

"Good."

There didn't seem to be much else to say and Valentina bade

Julian goodbye. As she walked away, she heard Julian murmur something to his friends, eliciting a burst of laughter from them. Her doubts about Julian's sincerity deepened.

Valentina was heading up to her bedchamber when on impulse she turned and took the staircase in the other direction, going down into the bowels of the castle. At the bottom, a dank passageway lit with a few guttering oil lamps led her to a wooden door reinforced with iron bracings. There was a bronze knocker set in its center and she rapped on the door with it. A moment later, a panel at the height of her head slid open and a pair of eyes beneath thick, black eyebrows peered back at her.

"What do you want?" a gruff voice demanded.

"I wish to see one of your prisoners. Don Pelayo."

The eyes studied her for a moment. "You got written permission?"

"Of course."

"Hold it up so I can see it."

Valentina pretended to search through her tunic. "I can't seem to find it. I must have left it in my bedchamber."

The gaoler's eyes narrowed. "Sorry, I can't let you in without a writ."

"Please, I just need to see him for a moment."

The panel slid shut.

"How dare you!" Valentina shouted furiously. "Open the door this instant!" When there was no response, she grabbed the knocker and let out her frustration by rapping furiously on the door with it. When her arm grew tired, she leaned her head wearily against the door, wondering what to do next. She thought of seeking out Commander Aurelio to ask him for permission to visit Pelayo, but in the end she decided that the quest would lead nowhere. *I should just bide my time and speak to Izaskun later at supper.*

For the rest of the afternoon Valentina wandered aimlessly through the castle. It was just getting dark when a young servant girl found her in the garden outside the walls and told her that Lady Izaskun had requested her company for dinner.

Most of the benches in the great hall were filled with diners by the time Valentina got there. A cacophony of laughter and conversations followed her as she threaded her way through the servants streaming down the aisles. As she neared the head table, she caught Lady Izaskun's eye.

"Oh, there you are, my dear," Izaskun said brightly. "Come sit here with me."

After greeting Izaskun, Valentina sat down beside her.

Julian broke off the conversation he was having with the man on his left and turned toward Valentina. "I'm glad to see you finally decided to join us," he said with a half-smile.

"I'm sorry I'm late," Valentina said perfunctorily, not really caring what Julian thought. She turned back toward Lady Izaskun and despite her best intention to wait for the appropriate moment, she couldn't refrain from broaching the subject uppermost in her mind. "I wonder if I could speak to you about Pelayo, Doña Izaskun. I don't know whether Julian has had the chance to —"

Lady Izaskun held up her hand, cutting Valentina off. "Not now, my dear. Let's enjoy our supper in peace, shall we? Try the rabbit, it's very good tonight."

Swallowing her impatience, Valentina pretended to take an interest in the food spread out before her.

Julian and Izaskun maintained a steady stream of polite conversation with Valentina throughout the meal. Valentina attempted twice more to raise the issue of Pelayo with Izaskun, only to be rebuffed each time. After her third attempt failed, she realized that she wasn't going to get anywhere that evening.

Telling herself that she would not be put off as easily the following morning, she finished her wine, then, pleading exhaustion, retired to her chamber.

Night had fallen and the servants had lit several candles in Valentina's bedchamber, allowing her to enter without stumbling around in the dark. Walking past the chair next to a small table, she sat down on the edge of the bed.

Her thoughts turned to Pelayo. It was difficult to think of him sleeping on a hard-stone floor in complete darkness, caged like an animal in the bowels of the castle. She wished she had Carmela to talk to; it would have been a comfort to have had a friend to keep her company on this dismal night.

Feeling restless and unsettled, Valentina went to fetch the travel bag she had brought with her. After searching through its contents for a moment, she pulled out a plain woolen smock she had purchased in one of the towns they had passed through. She changed into the garment, then began snuffing out the candles. At the last moment, fearing being left in the dark in the unfamiliar chamber, she decided to allow herself the luxury of keeping one candle burning through the night.

Valentina slipped off her sandals, pulled down the blanket of her bed, then laid down on the wool-stuffed mattress. After weeks of sleeping on a straw pallet, the bed felt wonderfully soft. The day had been long and trying and she thought that she would drift off to sleep immediately. But she lay awake, staring at the ceiling, unable to still the thoughts racing through her head.

At last her eyelids grew heavy. She was in that hazy state between sleep and wakefulness when a sound intruded into her consciousness. At first, she thought there might be a mouse in the room. The faint, scratching noise came again. This time it sounded more like a metallic rasp rather than the furtive scurrying of a rodent. At last it dawned on her what it was: a key being inserted rather clumsily into the lock of her door.

Valentina came fully awake. In the dim light cast by the single candle on her bedside table, she watched the door swing open. Her first thought was that it was a servant girl bringing her something, perhaps another blanket. But she couldn't understand why the girl hadn't bothered to knock.

The corridor was awash in torchlight and Valentina could see the outline of a man standing in the doorway. He just stood there, his face shrouded in shadows, staring at her in silence. His menacing stillness sent a shiver of fear down her spine. "Who's there?" she called out, her voice strained with tension.

"It's me, Julian," came a slurred voice. Without waiting for acknowledgement, he walked in and closed the door behind him.

Valentina sat up and pulled the blanket up around her. She told herself that Julian probably just wanted to speak to her about Pelayo. "What are you doing here at this hour?"

"I thought you'd still be up," Julian said, making his way unsteadily toward her bed.

"I was sleeping. You should know better than to enter a lady's bedchamber without knocking."

"I just wanted to give my future bride a goodnight kiss before she turned in," Julian said, coming to a stop by the bed. "Nothing wrong with that, is there?"

Valentina could smell the reek of wine on his breath. "You're drunk, Julian. Go to bed. We'll talk in the morning."

"It's not talking I'm here for," Julian said.

His words made Valentina's stomach lurch. "Leave my room at once," she said, hearing the fear in her voice.

Julian's lips quirked up in a drunken smile. "Don't be such a cold fish. You're going to be my wife in a few months."

"We should wait till then," she said, trying to keep her voice calm.

"Why? I'm in the mood now," he said, fumbling with the buckle of his belt.

Valentina's eyes darted toward the door, wondering if she could reach it before he caught up to her.

As if knowing what she had in mind, Julian edged to the side of the bed, blocking her path to the door. Unfastening his buckle, he let his belt fall to the floor.

"What do you think you're doing?" she asked, her dread mounting.

Julian took off his tunic and flung it away. He stood naked before her, his eyes gleaming in the candlelight. "I just want a taste of my conjugal rights."

Julian reached down and yanked the blanket off her bed in one violent motion.

Valentina edged away. "Don't do this, Julian, I beg you."

Julian sat heavily on the edge of the bed, making the wooden slats groan. "I know how you feel about me. I saw the way your eyes slid away from mine this afternoon, like I was some foul beast you couldn't stand to look at."

"You're imagining things. I like you, I really do," she said, her tone desperate.

Julian laughed mockingly. "Do you? Well then, this is your chance to prove it to me."

Valentina scrambled to the other side of the bed. Julian lunged after her and grabbed hold of one of her ankles just as she was about to get off the bed.

Her heart pounding, Valentina kicked at him with her other foot, trying to free herself.

Julian clambered on all fours across the bed and grasped

Valentina by the hair. Pulling her back on the bed, he forced her on her back, then sat astride her.

With the desperation of a trapped animal, Valentina flailed at him with her fists.

Turning his head away to avoid her blows, Julian grabbed her wrists then, pushing himself higher up her chest, pinned both her arms with his knees.

Though Valentina continued to struggle, she realized that she was under his complete control.

Julian grabbed the neckline of her smock, then tore it violently down the middle. A look of sensual pleasure suffused his face as his eyes feasted on her naked body. He reached out a hand and squeezed one of her breasts so painfully that she let out a groan.

With a sudden burst of force that caught Julian off guard, she bucked and twisted and managed to free her right arm. Before he could stop her, she reached up and raked his cheek with her fingernails.

Julian grunted with pain, then with a snarl of anger, slapped her hard across the face.

Valentina's head snapped to the side, pinpoints of light dancing before her eyes. She tasted blood from her cut lip.

Julian grabbed both her wrists again then laid down flat on top of her. She tried to wriggle free of him, but he was too heavy. He began prying her legs open with his knees.

"For the love of God, Julian, I beg you...don't do this..."

"Come on, you bitch," Julian panted, his voice thick with desire, trying to find her mouth. "Give us a kiss."

Valentina felt caught in a nightmare. A scream from somewhere inside her seemed trapped within her. Julian's face, flushed with the heat of arousal, filled her vision. His mouth ground painfully against her lips.

Valentina let out a cry as she felt him thrust into her.

Izaskun burst into Julian's bedchamber, stalked across the floor to the window, then threw open the shutters. Morning light flooded in.

Needles of pain shot through Julian's head. He covered his eyes with his arm and felt the sting from the scratches on the left-hand side of his face.

"You dim witted fool!" his mother raged, storming toward his bed. "Do you have any idea what you've done? How could you be so infernally stupid?"

Julian tried to focus his bleary gaze on his mother. The inside of his mouth felt like dried leather and he was dying for a drink of water. He was also badly in need of a piss. Though his present condition was not a novel experience, his mother's tirade was making the pain in his head worse. "Do you mind not shouting, mother? My head is splitting."

"I don't give a pox about your head! I've turned a blind eye to your debauchery for years, but this time you've gone too far."

Julian stared at his mother. "What the devil are you going on about?"

"Don't play the innocent with me, Julian. Did you really think you could treat a baron's daughter as though she was a common whore and get away with it?"

Julian sat up, took a deep breath, then threw his legs over the bed. "Didn't take the bitch long to go crying to you, did it?" he said sourly, looking at his mother through bloodshot eyes.

"She didn't come to me; it was the chamberlain who told me. One of the servants saw you going into Valentina's chamber, then heard her crying out. Now the entire household is talking about what you've done. It's too bad I wasn't told about it until this morning. I would have come into the room and taken a whip to you."

"What's got you so riled up? Nothing wrong with a man getting a taste of his bride-to-be, is there?"

"A taste? Is that what you call it? You stole into her room in the middle of the night and forced yourself upon her. What do you think Baron Ernesto will do when he hears what you've done to his daughter?"

"I don't know, lay siege to the city?"

"You find this amusing, do you? Well it's not, damn you! We're trying to form alliances to wrest back the crown. If word of this gets out, we'll be lucky to have the stable boys fighting under our banner."

"All right calm down. I'll go find Valentina and apologize to her."

"Apologize? You think she's going to forgive you after what you've done to her? Do you really know so little about women?"

"I know enough," Julian said sullenly.

"Oh yes, I can see that." His mother shot him a withering look. "You'd better fix this, you hear me? I don't care what you have to do. Get on your knees and grovel. Or promise her the moon. Just make bloody sure you clean up this mess."

When Julian didn't answer, Izaskun stalked out of the room and slammed the door shut behind her.

Julian stared moodily at the door. His mother was right, of course; what he had done was stupid. He had been drinking all afternoon, but that was no excuse. He tried to recall what had happened, but everything was a bit of a blur. He lay back on his bed, gazing up at the ceiling, trying to piece together the fragments of his memories. Despite his best efforts, however, most of the encounter with Valentina remained hazy. But one detail did stand out, something that he had registered even in the heat of passion. He had had plenty of experience in such matters and even drunk, he had noticed there had been no resistance when he had first penetrated her. Though he'd heard one couldn't always rely on this as a test of virginity, the ease with which he had entered her left him wondering.

He mulled over the matter as he rose from his bed and relieved himself into the chamber pot. A high-born bride was expected to arrive at the conjugal bed a virgin. If she wasn't, that was cause for a scandal. Of course, there was now no way of finding out whether his suspicion about Valentina was true or not. But the more he thought about it, the more he began to see her concern for Pelayo in a different light.

Standing naked by the washbasin in her room, Valentina dipped a cloth into the water and washed herself again. She felt terribly weary and every movement she made required an effort of will.

After Julian had left her chamber, she had lain in the dark, unable to muster the courage to rise. She had told herself that it wasn't her fault, that she had done everything in her power to fight him off. Yet she could not rid herself of the shame and self-loathing that had taken hold of her. She had wept bitterly for a time, but now she felt drained of tears.

Outside her window, the castle was slowly coming to life, reminding her that she had to get a hold of herself. Though she wanted to crawl back into bed and stay there all day, she forced herself to get dressed. Every fiber of her being was urging her to flee the castle and join Carmela at her sister's house. But that was not something she could allow herself to do, at least not yet. Though she suspected that the effort would lead nowhere, she had to find Lady Izaskun and plead with her to release Pelayo. Though she dreaded the encounter, given her fragile emotional state, she felt she couldn't leave any stone unturned in her efforts to save Pelayo.

Summoning up all her willpower, she gathered herself, then went looking for Lady Izaskun. The first place she tried was the study where they had met the previous day. The door was ajar, and she heard the sound of a chair scraping against the floor. "Is that you, Lady Izaskun?" she called out, pushing the door open.

"I'm afraid not," Julian said, looking across at her from behind the desk.

Valentina froze at the sight of Julian. It took all her courage to stand there and face him. "I'm looking for your mother," she said, her heart pounding. "Where is she?"

Julian waved his hand vaguely. "Outside somewhere."

Valentina turned to go.

"Wait," Julian called out, rising to his feet. "I want to apologize for last night."

Valentina turned back to face him, her composure crumbling. "You are a loathsome swine," she said fiercely, trembling with emotion. "You're going to pay for what you did to me last night."

"You have every right to be angry," Julian said, walking toward her. "What I did was unforgivable."

Valentina shot him a look of utter contempt. "Once I've spoken to your mother, I'm going to leave this place and hopefully never lay eyes on you again."

Julian came to a stop in front of Valentina. "I told you I'm sorry. I swear to you that if you —"

"Goodbye, Julian," Valentina said, cutting him off.

As she turned to leave, Julian's arm shot past her and he slammed the door shut, blocking her way out.

"Last night, I wasn't the first man to have you, was I?" Julian asked.

Valentina flushed. "How dare you! Have you no shred of decency in you?"

Julian's eyes bore into hers. "It was Pelayo who plucked your flower, wasn't it?"

"That's none of your affair!"

"That's arguable, isn't it, considering we're betrothed?"

"We're not," she said. "Not anymore."

"Because I was drunk and did something foolish?"

"Get out of my way," Valentina said.

Julian stared into her eyes. "I still want you for my wife," he said quietly, reaching out a hand to touch her face.

Valentina turned her head away, as if avoiding a red-hot iron. "You must be raving mad. You're the last man on earth I'd marry now."

"I have a proposition for you, something that might make you change your mind," Julian said, dropping his arm that was holding the door shut.

Valentina looked at him, her eyed fill with loathing. "Save your breath! I'm not interested in anything you have to say to me."

"Are you certain of that? It concerns Pelayo."

Late that night, after everyone had retired to their beds and sleeping mats, Julian and Valentina slipped out through the front door of the castle. After crossing the deserted courtyard, they took the stone staircase leading to the top of the ramparts. As they climbed, the full moon dimmed behind a cloud, making their ascent a treacherous affair.

When they reached the top, Julian waited for Valentina, then walked alongside her down the narrow causeway in silence. They came to the first of the two towers flanking the main gates and Julian opened a small door, then led Valentina up the spiral stairway to the summit. Feeling their way in the dark, they exited into a circular area ringed by a chest-high, crenellated wall.

Valentina gazed at the dark panorama around her, then leaned over one of the open spaces between the merlons and looked down. Some fifty feet below, a set of torches cast a ruddy glow over the area immediately outside the main gates of the castle. Beyond, stretching into the darkness, lay the road leading to the city, its boundaries now undistinguishable. Valentina walked to the other side of the tower and looked down again. The view this time was of the inner courtyard of the castle. The torches at the entrance doors of the main building had long burned down, leaving the area barely discernable in the moonlight.

A feeling of desolation swept over Valentina as she stared out into the night, feeling the bite of the north wind through her woolen cloak. She wrapped her arms around herself, her gaze fixed on the courtyard below her.

"On your feet, lad," Aurelio called out as he led a small squad of soldiers into Pelayo's cell.

Sitting with his back against the wall, Pelayo shaded his eyes from the torchlight. "What day is it?"

"Thursday. You've been here for four days. Seems longer doesn't it? That's how it is down here."

"Where are you taking me?" Pelayo asked.

"Outside; we're going to set you free," Aurelio said.

Pelayo didn't believe Aurelio, but he rose to his feet anyway. Anything was better than being caged up in the darkness. Wondering where they were really taking him, he followed the soldiers out of the dungeons, then up a staircase that led to the courtyard. Once outside he filled his lungs with the cool, night air and gazed up at the expanse of stars above him. It was an incredible feeling to be out in the open again.

Up on the watchtower, Valentina saw a rectangular patch of light materialize in the darkness below her. With torches held high, several soldiers began emerging from a doorway in the castle. They marched across the courtyard, then came to a stop by the gatehouse directly below her. One of the soldiers raised his torch up high, illuminating a figure in their midst. Though she had prepared herself for this moment, her breath still caught in her throat at the sight of Pelayo.

She wanted desperately to call out to him, to get his attention, to have him look up at her, so she could at least say goodbye to him. But the words stayed locked inside her as Pelayo continued walking, gazing straight ahead of him, oblivious to her presence up on the tower.

"Can you tell who it is?" Julian asked quietly from behind her.

"Yes," she answered, feeling a dull ache in her heart.

Julian leaned over the crenellated wall. "Carry on!" he called out to the men below.

The soldiers and Pelayo disappeared into the short passage that ran through the wall beneath her. She walked to the other side of the watchtower and saw Pelayo emerge, this time unaccompanied. He stopped, gazed back as if in puzzlement for a moment, then set off at a steady stride down the darkened road.

Valentina stood motionless on the watchtower, gazing out into the night long after Pelayo had disappeared from sight.

Behind her, Julian finally broke the silence. "As you can see, I've upheld my end of the bargain."

Valentina turned toward Julian, moonlight washing over her face.

Julian must have seen her tears glistening on her cheeks. "I hope you will love me like that one day," he told her.

"I shall never love you, Julian," Valentina said, her voice filled with loathing. "You should have no illusion about that. I will go to my grave despising you."

Julian's expression turned hard. "So be it. You can hate me all you want, but I expect you to perform your wifely duty. I want an heir, and by God, you shall provide me with one."

Pelayo picked his way through the gloom, the castle receding into the darkness behind him. His gaze occasionally strayed to the moonlit fields bordering the road. The sound of rustling leaves seemed implausibly loud. The breeze felt like a gentle caress on his skin. After the black void of his cell, every sensation was a precious gift.

Commander Aurelio had let him keep his purse and the jingling sound of coins followed his every stride. Despite the late hour, he thought he'd be able to find an inn in town still open, or at least find one whose owner was amenable to being roused in the middle of the night. As he continued walking, the elation he had felt at being freed began to fade. Questions about the odd events of the past hour began to nag at him. Why had Julian suddenly decided to let him go? And what was that business of stopping him in the middle of the courtyard and holding a torch up over his head? The one thing he knew for certain was that the voice he had heard coming from atop the tower had been Julian's.

He was following the road through a cluster of farmhouses, when the moon began clouding over and what little light there was dissolved into darkness. Relying on his instinct more than on his eyesight, he proceeded cautiously along the barely discernible ribbon of road. He was trudging up a rise, his mind drifting, when from somewhere ahead of him came a metallic clink. He stopped in mid-stride, a feeling of foreboding stealing over him.

The moon began brightening again, revealing several armed figures emerging from behind one of the houses. Silent as wraiths, they fanned out across the road, moonlight glinting off their helmets and swords.

Pelayo's heart began to pound, every instinct he possessed urging him to run in the opposite direction. As he spun around, preparing to flee, more soldiers came streaming out from behind another house. Swiftly they spread out across the road, cutting off his escape. By the uniforms the men were wearing, Pelayo could tell his assailants were Julian's house guards.

The bizarre turn of events left him reeling. Why the pretense of letting him go, followed by what seemed to be a carefully planned ambush? What he knew for certain was that this twisted exercise could only have come from Julian's devious mind. The only question remaining was why Julian had felt the need to carry out such an elaborate deception. Whatever the answer, he suspected that if he allowed himself to be recaptured, he might never see daylight again.

The last thing the soldiers expected was for their quarry to turn the tables and charge at them.

Driven by desperation, Pelayo rained blows about him, trying to break through the cordon of soldiers. Muffled curses and shouts filled the air as Julian's men wrestled him to the ground. Just before darkness closed in, he caught a glimpse of a sandaled heel descending upon his head.

CHAPTER 20

A SHEEN OF sweat glistened on Julian's forehead as he walked along the path encircling the castle. It had been an unusually warm spring and though it was only early March, the bushes in the back garden were already flowering and the air was scented with the fragrance of their blooms. Turning down a side path, he spotted Valentina sitting on a stone bench under a tree. She had her head down, her attention on a piece of cloth she was embroidering.

Julian noted that the swelling of her belly was growing more pronounced every day. Though she was seated, it was clear even from a distance now, that she was with child. In a few months time he would find out whether he'd have a son or a daughter. Truth was, he didn't really care which. Valentina had just turned nineteen and there was plenty of time for her to bear him a son.

As he walked toward her, he went over in his mind what he was going to say. He could not afford to strike a false note.

Hearing his footsteps, Valentina looked up from her embroidery and stiffened when she caught sight of him. He had paid her one of his conjugal visits the previous night. As usual, she had shut her eyes and turned her face away, no doubt imagining herself to be somewhere else. Seeing him now, invading what she probably considered her personal sanctuary, her eyes turned cold with contempt.

"There you are," Julian called out. "I've been looking everywhere for you."

"Well, you've found me. What is it you want?"

Julian was so used to her curt manner by now that he didn't even bat an eyelash at the lack of a proper greeting. In fact, there was never any attempt on her part to be civil with him, be it in private or in public. And her disrespect for him had not gone unnoticed with the servants and members of his retinue. The amusement he detected beneath their polite smiles infuriated him to no end. But he always made sure that she paid a price for her insolence, in the bedroom, when he had her alone to himself. There he would take her hard and fast as he would a common whore.

"Well?" Valentina said, looking up at him.

"A messenger arrived this morning from my great-uncle Siberto," Julian told her.

Valentia stared blankly at him, making her lack of interest in anything he had to say evident.

Julian reached into the pouch on his belt and drew out a glinting object. "The messenger brought this along," he said, extending his hand toward her.

Valentina's gaze fell upon a medallion in Julian's palm.

"Recognize it?" he asked.

Valentina looked up at him. "How did your great-uncle come by it?"

"One of his patrols came upon the body of a man lying in a ditch. They found this around the man's neck, under his tunic,"

Valentina's face went white.

"I'm afraid Pelayo's dead," Julian said, putting on a pained expression.

"No, it can't be true," Valentina whispered, looking shaken to her core.

"There's no mistake. My great-uncle identified his body when the soldiers brought him back to give him a proper Christian burial."

"Oh my God," Valentina moaned.

"It's terrible news, I know," Julian said in a solemn voice. He extended his hand and offered her the medallion. "Here, you can have this as a keepsake."

When there was no reaction from Valentina, Julian dropped the medallion on her lap, then turned and walked away.

Valentina's chest rose and fell as she stared at the medallion, paralyzed by the anguish engulfing her. The thought that she would never see Pelayo again, feel his arms around her or hear his laughter, tore at her heart. Her eyes welled with tears. Something gave way inside her and she began to weep, shuddering sobs that seemed to come from the deepest core of her being.

CHAPTER 21

THE WAIL OF the newborn infant rang throughout the bed-chamber, drawing smiles from the women gathered around Valentina's bed.

"It's a girl," the midwife said, beaming at her.

Valentina knew that the woman was relieved that the birth had gone well. As the midwife, she would have been blamed if either she or her child had died in labor, an event that was far from rare. She would now be paid, though less handsomely than if the baby had been a boy.

"She seems perfectly healthy, Doña Valentina," the midwife called out cheerily over her shoulder as she carried the infant to a basin filled with tepid water.

A servant girl caught Valentina's eye. "Doña Izaskun asked that we notify her the moment the baby came. Shall I go and tell her, my lady?"

Lying on her bed, her face etched with exhaustion, Valentina shook her head. "Not yet."

Carmela leaned over and wiped Valentina's brow with a wet cloth. "We're going to raise you a little, so we can pull away the birthing pad."

Valentina nodded.

One of the servant girls walked to the window and drew back the heavy, damask curtains. Sunlight streamed into the chamber. Carmela motioned to the servants and together they raised Valentina, then removed the blood-stained pad beneath her.

The midwife waited for the women to finish, then approached Valentina with the infant swaddled in a small blanket.

Valentina looked at the baby in the midwife's arms but made no effort to take her.

The midwife appeared puzzled by Valentina's disinterest. "Do you not wish to hold your daughter, my lady?" she asked, a faint note of disapproval in her voice.

Valentina had first begun to suspect she was with child sometime in November the previous fall. It had been a few weeks after her wedding, one and half months or so after Julian had come into her room and forced himself upon her. The realization that her violation might have resulted in the conception of a child had plunged her into despondency. She had always known she would have a child one day, but she never imagined she would have one conceived in such a hateful and violent manner.

From that day in November onward, throughout the entire month, she had woken up each morning, hoping she was wrong, that perhaps it was just that her monthly flow was late. But when her belly began to swell, she had been forced to confront the truth.

Now, realizing that her every move was being scrutinized by the servants and would later be the subject of gossip amongst them, Valentina took the bundle from the midwife and cradled the tiny creature in her arms. Despite the months of chafing at her condition, she could not deny that she was captivated by the small, pink face, the button nose, the delicate, nearly translucent eyelids and the damp wispy hair.

Valentina loosened the blanket, releasing a tiny arm that waved aimlessly in the air, as if swatting at some unseen insect. Despite herself, she reached out and gently grasped the miniscule hand that was the size of an acorn. *Why, she's lovely*, she thought in wonder. Something thawed inside her and to her utter surprise, she felt her eyes welling up with tears. *How foolish I've been. What does this innocent, little creature have to do with the manner of her conception?*

The baby grew restless in her arms.

"She wants to feed," the midwife murmured above her.

Valentina dutifully opened her robe and the tiny, squirming face found her breast. The sensation of the baby's suckling felt strange, though not unpleasant.

Valentina gazed thoughtfully at the infant in her arms. By her calculations it had only been a little over eight and half months since Julian had forced himself upon her. The baby had come early, but only by a few weeks. *Was that normal?* she wondered.

All throughout her term she had been convinced that she was carrying Julian's child. But now, the timing of the birth allowed for another possibility.

The baby could be Pelayo's.

She studied the tiny face pressed against her breast, trying to see if she could detect a resemblance to either Pelayo or Julian. But the little cherub looked nothing like either of them. After a moment she realized that there was simply no way of telling who the child's father really was. *Did it really matter anyway?*

A voice inside her whispered: *you know it does.*

After having learned of Pelayo's death that spring, Valentina had thought herself free of Julian, as he could no longer wield the threat of recapturing Pelayo to keep her in Gijón. For weeks she had worked in secret on an elaborate plan to slip away from the castle with Carmela and return home to her father and mother. Unfortunately, it had taken far longer than she had expected to find men who were both trustworthy and courageous enough to risk their lives in a venture to help the duke's wife steal away. But her persistence had eventually paid off and everything had fallen into place. A week or so before her planned departure, she had watched a group of house guards returning from a patrol. They had looked weather beaten and weary as they pulled up to the stable. It had dawned on her at that moment that she was too far along in her pregnancy to make the arduous, weeks-long journey home on horseback. She had heard stories of women in her condition miscarrying and bleeding to death and the thought that she might meet the same fate had given her pause.

Having to put aside her dream of escaping and returning home had been a heart-wrenching experience and she had wept over it for days.

Now with the birth of her child, Valentina realized that Julian had now another means of controlling her. He might let her go back to Girona alone, but she suspected that he would go after her with all the means and power at his disposal if she dared take their infant along with her. She might have entertained the notion of leaving the baby to Julian before the birth. But now, she knew with absolute certainty that she could never bring herself to abandon her newborn daughter.

Holding her infant against her breast, Valentina closed her eyes to rest. She lay in a drowsy daze until Julian's voice boomed across the chamber, jolting her awake.

"Boy or girl?" Julian called out as he strode toward her.

"It's a girl, Don Julian," the midwife answered.

Valentina was surprised to see Julian there. It had been over a month since he had set off with the Third Legion on some mysterious campaign. Two weeks after his departure, Carmela had told her she had heard a rumor that Julian was involved in a rebellion against the King. The idea had seemed so preposterous that she had dismissed the rumor out of hand. But a few days later, she had seen soldiers piling up sacks of grain in a corner of the courtyard under a lean-to. Then she had noticed the urns of oil and casks of wine stacked against one of the walls. Even to her inexperienced eye, it had been clear that the castle seemed to be girding for a siege, or at least for the possibility of one.

"I didn't know you were back," Valentina said tonelessly.

Julian came to a stop by the side of Valentina's bed. His face was gaunt, his eyes sunken, his tunic stained with sweat and dirt. "You didn't think I'd miss the birth of my first child, did you?" he asked, a rare spark in his eyes.

"How did you find out the baby was coming?" Valentina asked.

"Mother sent messengers to scour the countryside for me. Luckily we were encamped a short distance away."

Julian's face suddenly lit up. "Is that little bundle of rags my daughter?" he said, grinning from ear to ear. Reaching down, he took the infant from Valentina and cradled her in the crook of his arm. "She looks like a little angel, doesn't she?" he said in a voice filled with awe.

Valentina gazed wordlessly at Julian. The idea of him as a doting father was hard for her to reconcile.

What do you think we should call her?" Julian asked.

"How about Ulrika?" Doña Izaskun called out as she walked into the chamber. "It was my mother's name."

Julian looked at Valentina. "What do you think, shall we name our daughter Ulrika?"

"I don't like it," Valentina said. "It sounds harsh to my ears." She was damned if she was going to name her daughter after Izaskun's mother.

Izaskun threw Valentina a look of pure venom which bounced off her like a spent arrow on an iron shield. The rest of the women pretended to busy themselves at the other end of the chamber.

"Well then, what name would you like?" Julian asked Valentina.

Valentina thought for a moment. "Ermesinda." It was her grandmother's name.

"Yes," Julian said, nodding. "The name pleases me. We shall call her Ermesinda."

CHAPTER 22

GENERAL OLIVAR LAY on his bed, eyes half-closed, listening to the sound of gurgling water from the fountain in the courtyard below his window. He'd been awake for some time, but he had not felt the need to rise. Such indolence felt sinful and decadent, but the truth of it was that at this stage of his life he quite enjoyed it.

After some time he threw off his blanket, rose to his feet then padded barefoot to the window and threw open the shutters. Morning light flooded into his large, second-story room. A soft breeze redolent with the fragrance of jasmine drifted in from the garden below. Judging by the relative coolness in the air, he figured it was still early morning.

Outside his window, the flat roofs, the golden dome of the great Mosque, and the scores of needle-like minarets filled the skyline. Of all the strange and exotic places he had seen on this journeys, this cosmopolitan city, with its diverse culture and citizenry, struck him as the most wondrous of all. No doubt the city's charm and mild Mediterranean climate explained why Musa ibn Nusayr, the powerful governor of North Afriqiyah, had chosen Carthage as his summer residence.

Olivar was wondering how he was going to pass his day when he heard a discreet knock at the door.

"Who's there?" he called out in Arabic, a language he had learned during several postings as a young man in the garrison towns in North Afriqiyah, thus making him the ideal candidate for his current mission.

"It's me, Haman, Master," a sonorous voice answered.

Olivar unbolted the latch and pulled the door open. Before him stood the portly figure of the innkeeper, wearing a turban and a white robe that fell to his sandaled feet. This morning, his usually smiling, plump face was creased in an expression of regret.

"I'm sorry to have disturbed your rest, Master," Haman said.

"That's all right, I was awake," Olivar said. "What is it?"

"There are four soldiers waiting for you downstairs. It seems Governor Musa has finally granted you an audience."

At bloody last, Olivar thought. "Good. Tell them to wait. I'll be down as soon as I get dressed."

After closing the door, Olivar went to the chest at the foot of his bed and fished out the new tunic he had bought for the occasion. He placed it on the bed, then smoothed out the creases. There was no need to rush; he would probably have to wait all morning at the palace for his audience. That was to be expected, of course. He was just one more supplicant on a probably long list, while Governor Musa ibn Nusayr was one of the most powerful men in the Mohammedan world, second only to the Caliph in Damascus.

As Olivar dressed, he realized that his mission for Julian was coming to an end. Truth be told, he was surprised at how much he had enjoyed the venture. All the hardships he had endured, the stormy days at sea, the flea-infested beds, the strange and often disagreeable food, all that in retrospect seemed like spice sprinkled on the grey existence that had been his life in exile with Julian.

Olivar knew of course that he had no one to blame but himself for the way his life had turned out. Siding with Julian in the rebellion against the King had been one of the worst decisions he had ever made. In his own defense, he had felt at the time that he owed Fáfila's son his loyalty. But he now regarded that choice as a monumental lapse of judgment, and not just because scores of good men under his command had died. No, it was because as head of the Northern Legion, he had taken a vow to serve the King, a pledge that he had broken. Perhaps he might have felt differently if Roderic had turned out to be a tyrant or a fool. But the man had proven himself to be a wise ruler who had brought peace and prosperity to his people.

There was no use regretting the past now, Olivar told himself with an inward sigh. He had chosen his path and he would abide by the consequences.

After lacing up his sandals, Olivar put on his tunic then combed his thinning, gray hair. Satisfied that he was as presentable as he was ever going to be, he rummaged through his travel chest again and pulled out a foot-long, cylindrical case wrapped in oilcloth.

Holding the case, he ran a finger along its single seam, stitched together to keep its contents from prying eyes. Its only other distinguishing feature was a red wax seal with the family coat of arms of Lord Julian, once the Duke of Asturias, now banished to govern the fly-specked garrison town of Ceuta on the northwestern coast of Afriqiyah.

As wretched as Ceuta was, Olivar figured that Julian had gotten off easy for his part in the rebellion that had engulfed the kingdom. The rumour was that Valentina's father, Baron

Ernesto of Cantabria, had petitioned King Roderic to show clemency to his daughter's husband. If not for the baron's intercession, Olivar imagined things might have turned out far differently for Julian. And for himself, as well.

Olivar studied the cylindrical case, the delivery of which had entailed so much trouble and expense. By its size and weight, he suspected it contained a rolled-up parchment. During the previous two months, not a day had gone by without him wondering why Julian would want to send anything to the Mohammedan governor. Whatever the reason, he knew that Julian had gone to great lengths to ensure that the entire matter was handled with the utmost secrecy.

It was strange to think that in a few hours time, the mysterious cylinder would be out of his hands and no longer of concern to him. Once he concluded his assignment, he would head back to Ceuta to receive the payment that Julian had promised him upon the completion of the undertaking. Perhaps he would use part of his earnings to return here to Carthage and buy one of the hilltop villas overlooking the bay. He would enjoy that, he thought, spending the rest of his days sitting on a terrace, growing fat and gazing out at the deep blue waters of the Mediterranean.

Olivar locked the chest then pocketed the key. After making sure he'd left nothing of value lying about, he left the room and took the stairs down to the main floor.

Four turbaned soldiers in thigh-length leather vests and loose-fitting pantaloons, were waiting for him in the courtyard. One of the four, a stocky, bearded man with an air of authority about him, addressed Olivar, "Are you the one seeking an audience with Governor Musa?"

Olivar nodded. "Yes."

"You will come with us, please."

With the cylindrical case tucked under his arm, Olivar followed the Saracen soldiers out through the wooden door that led to the street. As usual, the noise and bustle outside made him feel as if he had just stepped into a different world.

The soldiers led Olivar down a series of twisting, narrow alleyways. Their path took them through one of the canopy-covered markets the locals called *souks*. The scents of spices, flowers and exotic fruits filled the air. Swarms of flies droned around tables laden with animal carcasses. Women wearing black veils, with only their eyes showing, bartered noisily with the apron-clad vendors. The soldiers escorting Olivar cut through the crowd as smoothly as a ship parting water.

They finally reached a sprawling palace of sandstone and white marble. Judging by the building's opulence, Olivar figured they had arrived at their destination: Governor Musa ibn Nusayr's summer residence. The guards at the gate questioned the officer in charge of Olivar's escort, then let them through. Once inside, the soldiers led Olivar down a garden path filled with fruit trees, shallow, rectangular pools of water and gushing fountains. Reaching the palace building, they entered through a door flanked by another pair of guards.

Olivar found himself in a marble-floored hall filled with lattice windows that allowed just enough air and light in to make it a welcome refuge from the glare and heat outside. A turbaned official wearing a silver medallion of office walked over, his appraising eyes scanning Olivar.

"What is your business here?" the man asked.

"I have an audience with Governor Musa. My name is General Olivar."

The official consulted a list on a parchment, then dismissed Olivar's escort. "This way," he said to Olivar.

The official led him to a small antechamber, then told

him to wait. Some time later, a man in a flowing, black robe appeared at the door. He had deep set eyes, a swarthy complexion and features that Olivar recognized as typical of the people from the northwestern corner of the Maghreb.

Olivar was not generally given to making quick judgments of character, but something about the tall Berber made him take an instant dislike to the man.

"What do you want with Governor Musa?" the black-robed man asked.

Olivar held up the cylindrical case. "I have been entrusted to deliver this to him."

"Give it to me; I will ensure the governor receives it."

Olivar held on to the case. "My instructions are to hand this over to him personally."

The Berber eyed Olivar for a moment then nodded. "Very well, come with me."

Olivar followed the man through a series of hallways, until they reached what seemed to be the inner sanctum of the palace. Opening a door, the Berber ushered Olivar into an airy chamber with arched windows facing a garden. Intricately patterned carpets in hues of reds and blues covered the floor. Brass urns and colorful ceramic vases lay in niches in the walls. At the far end of the chamber, a turbaned, middle-aged man sat cross-legged on the floor before a low-slung table, scribbling on a parchment.

Musa ibn Nusayr, governor of Afriqiyah, looked nothing like Olivar had imagined him. Plump and stoop-shouldered, the man had a roundish face and a short, black beard streaked with gray. Olivar could have passed him on the street a dozen times and not given him a second look. It was difficult to tell the governor's age and Olivar settled on somewhere between fifty-five and sixty years old.

Waiting to be acknowledged, Olivar glanced about him. There were two Saracen soldiers standing guard by the door through which he had entered. The only other person in the audience chamber was the tall Berber who had taken position behind Governor Musa and was now watching his every move. *Must be the governor's personal bodyguard*, Olivar thought to himself.

Governor Musa finally put down his quill and sat up straight. The tall Berber leaned down and said something in his ear. Nodding, the governor turned his attention to Olivar. "You may sit," he said, pointing toward the cushions on the floor on the other side of the table.

"Thank you, Your Excellency," Olivar said, easing himself down.

"I am told you have something for me," Governor Musa said.

"I do indeed," Olivar said, handing the governor the cylindrical packet. "It is from my patron, Lord Julian, the governor of Ceuta."

Governor Musa's brow furrowed. "I do not think I have heard of the place."

"It lies on the north coast of Mauritania, across from the Pillars of Hercules."

"Ah yes, the Christian garrison." Without further comment Governor Musa picked up a dagger from the table, slit open the seams of the cylinder, then fished out a rolled parchment.

"I can translate the missive for you if you wish, Your Excellency," Olivar said.

"No need. It's in Arabic."

"Oh," Olivar said, surprised. As the governor began to read, he glanced about, feeling the Berber's eyes on him.

Finally, Governor Musa put down the parchment and looked across at Olivar. "How long have you known Lord Julian?"

"Since his birth."

"Mmm. I find that surprising. Tell me about him."

Olivar found the comment odd, but he dismissed it from his thoughts and gave the governor an overview of Julian's life, leaving out his role in the uprising against King Roderic and his consequent exile to Ceuta.

As it turned out, Governor Musa had heard about the war over the Iberian succession and he asked Olivar whether Julian had sided with any of the factions. Thinking it unwise to lie outright, Olivar revealed Julian's role as one of the leaders of the rebellion.

"Your lord is not lacking in ambition," Musa said with an ironic lift of an eyebrow.

"No more so than any other man," Olivar said, knowing he was stretching the truth.

Musa studied Olivar for a moment. "He wants my help to overthrow your King Roderic and place the former king's son on the throne."

Alarmed, Olivar stiffened. "Your pardon, Your Excellency, I do not think that my lord meant for me to know that."

"It doesn't matter; you would have guessed the truth anyway, in light of the questions I am about to ask you."

Olivar didn't feel the least bit mollified by the governor's answer.

"Has your King Roderic consolidated his hold over the kingdom since the rebellion?" Governor Musa asked.

"I believe he has, yes. The King has proven himself quite adept at knowing when to use the carrot and when to use the stick."

Governor Musa nodded. "Your lord says that he is willing to provide us with ships to transport our troops across the strait of Al-Zuqaq. I assume he would need to commandeer dozens of merchant ships. How many are normally at anchor at Ceuta's harbor?"

Olivar belatedly realized that he was being asked for information that could be used to defeat Iberian forces. *Damned if I'm going to be a party to Julian's schemes again*, he thought to himself, furious at the way he was being used. The conversation with the governor suddenly took on a different light. "It depends on the season," he said carefully, buying himself time to think things through.

"You can just give me an approximate number of ships."

Olivar knew that any answer he gave the governor would be taken as fact. The problem was that he didn't know whether it was better to exaggerate the number or to minimize it. In the end he decided that the wisest strategy was to sow as much uncertainty as possible in the mind of the Saracen governor. "Sometimes as few as five." he said at last. "Other times more."

"How many more?"

"Dozens."

Governor Musa held Olivar's gaze. "Your lord claims that he can persuade some of the barons to turn against the king. Do you agree with his assumption?"

"It's difficult to say. The barons are an independent lot. Those that sided with him in the past suffered grave consequences when they lost. But I think some of them would probably be willing to cast the dice again, if they judge the benefits to be worth the gamble."

"How many soldiers does your King Roderic have under his command?"

"I have been in exile in Ceuta for many years, Your Excellency. I do not know whether the king has added or reduced the number of legions."

"Let us stay with something you know then. What is the size of your garrison in Ceuta?"

"Troops are continuously coming and going, the number varies so much from month to month that any number I give you would be misleading."

"And of course you wouldn't want that to happen, would you?" the Saracen governor said with a tight smile, obviously losing patience with Olivar's evasiveness.

Leaning back, the governor muttered something inaudible to the tall Berber, who immediately left his side. Governor Musa turned his gaze back to Olivar. "It seems I'm not going to get anything else out of you."

"I assure you, Your Excellency, I—"

"It doesn't matter," Governor Musa said, waving a languid hand. "I can find out what I want to know through other means."

Olivar breathed a quiet sigh of relief, expecting the audience would soon be over. As he stared at the governor, something flickered across his eyes. Before he could make sense of what he'd seen, he felt a cord tighten around his windpipe, cutting off his breath.

Instinctively he clawed at his neck, trying to insert his fingertips under the cord biting into his flesh. His nails raked bloody gouges down his skin as he twisted and squirmed, frantically trying to free himself. His lungs began to burn, and his chest fluttered in spasms. His terror mushrooming, he kicked his legs wildly about him, striking the table and sending it crashing away. His agony stretched on until a red haze began to fall like a curtain over his vision. His mind registered a final impression of the Saracen governor looking at him with cold detachment.

Governor Musa ibn Nusayr turned away and gazed out the window at the garden beyond. There was peace and beauty there and the unpleasantness he had just witnessed began to fade. Unlike many men who wielded unquestioning power, he took no pleasure in causing pain or meting out death. But he understood its necessity when the situation demanded it.

As the guards dragged away the body of the infidel, Musa picked up the parchment the man had brought him and reread the last few lines of the missive.

"I have no doubt you will treat this matter with the discretion it merits. The success of our endeavor relies on maintaining absolute secrecy. If my proposal is of any interest to you, I would advise you to eliminate the carrier of this letter. I shall await your answer through a courier that you regard as equally expendable."

Musa stared pensively at the words on the parchment. The Christian's proposal was like a double-edged sword. On the one hand it represented a golden opportunity to push northward into the soft underbelly of the Christian continent. Yet the undertaking was also fraught with danger and could end in failure. More importantly, it could bring about his personal ruin.

Musa mulled over the proposal for days, wondering whether he should take the bait that the lord of Ceuta had dangled before him. As time passed, he found himself leaning toward accepting the offer. When in his lifetime would another Christian lord be foolish enough to invite his enemy into his country and then demonstrate his sincerity by sacrificing the life of a trusted retainer? And was the challenge really any different from the others he had faced in his rise to power? It all boiled down to controlling the events so that he took the credit for the success, or if the effort proved disastrous, to shift the blame onto an underling.

With his decision made, Musa began formulating a plan

involving the troublesome Berber tribes that were growing restless in the western territories of the caliphate.

Over the next few weeks he worked diligently on the details, fleshing out the plan and making provisions for every eventuality. When he was satisfied that he had accounted for every component, he summoned his most trusted advisor, Khurram.

"You sent for me, Your Excellency?" the gray bearded counselor asked as he walked into the audience chamber.

"Do you remember the Christian envoy from Ceuta whom I spoke to you about last week?" Musa asked.

Khurram stared blankly at him. "Can you remind me, Your Excellency?"

Musa handed him Lord Julian's missive. "Here, read this."

Khurram read the document then handed it back, his brow knitted with worry. "It's dangerous to trust a man who is willing to betray his king, Your Excellency. How do we know he won't do the same to us?"

"I fully expect he will try," Musa said. "But he will find it difficult to get rid of the wolf once it has been invited into the fold."

"You're going to agree to the request then, Your Excellency?"

"I think so, yes."

"Where will you find the soldiers for the undertaking? Our armies are already stretched beyond what is prudent. Recalling even a single company could leave us vulnerable to a rebellion on the borderlands."

"We're not going to use our soldiers, Khurram. We'll send out an army of Berbers. As you know, they've been stirring up trouble on our western flank for months. Providing a target for their destructive energies will deflect the threat they posed to the caliphate."

"So, if the Berbers fail, we eliminate them as a threat; if

they succeed, you ask the Caliph for reinforcements and take control of the occupation."

"Exactly," Musa said with a smile. "In either case, we win."

"Very clever," Khurram said. "How can I be of service, Your Excellency?"

"I want you to go to al-Maghreb as my emissary and find a tribal chief called Tariq ibn Ziyad. Your task is to persuade him to gather his warriors and launch an invasion on the Iberians."

"The honor you bestow upon me is great, Your Excellency, perhaps too great. There are others who would be far more effective in carrying out your wishes. For instance—"

Musa waved a hand, silencing Khurram in mid-sentence. "There's no one I trust more to be my mouth and ears than you."

"I appreciate your faith in me, Your Excellency, but how do you expect me to convince a Berber chieftain whom I've never met to raise an army and launch a war on our behalf?"

"You offer him the one thing that no man can resist. Gold, the cartloads he'll find in Hispania, enough to make every warrior under his command wealthy beyond his wildest dreams."

"That would certainly be an effective inducement, Your Excellency...if it were true. But Hispania is not a rich land, as we have learned from our sorties. There is no gold in the quantities you suggest."

Musa smiled. "Have you not heard of King Salomon's gold, Khurram? Everyone knows his treasure lies buried beneath the king's palace in Toledo."

"That's nothing but a child's tale, Your Excellency, as you well know."

"Ah, but that's exactly what the Berbers are, unworldly children. They live in huts made of ox hides and mud in one of the most wretched corners of the world. If you tell them there is gold in Toledo, they will believe you."

Khurram looked like he had grave reservations about the idea, but he nodded. "Very well, Your Excellency. When would you like me to set out?"

"Tomorrow."

When Khurram took his leave, Musa began thinking about whom to send to Ceuta as his emissary. Finding someone to explain his plan to Lord Julian was not all that difficult a task. However, sending someone to his death was more problematic, if only because he did not feel he could afford to spare anyone from his inner circle, the only people he trusted to carry out the task.

As Musa strolled around the garden, he pondered over another problem for which he had not yet found a solution. If the invasion succeeded and Hispania fell to them, he would have to arrange for the elimination of the Berber chieftain in order to take control of the occupying force. Despite that particular detail, and one or two others of lesser importance, he was satisfied that the plan was as sound as it needed to be at this stage. Though experience had taught him that unforeseen events could unravel even the most carefully crafted plan, he had done his best and the rest was now up to Allah.

CHAPTER 23

A LIZARD SCUTTLED down the side of the wall, then paused, moving its head from side to side, assessing its surroundings for danger or perhaps searching for its next meal. Its quick, darting movements and sightless eyes seemed perfectly adapted to the darkness of its underground world. Occasionally it had to share its home with a human tenant, such as the one curled up on the stone floor, a ragged, miserable creature chained to an iron ring bolted to the wall. Like all the other cells facing out onto the dank, subterranean corridor, this one was empty of furnishings save for a wooden bucket. The only source of light and air came from a viewing slot in the door situated at head level. The opening was small and very little of the torchlight from the outside corridor filtered in, leaving the cell in perpetual twilight. As the passage of time was all but unknowable, it remained unmarked by its sole, human inhabitant.

Curled up on the floor, the man stirred, then rubbed his bearded face with his hand, brushing away at whatever had disturbed his sleep. His movement dragged the chains affixed to the iron manacles across his chest.

He lay with his eyes open, mustering his strength for a moment. With a groan, he sat up and leaned back against the stone wall of his cell. Having learned to ration his water, he licked his dry lips and gauged his thirst. It was time to drink. Stretching out his hand, he felt for his metal cup. There was no fumbling; he knew exactly its position on the floor. Carefully he lifted the rim of the vessel to his lips and took two measured sips. The cup was nearly empty. Another day had passed.

The shuffling sound of footsteps drifted in from the corridor outside his cell. Idly he wondered which of his three jailers was going to bring him his rations today. He had nicknames for all of them. 'Cyclops' was a horse-faced man with a patch over one eye and a scar running from his hairline down to his jaw. He liked to make jokes, usually about the food he brought, and would snicker with amusement at his own wit. 'Hobbler' was a stooped-shoulderered man in his mid-forties who walked with a pronounced limp. He had the vacant look of someone not quite right in the head and he hardly ever said a word.

His third jailor, and by far the worst of the lot, was 'Ferret', a small, wiry man with sharp features and the mean disposition of his namesake. Unlike the other guards who treated him with bored indifference, Ferret seemed to take delight in tormenting him. The man would sometimes place his food and water just beyond the reach of his chains. Other times he would leave a piece of dung floating in the water cup or pretend to trip and spill the slop that passed as his rations on the floor. Whatever the antic, if Ferret came through the door of his cell, there was a better than even chance that he would not eat or drink that day.

The light from an approaching torch began filtering in through the viewing slot in his door. Gradually his cell filled with a rosy luminance. Dim as it was, to him it felt as glorious as a sunrise. The guard passed by his cell and all too soon the light waned. Darkness like a shroud enveloped him again.

A fit of coughing suddenly seized him. Dragging his chains along, he wrapped his arms around his knees until it subsided. Afterward he sat in a mindless stupor, staring sightlessly into the darkness. After a time, he rose to his feet, the exertion making his heart pound. With the shuffling gait of a man many years older, he began walking back and forth along his cell floor, at least as far as his chains would allow him. Forcing himself to stand or to walk regularly required an effort of will, but he had learned that it was the only way to avoid getting painful sores on his body.

As he contemplated the endless hours stretching before him, entombed in darkness, a familiar sense of despair began encroaching upon him. It was as if there was some malignant creature lurking inside him, waiting for him to ease his guard, so it could drag him down into some abyss from which he knew there would be no coming back. But he had not succumbed, at least not yet, and over time he had grown adept at fighting back against the creature. He had used the only possession they had not been able to take away from him: his memory and his imagination.

Now, feeling himself tested once again, he focused his thoughts and began to conjure up an image in his mind's eye.

Thanks to the military lore that he had been taught as a youth, he could remember a dozen major battles that had shaped human history. For every encounter, he could recite by rote the location as well as the size and deployment of each side's cavalry and infantry units. He knew the tactical brilliance and the follies of the respective commanders, as well the accidents of fate that had determined which side became the victor, and which the vanquished. He had played and replayed each battle countless times in his mind. Sometimes he took the part of Scipio, other times that of Julius Caesar, or of Hannibal, or of the hapless Gaius Terentius Varro.

Today he decided he would be the Roman consul, Lucio Aemilius Paullus. But this time, Hannibal would not crush his legions and slaughter all 70,000 of his men.

The semi-arid valley of Cannae slowly began forming in his mind, or at least the version that his imagination conjured up for him. Slowly, painstakingly, he filled in the details, fashioning a terrain covered with thick, yellowed grasses, swaying gently in the warm breeze. Stunted olive trees withered on the parched hilltops. His legions, the largest expeditionary force that Rome had ever fielded, stretched out behind him, stirring up clouds of choking dust. In his mind he could hear the rhythmic pounding of their feet as they marched. The supply wagons rumbled behind him. Sitting on his horse, he scanned the horizon for the quarry he and his legions had been chasing for days. In the distance, emerging from the mouth of the narrow valley, a column of Hannibal's soldiers began to flow forth.

A murmur of voices intruded into his consciousness, dissipating his carefully constructed imagery.

The interior of his cell gradually brightened, as light flowed in through the viewing hole. He listened to the approaching footsteps until they stopped outside his cell. *Was it already time for his food and water?*

There came the sound of a key being inserted into a lock, then his cell door swung open with the usual metallic groan of rusting hinges.

Holding up a torch, Hobbler, the jailor with the limp, entered his cell. Behind him, a man in a hooded cloak, holding a rag over his mouth and nose, followed him inside.

"Raise the torch a little higher," the hooded stranger said in a muffled voice.

Hobbler lifted the torch over his head and the hooded man studied him for a moment.

"I'm afraid it's not him," the hooded stranger said, a note of disappointment in his voice.

"Too bad," Hobbler said. "Sorry you wasted your time."

The hooded figure shrugged. "There was no other way to find out for sure."

"True enough," Hobbler said, heading for the door.

As the hooded man turned to follow Hobbler, the prisoner called out in a voice hoarse with disuse, "Going to leave without saying goodbye, Theo?"

Theodosius froze, then turned back slowly. "Mother of God!" he breathed, his eyes wide with shock. "Is that you, Pelayo?"

"Am I that hard to recognize?" Pelayo said, rising slowly to his feet.

Theodosius hurried forward and clasped Pelayo in a fierce embrace. "I'm so glad to see you, my boy," he said, his voice thick with emotion.

"How long have I been here?" Pelayo asked in a raspy whisper.

Theodosius released Pelayo. "It's coming on three years."

Pelayo stared at Theodosius, his expression all but hidden under the tangled rat's nest of his beard. "Seems like a lot longer."

Hobbler cut in, his voice pitched low, "We should get going. We only have until sunrise to put this place behind us."

"You're right, Ordonez; time is not our friend," Theodosius said. "Let's get those chains off of him."

It was then Pelayo understood that Theodosius had come, not for a visit, but to help him escape. A storm of emotions, raw and powerful, battered at him. The thought of regaining his freedom seemed almost inconceivably wondrous.

Ordonez, the man he had called Hobbler for years, handed Theodosius the torch, then took out a ring of keys and unlocked his manacles.

When the chains fell away, Pelayo rubbed his wrists, feeling the toughened skin that had developed as a result of the constant chaffing. His hands felt strangely light, as if they wanted to float upward. A sense of unreality gripped him and for a moment he wondered if this wasn't just all a cruel dream.

Ordonez went to the door, stuck his head out to make sure the area was clear, then stepped out into the corridor. Theodosius and Pelayo followed, close on his heels. When everyone was out, Ordonez locked the cell door shut again. He took the torch back from Theodosius, then led the way toward a brightly lit area down the corridor.

Ordonez turned to Pelayo, put his finger to his lips, then proceeded cautiously into what looked to be the guards' room.

Two men lay slumped over a table, their heads cradled in their arms. Dishes of half-eaten food, a wine jug and two upended cups lay strewn about on the table.

Theodosius leaned over and whispered to Pelayo, "I gave Ordonez a sleeping potion to put into their wine. Looks like it's working."

Unconsciously holding his breath, Pelayo followed Theodosius and Ordonez across the guards' room.

They were halfway through when the door at the far end swung open. A stocky, broad-shouldered man wearing an officer's cloak halted in mid-stride and looked at them with a look of surprise.

"Ordonez, what the devil are these men doing here?" the officer called out.

Ordonez stared mutely at the officer, seeming unable to come up with a credible answer to his question.

The officer's eyes narrowed, obviously having figured out there could only be one possible explanation for catching Ordonez in the company of two civilians, one clearly a prisoner. Throwing back his cloak, his hand flew to the hilt of his sword. "Wake up, you drunken fools!" he bellowed to the two guards slumped over the table. "There's a prisoner escaping!"

No doubt aware that he would be facing the gallows if captured, Ordonez threw his torch at the officer's face, buying himself time to draw out his sword. Theodosius unsheathed his blade and went to Ordonez' aid.

Weaponless, Pelayo edged back against the wall, watching the ensuing confrontation as the three men began going at each other. He wasn't surprised to see that the officer of the watch was more than a match for his two opponents.

The sound of clashing steel rang out with a din that reverberated in the confines of the guards room. Pelayo cast a worried glance at the two guards slumped over the table. To his dismay, one of them slowly raised his head.

It was Ferret.

Looking blearily around the room, Ferret rose unsteadily to his feet. He seemed to be struggling to make sense of the commotion around him. Then his gaze fell on Theodosius and Ordonez who were trading blows with the officer of the watch.

The sight seemed to clear the fog in Ferret's head and with a snarl, he drew out a knife from his belt and launched himself forward.

Standing too far to intercede, Pelayo guessed at once Ferret's intention. "Theo!" he cried out. "Watch out, behind you!"

Before Theodosius could act on the warning, Ferret closed in and with a thrust of his arm, knifed Theodosius in the back.

Across the room, the sight seared into Pelayo's eyes and his blood turned to ice.

Ordonez must have seen that Theodosius was out of action, and he threw himself at the officer with renewed vigor.

Pelayo looked around desperately for a weapon. There was nothing in the chamber save for a stool lying by the side of the guard's table.

Ferret was trying to sneak up behind Ordonez when Pelayo yelled at the guard to get his attention.

Catching sight of Pelayo heading his way, Ferret gripped his knife in his right hand and crouched in a typical fighter's stance.

The moment Pelayo stepped in range, Ferret sprung into action. But his movements were just a bit sluggish and unco-ordinated. The look of horror on his face revealed his dawning realization that he was still under the effect of whatever Ordonez had put in his wine, and that he was not going to be able to evade the stool descending upon him. At the last instant, Ferret tucked in his chin and took the blow on his head.

There came a dull thunk followed by the sound of crunch-ing bone. Ferret's eyes rolled back in his head and he collapsed senseless to the floor.

Pelayo stood over Ferret's prone body, his chest heaving form exertion. *Rot in hell, you black-hearted bastard!* he thought to himself as he leaned down and pried the knife out of Ferret's lifeless hand. As he straightened, he turned his gaze toward Ordonez and the officer who were slashing at each other with deadly intent. Incredibly, Ordonez seemed to be holding his own.

With Ferret's knife in one hand and the stool in the other, Pelayo set off to help Ordonez.

The embattled officer caught sight of Pelayo coming toward

him. Seemingly not liking the odds, he spun on his heels and crying out for help, bolted for the door.

Using both hands, Pelayo threw the stool at the fleeing officer, striking him in the back. The force of the blow knocked him off his course. With surprising alacrity for a man with a limp, Ordonez closed in on the officer and ran him through in the back.

The stricken officer let out a tortured cry then collapsed to the ground. After twitching for a moment, he lay still.

Silence settled over the guards room.

Ordonez and Pelayo stared at each other, their faces etched with tension. After a time they both let out their breath.

"We should get the hell out of here," Ordonez whispered.

"I agree," Theodosius said quietly from behind them.

Pelayo turned and saw that Theodosius was holding on to the edge of the table for support. "We're not going anywhere until we've taken care of your wound, Theo."

"There's no time for that," Theodosius protested.

Ordonez interjected, "Pelayo's right, there shouldn't be anyone else coming down here for a while. Our replacements are only due in the morning."

After a moment's hesitation, Theodosius nodded. Without further word, he turned and pulled away his cloak, revealing his back.

Ferret's knife had punched through the links of Theodosius' chainmail, splitting open a thumb's length section of the iron rings just above his waist.

"We'll have to get the chainmail off of him," Pelayo told Ordonez.

Not bothering to argue this time, Theodosius sat down on the edge of the table, allowing Pelayo and Ordonez to remove his chainmail shirt and his tunic in order to bare his back.

There, on his lower back, a small, puncture wound was oozing blood, staining the waistband of his undergarment a dark red.

Pelayo's heart sank in dismay at the sight of the puncture. He had hoped that Theodosius' chainmail might have stopped the tip of Ferret's knife from plunging in too deeply, but the wound looked deep and serious, obviously necessitating stitching. Unfortunately, that required a needle and either catgut or silk, all three unavailable at this point in time. That only left them with one alternative. "Is there anything down here we can use to bind the wound?" he asked Ordonez.

"There's some old blankets we can cut up."

"All we need is one, I think," Pelayo said.

Ordonez went off and returned a with a smelly, brown blanket, which they proceeded to cut into long strips. Afterwards, they used the strips to bandage Theodosius' wound.

"This will have to do for now, Theo," Pelayo said when he finished.

Theodosius nodded stoically, then slid off the table and rose to his feet. After helping him put on his tunic and chainmail, Ordonez put his arm around Theodosius and helped him to the door, then up the stone staircase.

Pelayo was the last to step out into the courtyard. The sky was cloudless and full of stars, with a three-quarter moon that cast a pale light over the grounds of the castle. Save for two soldiers standing guard by the torch-lit gates some hundred paces away, the entire area was deserted. *Must be the middle of the night*, Pelayo thought.

Half carrying Theodosius, Ordonez edged forward, staying close to the walls, keeping to the shadows as he made his way around the courtyard toward the stable. Once they reached the building, they slipped inside through one of the large doors that had been left ajar. The pungent smell of hay and horses closed in around them. Two candles on a shelf provided a weak, orange glow. A horse snorted from somewhere deep inside.

Leaving Theodosius behind, Ordonez grabbed one of the candles and went off toward the back of the stable. He reappeared a moment later with two cloaks and a gilded, bronze helmet. "Here, this one's for you," he whispered to Pelayo, handing him one of the cloaks.

Pelayo took the garment, noticing it had a military look about it, then draped it over his shoulders.

Ordonez stood back and studied Pelayo with a critical eye. "Pull the hood down over your face as much as you can."

Pelayo tugged the hood over his forehead until he could barely see out.

Ordonez turned toward Theodosius, who was leaning against a post, obviously in some discomfort. "I have to ask you, can you still carry out your part in this?"

"Yes," Theodosius answered.

Ordonez stood unmoving, appearing skeptical of Theodosius' assurance.

"I said I can do it," Theodosius said, this time with an edge in his voice. "Let's get on with it."

Ordonez nodded, then turned toward Pelayo and handed him the second cloak, as well as the ornate helmet. "Can you help Theodosius put these on while I'll go fetch the horses?"

"Of course."

Ordonez went off, then came back a moment later with three saddled horses in tow. He separated a chestnut gelding, then with Pelayo's help, got Theodosius mounted.

When it appeared that Theodosius was managing to sit on his horse unaided, Ordonez turned and addressed Pelayo, "All right, let's get out of here."

"How are you planning to get us past the guards at the gates?" Pelayo asked.

"Theodosius and I have it all worked out. Just stay quiet and don't draw attention to yourself."

The answer did nothing to quell Pelayo's misgivings, but it seemed he had little choice but to follow Ordonez's instruction.

When they were all mounted, Ordonez led them out in single file through the stable doors. Once outside, they steered their horses toward the torchlit area around the gates.

Expecting that they wouldn't be getting out without a fight, Pelayo slid his hand under his cloak and gripped the hilt of the sword that he had taken from the dead officer. The feel of the weapon made him feel less helpless.

As they approached the gates, the two guards peered across at them. "Is that you, Ordonez?" one of them called out.

Ordonez reined in his horse in the pool of torchlight, pretending to stifle a yawn. "I'm afraid so," he answered.

"Where are you all going at this late hour?"

"I have orders to escort these gentlemen to the coast," Ordonez said.

"In the middle of the night?" the second guard asked, eyeing the two cloaked horsemen behind Ordonez.

Theodosius nudged his horse forward into the torchlight, revealing his gleaming helmet and crimson, military cloak. "We need to get to the port by sunrise, soldier. We have to catch a ship before the tide goes out."

The guard immediately straightened. "Beg your pardon, sire. I didn't know we had a general visiting us."

"Lord Siberto is hoping to keep our meeting private," Theodosius said.

"Yes, of course, sire." the guard said, seemingly understanding why the general was traveling without a larger escort.

The second soldier spoke out, "The Officer of the Watch didn't mention there'd be anyone leaving so early in the morning."

"Don Siberto and I talked late into the night. I imagine it must have slipped his mind to advise your superior."

The two guards looked at each other.

"I'm afraid our time is short," Theodosius said with obvious impatience. "Either open the gates or go rouse Don Siberto and get his approval." He gave both guards a tight smile. "I'm certain he'll be properly thankful for your conscientiousness."

At Theodosius side, Ordonez snickered.

The first guard turned toward his companion and said quietly, "I don't think this is worth waking Don Siberto up in the middle of the night."

The second guard nodded. "I agree."

Pelayo pulled away his hand from the hilt of his sword as the guards withdrew the bar and opened the gates.

"Have a safe journey, general," the first guard called out as he waved them onward.

Pelayo kept his head down and his chin tucked in as he rode past the guards, trying to keep his bearded face in the shadow of his hood.

Once through the gates, Ordonez broke into a canter, leading Pelayo and Theodosius into the night.

A feeling of exultation swept over Pelayo as the castle fell away behind him. Though he wanted to shout out with the sheer joy of it, he reminded himself that he had tasted freedom once before, only to have it taken away from him within hours. If anything, his current situation was even more precarious. Once his escape was discovered, Siberto would send out every man he could muster to scour the countryside for him.

The road led Pelayo and his two riding companions to the

nearby town of Ribadesella. The streets were deserted, and they rode through at a gallop, the sound of their horses shattering the quiet of the night. Soon the warren of alleyways turned into a moonlit landscape of empty fields. They rode on without stopping, the leagues falling away beneath their horses' hooves.

Pelayo kept a close watch on Theodosius, who despite the seriousness of his wound, seemed to be holding up well. He was beginning to think that they just might make it to wherever they were going when he saw Theodosius slump over his horse. Fearing his old tutor was going to fall off, Pelayo sped forward until he was riding alongside Theodosius. He then reached across, grabbed the reins of Theodosius' gelding and brought both their horses to a stop.

"Are you all right, Theo?" Pelayo asked.

Theodosius turned his head toward Pelayo. "I'm not sure how much longer I can go on," he said, his voice strained with fatigue.

"What's wrong?" Ordonez called out, riding back toward Pelayo. "Why are you stopping?"

"It's Theodosius," Pelayo said. "This ride is hard on him. We need to stop."

"We're dead men if we do," Ordonez said. "The sun will be up soon. We'll stick out like a thumb in these plains."

"why don't we find somewhere to hole up for a while then?" Pelayo said.

"There's nothing but flat scrubland for a dozen leagues in any direction,"

"Ordonez is right," Theodosius said, his voice weak. "We have to keep moving. I'll try to hold on."

Pelayo said, "How about we ride double? I'll hold on to you and Ordonez can lead my horse."

Ordonez nodded his approval. "That should work," he told

Pelayo. "You're all skin and bones. Theodosius' horse should be able to carry you both."

Pelayo slid to the ground, then mounted behind Theodosius on his horse. Putting one arm around his old tutor, he reached around with his other hand for the reins.

Ordonez took the point position again and they all set off at a canter.

After riding in silence for a time, it occurred to Pelayo to ask Ordonez where they were going.

"Somewhere that will allow us to stay out of sight for while," Ordonez answered over his shoulder.

"How much further is it?"

"It's still some distance, I'm afraid."

The three men rode on for what seemed like hours, Pelayo holding on to Theodosius, watching the sky gradually brighten. They were travelling through an area of parched foothills when Ordonez finally veered off the road and headed toward a nearby creek.

The horses picked their way upstream, the rushing waters scrubbing away their tracks. Gradually, the landscape began to change, becoming even more arid and craggy. By midmorning, they found themselves splashing through a narrow gorge flanked by ochre colored cliffs.

Pelayo began noticing that the area was pockmarked with caves. He was not surprised when a moment later Ordonez led them up the pebbled bank away from the creek.

The cave Ordonez chose for them lay at ground level. It was large, some twenty paces deep, with the bones of small animals scattered around the entrance. After following Ordonez into the cave, Pelayo dismounted, then helped Theodosius off his horse.

Ordonez spread a blanket over the ground, then with Pelayo's help, eased Theodosius down on it.

"I'm going to check your bandage, Theo" Pelayo said. "It looks like you're still bleeding."

"Don't bother," Theodosius said. "There's nothing more you can do for me without a needle and thread."

Pelayo nodded grimly, knowing Theodosius was right. "Very well, I'll go unsaddle the horses, then I'll come back to you."

"Stay with me for a moment," Theodosius said. "You need to know what's happened since you've been away."

"We can talk later, you should try to rest now," Pelayo said.

"I may not have the strength to talk later. I have an open knife wound. I think we both know what that means."

Pelayo let out his breath slowly. "All right, Theo."

Aware of the gravity of the situation, Ordonez put a hand on Pelayo's shoulder and said quietly, "I'll take care of the horses. You stay here with Theodosius."

Pelayo's heart was heavy with sadness as he sat cross-legged on the ground. "Very well Theo, what is it you want to tell me."

Theodosius gathered his strength for a moment, then began recounting the events that had occurred over the previous three years in the kingdom. Most of his story dealt with a single event: the attempt by Julian, his great-uncles, as well as a cadre of northern barons to depose King Roderic and replace him with King Witiza's young heir, Olmund.

The uprising against the King had been a short and brutal affair, exacting a heavy toll in lives and treasury on both sides of the conflict. After six months of skirmishes, Julian and his co-conspirators had finally faced off with the King and his legions on a field outside the city of Saragossa. Though by all accounts the battle had been a hard-fought contest, the King and his legions had, in the end, prevailed.

Julian and the northern barons had suffered crippling losses, however, when darkness fell, they had managed to slip away with several hundred of their men. The following day, they sent a messenger to the King with a proposal for a truce. The King rejected the baron's offer and demanded they surrender outright, or face being hunted down and killed. But Roderic handed the rebel barons an important concession: if they laid down their arms and swore allegiance to him, he promised to show them mercy.

Some three days after the battle of Saragossa, Julian and the northern barons surrendered to the King, thus bringing the rebellion to an end. True to his word, the King Roderic had treated the conspirators with clemency. Julian, however, as one of the acknowledged leaders, had been stripped of his lands and banished to Ceuta in North Afriqiyah to serve as the garrison commander there.

Bishop Oppas had been sent off to Rome, essentially in exile as well. The other leaders of the rebellion, including Siberto, had been allowed to keep their lands and their titles after agreeing to pay the king a yearly sum in restitution, thus limiting their ability to cause mischief in the foreseeable future.

When Theodosius finished his account, Pelayo asked him the question that had been foremost on his mind since the moment of his release. "Do you have any news of Lady Valentina, Baron Ernesto's daughter?"

"She's Julian's wife now," Theodosius answered. "They were married some three years ago, shortly after you disappeared."

Pelayo stared at Theodosius, refusing to believe his ears. "That can't be."

Theodosius saw the anguish in Pelayo's eyes. "I'm afraid it's true, my boy," he said gently. "They have a daughter now."

Pelayo felt something lurch in the pit of his stomach. *Married to Julian? For three years? How could she have gone back on everything she told me?* It was the thought of seeing Valentina again that had given him the strength to endure those long years of solitude in his cell. The realization that she had been warming Julian's bed all that time left him contemptuous of his romantic notions. *What a stupid fool I've been to have believed she ever loved me.*

"We all thought you were dead," Theodosius said quietly.

"Why?" Pelayo asked. "I understand that it must have appeared as if I'd vanished from the face of the earth but—"

"It was more than that," Theodosius said. "Some six months after your release, Baron Siberto sent word that his soldiers had found your body lying in a ditch. He said it appeared you'd been set upon by thieves. After that, no one questioned your disappearance."

How cleverly they played me, Pelayo thought bitterly.

"I'm sorry," Theodosius said quietly, as if guessing Pelayo's turmoil.

"Did you ever find out any other information about my father's death?"

"No. If anything untoward happened to your father, those responsible did a good job of covering up their tracks."

Pelayo sat there, staring sightlessly into the distance.

"You have to put all that behind you now, my boy. It's what your father would have wanted. He lives inside you now; this is your chance to start a new life and make him proud."

Theodosius' words had the ring of truth about them. He had never forgotten the argument he had had in the armory, when his father had accused him of besmirching their family's good name. His father had been right, the noble born weren't the enemy. It was the Saracens that posed a real threat to the kingdom's existence. He had squandered away his youth, and even more years had been stolen from him by Julian and Izaskun. The time had come now to give some purpose to his life.

"I'm going to sleep now," Theodosius murmured, closing his eyes.

Pelayo looked around the cave for Ordonez and saw him stretched out on the ground beside the tethered horses, an arm over his face. Giving in to his own exhaustion as well, he curled up on the dirt floor, as he had done for the previous three years, and immediately drifted off to sleep.

When he next opened his eyes, the setting sun's rays were flooding into the entrance of the cave. Theodosius was awake too, staring at the rock-strewn landscape outside. "How are you, Theo?" he called out

"A little thirsty," Theodosius replied in a raspy voice. "Could I have some water?"

"Of course." Pelayo got his waterskin, then, kneeling by Theodosius' side, he raised his head so he could drink.

After slaking his thirst, Theodosius gazed outside of the cave again. "The sun's setting, it'll be dark soon."

Pelayo nodded. "I should go gather up some firewood while there's still some light."

"You planning to make a fire?" Theodosius asked. "Is that's wise?"

"I don't think anyone is going to see the glow of the fire, not with all these cliffs around us."

"You're probably right," Theodosius murmured.

A silence settled over them for a moment.

"If you're up to doing some more talking, Theo, I'd like to know how you found out that Siberto was holding me prisoner."

"You have Julian to thank for that," Theodosius said.

"Julian?"

"Yes. Before being exiled to Ceuta, he sent me to help his great-uncle Siberto draw up the deeds to some lands he wanted to sell. Apparently Siberto was lacking the funds to pay the first installment of the King's fines. When I arrived at his castle, I tried to find out where they had buried you, so I could go and pay my respects. To my surprise no one there seemed to know anything about you, not even the local priest. I also couldn't track down any of the soldiers who had supposedly found your body. I could have gone to ask Lord Siberto about it, of course, but by then I was beginning to sense that something was not quite right and that he was probably at the center of whatever had happened to you. So I resigned myself to never uncovering the truth about your death. Then one day, as luck would have it, providence intervened."

"In what way?" Pelayo asked.

"I ran into some of Siberto's soldiers at one of the town's tavern," Theodosius answered. "I got talking to Ordonez, who was sitting next to me, and he told me that he was a guard in the dungeons. Making idle conversation, I asked him about his prisoners, what they were like, what crimes they had committed and so forth. Ordonez told me they were all cutthroats, the scum of the earth. Except for one, he said, that no one knew anything about. That piqued my curiosity. I asked him about the man, what he looked like and when he'd first been imprisoned."

"Ordonez said he was a young man and that he'd been brought to the dungeons under mysterious circumstances some years earlier. He told me the man's speech and manner pointed to a privileged upbringing. Though the description was rather vague, the hairs on the back of my neck had stood on end. From that moment on, I knew I would never find peace until I discovered the identity of Ordonez' mysterious prisoner."

Theodosius paused and closed his eyes.

"You want to stop and rest, Theo?"

"It's better if I talk. It distracts me from thinking about the pain."

Pelayo placed a comforting hand of Theodosius' shoulder. "All right."

"Where was I?" Theodosius continued, "Oh yes… I had just about finished drawing up the land deeds for Baron Siberto and was preparing to return home. Over the next two or three days, I spent as much time as I could with Ordonez, trying to gain his trust. On my last night there, putting my faith in God, I told Ordonez all about you. I explained to him that you were as fine a young man as I'd ever met and that you could not possibly be guilty of anything that might have merited your being thrown into the dungeons. I then asked Ordonez to help me find out if you were his mysterious prisoner. And if that turned out to be the case, to help me break you free. I had done well for myself as your father's chief steward, and I was able to offer Ordonez more money that he could have earned in his entire lifetime for his assistance."

Theodosius licked his lips before continuing in a voice noticeably grown fainter. "To my great relief, my gamble paid off and Ordonez agreed to help me. He was a twenty-year veteran in the King's Legion, and I could tell that he felt a kinship with you, knowing that you had served in the Third. Also, by then Ordonez had taken Siberto's measure and had come to despise him."

"After that day, we spent months and months trying to

figure out a plan. I'm sorry it took us so long to set everything in motion. I know every day in that cell must have seemed like an eternity to you."

"You don't need to apologize to me for anything, Theo. You took a grave risk coming for me. I wish I had the words to tell you how grateful I am."

"No words are necessary between us, my boy," Theodosius said softly. "I know you would have done the same for me."

Pelayo's throat tightened with emotion. He reached over and gripped Theodosius' hand.

When Ordonez awoke a short time later, Pelayo told him he was going to gather some firewood and asked him to keep an eye on Theodosius.

There were plenty of twigs and branches that had washed up from the creek and he was able to gather up several arm-loads of wood and kindling before it got too dark to see. Later he made a small fire near where Theodosius was lying. As the cave lit up with a flickering orange glow, Ordonez went off to fetch the provisions that Theodosius had packed for them in their saddlebags.

Accustomed to hunger, Pelayo had forgotten that he hadn't eaten that day. But when Ordonez handed him a chunk of bread that wasn't moldy and a link of smoke-dried sausage, his mouth flooded with saliva. He tore away at his food, the flavors bursting in his mouth. He gobbled it all down with animal-like intensity, until not a single crumb remained. He thought it was the finest meal he had ever eaten.

Theodosius passed up on his share of the food, offering it to Pelayo, who again wolfed it all down.

When they were done eating, Pelayo and Ordonez passed the time talking, keeping the fire going and watching over

Theodosius, who seemed to have fallen into a deep slumber. When their supply of firewood ran out, Ordonez went off to sleep at the back of the cave.

Pelayo decided to stay awake in case Theodosius woke during the night and needed anything. Soon after, the fire died out, leaving the cave in total darkness. The only sound was that of Theodosius' labored breathing.

As Pelayo sat in the dark, watching over Theodosius, his mind began to wander. The thought that Valentina was lost to him forever filled him with a deep sadness. He remembered how she had looked, drenched from the rain, the night he had kissed her for the first time. Another image of her, riding at his side, her hair swirling in the wind, formed unbidden. He tried to quell his thoughts, but memories of her kept stealing back to haunt him.

The sun finally rose, flooding the cave with light, rousing Pelayo from the light slumber to which he had finally succumbed. He was confused for a moment, puzzled as to why it was so bright. Then he remembered everything that had occurred and where he was. As he came fully awake, his eyes fell on Theodosius stretched out before him. His chest tightened with concern as he noticed his old tutor's unhealthy pallor. It was clear Theo had taken a turn for the worse during the night.

He placed a hand on Theodosius' forehead and discovered that he was burning with fever. At the touch of his hand, Theodosius' eyelids flickered open.

"How are you feeling?" Pelayo asked quietly.

There was a long pause. "Not good, my boy…" Theodosius said in a whisper.

Ordonez wandered over and gave Pelayo an inquiring glance.

"He has fever," Pelayo said quietly.

Ordonez nodded, his expression somber.

Pelayo turned back to Theodosius. "I'm going to get some cool water from the creek and put a cold cloth on your forehead. It should help with the fever."

"There's something I want you to do for me first," Theodosius whispered. "There are three purses of coins in my travel pack. Could you fetch them for me?"

"Of course."

When Pelayo returned, Theodosius asked him to give one of the three purses to Ordonez.

Ordonez took the pouch, untied the drawstring, then poured out a stream of gold coins into the palm of his hand. His thick dark eyebrows arched in surprise. "This is far more than we agreed upon, Theodosius."

"It's little enough recompense for the hardships you may have to endure in the future," Theodosius said

"I have no regrets," Ordonez answered. "Our cause was a just one."

"You're a rare bird," Theodosius said softly to him. "A man of honor."

"You are kind to say so," Ordonez muttered, looking embarrassed.

Theodosius turned his gaze toward Pelayo. "I had meant to keep one of the purses for myself, but it seems I won't have need of it now."

Pelayo remained silent, sadly recognizing the truth in Theodosius's words. There was greater pain than watching someone you love slip inexorably toward death.

"Go to Tarragona," Theodosius whispered to Pelayo. "Seek out the King's protection."

"I am nothing to the King, Theo," Pelayo said. "I doubt he'll even grant me an audience."

"He will. Promise me you'll go."

Pelayo hesitated then nodded. "Very well, I'll do as you ask, Theo."

"I knew if I lived long enough, I'd hear you say those words one day," Theodosius whispered.

"I'm sorry that my rescue has brought you to this end, old friend," Pelayo said, taking Theodosius' hand.

"I've had a long life, I'm at peace." After saying those words, as if he'd fulfilled his duty, Theodosius closed his eyes and drifted off again

Pelayo went out to the creek and refilled his waterskin. After returning to the cave, he found a washrag, poured cold water over it then placed it over Theodosius' forehead.

Ordonez wandered off and sat outside near the entrance of the cave, where he could keep an eye out for approaching horsemen.

Pelayo spent the rest of the day watching over Theodosius, leaving him only to gather more firewood when daylight began to wane. This time he stocked up enough wood to see them through until the following morning.

Evening turned to night. The hours passed, the light from a small fire kept the darkness at bay.

Pelayo woke up several times during the night and tried to rouse Theodosius to get him to drink some water. But his old tutor remained unresponsive.

Shortly before dawn, a soft rattling sound roused Pelayo from his light sleep. Sitting up, he reached out a hand to touch Theodosius. His old tutor's body was warm, but the rhythmic rise and fall of his chest had come to a stop.

A sense of loss swept over Pelayo as he looked down upon the still figure before him. He told himself that Theodosius had escaped his pain and that he was now at peace. But the thought did little bring him solace. Reaching over, he gently closed Theodosius' eyelids.

The finality of that act overwhelmed Pelayo with grief. He rose to his feet and walked to the entrance of the cave. He stood there for a long time, gazing out as the sky gradually brightened.

"He was a good man," Ordonez said coming up behind Pelayo. "The world will be a lesser place with him gone."

Both men stood in silence, their gazes fixed on the sun-drenched cliffs outside the cave, drawing comfort from each other's company.

Lacking shovels to dig a grave, Pelayo and Ordonez laid Theodosius to rest in a pit-like depression inside the cave, then covered his body with rocks to keep the animals away. It took them all morning to accomplish the task. Afterwards Pelayo said a few words in prayer over the mound of rocks, while Ordonez bowed his head in respect.

It was late afternoon when Pelayo finally got around to looking inside the saddlebag that Theodosius had packed for him. Inside, he found a clean tunic, a belt, a thin bladed knife, a bronze mirror, a pair of sandals and a small bar of soap smelling of tallow and ashes. He stuffed all the items back into the saddlebag then took it outside.

He propped up the mirror on a rocky ledge along the cliffside, then began hacking away at his hair and beard with his knife. Once he had finished, a thin, hollow-eyed stranger stared back at him from the mirror, reminding him of the years that had been stolen from him.

He took off his tattered tunic and sandals, grabbed the soap and saddlebag, then walked toward the creek. Wading in, he sat on his haunches in the deepest part of the stream and began scooping water over himself. Despite the heat of the day, the cold water had him chattering as he washed away the layers of grime from his body. When the water ran clear, he rose and headed back to where he had left the saddlebag.

He put on the new tunic and discovered it was much too large for his bony frame. The belt was also too big for his slim waist and he had to use his knife to pierce a new hole in the leather.

That night, while sitting around the fire and eating another simple meal of bread and smoke-cured sausage, Pelayo and Ordonez discussed their plans for the future. In the end they both decided that it would be safer for each of them to travel alone.

"The road to Tarragona will be crawling with soldiers searching for you," Ordonez said. "Keep an eye out for them. You don't want to fall into Siberto's hands again."

Pelayo nodded. "What about you? Where will you be heading?"

"I've been thinking of going back home," Ordonez said, staring at the fire. He told Pelayo that he was planning to reunite with his brother, whom he hadn't seen in some twenty years. As the eldest, his brother had inherited the family's farmstead near a small town that Pelayo had never heard of. Ordonez said he was planning to use his newfound wealth to buy a few stallions and get into the horse breeding business with his brother.

"Sounds like a sensible plan," Pelayo said.

The following morning, shortly after sunrise, Pelayo and Ordonez stuffed their belongings into their saddlebags, then led their horses outside.

"Why don't you take Theo's stallion with you?" Pelayo said to Ordonez. "He can be the first of your breeding stock."

Ordonez' eyebrows raised in surprise. "Are you certain you don't want to keep the animal for yourself?"

Pelayo patted his own horse. "This nag here is good enough to take me where I'm going."

"In that case, I'll take the stallion off your hands, of course." Looking pleased, Ordonez walked toward Theodosius' horse, then swung himself up onto the saddle. Once he settled on the horse, he nudged him forward a few paces, then reached down to take the reins of his other mount.

Pelayo walked up to him and extended his hand. "Farewell, Ordonez. Thank you for getting me out of that hellhole."

"I'm glad I was able to help." The old soldier clasped Pelayo's wrist. "Perhaps our paths will cross again one day, but if they don't, have a good life, lad."

"And you as well. God speed, my friend."

Ordonez steered his horse down the embankment, then turned and gave Pelayo a parting wave. It was then Pelayo noticed that the vague, empty look he had seen on the jailor's face during the previous three years had disappeared.

Pelayo mounted his horse, then gazed into the cave at the pile of rocks that marked Theodosius' grave. A feeling of great sadness washed over him, bringing tears to his eyes. *Goodbye, Theo. You've given me back my life. I swear before God I will not waste it.*

CHAPTER 24

IT HAD BEEN three weeks since Pelayo's escape from Siberto's dungeons. After parting with Ordonez, Pelayo had kept to secondary roads and had not seen any sign of armed horsemen. Thanks to the gold that Theodosius had given him, he had been able to buy food and pay for accommodation at a string of small inns along the way. As a result he had regained some of the weight he had lost while imprisoned. Also, his strength and stamina were coming back.

It was early afternoon when he caught his first sight of Tarragona. From the distance, the king's capital looked more like a walled fortress than a city. Perched atop a promontory and surrounded by high, stone walls, it appeared as if it had been built to serve a single purpose. To be impregnable to anything man could throw its way. Grim though the city appeared, especially under the harsh light of the summer sun, Pelayo was glad that his journey had finally come to an end.

The guards at the gates waved him through and he steered his horse along a stone archway, then emerged into a large square ringed with shops. The smell of freshly baked meat pies brought him to a stop by an outside stall. He paid two copper pennies for one of the pastries, then munched on it as he rode on. He made another stop at a barber's stall and had his hair and beard trimmed.

It was mid-afternoon when he reached the king's citadel. Squatting on the highest point of the city, King Roderic's administrative center was a complex of interconnected buildings of quarried granite encircled by thick walls. He must have appeared presentable enough with his new tunic, as the guards at the gates waved him through after only a few cursory questions.

He left his horse with a groom at the stable, then walked across the courtyard toward the main entrance of the castle. There were two more guards standing outside the iron-braced entry doors. He explained to them that he was seeking an audience with the King. One of the guards escorted him inside the building, then led him down a hallway into an audience chamber.

A distinguished-looking man with the air of a high-ranking official about him sat behind a marble-topped table. Around his neck hung a heavy gold chain bearing a medallion of office. Barely glancing up from the document he was reading, the gray-haired man gestured for Pelayo to sit down on one of the two empty chairs facing the table, then introduced himself as the King's chamberlain.

"So, what brings you here?"

"I'm seeking an audience with the King," Pelayo told him.

"The King, you say," the chamberlain said, looking at him with bemusement. "And why do you wish to see him?"

As he began to explain, the chamberlain's eyes slid away from him and wandered aimlessly around the room.

When Pelayo had finished, the chamberlain turned his attention back to him. "The next public audience with the King is on the last Sunday of November."

"That's nearly three months away," Pelayo said.

"I'm glad to see you can count," the chamberlain said dryly.

Pelayo hid his irritation, aware that such a display would not serve him well. "I'm afraid that my business with the King is pressing. I can't wait that long."

"I'm sorry to hear that," the chamberlain said distractedly, searching for some item amidst the clutter on his desk.

Pelayo tried again. "Is there some way you can arrange for me to see the King before November?"

The chamberlain frowned. "Do you think the King grants an audience to every man in the kingdom who takes it into his head that he has been wronged? He would not have time to do anything else, now would he. Luckily, I am here to guard his privacy."

"Such a responsibility must weigh heavily on your shoulders," Pelayo said.

The chamberlain's eyes went flat. "Well, I think we're done here."

Pelayo remained seated. "I need a private audience with the King. I'd be most grateful for any help you'd care to give me."

The chamberlain leaned back. "Well, perhaps there may be other possibilities we could explore…" He stopped and stared at Pelayo expectantly.

Pelayo reached for his purse, counted out five silver coins, then placed them on the desk.

The chamberlain reached out a languid hand and took the coins. "The King is about to leave on a journey, but I can arrange an audience for you when he returns."

"When is that likely to be?" Pelayo asked.

"It's difficult to say. A few weeks, perhaps."

"Or maybe a few of months?"

The chamberlain shrugged. "Possibly."

Pelayo stilled an impulse to reach over and wrap his hands

around the chamberlain's neck. Instead, he fished out five more coins and placed them on the table. "I need to see the King sooner than that."

The chamberlain eyed the coins. "Yes, I think that could be arranged." When he reached out for the coins, Pelayo covered them with his hand.

"When exactly?" Pelayo asked.

"How about right now?"

Pelayo withdrew his hand and the coins disappeared from the desk.

"What did you say was your reason for seeking an audience?" the chamberlain asked.

"A dispute over succession."

"I see." The chamberlain wrote something down on a piece of parchment. "And your name?"

"Pelayo, son of the late Duke Fáfila of Asturias."

The chamberlain stopped and looked up. "You should have mentioned from the start that you are Duke Fáfila's son."

"Would that have saved me the money for the bribe?"

The chamberlain gave him an enigmatic smile. "Come with me."

Pelayo followed the official out of the chamber, then along a columned hallway that opened onto a large courtyard where several stone benches were spaced at regular intervals along a rectangular pool of water. There, a dozen or so men were gathered in small groups, some standing, some sitting, all appearing bored.

"Have a seat," the chamberlain told Pelayo. "Your name will be called when your turn comes."

"Should I expect a long wait?"

The chamberlain shrugged. "I simply give the King the names of those waiting to see him, as well as their grievances. The King then decides whom he wishes to see and when."

"I could be here for days then," Pelayo said.

"Possibly," the chamberlain replied with another tight smile.

Pelayo stared at the chamberlain as he retreated, then with a shake of his head, he walked along the colonnade toward one of the benches that had some free space. He nodded in greeting to the two men there, then sat down between them. "How long have you two been waiting?" he asked.

A bald-headed man who smelled faintly of lye met his eyes. "Three days."

"Just one for me," the second man said.

"You should have brought food and something to drink," the first man said, pointing to a small wicker hamper at his feet.

Pelayo let out a sigh. *I guess I should have thought things through a bit more carefully before coming here.*

Pelayo had always found it difficult to wait and the afternoon dragged by slowly. Shadows began lengthening over the garden and the temperature cooled. He was staring sightlessly into the distance when a door at the far end of the courtyard swung open. A richly attired man came striding out, the chamberlain hurrying behind him. The eyes of everyone in the garden followed the men as they strode along the colonnade toward where Pelayo and his two companions were sitting. To Pelayo's surprise, the two came to a stop by his bench.

"That's him, my lord," the chamberlain said, pointing a finger at Pelayo.

Having surmised they were facing the King, Pelayo and his two companions rose to their feet and bowed.

Hands on his hips, King Roderic studied Pelayo with a look of open curiosity. "So, you're Fáfila's second son," he said in a deep, sonorous voice.

"I am, my lord," Pelayo said.

"I can see the family resemblance," the King said. He

dismissed the chamberlain, then turned back toward Pelayo. "I heard that you had vanished after your father's death."

"I did indeed, my lord, straight into Baron Siberto's dungeons."

King Roderick cocked an eyebrow. "Sounds like there's a story there. Why don't you walk with me and tell me about it?"

"It would be an honor, my lord."

Pelayo fell in step beside King Roderic and together they walked back toward the door at the far end of the courtyard.

"So," King Roderic said, "What mischief did you get into that warranted your being thrown into the dungeons?"

"It seems I asked too many questions," Pelayo said.

"Oh?"

Pelayo told the King about the events leading up to his imprisonment, beginning with his homecoming to Gijón and his learning about his father's death. They both walked slowly and Pelayo finished his story just as the two entered the King's audience chamber.

"Are you telling me that Julian imprisoned you to stop you from asking questions about your father's death?" the King asked.

"I've had three long years to mull that over. I can think of no other reason why Julian would have wanted to silence me. The only question for which I've yet to find an answer is what drove him to murder our father."

"I think I can guess," the King said. "The rebellion Julian was planning against me would not have been possible without the backing of the Asturian legion. Had your father lived, he would never have agreed to use it against me."

"With all due respect, my lord, how can you be so certain? My father might have felt an obligation to side with his wife and her uncles."

"I don't believe that for a moment, and I'll tell you why," the King said. He recounted the story of how Pelayo's father had played a pivotal role in swaying the Council of Barons. "So you see, if your father had not thrown his support behind me, I would never have been elected king."

Pelayo was surprised to hear that his father had chosen to side with Roderic rather than to back Witiza's son, Olmund, who was related by blood to Izaskun and Julian. But knowing his father's moral rectitude and uncompromising character, the story rang true to him. While realizing those same virtues had brought about his father's death, Pelayo couldn't help but feel a certain pride in him. "That all makes sense, in a terrible kind of way."

King Roderic studied Pelayo. "So, tell me, why have you come to see me?"

"To ask for justice," Pelayo answered promptly. "I want anyone who's had a hand in my father's murder punished."

"That's probably every baron who took part in the rebellion," the King said.

"Whoever they are, they deserve to be hung."

The King shook his head. "I'm sorry, I can't help you. Even if you had a dozen witnesses to support your accusation, I cannot afford to shatter the peace and plunge the country into another war."

Pelayo nodded, feeling deeply disappointed despite having anticipated the King's refusal. "I understand, my lord," he said woodenly.

"What I can do, however," King Roderic added, "is give you back the townships that your father left you."

Pelayo' spirits lifted somewhat. Owning land and having a source of income for the rest of his life was no small matter. "I appreciate that, my lord, thank you."

The King nodded. "I was very sorry to hear about your father's death; I could have used his friendship and his counsel during these difficult times."

"I miss him as well, my lord."

"I'm sure you do." The King gazed at Pelayo with a thoughtful expression. "I'm planning to strengthen the Fifth Legion, which has been undermanned for years. I'm going to need competent officers whose loyalty I can count on. Would you be interested in a command post?"

Pelayo was taken aback by the offer.

"Why don't you join me tonight as my guest at supper?" the King said. "You can me give your answer then."

"Of course. It would be an honor."

"Very well, off you go then. There are others waiting to see me."

Pelayo took his leave from the King, then left the chamber. As he was walking away, he realized that he wasn't entirely disappointed with the outcome of the audience. The King's offer would help settle the question of what to do with his life. He would accept the King's offer of a military command and serve his country as best as he could. His father would approve of that, he thought.

The twin blows of Theodosius' death and the news of Valentina's marriage to Julian had affected him deeply. Everyone he had ever truly cared for in his life was gone now. He would keep their memory alive for the rest of his days, but there was only sorrow in thinking about them now. He would force himself to look only to the future. He'd start life afresh, make new acquaintances, and grow new roots.

For the first time in years, he felt at peace.

PART II

CHAPTER 25

THE RANKS OF soldiers waited in silence, oblivious to the light rain that had been falling through the night. Except for the occasional command given in hushed tones, all was quiet and deceptively peaceful.

"The enemy seems to be on the move, sire," Pelayo's adjutant remarked tersely.

Wrapped in the red military cloak of a field commander, Pelayo turned in the saddle and peered at the enemy horsemen crawling across the far side of the Guadalete valley.

"They're just getting into position," he said, his voice calm. "It'll be a while yet."

The two continued riding by the rows of soldiers assembled in battle formation. A centurion, standing in front of his men, called out, "How are you this morning, commander?"

"I'm well, Velasco," Pelayo said, reining in his horse. "And you, how's the shoulder?"

"Much better," the centurion said, flexing his arm.

"Glad to hear that; we need you in fighting form today."

"I won't let you down, commander."

"I know you won't," Pelayo said. He eyed the soldiers arrayed behind the centurion. "Your men ready for battle?"

"I hope so, sire, the long march has taken a toll on them. It's unfortunate we couldn't have had a few more days to rest. Rotten luck we got caught so far north."

"I don't believe luck had anything to do with it," Pelayo said. "I'd wager a month's salary the Moors knew exactly where we'd be."

King Roderic had launched a major offensive against the Basques a month earlier. As the legions had been marching through the Pyrenean mountains, the King had received word that a Moorish army had landed on a southern beach near the Pillars of Hercules. Fearing any delay in countering the incursion would allow the invaders to swallow up more territory, the King had immediately ordered his forces to turn around and head southward. The long and arduous journey had been accomplished with remarkable speed, but it had come at a cost.

"The enemy has had days to prepare for battle," Velasco said, gazing in the direction of their opponent's camp. "I wonder what unpleasant surprises they have in store for us."

"Whatever they are, we won't have long to find out," Pelayo said.

Velasco nodded grimly. "Good thing the northern barons showed up when they did."

"No question about it; their troops should give us the edge."

The previous day, while Pelayo and his soldiers had been setting up camp, a column of some three thousand men had appeared over the horizon. At first no one had been able to tell whether or not the force was friendly. After a tense moment, they had finally been able to make out the troops' pennants. At the sight of the Iberian banners, the men had broken into raucous cheers.

Only Pelayo had remained silent. He had spotted Siberto's standard amongst the others in the distance and memories of the three long years he had spent entombed in the baron's dungeons had come flooding back.

Pelayo had joined an honor guard that had ridden out with the King to meet the northern barons, all of whom had taken part in the rebellion against the newly appointed monarch some years earlier.

Speaking on behalf of the northern barons, Siberto had explained to the king that given the common threat they were now facing from the invaders, all five of them had decided to cast aside their differences and stand as one with him.

Looking deeply moved, King Roderic had vowed to the northern barons that he would never forget their timely aid.

A horseman galloping toward Pelayo brought him out of his thoughts.

"A message from the King," the rider called out, bringing his horse to a halt. "With the addition of the northern barons' men, the King feels he has enough troops to hold back three cohorts in reserve. If at any time you require reinforcements, you are to give the signal of two long trumpet blasts, repeated at intervals."

"Two long blasts," Pelayo said. "Understood."

"One more thing, commander. The King says it is imperative that you and your troops stand fast and hold the left flank at all costs."

"Tell the King my men and I will do as he asks or die trying."

"I'll pass on your words to him. Good luck to you today, Commander Pelayo."

Pelayo turned back to the centurion as the King's messenger rode off. "I guess I'd better be on my way. Stay safe, Velasco."

"You as well, sire."

After finishing the inspection, Pelayo and his adjutant headed back to the barren hilltop they were using as their command post. After dismounting, they joined the four staff officers standing at the crest of the hill alongside their horses. From there, they had an unobstructed view of the Iberian legions lined up in battle formation across the mouth of the valley.

Directly below them, making up the left flank of the King's forces, stood the two legions under Pelayo's command. To their right, occupying the center of the valley, lay the bulk of their force: five legions, each comprised of eleven hundred men under the command of King Roderic. Stretching from the King's position to the far end of the valley, making up the right flank, stood the northern barons' three thousand men.

Pelayo turned his gaze to the other end of the valley, where the Berber horsemen seemed to be amassing on a ridge in the distance. Due to the rainy conditions, it was difficult to judge precisely the size of the enemy force, but he estimated them to be some twelve to thirteen thousand men.

He had fought a number of battles in the last five years, but this one felt different. The threat he and his men were facing was more serious and the stakes far higher than any in the past. The fate of the kingdom hung in the balance. If they won, they would deal the Moors a decisive blow. But if they lost…his mind could not conceive of the horrors that would follow. The Saracens and their allies had so far toppled every kingdom that had stood in their way. And now it was Hispania's turn to be tested.

Pelayo tried to ignore the sense of dread that had come over him that morning when he had realized that the Moors were going to attack them on horseback. Every general since Roman times had used the cavalry to harass the enemy, then had relied on the infantry to bear the brunt of the fighting. An attacking force made up solely of horsemen seemed as heretical to the rules of warfare as did intentionally choosing the low ground. Whether ultimately a mounted charge proved successful or not, the sheer unpredictability of the maneuver would make it difficult for the King and his forces to counter it effectively.

To make matters worse, the previous evening at the war council, the northern barons had proposed that the King deploy his forces in a straight line across the mouth of the valley. He had argued against the idea, pointing out that lining up the legions like that would make their units difficult to maneuver in the changing conditions of battle. But the King, no doubt feeling indebted to the northern barons, had in the end taken their advice.

Now watching the enemy milling about in the distance, Pelayo suspected that the battle formation the King had chosen for them was going to prove even more ineffective against a cavalry driven attack. However the moment to do anything about it had passed. Turning, he singled out one of his officers.

"The lancers are standing too far apart," Pelayo said. "They're creating gaps that the Moors could slip through. Ride down and tell the squad leaders to tighten up their ranks; keep the men at arm's length and no more."

"At once, commander."

A series of trumpet blasts drifted in from across the valley. For a moment nothing happened, then the enemy horsemen began sweeping down from their position.

A third of a league away the Moors broke into full gallop. Their strange, ululating cries drifted in from across the valley, making the hackles rise at the back of Pelayo's neck. As they narrowed the distance to his position, he began to feel the rumble of their horses' hooves through the soles of his feet. He waited until the right time, then raised his fist in the air.

Arrayed behind the lancers, Pelayo's archers lifted their bows, took aim, then released their first salvo. A buzzing sound like that of a thousand partridges taking flight rippled through the air. The feathered shafts traced arcs through the sky, then began plummeting down on the charging horde. Scores of Moorish riders went tumbling off their horses, their bodies swallowed up by the successive waves of horsemen thundering behind them.

Engrossed in the scene playing out below him, Pelayo heard someone at his side let out a gasp.

"Commander!" his adjutant cried out, grabbing his arm and pointing toward the distance. "Look over there, at the far end the valley!"

Pelayo peered through the drizzling rain to where his adjutant was pointing. The sight that met him was so unexpected that for a moment he couldn't believe his eyes. The entire right flank, made up of the troops under the command of Siberto and the northern barons, was melting away.

"What the devil are they doing?" one of the staff officers cried out in consternation.

Pelayo wrenched his gaze back to the charging horde. The leading edge of the swarm had begun splitting in two. One group was veering to the left, heading toward the now undefended space that had opened up on the far side of the field. The other half was continuing its charge toward his and the King's legions.

It suddenly dawned on Pelayo that he was witnessing a carefully planned and well-executed maneuver. *We've been betrayed*, he thought, a sickening dread washing over him and chilling him to the marrow. It was hard to believe that Siberto and the other barons were colluding with the enemy against their own people, but the proof of it lay before his eyes. His dismay turned into a cold rage. All his half-forgotten hatred of Oppas and Siberto came rushing back with a stomach-churning intensity. *You treacherous bastards! May you all burn in hell for this!*

"They're going to circle around and attack us from behind!" his adjutant shouted, a note of barely controlled panic in his voice.

Pelayo had already come to the same conclusion. Turning toward his staff officers, he began shouting orders.

"You, ride down and get our two back lines to turn and face the rear. Llorca, go warn the archers of a coming attack from behind." He turned and grabbed another man by the arm and pointed into the distance. "Reposition a cohort up there on the rise. Have them face south, toward the mouth of the valley. Go!"

The enemy swept closer, the pounding of their horses' hooves growing louder and louder. Down on the front lines, Pelayo's lancers braced their spears on the ground, presenting a bristling, iron-tipped barrier to the charging horde.

The first wave of horsemen smashed into Pelayo's battle lines with the ferocity of a blow from an iron mace. The din of clashing steel, screaming men and neighing horses rang through the air. Pelayo's front lines dissolved into a jumbled mass of horsemen and foot soldiers locked together in mortal combat.

Pelayo turned his gaze to the other end of the valley, to what had once been their right flank. The enemy horsemen had entirely pushed through the gap and were beginning to wheel about. As he watched, the Moorish force started to split again. Their intention became clear a moment later. A group of some four thousand horsemen were heading toward the back of the King's formation. A second band, composed of some two thousand horsemen, was circling toward his own rear.

The sky grew darker and the drizzle turned into a steady

downpour. Pelayo tracked the Moors with his eyes as they closed in on the King's legions. He couldn't quite see what measures, if any, the King had taken to ward off the two-pronged assault to which he was now subjected.

Pelayo turned his attention to the second wave of Moorish horsemen bearing down on him and his men. When the enemy came within range, he gave the signal to the archers who had turned to face the rear. A salvo of arrows buzzed through the air and began raining down on the charging horsemen. Scores of Moors went tumbling down, but the vast majority continued their run toward the cohort that Pelayo had deployed on a nearby rise to protect his rear lines.

Shouting hoarse cries, the enemy riders smashed into Pelayo's cohort. The line of lancers wobbled, then firmed, forcing the Moors to ride around the cohort, thwarting their attempt to split and scatter Pelayo's men.

Knowing he had bought himself some time, Pelayo stole a quick glance at the unfolding tragedy that had ensnared the King's legions. Attacked from both the front and the rear, the King's men were trapped, unable to move forward or to fall back. Slowly, inexorably, like two ends of a vice closing, the Moors drove forward, pressing the King's legions, constricting them in an ever tightening and deadly embrace.

"Is there anything we can do to help the King, commander?" Pelayo's adjutant called out in a voice strained with tension.

"No," Pelayo answered, forcing the word out. Every man under his command was engaged in combat. Withdrawing any number of them would fatally weaken their defenses and hasten their defeat. Even if he could manage to pull together a few hundred men, there was simply no way they could reach the King without they themselves being cut down by the Moors who were now firmly in control of the battlefield.

As the morning wore on, Pelayo watched the gradual but steady decimation of the legions, feeling as if part of him was dying. At last came the moment when he realized that there was no longer any need to maintain a command post. The battle had changed from a contest of carefully thought-out tactics, of thrusts and counterattacks, to simply trying to hold back the Moorish onslaught. *We're done for*, he thought to himself, the terrible admission bringing a bitter taste to his mouth. Steeling himself, he turned toward his officers and met their gazes.

"It's time for us to join the battle," Pelayo said.

His officers stared at him silently, their bleak expressions revealing they understood the import of his words.

"Do you have any specific orders for us, commander?" his adjutant asked.

"Yes," Pelayo said remembering his promise to the King. "Fight with courage and die with honor."

Every man there nodded, their faces somber.

After mounting, Pelayo turned his horse to face his officers. "It's been an honor serving with you." He unsheathed his sword and raised it in the air. "For God and King!" he shouted.

"For God and King!" his men shouted back.

Pelayo dug his heels into his horse's flanks and galloped down the hillside toward a section in their lines where the enemy had broken through. He felt no fear now, nor regret. There was just a burning need in him to strike back at the enemy and exact a measure of revenge.

Several Moorish horsemen spotted him coming and immediately began converging on him.

Pelayo suddenly found himself fighting for his life. He slashed to his left and right with his sword, carving out a circle of safety around himself. He narrowly avoided a spear thrust, then hacked away at his attacker. Warm blood sprayed onto his face. Another Moorish rider closed in, his sword scything toward him. Pelayo blocked the blade with his shield and struck back, a swift, hard blow that caught the warrior on the side of the head with such force that it knocked him off his horse.

Another rider bore down on him from the right. Pelayo traded blows with him as their horses circled around each other. When he saw an opening, he thrust his sword into his opponent's midriff. The tip of his blade punched through the man's chainmail, then sank into flesh.

Several Moorish horsemen broke away from the fighting and headed toward him, no doubt having identified him as a high-ranking officer. As the riders closed in, his adjutant and another of his officers galloped into view, intercepting two of the enemy horsemen. With only the third man left to fend off, Pelayo guided his horse with his knees, deflected a blow on his shield, then struck back with a slashing sweep of his sword. He missed the man's throat by less than a palm's width, then had to ward off several blows before he found an opportunity to strike out again. This time his aim proved true.

The fighting continued throughout the afternoon, the Moors pressing hard, meting out death from atop their horses. The screams of agony, and the clash of steel became a constant roar that assaulted the senses. Swords and axes, maces and spears slashed and tore, pounded and pierced. Blood mixed with rain, stained the mud an ochre red. Pelayo felt as if he'd been cast into the deepest pit of hell.

Pelayo's right arm began to ache. Each swing of his sword became more difficult than the last. On the verge of exhaustion, he suddenly found himself in a pocket of relative calm. His chest heaving, he gulped breaths of air into his burning lungs. As he recovered, he took stock of the battle churning around him. He had lost roughly half his men. At the current rate of attrition, he figured that less than a hundred of his men would survive to see nightfall.

Beyond, in the center of the valley, the king's standard was no longer flying. Realizing what its absence meant, Pelayo felt a stab of sadness. Roderic had been more than a good king; he'd been a mentor and a friend.

The rhythmic pounding of a galloping horse cut short Pelayo's mourning. Turning to his left, he caught sight of a Moorish horseman bearing down on him fast. Before he could lift his shield, something blunt and heavy smashed with a deafening clang onto the side of his helmet. A flash of light exploded behind his eyes. He swayed in the saddle, bolts of pain radiating down the side of his head. Sound dimmed, and the world darkened. He was vaguely aware of slumping over his horse. Thankfully, his mount instinctively began prancing away from the enemy horseman. Knowing that he'd never wake up from his swoon if he gave into it, he willed himself to hold on to consciousness. Though the pain in his head continued throbbing, the darkness receded a little and gradually his surroundings sharpened into focus.

Some half dozen paces ahead of him, a Moorish chieftain, wearing chest armor over a black military tunic, was guiding his horse toward him. On his left arm hung a small, round shield gilded with intricate designs. From his right hand dangled an iron ball and chain that he was swinging back and forth.

The sight did wonders to clear Pelayo's head. With dismay, he suddenly realized that he had dropped his sword. Somehow, he had managed to hold on to his shield, no doubt due to the leather loops snugly encircling his forearm. But the shield wasn't much use to him without a weapon. He scanned the area around him and spotted his sword lying in the mud a half-dozen paces away. It may as well have been on the moon for all his chances of reaching it before the Saracen horseman closed in on him.

Pelayo's first instinct was to give his horse its head and bolt away. But he knew that the Moorish chieftain would never give him the time to get to speed. With no other recourse than to fight, he drew his dagger from its sheath. It wasn't much of a weapon against a ball and chain, but it was better than nothing.

The Moorish chieftain closed in, a faint smile revealing his contempt for his adversary's chances. With a sweep of his arm, the chieftain sent the spiked iron ball hurtling forward.

Pelayo lifted his shield, knowing that it was no match for the iron ball. With a loud crack of splintering wood, his leatherbound shield broke asunder. A painful shock radiated down his arm, numbing him to the shoulder.

The Moorish chieftain circled around. Pelayo threw his dagger, aiming at the bearded face, the only part of the man's upper body not sheathed in armor.

The chieftain jerked back. Though he narrowly avoided the dagger, his sudden movement unsettled his horse, sending it skittering away.

The ebb and flow of the battle drove some of Pelayo's soldiers in his direction. As his men swarmed around him, the Moorish chieftain gave Pelayo a mocking wave before riding away.

A centurion Pelayo did not recognize shouted at him over the din of battle, "There's blood running down the side of your face, commander. Are you all right?"

Pelayo threw away his broken shield, then eased his fingers under the right-hand side of his helmet. His hair was sticky with blood and his temple felt painful to the touch.

"It's nothing serious, I'm fine," Pelayo called out. "You've done well to keep your men in formation."

"I've tried my best, sire, but we're in a desperate situation now. Do you have any orders for us?"

"Whatever you're doing, just keep at it," Pelayo answered, throwing his leg over his horse and dismounting.

The centurion looked crestfallen. "Is the battle lost then, commander?"

Pelayo retrieved his sword from the ground, then turned and met the centurion's eyes. The man deserved more from him than inane platitudes, a voice said inside his head. He turned and studied the corpse-strewn field around him, considering the battle in tactical terms again. Thanks to the wedge-shaped defense that he had deployed to protect his rear, the two legions under his command had managed to withstand the onslaught far better than the king's forces. But it was a hollow achievement. They were surrounded, with no hope of breaking through the cordon of enemy horsemen encircling them.

Pelayo turned and scanned the area around him. There was no sign of the King's men to be seen anywhere, just turbaned horsemen roaming unimpeded over the battlefield. He was overcome with sadness at the realization that the two thousand or so soldiers still remaining were all that was left of the once mighty Iberian legions. He thought of all the good men that had fallen that day. Faces of friends and comrades flashed across his mind's eye. Strangely, he felt no fear as he contemplated the near certainty of his own death. There was only a grim determination to see the battle through to the end. Squaring his shoulders, he turned toward the centurion.

"Do you have any men in reserve?" Pelayo asked, mounting his horse.

"There's a company of archers behind us."

"Good," Pelayo answered. "We'll make our stand over there,

by the knoll. Let's reposition the men. You get the archers, I'll draw back the lancers."

The centurion's eyes filled with purpose.

"At once, sire."

Pelayo began the delicate maneuver of pulling back the men fighting on the front lines. "Draw back, slowly!" he shouted as he rode up and down behind the rows of soldiers. "Keep your lines tight! Don't turn your back to the enemy!"

Maintaining a running battle with the Moorish horsemen, Pelayo's men drew back in an orderly retreat. The archers, already in position on the knoll, began laying out a cover of arrows for them.

Pelayo began positioning his men in concentric circles around the knoll, the outer ring keeping the Moors at bay with their spears. The maneuver was similar to the one he had used many years ago in the mock battle against Julian. Back then, he had snatched victory from defeat, but he knew that this time his attempt would ultimately fail. They were too greatly outnumbered, and their fate was all but sealed. All he and his men could do now was exact as high a price as they could for their lives. After abandoning his horse, he joined his men up on the knoll.

The attack of the Moorish horsemen stopped for a moment, as they contemplated the bristling wall of spears facing them.

Sweeping back his cloak over his shoulders, Pelayo walked through his men until he was facing the sea of Moorish horsemen.

"Come on, you sons of whores!" Pelayo shouted, raising his sword in the air. "What are you waiting for? Come and get a taste of our steel!"

As if understanding the challenge hurled at them, the Moors stormed forward with swords drawn.

Sitting atop his horse, Tariq ibn Zayad watched his men finish off the last pocket of Christian soldiers who were making a stand on the hillock before him. Though the sky had finally cleared, dusk had set in and now the light was fading fast. He could not be certain, but he thought that the embattled, red-cloaked Iberian officer who was fighting for his life in the distance was the same man who had thrown a dagger at him earlier in the day. The man was one of four Christians standing in a knot, back-to-back, trying to keep at bay a ring of his warriors who seemed in no hurry to finish off their quarry.

Tariq's men were shouting taunts and prodding the Christians with their lances. One of his warriors darted in and with a quick sweep of his sword struck off the head of one of the infidels. His men cheered, then began kicking the head across the muddy ground.

Though there was much to do before nightfall, Tariq did not interfere in the scene unfolding in front of him. His warriors had earned the right to a little entertainment.

Unexpectedly, the remaining three Christians soldiers charged the ring of warriors surrounding them. Shouting in defiance, they managed to catch some of Tariq's men flat-footed, before they themselves were finally cut down in a flurry of blows.

It is done, Tariq thought to himself, awed by what he and his men had accomplished. *Allah has smiled on us today.* He could scarcely believe, that despite all the possible complications that could have arisen, the plan he and his council had devised had gone smoothly and victory had been won. They had not only defeated the Christians, but more importantly, they had annihilated their army. That was an achievement worth savouring. But he realized that the conquest of Hispania was far from over. For one thing, there was still the question of what to do with the Christian barons, their allies for the moment.

There was also another problem, more of a complication really, that he had not foreseen. The Iberian monarch had slipped away during the battle. That by itself was no reason for concern, as they were in the middle of an uninhabited area and the man was apparently on foot. Still, he would have to send out some of his already exhausted soldiers to track the wretch down before he got too far. Tariq was confident that in two-or three-days' time, the monarch's head would lie impaled on a spear outside his tent. The head would make a fine trophy and a fitting accompaniment to the letter he would send to the Caliph, apprising him of the day's great victory. The dispatch would also include a request for reinforcements; not only of soldiers, but also of men skilled in the art of governing.

The greatest challenge facing Tariq now was how to circumvent the Saracen governor, Musa ibn Nusayr, and stop him from taking credit for today's victory. Thwarting the governor's ambitions would be difficult and the attempt itself would undoubtedly pose a risk to him. But now was the time to be bold and to reach out for the prize, before it was taken away from him. And the prize wasn't King Salomon's gold, the reward that the governor had promised them for defeating the Iberians. Everyone knew the story to be nothing more than a myth and the offer itself was clear evidence that the Saracen governor viewed him and his Berber people with contempt. He had done nothing to dispel Governor Musa's assumption, but he had known from the start that the real prize was Hispania itself. Now that the battle had been won, who was more deserving than him to become the governor of the empire's newest jewel?

Tariq knew that in the coming days, one or more of the advisors Governor Musa had sent him would try to slip away and report the news of the victory to their master. He would not allow that to happen. It was imperative that his own envoy reach the Caliph first, in order to give the man a truthful report of the day's events. That night he would issue orders to have all the Saracen advisors watched. Any of them attempting to leave the camp would be intercepted and killed.

Despite all the measures Tariq had taken, uncertainty still gnawed at him. Had he thought of everything? Could the Christians gather a new army and mount another offensive? Could Governor Musa catch wind of the victory and get to the Caliph first? Did he have enough men and siege weapons to take all the Iberian cities by force?

Only Allah knew.

CHAPTER 26

THE SHEPHERD BOY stood motionless, his flock of sheep foraging on the mountainside, all but forgotten. An oiled leather cowl kept the rain away from his eyes as he gaped at the scene unfolding in the distance below him. He was too far away to see clearly what was happening, as the tiny figures crawling along the valley floor were the size of ants. Nonetheless, he knew that what he was witnessing was a battle of monumental proportions. When he finally managed to tear his gaze away from the valley, he saw with dismay that he had allowed his flock to wander off. He whistled several times, the piercing sound carrying down the mountain slope to the sheepdogs some distance below him.

It was getting dark by the time the young shepherd reached the village. There was an elderly couple just about to enter their house and he told them what he'd seen, his words tumbling out of him in a rush.

His story was met with murmurs of astonishment. Others came out of their homes and soon a crowd began to gather. The shepherd kept recounting his story until an elderly priest in a brown cassock pushed his way through the throng.

"What's this I hear about a battle?" Father Ignacio asked, wispy strands of white hair flying in disarray around his head.

A man in the crowd pushed the young shepherd forward.

"Go on, boy," the man said. "Tell the good Father what you just told us."

"It's t-true," the shepherd boy stammered. "I saw it with my own eyes."

"Where were you, Tulio?" Father Ignacio asked, recognizing the boy.

"I was up on a mountainside by our farm, Father. I was watching our sheep."

"Were you alone?"

"Yes."

"Tell me what you saw."

"There was a battle taking place in the valley, Father, a big one."

"What do you mean 'big'? Were there a few dozen men, a hundred... five hundred?"

"More than that, Father. There were fighting men from one side of the valley to the other."

"Could you tell who they were?"

"No. But one side had horses, the other side didn't."

"Did you see banners or flags of any kind?"

"I was too far away to see any if they had them. I'm sorry."

"That's all right, Tulio. Were they still fighting when you left?"

"Yes, but the side with the horses seemed to be winning."

Father Ignacio continued to quiz the young shepherd, but it soon became clear that the boy had nothing further to add. After reflecting for a moment on what he'd just learned, Father Ignacio turned toward the crowd.

"It's best none of you venture outside the village tonight," he said. "Close your shutters and don't bang your pots or ring any bells. We don't need to announce our presence to anyone out there."

The villagers murmured their assent, then casting fearful glances around them, began to disperse in all directions.

The following morning Father Ignacio awoke at sunrise. He stuffed some rags and strips of cloth along with a bottle of holy oil into a canvas satchel, then slipped his prayer book into the pocket of his cassock. After a final look around his humble quarters, he slung his satchel and a waterskin over one shoulder and walked out the door.

The sun was rising over the mountain tops as he began the long walk down the hillside to the village. As he neared, he spotted a group of some twenty men and women waiting with their handcarts by the side of the road. Behind them stood a large hay wagon, yoked to two oxen, that he had arranged for the previous evening. Its owner, a local farmer, was sitting on the driver's bench ready to set out.

The villagers began calling out to him as he drew near, "Good morning, Father."

Father Ignacio's eyes swept over the group. "What are you all doing here?"

One of the village elders answered, "If you don't mind, we'd like to come along with you to the valley. We thought there might be some metal we could scavenge from the battlefield."

Father Ignacio hesitated. There was an element of grave robbing about the request that he didn't like, but he knew that sooner or later news of the battle would leak out and everyone within walking distance would flock to the site. *Why not give the villagers the first go at it?*

"You can come, under one condition," Father Ignacio told the man. "You help me carry any wounded to the wagon."

"Yes, of course, Father," the elder answered quickly. "We'd be glad to."

It took Father Ignacio and the accompanying villagers the better part of the morning to reach the Guadalete valley. As they walked through the canyon-like entrance, the apocalyptic carnage that had taken place in the valley opened up before them. A gut-churning smell of putrefaction permeated the air. Father Ignacio, though no stranger to death, felt the gorge rise at the back of his throat.

Clutching burlap bags, the villagers dispersed in all directions, on the hunt for swords, knives, spear heads, belt buckles or clasps that the victors might have missed or not bothered to take.

Leaving the villagers to their own pursuits, Father Ignacio began walking through the muck along the corpse-strewn field. Around him, vultures and crows pecked at the banquet before them. As he passed, swarms of black flies took to the air, only to settle down again a moment later around the mouths, noses and eyes of the dead.

Doing his best to ignore the stench, Father Ignacio concentrated on the task at hand: to find survivors that might still be clinging to life. Though primarily relying on sight, he also kept an ear out for any sound, be it a groan, a murmur or a sigh. As his eyes swept the ground from side to side, he began to notice that many of the dead soldiers had small, rectangular holes punched through their helmets. It appeared as if the victors had used some sort of pickaxe to finish off their wounded opponents. He doubted he would not find many survivors.

Hearing someone coming up behind him, Father Ignacio

turned and saw a village elder by the name of Octavio walking in his direction.

"You reckon these are the King's legions we're looking at here, Father?" Octavio asked, gesturing to the bodies lying around them.

"I imagine so, given the numbers," Father Ignacio replied.

"Another rebellion, like the one we saw a few years ago?"

"No, not this time. These soldiers were battling Saracens."

Octavio looked sceptical. "I don't know about that, Father; none of these poor wretches look like Saracens to me."

"They're not," Father Ignacio said. "These men were part of the King's legions. The reason we're not seeing Saracens is because they took away their dead. My guess is we're going to find a great mound of freshly turned earth somewhere further down in the valley."

"We may find a mound, but that won't prove that there are Saracens buried there."

"See the dead horse with the spear sticking out of its chest?" Father Ignacio asked, pointing. "Have you ever seen such a breed of horse before?"

Octavio hesitated then shook his head.

"And that shield over there in the mud with the pointy, iron roundel. Have you ever seen one of our soldiers carrying anything like that?"

"I don't think I have, no."

"That's because they are only used by the Saracens and their allies."

Octavio studied Father Ignacio. "You seem to know a lot about the heathens, Father."

"I've read accounts about them; they've been raiding our churches along our eastern coast for years now."

"This here was no common raid though, was it?"

"No, Octavio, this was a major battle."

"And by the looks of it, the heathens won."

"Quite decisively I'd say," Father Ignacio answered.

Octavio shook his head. "I thought I might be able to have some peace in my old age. No such luck I guess," he added bitterly.

"The world we know is coming to an end, Octavio. We're in for darker times ahead."

"What do you think we should do, Father? Should we seek refuge in the city?"

"Probably not, Octavio. My guess is that the village might be as good a place as any to weather the coming storm."

Octavio nodded somberly, muttered something, then wandered away.

Father Ignacio continued on his way, occasionally bending down to touch one of the bodies. Each time he would be met with the clammy touch of cold flesh. There was a lot of ground to cover and he moved quickly. He didn't want to miss anyone still clinging to life, but he also knew he could not afford the luxury of making too thorough a search.

The morning ended without Father Ignacio finding anyone alive. A sense of hopelessness was stealing over him when he caught sight of movement. A soldier lying face down in the mud had stirred.

Rushing to his side, Father Ignacio knelt down and touched the young man's hand. It was warm.

At the touch, the soldier stirred.

"Rest easy, my son," Father Ignacio murmured. "I'm a priest."

Moving slowly, Father Ignacio turned the soldier onto his back. The man's stomach had been slashed open. The fact that he'd had been lying face down on the ground had kept the wound closed, but now a mix of bile and innards came spilling out. It was clear that the young soldier was at death's door.

"I'm going to give you the last rites, my son," Father Ignacio said quietly.

The soldier's eyes fluttered opened.

"Don't be afraid," Father Ignacio told him. "God is by your side."

Making no attempt to speak, the soldier looked up at him with eyes glazed with pain.

Father Ignacio reached into his pouch for the vial of holy oil. He poured a small amount of the amber liquid into his cupped palm, dipped a finger into the oil, then made the sign of the cross on the soldier's forehead. Just as he finished, a tremor went through the young soldier's body.

Father Ignacio placed two fingers at the side of the soldier's neck. Finding no sign of a pulse, he closed the young man's eyelids. He said a brief prayer, then with a heavy heart, he rose to his feet and continued his search.

By midday, the sun had baked the muddy ground into a hard surface of ridges and furrows. Father Ignacio was trudging along the scarred landscape when he heard one of the villagers calling out in the distance.

"Father; come quick! I found someone still breathing."

As the afternoon wore on, the villagers found four more men alive at different locations on the field. The survivors were taken to the wagon. There, Father Ignacio gave them water, then cleansed and bandaged their wounds.

When the light began to wane, Father Ignacio decided it was time to end his search. There was still a sizeable portion of the field that he had not yet covered, but if he and the villagers didn't head back to the village soon, they'd be caught out on the open road when darkness fell. He didn't like the idea of

abandoning whatever poor soul might still be out there clinging to life, but it would soon be too dark to see anyway. He
would return in the morning, though he doubted that anyone
seriously wounded would survive another night in the open.

He was circling back to the wagon when he heard what
sounded like a moan coming from somewhere close by.
Scanning the surrounding bodies, he narrowed down the possible source to a soldier lying on his side, a broken spear-shaft
protruding from his back. A raven sat perched on his leg, pecking away at an open wound on his thigh. The soldier appeared
unconscious, though Father Ignacio figured that at some level,
the poor wretch must be feeling pain, thus accounting for his
intermittent groans.

Father Ignacio shooed away the raven, then knelt down by
the man's side. Unlike most of the other fallen soldiers who were
clad in chainmail shirts, this man was wearing chased, bronze
breastplates. Judging by his expensive armor as well as his mud-
encrusted red cloak, the priest figured the man was an officer of
high rank, which was surprising, given that he appeared to be
relatively young, mid-twenties Father Ignacio's guessed.

Father Ignacio realized he needed help to deal with the
wounded officer. Rising to his feet, he hailed two villagers in
the distance. "Hey, you there!" he called out to the men who
were pulling a handcart behind them. "Can you come and give
me a hand?"

One of the villagers hollered back, "Be right with you,
Father."

When the two men approached, Father Ignacio wasted no
time giving them instructions. "We need to pull the spear out
of this man's back before we move him. Hold him down in case
he come to his senses."

The two men nodded their assent and got ready. Father

Ignacio grasped the shaft of the spear and pulled out the steel head that had punched through the officer's armor at a point below his left shoulder blade. Thanks to the bronze armor, the spearhead had not penetrated too deeply. The underpadding beneath the breastplates had also kept the spearhead wedged in, keeping the man from bleeding profusely. Now free of the spearhead, the wound started leaking blood at an alarming rate.

With the two villagers helping him, Father Ignacio stripped the officer of his armor, belt and tunic, then bound the wound with one of the bandages he had brought with him. Once he had finished, he turned his attention to the gash on the man's leg. After uncorking his waterskin, he poured some water over what looked like a sword cut to rinse off the dirt, then wrapped a bandage around the wound.

When Father Ignacio had done all that he could, the two villagers placed the unconscious man in their handcart, then wheeled him off to the hay wagon. As Father Ignacio was walking behind them, he noticed that the bandage he had just wrapped around the officer's back was already soaked through with blood.

"He seems pretty far gone," one of the men remarked. "Do you think you can save him, Father?"

"I can set a bone or stitch a small cut, but treating a deep wound requires someone with knowledge of the healing arts, otherwise rot will set in."

"The nearest physician is in Córdoba. This man will be long dead before we ever get him there."

"I know."

"So, what do we do?"

"We are going to take him to Eleni's house."

The villager looked at him in surprise. "The old woman living with her daughter at the river's bend?"

"Yes."

"She's just a midwife, Father. And from what I hear, she only does that on the rare occasion."

"She knows a lot more than midwifery, trust me. The woman's a wonder with healing plants. She can identify everything growing in these parts by its proper name."

"Where did she learn that?" the villager asked.

"It's been passed on through her family, apparently, mother to daughter."

They set off for home well before the sun started sinking beneath the mountain tops. Father Ignacio sat in the wagon with the wounded soldiers, his back pressed against a sideboard. Behind him trailed the villagers, their handcarts creaking under the weight of their scavenged treasures.

Once out of the valley, the caravan continued along the road until they reached the first crossroad. Father Ignacio and the wagon driver bade the villagers farewell, then headed off in a different direction.

It was nighttime when the lumbering wagon rolled up to a small, sod-roofed cottage with lamplight spilling out from its two shuttered windows. Father Ignacio climbed down from the wagon and stretched his aching back. A near full moon in a starry sky provided just enough illumination to guide his way up the path to the front door. The sound of barking erupted from inside the house.

"Eleni, it's me, Father Ignacio," he called out.

After a moment, the door opened a crack and the face of an elderly woman peered out at him. She swept away a lock of gray hair from her eyes and frowned, making no attempt to hide her annoyance.

"Goodness, you gave us a fright, Father. What are you doing here at this hour?"

"I'm sorry to intrude on you like this, but I need your help. There's been a battle in the Guadalete valley. We've found five survivors. They're in the wagon. I thought you could-"

"I'm not running a hospice here," Eleni cut him off brusquely. "Take them somewhere else."

"There's no time for that, Eleni. They'll die if they don't receive immediate treatment."

Eleni's frown stayed in place. "You ask too much, Father. Blanca and I have enough to do around here without having to care for dying men."

"One of the soldiers has some coins hidden inside his belt. They feel heavy, probably gold. I'm sure he wouldn't mind parting with one or two as payment for you saving his life."

Eleni's expression thawed a little.

"I'm sure you could put the money to good use," Father Ignacio said, pressing her.

Eleni hesitated, then opened the door fully. "I suppose I could take a quick look at them."

"God bless you, Eleni."

"Wait here." She said curtly. She disappeared inside, then came out a moment later cupping a lit candle. Behind her followed a large dog that immediately went up to Father Ignacio and began sniffing him.

Ignoring the farmer standing by the oxen, Eleni climbed onto the wagon bed, then beckoned to Father Ignacio to follow her. After he did so, Eleni handed him the candle, then began examining the wounded soldiers, who were all either unconscious or in a daze. With sure, quick movements, she peeled back their bandages and inspected their wounds. When she finished, she straightened and turned back toward Father Ignacio.

"This man and that one over there have lost too much blood. They won't make it through the night," she said in a matter-of-fact tone.

Father Ignacio sighed and nodded.

"That one there with the stomach wound," Eleni said. "He may live a day or two longer but there's nothing I can do for him. The one there in the corner just needs some stitching. You can do that yourself or get one of the women in the village to do it. He should be fine once he regains his senses. Now this man over here has several wounds, most of them minor. But the one in his back is deep and might fester. Probably will, but I think I can help with that."

"You'll be well rewarded if you do, Eleni. He's the one with the coins stitched inside his belt.

Noticing something, Eleni took the candle from Father Ignacio, then held it up close to the head of the soldier they were speaking about. The hair around the man's right temple was matted with blood. She prodded the spot carefully with her fingers.

"Looks like he's also suffered a nasty blow to the head," Eleni said. "Mmm. I can't tell if his skull is broken. If it is, he may never recover. I knew a man once who got kicked in the head by his horse. He never spoke another word again."

"You'll still take care of him though, won't you?" Father Ignacio asked anxiously.

"I'll do what I can."

"Good. I shall pray for his recovery."

His words seemed to irritate Eleni, and she turned away from him impatiently. "Bring him inside. Heaven knows where I'll put him."

CHAPTER 27

HE COULDN'T TELL how long he had been floating in the void, but for the first time it occurred to him to wonder. It could have been a day, a week or a month; it didn't really matter all that much; he had no great need to know. In the void, there was neither fear nor loneliness, nor discomfort of any kind. Yet the thought, like a breeze rippling across the surface of a pond, caused a disturbance in his consciousness. It was faint at first, the merest sensation of unease, then it grew, becoming more insistent. There came the impression of light, followed by a sense of floating upwards, as if from the bottom of a deep well, toward an area of glowing luminescence.

Pain suddenly tore at him. In shock, he opened his eyes. His head was throbbing, and his entire body felt bruised, as if he had been trampled by a horse. The worst of the aches and pains assailing him was a well-defined area of agony halfway down his back. He wanted to sink down into the void again and be free of his misery. But the way back was barred to him now and to his dismay, he was stuck in this harsh, new reality.

Moving slowly, he lifted his head and looked around. He was lying on his side, on a pallet of straw, in what appeared to be a peasant's cottage. The ground was of hard-packed dirt covered with rushes. Light streamed in from two small windows situated on both sides of the door. There were no furnishings, save for a roughly hewn plank table and four stools. Clothing, cooking pots and farm implements hung from hooks nailed to the rafters. At the far end of the cottage, a ribbon of smoke from an open fire spiraled upward toward a hole in the roof. Near the fire by the second window, a young woman sat on a stool. She was mending a garment and seemed unaware of his presence.

The door opened, and an elderly woman walked in. She was stoutly built, with unkept gray hair and a face lined with wrinkles. Upon entering, she noticed him looking at her.

"I was wondering if you'd ever wake up," the woman said.

"Who are you?" he asked, hearing his words come out in a raspy whisper. "How did I get here?"

"My name is Eleni. A village priest found you lying unconscious on a battlefield and brought you here. Do you have any recollection of that?"

With his brow furrowed in concentration, he searched his mind for an answer. In shock he realized that he couldn't remember anything about his past. Every memory seemed to have been expunged from his head. An eerie feeling, as if he was a disembodied ghost, detached from everything and everyone, swept over him. "I don't remember anything," he said finally.

The elderly woman came toward him, holding a cup in her hand. "I've been spooning water into you for three days. See if you can manage to drink on your own."

His hand trembled a little as he reached out for the cup. It was difficult to drink while lying on his side, but he managed to swallow a few mouthfuls of water. After the woman took his cup away, he slipped back into unconsciousness.

The next time he opened his eyes, it was dark outside, and

the cottage was aglow in lamplight. The two women he had seen earlier were sitting around a small table, eating what he guessed was their supper. He tried to remember the name of the older woman. *Helena? Alana?* Whatever her name was, the woman glanced in his direction and noticed that he was awake.

"Feeling any better?" she asked, rising from the table.

"About the same," he said, his voice little more than a whisper. "How long have I been here?"

"Four days."

The woman stood over him, studying him with a critical eye. "Can you recall your name now?"

Though his head still felt as if it was stuffed with wool, the answer came to him after a moment.

"Pelayo," he said. He suddenly remembered the old woman's name too: Eleni.

"Well, Pelayo, you need to build up your strength. Are you up to having a bowl of broth?"

He wasn't hungry, but he supposed that after four days of not eating, he should try to put something in his stomach.

"I think so."

"Good."

Eleni went to fetch a bowl of broth, then came back and knelt at his side. As she helped him sit up, she noticed him wince.

"Your side hurts?" she asked.

Pelayo nodded.

"You probably have one or two broken ribs. Do you have pain anywhere else, besides your back?"

"My head."

"That's not surprising. Someone gave you such a nasty blow. It's a wonder you survived at all. You must have a thick skull."

"My old tutor used to accuse me of that," he answered, moving his right hand up and touching his bandaged head.

Eleni handed him the bowl of broth. "Here. See if you can finish this."

The broth was hot and tasty and Pelayo had no trouble downing it all. Afterwards Eleni eased him down on his side again.

"Can I ask you a question?" Pelayo asked.

"Ask away."

"How many other men besides me survived the battle?" he asked.

Eleni met his gaze. "Only four others, to my knowledge."

Pelayo's mind reeled at the answer. A moment later he lapsed into oblivion again.

When he next awoke daylight was streaming in through the windows. His aches and pains seemed undiminished from the day before. He tried to raise himself up on his elbow, but the effort proved too much for him.

The face of a young woman floated above him, her brow creased with concern.

"You mustn't try to get up yet," she said in a soft, lilting voice. "You have to let your body heal."

The young woman was very pretty up close, with almond-shaped eyes and long, brown hair that fell down her back. She appeared to be much younger than he had first judged, perhaps seventeen or eighteen years of age.

"My name is Blanca," she said. "Are you hungry?"

"Not really."

"You should try to eat anyway. I'm going to prop you up. Ready?"

Pelayo nodded, thinking that the girl had the same no-nonsense character as her mother.

When he was sitting up, Blanca bunched up his blanket and placed it behind him so he could lean back against the wall. "I'm going to get you some food. Try not to fall asleep on me," she said walking away.

Blanca returned and handed him a dish containing some cheese, a few olives, and a slice of dark bread. He was making his way through the meal when Eleni walked in through the door.

"Eating real food?" Eleni remarked. "Good. You must be feeling better."

"Yes, a little," Pelayo said, deciding not to tell her about the burning pain in his back which had gotten worse. Despite his best intentions, he only managed to eat a small portion of the food on his plate.

"I don't think I can eat anymore," he told Blanca. When she came over, he handed her his dish to take away.

Eleni knelt at his side. "I'd like to change your bandage while you're sitting up. It's going to hurt a little. Are you up to it?"

"I think so," Pelayo said.

"Turn around, so your back is to the window."

When Pelayo turned, Eleni peeled away his bandage. Though she tried to do so gently, she tore away the scab sticking to the cloth.

"Hmmm," Eleni said enigmatically from behind him. "I need to put a poultice on this. Hold still, I'll be back."

By nighttime the wound in Pelayo's back was throbbing with pain. He was clammy and his head felt as if it was stuffed with wool. Nobody needed to tell him that the wound in his back was festering.

Night slipped into day, then into night again. In the grip of a high fever, Pelayo lay on his side, drenched in sweat. At other times, he shivered violently from cold. The cycle of day into night repeated itself over and over. Grotesque figures haunted his dreams. Occasionally someone would place a wet cloth on his forehead, and he'd feel a moment's respite.

At last, one morning he opened his eyes and felt wonderfully cool. More importantly, the throbbing pain in his back had receded to a tolerable level.

Noticing he was awake, Eleni came over and touched his forehead. "Your fever's gone. You'll be mending now."

Pelayo nodded mutely.

"Why the long face?" Eleni asked. "You should feel happy you've pulled through."

"My men didn't. The King, my comrades, almost everyone I knew in the world is dead."

"All the more the reason to be grateful that God spared you," Eleni said. "He must have a very special purpose for you."

Yes, Pelayo thought bitterly. *To bear witness to the horrors the Saracens will unleash upon our land.*

CHAPTER 28

STANDING ATOP THE ramparts of the city of Córdoba, bored from staring out at the empty countryside, the sentry caught sight of his replacement striding along the walkway toward him. With luck, he would have enough time to get back to the barracks before the approaching storm hit the city. Already the wind had quickened, and he could taste the rain in the air. "Looks like you're going to get drenched soon," he called out to the bearded soldier approaching.

His replacement shot him a sour look. "You needn't sound so bloody happy about it."

"Probably be some thunder and lightning too."

"Oh, piss off."

"Glad to. See you back at —" The young sentry's smile faded. "Mother of God!"

"What the hell's wrong with you?" the bearded soldier asked, coming to a stop.

"Look behind you!"

The fear in his comrade's voice was contagious and the bearded man turned and scanned the arid landscape stretching out beyond the wall. Except for a couple of horse-drawn carts, every road leading toward the city was deserted. Then his gaze strayed further out, toward the horizon. There, like a carpet of black locusts, thousands of horsemen were swarming across the plain, heading toward the city.

The rhythmic tramping of metal-shod sandals echoed down the hallway, growing gradually louder. Attending Sunday mass in the chapel, Baron Augusto and his retinue found the sound increasingly difficult to ignore. A helmeted officer emerged from the corridor and, ignoring the curious stares of the people gathered there, walked up to the baron standing at the front of the chapel.

Standing before the altar, the priest paused in mid-sentence.

"Forgive me for disturbing you, sire," the officer said, pitching his voice low. "I wonder if I might have a word with you in private."

Known for his quick temper, Baron Augusto frowned at his captain of the guard. "Could this not have waited till later?"

"Unfortunately not, sire."

Baron Augusto followed the captain out of the chapel and into the corridor. Once they were out of earshot, he turned and fixed the officer with a stern look. "All right, let's hear it. What is so important that you needed to interrupt me at mass?"

"There's a delegation of Moors riding toward us, sire."

The baron's peevish expression vanished. "Well then," he said quietly, "I suppose we should go see what they want."

"I took the liberty of ordering your horse saddled, sire."

"Good. I'll meet you at the stable."

Baron Augusto returned to the chapel, beckoned to two of his advisors to follow him, then led them out to the courtyard. After mounting their horses, the three followed the captain of the guard up to the ramparts.

Normally bustling with people at this time of the morning, every street and alleyway in Córdoba was deserted. Just two days after the sentries had spotted the Moors over the horizon, fear seemed to have sucked the life out of the city. There had been a panicked run on the food markets the previous afternoon and today all the shops were shuttered and every stall empty. In stark contrast, the area around the southern gates was thronging with soldiers

After securing their horses, Baron Augusto and his two advisors climbed up one of the ladders that were spaced out at regular intervals along the battlements.

Reaching the top, Baron Augusto stepped carefully onto the walkway, then looked out over the crenellated wall. Below him, some twenty paces away, a party of Moorish horsemen waited in silence.

Baron Augusto focused his attention on a turbaned warrior holding up a spear with a white cloth dangling from its tip.

"I am Lord Augusto," he called out, his deep voice carrying to the Moors. "Do any of you speak our tongue?"

The Moor with the lance nudged his steed forward. "I do. Salaam, my lord," he said in heavily-accented Iberian.

"What is it you want?" Baron Augusto asked.

"I bring you a message from our commandant, General Tariq. He says that he does not wish to spill any blood needlessly. If you open your gates to us, he gives you his word that no harm will befall your people."

Baron Augusto let out a laugh. "That's all we have to do, you say! Just open our gates and everything will be fine? Are you certain you haven't left out any other terms? Like having to turn over our coffers to you or letting you steal our land?"

The Moorish horseman gazed up at Baron Augusto. "There are indeed other terms as you call them. I am certain General

Tariq will be pleased to tell you what they are when you face him on your knees. For now, all you need to know is that if you surrender, he will spare your city from destruction. Resist and you will watch it burn to the ground. You have until the sun goes down to give us your answer."

"You needn't wait," Baron Augusto replied. "I can give you my answer right now. Tell your general that it will be a cold day in hell before I surrender Córdoba to a pack of heathen dogs."

At the baron's side, one of his advisors drew a sharp breath. "Baron Augusto, you should at least consider the offer. We are seriously outnumbered and our supplies—"

Baron Augusto turned to face the advisor, his eyes flashing with anger. "Stiffen your spine, man. Our walls have never been breached. We're going to stand our ground and fight."

Beyond the ramparts, the Moorish horseman lowered his lance. "I will relay your message to General Tariq," he called out. "Farewell for now, foolish lord."

Baron Augusto shouted back, "You and your men have until the count of five to ride away. Then I'll order my archers to shoot you down like the vermin you are."

CHAPTER 29

IT TOOK TEN days before Pelayo felt strong enough to leave his bed. Eleni and Blanca had gone outside to work in the garden, and he was thoroughly bored with staring at the walls. The wound in his back still troubled him, but his other injuries were mending nicely.

Throwing off his blanket, he sat up on his pallet, then slowly rose to his feet. He felt as weak as a newborn infant and he had to husband his strength for a moment before taking a tentative step forward. Feeling as if he might topple over at any moment, he made his way slowly across the room toward the door. He pulled up on the simple latch, pushed the door open, then got his first look at the outside world since he had been brought to Eleni's cottage.

Eleni was on her knees, using a trowel on a small patch of garden near the front door. Catching sight of him, she straightened and gave him a smile. "You're up? Good. How does it feel to be back in the land of the living?"

"I have to say it's nice to feel the sun on my face again," Pelayo answered.

"Yes, I can imagine. It's the little things we miss when we're cooped up inside for too long."

"True." Pelayo looked around. "Where's Blanca?"

"She's gone into town to buy a few things," Eleni said.

"How far is the town from here?"

"It's a morning's walk, there and back."

"Walk? Don't you have a horse?"

Eleni snorted. "Horses are for rich folk. I wager you haven't had to do much walking in your life."

"I've done my share."

"Is that so? How old were you when you got your first horse?"

"Five or six," he admitted.

Eleni raised an eyebrow. "Born with a silver spoon in your mouth, were you?"

"I suppose you could say that."

"I'm sorry, I didn't mean to pry," Eleni said.

"That's all right. I don't mind."

"Are you hungry?" Eleni asked.

"I can wait until you finish."

"In that case I'll get back to the garden. Let me know if you need anything."

Pelayo eased himself down onto a wooden bench by the side of the cabin. Eleni's hound, lately his constant companion, padded over to him and settled at his feet. He leaned back against the wall of the house and studied his surroundings.

Eleni's farm appeared to be rather small and humble, at least by Asturian standards. There was a path that led from the cottage to a dirt road. Beyond was a forest that spread in all directions. To the left of the garden lay a fallow field of about two or three acres. Even from a distance, he could tell that the soil appeared rocky, and dust blown. *It can't be easy for Eleni and Blanca to scratch out a living from this farm.*

As his eyes wandered over the peaceful surroundings, it struck him for the first time since he'd woken up in the cottage that he was glad that he had survived the battle. He did not know what irony of fate had spared him while so many good men had died. But as Eleni had said, who was he to question the will of God?

The days passed and Pelayo grew stronger. Eventually, he began helping Eleni and Blanca with some of the farm's chores.

Pelayo was outside stacking firewood one afternoon when he spotted a figure with a bundle under one arm trudging up the road. To his surprise, the man took the path that led toward the farm. When the figure drew closer, Pelayo saw that he was wearing a priest's brown cassock.

"Looks like you ladies are going to have company," Pelayo called out to Eleni and Blanca who were inside the cottage preparing supper.

The two women came out, wiping their hands on their aprons.

"That's Father Ignacio," Eleni told Pelayo. "He's the one who brought you here."

Pelayo gazed curiously at the priest. "I suppose I owe him my life, don't I?"

"I doubt you would have survived another night in the open."

Father Ignacio gave them a cheery wave as he approached the cottage. "Good morning to you all."

"Good morning, Father," Eleni answered. "What brings you our way?"

"I thought it was high time I checked on my charge."

"Judge for yourself," Eleni said. "His name is Pelayo."

Father Ignacio smiled. "Well met, my son. I must say you're looking better than the last time I saw you."

Pelayo chuckled. "I can well believe that. Thank you for saving my life, Father."

"Just doing God's work. How are you feeling now?"

"I'm on the mend, thanks to these ladies."

"I'm pleased to hear that," Father Ignacio said. "You're a very lucky young man."

"So I've been told."

"Here, I brought you this," Father Ignacio said, handing Pelayo the cloth-wrapped bundle he'd been carrying.

Pelayo took the bundle then pulled away the cloth. A smile spread over his face as he caught sight of a sword with filigreed metalwork on the pommel. "I thought I'd never lay eyes on this old friend again."

"It was half-buried in the mud near where I found you," Father Ignacio said. "I figured that even if it wasn't yours, you might have need of a weapon again one day."

"I just might at that, Father. Seems that I'm in your debt again."

"On the contrary, my son; it is I and everyone else in the land who owe you our gratitude."

"It's kind of you to say so," Pelayo said. There was a moment's silence. "How are the other soldiers you found?"

"I'm afraid three of them have died. There was nothing we could do for them. The fourth soldier recovered and moved on."

"Did he happen to mention where he was going?"

Father Ignacio nodded. "He told us he was heading to Córdoba."

"That's close to here, isn't it? I might just go there myself once I get my strength back."

"I don't think you're going to want to do that, my son," Father Ignacio said. "Córdoba has fallen to the Moors."

There was a sharp intake of breath from Eleni and Blanca.

Pelayo was far less surprised at the news than the two women. The assault on the city made tactical sense. The Moors could not afford to leave a fortified city the size of Córdoba in their wake as they swept northward. But the speed with which they had taken the city was remarkable. "I assume Córdoba surrendered without a fight," he said.

"They didn't surrender. The Moors took the city by force," Father Ignacio said. "They breached the walls in less than two weeks."

There was a momentary silence.

"Do we know what happened to the townspeople?" Blanca asked quietly.

"They slaughtered the men and enslave the women and children. No one was spared."

"Mother of God!" Eleni said, making the sign of the cross.

"You'd be wise to leave this place, Eleni," Father Ignacio said. "You and Blanca are no longer safe here. You should both come and live in the village."

"If the walls of Córdoba couldn't keep the Moors out, what makes you think the village stands a better chance?" Eleni asked.

"Forgive me, I didn't make myself clear," Father Ignacio said. "It's not the Moors that pose a danger to you; it's the people fleeing from them. They're a hungry and desperate lot. Some have formed into bands that are preying on isolated farms like yours, taking whatever they want by force. In the last few days, three farmsteads just west of the river have been sacked."

"We can't exist on air, Father," Eleni said with a note of exasperation in her voice. "What you're suggesting is impossible."

"It's not impossible. The villagers will do what they can to help you."

"You're wasting your time, Father," Eleni said. "I will not abandon my farm, it's the only thing I have in this world."

"Very well, Eleni, I won't press you further," Father Ignacio said. "But you should reconsider your decision, if not for yourself, then for Blanca's sake."

CHAPTER 30

SITTING ON THEIR horses, Rufio and his two men watched the women from the shadows, just inside the tree line, confident that the bright sunlight rendered them invisible. They had learned from their earlier mistakes and their actions now had an air of practiced routine.

One of the women they were watching appeared middle-aged, the other was young and slender, with brown hair that fell loosely down her back. From the distance they could not see if the girl was comely or not, but it didn't matter all that much. None of them were particularly choosy. There didn't seem to be any men around, which made up for the fact that the farm appeared humble and would in all probability yield poor pickings.

"What are we waiting for?" one of the men called Gorro asked in a hushed voice. "There's nobody else there."

Rufio cast a last look around, then gave a nod to Gorro and the second man, Heliodoro. "All right let's go."

Eleni and Blanca were down on their hands and knees in the garden, digging out the last of the turnips, when their hound rose up from his position by the door and began emitting a deep growl.

Shading her eyes with her hand, Eleni scanned the length of the road. *Strange*, she thought to herself, finding no one there. She was about to turn back to her work when she saw three horsemen emerging from the woods in the distance. A shiver ran down her spine as she remembered Father Ignacio's warning about bands of marauders preying on local farmsteads. She suddenly wished that Pelayo hadn't gone to town that morning; not that he would have been able to do much against three men. But having a man at her side would have given her comfort.

She rose to her feet, her gaze fixed on the horsemen as they came toward her and Blanca. Her heart pounding in her chest, she called the hound to her side, then told Blanca to go inside the house and stay there. For once, Blanca did as she was told.

The three horsemen cut across her garden toward her, not caring that they were trampling on her neat furrows. When they got within a few paces from her, they reined in their horses.

"Good morning, Señora," the man in the lead called out." My name is Rufio. How are you today?"

Determined not to let any of the men see her fear, Eleni forced a smile on her face. "I'm well, thank you. Are you looking for directions to the village?"

The man who had addressed her, Rufio, threw a leg over his horse and slid to the ground. Arching his back, he let out a grunt of contentment. He had a strong, powerful body though his waist had begun to thicken, and his dirty, sweat-stained tunic was stretched tightly around his paunch.

Eleni turned her gaze to the other two men as they dismounted. Both were heavy-set, with broad shoulders and corded muscles. *Cut from the same cloth*, she thought. Not having received an answer to her question, she tried again. "Is there something I can do for you?"

"You ladies run this farm by yourselves?" Rufio asked, as he and his men tied their horses to one of the posts holding up the roof-like canopy over the well.

"My husband and son are in town on an errand," Eleni answered, trying to sound casual. "I expect they'll be back any-time now."

"Is that so?" Rufio said, scratching the side of his nose, and looking around.

"If its food you're wanting, I can spare a loaf of bread for you," Eleni said.

"That's kind of you, but we're grown men, not boys" Rufio said good-naturedly. "We need meat."

At Rufio's side, one his men grinned, revealing blackened teeth. "That's right, pink, raw meat."

Eleni's smile wavered. "I have some sausages drying in the house. I can fetch a link or two for you if you'd like."

"I got a better idea," Rufio said. "Why don't you invite us inside? Then we can sit down to eat with that pretty young thing we saw running into your house."

Eleni let out her breath slowly. "You're not here for food, are you?"

Rufio inclined his head in acknowledgement. "Let's say... not just for food."

His two companions snickered.

"I think you'd better leave," Eleni said, hating the quavering note that had crept into her voice.

"Leave?" Rufio said, his eyebrows arching in mock surprise. "We just got here."

"We have nothing of value," Eleni said. "You're wasting your time with us."

Rufio's veneer of pleasantness slipped off like a mask and his eyes turned cold and hard. "The only waste of time is talking to you, old woman," he said, taking a step toward Eleni.

Sensing her distress, the hound at her side bared its teeth and began to growl.

Rufio stopped dead in his tracks.

Eleni grabbed the fur around the hound's neck, holding it back. "Take one more step and I'll set the dog on you."

Rufio stared at the snarling animal, whose eyes were fixed malevolently on him. "Kill the hound," he told his companions.

Before any of the men could carry out Rufio's order, the door of the farmhouse flew open and Blanca came running out.

"Stop!" Blanca yelled at the men, her voice strained with desperation. In her hand she held the sword Father Ignacio had given Pelayo. "Don't hurt my mother!"

"Blanca!" Eleni cried out in dismay. "I told you to stay inside."

"Don't listen to her, Blanca," Rufio called out, his good humor returning. "Come over and join us."

"Go to hell!" Blanca shot back, her chest heaving as she came to a stop at Eleni's side. Though her tone was defiant, she was trembling so much that the tip of the sword she was pointing at the men was bobbing up and down erratically.

Losing patience, Rufio turned toward Gorro, wondering why the devil he hadn't dispatched the hound. But Gorro's attention wasn't on the animal; he was gazing over Rufio's shoulders at something that had caught his eye in the distance.

Rufio turned and saw a man trudging down the road toward the farm. By the weariness evident in the man's slow pace, he was either old or afflicted with some sort of illness. As the man neared, Rufio saw that he was wearing a cheap, threadbare tunic that hung loosely on his lanky frame. Though the man appeared to be in his prime, Rufio dismissed him at once as a potential threat.

Pelayo had spotted the three men talking with Eleni from a distance, but it was only when he saw Blanca running out of the house with a sword in her hand that he realized the seriousness of the situation. As he approached the group, now gone silent, their eyes fixed on him, he could feel the tension hanging in the air.

"This your farm?" one of the three men called out to him.

Pelayo ignored him. "What's happening here?" he asked Eleni and Blanca as he came to a stop before them.

Looking frightened, Eleni answered him in a low voice, "I think these are the people Father Ignacio warned us about."

The rough-looking lout that seemed to be the men's leader called out to him again, "You deaf? I asked you a question."

Pelayo turned to face the thickset man and studied him for a moment before answering. "You and your men should get back on your horses and ride on. There's nothing worth your while here."

The man's gaze slid toward Blanca. "I have to disagree with you on that," he said with a lecherous smile.

"I can see why you'd think so," Pelayo said. "But you'd be dead wrong."

Rufio took a second look at the stranger. Dispassionate gray eyes stared back at him. Despite his shabby appearance, Rufio suddenly felt certain that the man was no ordinary farmer. For one thing his manner was too confident. For another, his stance and the way he was balancing his weight on the balls of his feet, his arms loose by his side, those were all signs of someone who knew how to handle himself. He had ejected many a drunk from the tavern he had once owned, and he recognized trouble when he saw it.

"Last chance to move on, friend," the lanky newcomer said.

Rufio stared at the man, wondering what sort of game he was playing.

"Release the hound, Eleni!" Pelayo shouted, reaching behind his back for the dagger he had tucked into his belt.

Eleni didn't hesitate. "Go Chulo!" she cried, urging the hound forward. "Get him!"

The hound took one bound forward, then leapt into the air.

The thickset ruffian raised his arm instinctively against the hurtling animal, trying to protect his face. The hound clamped its jaws around his forearm, its fangs sinking into his flesh, crunching into bone. Howling with pain, the man made the mistake of trying to shake his arm free. This just made the hound hold on tighter, like a terrier worrying a rat.

Attempting to come to his companion's aid, one of the men skirted around, trying to get a clear strike at the dog.

Pelayo lunged forward and grabbed the man's wrist, immobilizing his sword arm. Before the man could pull himself free, Pelayo rammed his dagger into the man's belly. When the blade sank in up to the cross-guard, Pelayo ripped upwards, cutting the man open.

The third man fumbled feverishly for his sword, appearing stunned at how quickly the situation had spun out of control.

"Here!" Blanca shouted at Pelayo, handing him his sword.

Pelayo grabbed the weapon, then assumed the classic fighting pose: left foot slightly ahead, both hands gripping the pommel of the sword at chin level, blade raised, pointing at the sky.

The man eyed Pelayo warily, then slowly backed away toward the horses. Pelayo followed him, determined not to let him get away, forcing him to turn and defend himself.

Pelayo knew that, when cornered and forced to fight, a man untrained in swordplay will instinctively try to protect his head and chest, forgetting that his legs, ankles and feet were all equally vulnerable.

Stepping in, his sword a blur, Pelayo struck twice. The first blow sliced through the man's left ankle; the second slashed open his right shin. Neither was a killing blow, but they were enough to put the man out of action.

Caught in the hound's vice-like jaw, the third man's forearm was covered in blood. Despite the intense pain he must have felt, he had the presence of mind to reach out for his sword with his left hand. He was on the point of drawing it out when Eleni and Blanca ran up to him and grabbed his arm.

The women's intervention bought Pelayo the time he needed to reach the man. Careful to not injure the women, he thrust his sword into the man's back, between the ribs, aiming at the heart. Pelayo's aim proved true and man went limp then crumpled to the ground.

Blanca covered her mouth with her hands and stared ashen-faced at the blood-soaked scene around her.

Eleni wrapped her arms around Blanca's shoulders and held her tight. "It's all right, Blanca, it's over now," she murmured.

From the corner of her eye, she saw Pelayo walking toward the third man who was on the ground, moaning with pain. Suspecting what was coming, she held Blanca's head down, blocking her view.

Pelayo dispatched the wounded man with a sword thrust to his chest. By the way the man grew still, Eleni knew that the sword tip had pierced his heart. Justice had been meted out, she thought, feeling a grim sense of satisfaction.

"Are you and Blanca all right?" Pelayo called out, walking toward them.

Eleni nodded mutely. She told herself that the nightmare was over and that she and Blanca were safe. But that understanding did little to stop the uncontrollable shaking that had taken hold of her.

It took Pelayo the rest of the day to bury the three men. After returning to the farm, he unsaddled and secured the horses that he had used to haul away the bodies. Taking the men's saddlebags with him, he headed for the cottage.

Eleni was sitting by the table, a shawl draped over her shoulders, mending clothing by the light of a candle. Blanca was sitting on a stool next to her, grinding something in a mortar.

Eleni looked up from her sewing. "You were gone a long time. I was beginning to worry about you."

"I wanted to bury the bodies as far from here as possible."

"That was thoughtful of you, thank you," Eleni said.

"I left the graves unmarked. In a year or two there'll be no trace of the site."

"Good. That's what they deserve, to be forgotten like the animals that they were."

Pelayo slipped the three saddlebags off his shoulder and let them drop to the floor. Eleni and Blanca stared at them as if they were unwelcome intruders in their home.

Pelayo nudged one of the saddlebags with his foot. "They're filled with trinkets, mostly of silver items; pins, clasps, spoons and the like. I thought Father Ignacio might be able to figure out what to do with them."

Eleni nodded.

"You've been gone all day," Blanca said, rising from her stool. "Let me get you something to eat."

Pelayo eased himself down on a stool by the table, feeling really tired. Walking to town that morning, then fighting the three men and burying their bodies had just about drained him of his last reserves of strength.

Blanca placed a bowl of stewed vegetables in front of him and he attacked it with relish, savouring each spoonful. When he was done, he rested his elbows on the table and gazed at Eleni, who had resumed her sewing.

"Is that my military tunic you're mending?" he asked her.

Eleni smiled at him. "I thought you might be getting tired of that old rag we bought you."

"It'll certainly be nice to wear something that actually fits me when I take to the road next week."

Eleni's eyebrows arched in surprise. "You're leaving already?"

Pelayo nodded. He had thought he could ignore the strife plaguing the country by cutting himself off from it. But the attack on Eleni's farm had shown him that trouble was going to find him wherever he was. "I'm pretty well all healed up, Eleni. It's time for me to move on."

"Have you decided where you're going to go?"

"Girona," he said. "I plan to take one of the men's horses with me, the Arabian. You and Blanca can have the other two for yourselves."

Eleni considered the offer. "I suppose one horse might be useful to plow the field," she finally said. "I don't know what we'd do with a second one though."

"You could buy a wagon and use the horses to pull it," Pelayo said.

"Why would I want to do that?"

"So you could pile your belongings into it and find a new place to live."

"And leave behind everything I've worked my entire life for?"

"This farm isn't worth your life, Eleni. You've seen for yourself how dangerous it is for you and Blanca to live here on your own."

"I realize you have my best interests at heart, Pelayo, but what you're suggesting is impossible. We don't have the means to buy a wagon, never mind what we would need to buy land elsewhere. As I told you before, Blanca and I can't exist on thin air."

"You won't need to."

Eleni peered at him with a quizzical expression.

Pelayo unfastened his belt, took out his knife then began snipping away at the stitches running across the bottom seam. Once he'd finished a section, he held the belt by one end and shook it carefully over the table. A stream of coins began spilling out.

Blanca stared at them with round eyes. "I've never seen so much gold in my life," she said in awe.

Pelayo divided the coins into two piles, then pushed one toward Eleni. "This is for you and Blanca, for bringing me back from the land of the dead."

"Goodness, no!" Eleni exclaimed. "That's too much. We appreciate the gesture, but you'll be needing this for yourself."

"There's enough here for all of us, Eleni. Besides, I won't have need of gold where I'm going. I've decided to join Girona's garrison as a soldier. With the threat posed by the Moors, and the inevitable next confrontation with them, I reckon I won't need to worry too much about setting aside funds for my old age."

Eleni looked as if she was going to protest again, but Blanca interjected. "For God's sakes, Mama, Pelayo wants us to have it. It's our one and only chance to start a new life."

"She's right," Pelayo said.

Eleni seemed to wrestle with the question for a moment, then the tension went out of her shoulders. She gazed at Pelayo, her eyes welling with tears. "I don't know what to say, except thank you."

Blanca came around the table, threw her arms around Pelayo and squeezed him tightly. "You've just saved us once again," she murmured, her eyes aglow in the lamplight.

Pelayo smiled. "Consider us even then."

CHAPTER 31

THE WINTER HAD arrived early in the north and the cold weather had made Pelayo's journey to Girona a rather unpleasant affair. The few inns along the road where he might have found shelter for the night were all boarded up. The war with the Moors had killed off trade, and with it the need to provide food and shelter to the merchants and traders who made up the bulk of the inns' regular customers. Luckily, he'd been able to buy food at the villages he had passed through, and most of the time he had found shelter at the churches there as well. Other times he had curled up on the ground with a blanket and slept on the leeward side under a tree.

There was no shortage of travelers on the road however, but most were impoverished farmers and their families whose crops and livestock had been seized by the Moors. With their winter supplies gone, they had been left with little choice but to flee northward, hoping to find sanctuary in the cities that remained free.

Pelayo knew there was a good chance that many of his fellow travelers would die of starvation that winter. And judging by the despair he read on their faces, the farmers themselves were aware of that possibility. He found it difficult not to slip a coin into the hands of men with families, at least those he judged to be in dire straits. After several weeks of this, he found himself with a much-depleted purse and he was glad when he finally reached his destination.

The city of Girona lay at the confluence of two rivers, about a two-day ride inland from the Mediterranean coast to the east. The rivers provided the city with a natural, defensive barrier on three sides. In the south, however, an arid plain left the city vulnerable to a land attack. The city was encircled by stone walls, which from a distance, did not look particularly impressive. He suspected the Moors would have no trouble scaling them with ladders.

As he drew closer to the city, the road began filling with people walking and wagons rolling by. When at last he reached the gates, he dismounted and joined the tradesmen and farmers milling around the armed guards who were questioning everyone before letting them through. When his turn came, the guard's bored expression turned to one of suspicion.

"You're not from these parts, are you?" the guard asked.

"What gave me away?"

"Your horse. Never seen one like it before. It's an Arabian, isn't it?"

"That's right."

"The Moors give it to you?"

"No. I got the horse from an Iberian."

"How did he come by it?"

"I don't know," Pelayo answered. "He didn't say."

"Most people would have thought to ask, don't you think?"

"I guess I'm not the curious type."

"What type are you then?"

Pelayo let out his breath. *That's all I needed, an officious idiot.* "Not the spying kind, if that's what you're implying."

The guard studied Pelayo for a moment. "Wait here," he said, walking away to speak to his superior.

Pelayo cooled his heels until a young, competent-looking officer came marching toward him.

"What's your business here in Girona?" the officer asked him curtly.

"There's a war coming," Pelayo answered. "I thought the city could use another soldier to man the walls."

"Where did you get your horse?"

"From a man near the Guadalete valley," Pelayo said. "He must have found the animal wandering around. The original owner was probably killed in the battle that took place there."

"You're wearing a military tunic. You get that from the man too?"

"No, the tunic is mine."

"You're a soldier?"

"Was, up until a couple of months ago. Third Legion."

The officer's brow furrowed. "Are you saying you fought with the King at Guadalete?"

"Fought and lost," Pelayo answered.

The officer's expression subtly changed. "We heard not many soldiers survived the battle. How did you manage to escape unscathed?"

"I didn't say I escaped unscathed, commander," Pelayo said. "I got the sharp end of a spear in my back."

"Mind showing me the wound?"

Pelayo hesitated, then shrugged. He unbuckled his belt, then along with his sword, he let both drop to the ground. He then turned and pulled up his tunic to bare his back.

"Nasty-looking scar you got there," the officer said. "You're lucky to be alive."

"You're not the first person to point that out to me," Pelayo said, retrieving his belt, scabbard and sword. "The priest that found me said I was only one of six soldiers that survived the battle."

"Those are some odds," the officer remarked. He looked at Pelayo for a moment, then extended his hand. "I'm Commander Lugo."

Pelayo clasped the officer's wrist. "Pelayo."

"Welcome to Girona, Pelayo. Sorry about the interrogation."

"No need to apologize. I know one can't be too careful these days."

Commander Lugo turned toward the guards who were standing nearby. "He's fine."

The guards stepped aside, allowing Pelayo to walk his horse through the gates.

Commander Lugo fell in step beside him. "Mind if I ask what rank you held in the King's legions?"

"Field commander."

Lugo raised an eyebrow. "That's a stroke of luck for us. I'll take you to meet General Forlan. He'll be pleased to have an officer of your rank and experience join us."

"I appreciate the offer, commander, but I've come to enlist in the ranks."

Commander Lugo looked at Pelayo as if he'd just grown two heads. "Why on earth would you want to do a crazy thing like that?"

"I've had my fill of leading men to their deaths. I'd rather let someone else bear that burden for a while."

"It's going to be quite a comedown for you, isn't it?"

"Oh, I don't know, I've gotten used to the simple life lately."

Commander Lugo snorted. "We'll see if you still hold that view once you've tasted the slop they serve to the rank and file."

Pelayo smiled. "I haven't eaten since yesterday morning. Any food is going to taste just fine."

Commander Lugo looked as though he wanted to argue the point further, but then he shrugged his shoulders. "It seems like a waste of your talents to me, but it's your choice I suppose."

They came to a stop in front of a square. Commander Lugo pointed at a building with a wooden sign over the door. "If you're looking for a decent inn, that one there is about the best in the city."

"Looks expensive," Pelayo said.

"You could always enlist today and save yourself the price of a room."

"I might just do that," Pelayo said. "Where does one go to enlist?"

"You can do that in the armory. It's on the other side of the city, by the eastern wall. You'll have to go through an unsavory part of town though, so if you go there, keep an eye on your money pouch, and your horse, of course. These days any animal that can pull a cart is worth a small fortune."

"I'll remember that," Pelayo said, mounting his horse. "Thanks for your help."

The young officer nodded. "Good luck to you, Commander Pelayo."

Pelayo nudged his steed forward and headed down the first of a number of small winding streets. He got lost for a while and found himself going around in circles. At last, he spotted a section of the city walls looming over the rooftops. Shortly after, he came across an inn with a stable next to it. Making a quick decision, he sought out the inn's owner, then negotiated a price for the feeding and sheltering of his Arabian. When he was done, he slung his saddlebag over one shoulder, gave his horse a farewell pat on the rump, then set off on foot toward the armory.

The sun was setting by the time Pelayo reached a squat building with iron-studded doors guarded by two armed soldiers. As he walked up the stone steps to the landing, one of the men threw him an inquiring glance.

"You here to enlist?" the guard asked.

"Thought I'd give it a try."

"Don't worry, they'll take you," the guard said, pulling the door open to let Pelayo in. "You should see the sorry lot we've been getting these days."

The cavernous hall that Pelayo entered was empty, save for a torchlit area where two soldiers were sitting behind a table, staring off into space. He walked over to them, answered a few perfunctory questions, then put his mark on a parchment. Without any pomp or ceremony, his brief stint as a civilian had come to an end.

"Congratulations, you're a soldier now," the recruiting officer said with a note of irony in his voice.

The second soldier at the table sized Pelayo up with his eyes, then handed him a tunic of coarse gray wool and a folded blanket. "Change into this, then go report to the base camp. Do you know where that is?"

"Sorry, I'm new in town."

"Cross the square, then take the road on the right. When you reach the wall, turn left and continue walking until you pass a large field of overgrown weeds. At the end of it, you'll see a bunch of tents."

Pelayo changed into the knee-length, gray tunic he'd been given and stuffed his old one into his saddlebag. With his new blanket tucked under one arm, his saddle bag over his shoulder, he nodded to the soldiers and left the armory.

It was dark by the time he reached the grounds housing the city's garrison. The camp looked like all the others he had seen. Built on the traditional model that stretched back to Roman times, the tents had been laid out on a square grid pattern that could only have come from builders using a groma, a cruciform wooden frame with plumb lines at four ends of the crossbars. The tool ensured that the camp's perimeter met at precise angles and that the pathways between the tents crisscrossed in neat, evenly spaced lines. Encircling the outer perimeter of the camp was a deep trench flanked by earthen ramparts. The only access point into the camp was through a swing gate structure that could be defended against a frontal attack. That night, two spear-wielding soldiers were standing guard behind the wooden barricade, eying his approach.

"I just signed up at the armory," Pelayo told the two men.

"Good for you," one of the guards answered.

"Where do I go now?" Pelayo asked.

The second guard, more helpful than his companion, pointed in the distance. "They've set up a tent for new recruits over there. It's the first one on the right, down the fourth row. See it?"

"I think so," Pelayo said, peering through the gloom at the rows of neatly set up tents, their interiors aglow in lamplight.

"There should be room in that tent for you, the guard said. If not, someone there will tell you where to go."

Pelayo had expected a more formal admittance procedure, but having never before enlisted as a common soldier, he supposed this sort of reception was normal. After being waved in, he headed down one of the paths running through the grounds. When he reached the tent the guard had indicated, he opened the flap and stepped inside.

His entrance drew the gaze of every man in the tent,

including the six on the floor who were playing dice. Ignoring their curious stares, he made his way along the central aisle toward a cot that appeared vacant. As he neared it, he caught the eye of a man lying on the adjacent cot.

"This one free?" Pelayo asked.

"So far."

Pelayo unbuckled his scabbard, took off his sandals, then shoved his belongings under the cot. The noise level in the tent returned to normal again. He lay down on the stretched canvas, drew his new blanket over himself, then with a sigh of contentment, closed his eyes. The previous twenty-four hours soon faded into a blur.

It seemed like only an instant later, when a sharp poke in his ribs jarred him awake.

"What do you think you're doing?" a bearded face snarled down at him.

Pelayo sat up, rubbing his recently healed ribs, as he stared at the person who had woken him up. The man had the scarred cheeks and flattened nose of a tavern brawler. The bad news was that the insignia of a squad leader was embroidered on the front of his tunic.

"Something wrong?" Pelayo asked, trying to get his mind working again.

"On your feet when you address me."

Pelayo rose, then stood by his cot facing the squad leader. The man was a hand's-breadth shorter than him, but heavier in build, with broad shoulders and a thick neck.

The squad leader pushed his bearded face close to Pelayo's. "You think you can just wander in here and do whatever you please without checking with anyone?"

"It was late," Pelayo said. "I thought I'd advise whoever I needed to in the morning."

"You're not here to think; you're here to follow the rules."

"That's hard to do when you don't know what they are."

"Then you shut your mouth and do as you're told until you learn them."

Pelayo said nothing.

"Seeing as you've already had your rest, you can go and stand first watch."

Pelayo kept his face expressionless. "I guess I can use the fresh air."

The squad leader's eyes narrowed. "Since you enjoy the outdoors so much, tomorrow you can dig out the latrines. Anything else you want to add?"

This time Pelayo decided to hold his tongue.

"Go find the officer of the night watch and report to him,"

Pelayo glanced around at the faces of the twenty or so men in the tent who were staring at him. Hitching his shoulders, he walked down the aisle toward the tent's exit. *It's going to be a long night.*

The following weeks dragged on with mind-numbing monotony, the hours filled with training exercises that Pelayo found both dull and physically demanding. Every day seemed more or less the same as the one preceding it.

A trumpet blast would rouse him and his tentmates at dawn. After putting on their uniforms, they'd hurry outside and join the recruits spilling out from the other tents. They would stand for a general inspection, then march out to the training grounds outside the walls. There, they would stomp up and down the field, drilling until they heard the noon bell tolling in the distance. That was the signal to break off and return to camp for the main meal. In the afternoon they would strap on their campaign packs and go out on patrol, a circuit that took them around the perimeter of the city.

They would return to camp around dusk, hungry and tired, many suffering from bleeding blisters on their feet. After a mandatory wash-up at the troughs, they'd line up at the food stations and wait their turn to be served by the cooks and their assistants. Once they'd eaten, they'd sit out by the campfires, then retire to their tents to spend their last waking hours talking or playing dice before someone snuffed out the candles.

Due to his military training, Pelayo adapted far more quickly to the daily routine than did his tentmates, who all struggled with the physical demands of the exercises, as well as with the execution of the maneuvers they were learning. He couldn't help but compare their bumbling performances with those of the King's legions, with their effortless efficiency and ironclad discipline. He realized it wasn't a fair comparison to make, of course, as it took months, if not years to forge men into soldiers. It also required officers who could not only teach their men the skills they needed to survive in combat, but who could also lead by example. Unfortunately, that last attribute, and others such as sound reason and good judgment, were completely lacking in Quintus, their squad leader.

Pelayo had Quintus pegged as a typical example of the sort of man one should never elevate to a position of power. These men had force of character and ambition but lacked compassion and self-restraint. They also tended to hold convictions rooted in ignorance. If they had any friends at all, they were of the same ilk, brutish and mean-spirited.

Putting these men in command of raw recruits inevitably turned them into petty tyrants. But Quintus' zeal for discipline as well as his penchant for cruelty far exceeded the norm. In the previous two weeks, more than a third of the men in the squad had been singled out for punishment, usually in the form of some menial task that required them to spend half the night carrying it out. This robbed the men of the restorative sleep they needed, which then made it difficult for them to perform well the following day. Quintus' idea of discipline ended up entrapping the physically weaker men in a cycle of failure and punishment from which it was difficult to escape.

Pelayo was confident he could get through the coming months, no matter how challenging the ordeal. But he wondered if the relentless pressure might prove too heavy a burden for some of his tentmates.

He didn't have to wait long to get his answer.

He first noticed that some of the men in the squad were spending more time in Quintus' company than was necessary. They hung onto his every word, laughing a little too loudly at something he said, clearly currying favor with him. Then they started baiting the men who had been singled out by Quintus as clumsy or lazy that day.

It soon became obvious that everything anyone said or did throughout the day was finding its way to Quintus' ears.

Their monotonous routine came to an end one November morning when Quintus lined up the men and informed them that they were now ready to start combat training. After passing out blunted swords and shields to everybody, he marched them off to the training grounds outside the city.

Bringing up the rear, Pelayo kept an eye on the youth Ramundo, marching at his side. Though they were only less than halfway to their destination, the lad already appeared winded.

"Try to match your breathing to the pace of your steps," Pelayo told the young overweight recruit.

Ramundo looked at Pelayo with a resigned expression. "I

don't think that's going to help," he answered, panting lightly. "I'm just not good at this soldiering business."

"You'll get better with practice," Pelayo said.

"You really think so?"

"Of course," Pelayo replied, looking away. The truth was that Ramundo wasn't cut out to be a soldier. It just wasn't in his bones. He should have stayed home and helped his father run the family farm.

Ramundo had only recently joined the squad. Within days of his arrival, it became apparent to everyone that he was slow and uncoordinated. When he started dragging down the standing of the squad, Quintus began riding him mercilessly. Most of the men felt sorry for him and left him alone, but Quintus' pack had gone after him like wolves on the trail of a wounded stag.

Pelayo couldn't recall a single day in the previous week that Quintus' sycophants hadn't pulled some sort of prank on Ramundo, such as hiding his sandals or unmaking his bed. Pelayo had done what he could to protect the youth, but he knew there was a fine line beyond which he would just be making things worse for the lad.

Now the squad came to a halt at the edge of the empty field they'd been using as a training ground. A few other squads were there already, doing drills with various weapons. At the far end of the field, a group of archers were practicing on straw targets. Up on a hillock, keeping an eye out on their men, stood a handful of squad leaders. Catching sight of Quintus' arrival, one of the men in the group broke away and began walking toward them. Pelayo recognized the man as one of Quintus' friends. Along with another squad leader called Morrisco, the three usually spent their evenings together, sitting and talking around a fire.

The man approached Quintus, exchanged a few words with him, then walked over to address Pelayo and his squad.

"My name is Habel, your new combat instructor. I'm going teach you how to use the sword, one of the most difficult weapons to master. I don't expect any of you to become great swordsmen, but if you work hard at it, you might just learn enough to survive your first battle. So pay attention, your life depends on it."

Habel proceeded to demonstrate the basic moves of sword play: the thrust, the parry, the block, the swing, the correct angle of the elbows, the position of the legs and feet, the shifting of the weight to give power and speed. Keeping his movements slow and deliberate, he demonstrated how to use the shield both as a defense and as a weapon. Next, he showed them the correct stance to fend off different types of attacks. When he had finished, he repeated all the movements again, slowly.

"All right," Habel called out when he was done. "Let's see what you've learned. Who wants to go first?"

Every man in the squad remained silent. By now they had all learned the folly of volunteering for anything.

The silence stretched on until Quintus called out from the side, "Ramundo! Get out there."

Appearing startled at having been singled out, Ramundo hitched his shoulders, marched forward and came to a stop before the combat instructor. Just like he'd been shown, he raised his shield and held his sword in front of him.

Habel circled around the youth, then closed in, swinging his sword in a broad arc.

Ramundo tried to parry the blow, but his sword went flying out of his hand.

Habel shook his head in disgust. "Pick up your sword, boy. Try holding on to it this time."

Looking embarrassed, Ramundo recovered his weapon, then assumed a fighting stance. He looked even more ill at ease than he had the first time.

The combat instructor feinted to the right, then unleashed a low, horizontal blow. The flat end of his sword smacked into Ramundo's thigh.

Ramundo let out a yelp of pain. Tucking his sword under his armpit, he vigorously rubbed his leg with his hand.

"Let's go again, boy!" Habel called out.

His face red, Ramundo nodded in reluctant assent.

With quick, nimble steps, Habel closed in again, raining blows on Ramundo. The youth cowered behind his shield, making no attempt to strike back with his sword. As he backed away, he stumbled over a rock and fell on his backside.

Standing over him, Habel shook his head in dismay. "You're pathetic."

Ramundo scrambled to his feet.

"Use your sword, you idiot," Habel called out. "Keep your opponent at bay."

Ramundo's head bobbed up and down in assent.

Habel went on the attack again. With contemptuous ease, he swatted away Ramundo's weapon, then struck him on the side of his helmeted head with the flat end of his sword.

Ramundo wobbled on his feet, his sword slipping to the ground from his slackened grip.

Watching from the distance, Pelayo felt his anger stirring. It was one thing to teach a recruit swordplay and quite another to humiliate him in front of his comrades. "Hey Quintus," he called out, "Anyone else going to get a chance to practice today?"

"Who said that?" Quintus called out, gazing at the squad.

"I did," Pelayo said, stepping forward.

Quintus's lips stretched in a tight smile. "Ah, Pelayo. Anxious to go next, are you?"

"I don't want to pass up on the chance to learn from a master swordsman," Pelayo said.

Quintus exchanged glances with Habel, who gave him a nod.

"It's your lucky day," Quintus called out. "You get to go next."

Pelayo strode forward. As he passed Ramundo, the youth caught his eye and gave him a grateful look.

Coming to a stop several paces away from the combat instructor, Pelayo unslung his shield, slipped his left arm through the first loop, then gripped the second tightly.

"This is just a training lesson, right?" Pelayo asked, unsheathing his sword and testing its balance.

Habel flashed him a smile. "What's the matter, getting cold feet already?"

Pelayo shrugged. "Just want to know the rules."

"You make a mistake, you learn a painful lesson. It's not complicated."

"Just so I know."

"All right…let's see what you've got," Habel said, testing Pelayo with a playful, darting jab.

Pelayo parried the blow with a compact flick of his wrist, then held steady.

Habel lowered his head, then launched a blistering attack, forcing Pelayo to give ground.

Pelayo waited until Habel began to tire, then planted his feet and struck back hard, putting every ounce of muscle into the blow.

Habel blocked Pelayo's sword with his shield, but the force of the strike sent him staggering back.

Pelayo could have gone after him then, disarming him or worse, but he held back.

Habel resumed his stance, looking far more wary than before. "I see you've handled a sword before."

Pelayo gave him a hard smile. "What's the matter, getting cold feet?"

Habel clenched his jaw as he came for Pelayo again.

As the two exchanged a few, exploratory blows, Pelayo studied the instructor's fighting style. Habel was an accomplished swordsman, no doubt about it, but his approach was more blunt force than guile. His Achille's heel, however, was the unconscious telltale sign he gave off before striking out with his sword.

When Habel next lowered his shield and shifted his weight to his right leg, Pelayo was ready. Instead of parrying the blow, he stepped nimbly to the side. Habel's sword flashed by in a downward strike. Encountering empty air, Habel stumbled forward, thrown off balance once more.

One of the men in Pelayo's squad let out a snicker.

Habel's eyes narrowed with anger as he brought up his shield. Weaving his sword from side to side, he went on the attack again.

The contest, for that was what it had become, grew more intense, as both men exchanged hard, swift blows. Strike, block, parry, strike, block, thrust, parry… The cycle went on and on. There was little pretense anymore that this was a training session.

Pelayo could have disabled Habel half a dozen times or inflicted some real damage. But doing so would have brought his newfound military career to an inglorious end. Instead he chose to go on the defensive, lulling Habel into a state of complacency, while he watched for another chance to strike back. When the opening came, he stepped out of the way from the downward sweep of Habel's sword.

For the second time, Habel found himself off balance.

"Shall we try that again?" Pelayo called out, repeating the words Habel had used on Ramundo.

More men in the squad laughed.

Habel's grim expression made it clear that he didn't like being mocked.

The clash between Pelayo and Habel began drawing the attention of some of the other soldiers on the training grounds. Even those who knew little of swordplay could see that one of the two men fighting was clearly dominant and was passing up many opportunities to put his opponent away.

Growing bored of being on the defensive, Pelayo decided he had had enough and went on the attack. Hammering blow after blow, he drove Habel back, forcing him to hide behind his shield.

Quintus finally held up his arm and cried out, "All right, that's enough."

Pelayo stopped his attack.

After a moment's hesitation, Habel lowered his shield, panting heavily, his face drenched with sweat.

Quintus walked up to Pelayo and stared at him, as if seeing him for the first time. "Where did you learn to fight like that?"

"I just picked it up here and there."

"Is that so?" Quintus said, the look on his face making it clear he thought Pelayo was lying. "All right, get back in line."

When Pelayo rejoined his squad, the man on his left whispered to him, "You fight like you were born with a sword in your hand."

Pelayo thought of all the instructors his father had provided for him over the years. *That's pretty close to the truth*, he thought to himself.

"Hey," the man on his right whispered. "Think you could teach me some of those fancy moves of yours?"

"I suppose so," Pelayo answered.

"How about me?" another man asked. "Could you teach me too?"

That night, Ramundo approached Pelayo as he was lying on his cot.

"Can I have your sword, Pelayo?"

Pelayo gazed at the youth in surprise. "What for?"

"I've got to file away the nicks on everyone's swords, because of how badly I did in training this morning."

"It's all right, Ramundo, you can skip mine. I'll do it myself."

Ramundo's expression brightened. "You sure?"

"Yes." Like most people who owned a knife, Pelayo kept a small steel rasp in his kit.

Ramundo thanked Pelayo, then moved on to the man in the next cot, a former blacksmith's apprentice called Ambrosio. He was about to hand over his sword to Ramundo when he sensed Pelayo staring at him. Though Pelayo's expression was neutral, Ambrosio seemed to think better of the idea.

"Ach, you'll only cock it up, Ramundo," Ambrosio said. "Best I do it myself."

Shortly after dawn the following morning, Quintus ordered the squad to form a line outside. After telling them to draw out their swords, he began inspecting the blades, checking the edge of each man's blunt weapon with his thumb. As he neared Ramundo, he grew puzzled by the boy's alert demeanor. *How did the idiot manage to accomplish the task I gave him and still look so well-rested?*

CHAPTER 32

THE DAY BEGAN as any other for Pelayo. After a quick breakfast of dark bread and honey, he spent the morning doing various drills. After four months, nearly every soldier in the squad could march the entire morning with a loaded pack on his back and handle a sword with a degree of proficiency. The lone exception was Ramundo, who continued to lag behind in every category.

By now, everyone seemed to have come to accept that Ramundo was going to keep them at the bottom of the squad rankings. They also realized it wasn't the lad's fault that he was slow and clumsy. In any case, his failings were more than offset by his qualities. The lad did not have a mean bone in his body, and that went a long way to endear him to most of the men in the squad. Instead of poking fun at him, or badgering him for his shortcomings, most everyone had taken him under their collective wing. Though they did what they could to protect Ramundo from Quintus and his group of sycophants, they weren't always successful as an incident that afternoon showed.

They were eating their midday meal at the camp when

Quintus had walked up to Ramundo and dumped an armload of waterskins at his feet.

"Didn't I tell you to fill these up?" Quintus asked, glaring at Ramundo.

Looking flustered, Ramundo scrambled to his feet. "I'm sorry, I thought it'd be all right if I took care of it after I finished eating."

"Did I say you could do it later?"

Ramundo shook his head mutely.

"What? I can't hear you."

"No, Quintus."

"All right, you're done eating. Go fill up these waterskins, then put them in your pack. You are going to carry them this afternoon. Next time I give you an order, you carry it out immediately, understand?"

"Yes," Ramundo mumbled, gazing down at the three waterskins belonging to Quintus and two of his toadies.

Sitting nearby, Pelayo saw the look of dismay on Ramundo's face. On a long march, every extra ounce of weight one carried made a big difference. By the end of the afternoon those three waterskins were going to feel as heavy as a millstone to Ramundo.

When they finished eating, Pelayo and the other men in the squad retrieved their campaign packs from their tent, then reassembled outside in a column of two abreast. Quintus assumed the point position, then led the squad out of the camp on their daily march around the city.

Bringing up the rear of the column as usual, Ramundo managed to keep up as they made their way out of the city. Soon after passing through the gates, however, he began to struggle to stay abreast of the man marching at his side.

Positioned in the column directly ahead of Ramundo,

Pelayo slowed down until he was walking between the youth and his marching companion.

"Do me a favor, Ambrosio," Pelayo said. "Take my place for a while."

Ambrosio gave Pelayo a curious look, then shrugged his shoulders. "Yes, sure, why not?" he said, picking up his pace.

Pelayo fell in step beside Ramundo. "How are you holding up?"

"Getting a bit tired, to be honest," Ramundo said, perspiration beading on his forehead.

"I have an idea. Let's trade packs. It'll give you a chance to catch your breath."

"You sure you want to do that?"

Pelayo nodded. "Let's do it quickly, so no one notices."

Ramundo craned his neck to peer at the front of the column where Quintus was marching along, seemingly oblivious to anything happening in his rear, then furtively switched packs with Pelayo.

Quintus kept the squad marching at a steady pace as they began their circuit around the city. After marching for several hours, they came upon a rise overlooking the river. The spot marked the halfway point in their march and they usually stopped there for a short rest. As they trudged up the grassy rise toward a stand of trees, Pelayo and Ramundo switched packs again.

After coming to a halt, everyone shrugged off their packs and sank to the ground.

"Ramundo!" Quintus called out as he strode toward him. "Break out the waterskins."

Getting to his knees, Ramundo reached for his pack, pulled out the waterskins, then handed them out to Quintus and the two men who came to join them.

After Quintus and his companions drank their fill, they handed the depleted waterskins back to Ramundo, who then stuffed them back into his pack.

When they were preparing to march out again, Pelayo and Ramundo surreptitiously traded packs once more. Pelayo thought no one had noticed the switch until Ambrosio, the man who'd originally been marching with Ramundo, sidled up to him.

"If you don't mind my saying so, Pelayo, you're looking a little spent," Ambrosio said, his face deadpan. "Why don't we trade packs for a while?"

Pelayo, whose shoulders were a little raw from the straps chaffing his skin, considered the offer. "It's rather heavy…"

"Well yes; that's the point, isn't it?"

Pelayo smiled.

The switch was made quickly and without anyone apparently taking notice. But some time later Pelayo saw Ambrosio switch packs with his marching companion. It seemed that the squad had finally come together as a single unit.

They were on their last leg of the march, heading back toward the city, when Quintus glanced over his shoulder to check on Ramundo. Remarkably, the farm boy seemed to be bearing the extra weight in his pack with admirable fortitude. Perhaps he had underestimated the progress Ramundo had made over the past few weeks. After all, he supposed even a donkey could learn a trick or two with enough prodding of the stick.

Coming to the end of their march, as was often the case when the weather permitted, Quintus called for a rest by the bank of the river, just outside the city walls. The stop was meant to give his men a chance to wash away the dust and grime of the road before making their way back to camp.

Habel and his squad had beaten him to the riverbank that afternoon, and he gave Quintus a friendly wave.

As the men began collapsing on the ground, Quintus spotted Ramundo some distance away. The youth looked tired, but no more so than anyone else. This just didn't smell right to him. As he pondered over the mystery, a possible explanation occurred to him. Letting his pack fall to the ground, he made his way through the seated men toward the farm boy.

Everyone around Ramundo seemed to find something with which to busy himself. The lone exception was Pelayo, who was sitting on the grass next to Ramundo, gazing back at Quintus with his usual thinly veiled insolence.

Quintus had, over the years, honed his ability to sense when his men were trying to pull the wool over his eyes. And that feeling was strong in him now. He was fairly certain that someone in the squad had helped Ramundo carry his pack. He had obviously made a mistake by not ordering Ramundo to march at the front with him. *Well, we'll see who gets the last laugh, you little bastard.*

"You held up pretty well today, Ramundo" Quintus called out, smiling, as if in admiration. "All that extra weight and you hardly look winded."

Sitting on the ground, untying his sandal, Ramundo looked up warily at Quintus. "I just paced myself, like you always tell us to do."

Quintus' pleasant expression vanished. "Open your pack." he said, his tone hard and flat.

Ramundo hurried to comply.

Quintus reached down and upended the pack, spilling its contents on the ground. Amongst the scattered items were several nearly empty waterskins. Straightening, he fixed his gaze on Ramundo. "I know you didn't carry your pack all this way by yourself. Who helped you with it?"

Ramundo flushed red. "N-no one," he stuttered.

"You're lying; I can see it on your face."

"I'm not," Ramundo said unconvincingly.

Quintus' eyes bored into Ramundo. "I'm going to give you one last chance to tell me the truth."

Ramundo said nothing, but as the silence stretched, he began squirming under Quintus' piercing stare.

"All right, we'll do it the hard way," Quintus said with an ominous shake of his head. "I'm going to get to the truth, and when I do, I'm going to come down hard on you, boy. You can count on that."

After Quintus stalked away, Pelayo caught Ramundo's eye and gave him a nod of approval. The lad had done well, he thought. If he could keep his nerve and say nothing, Quintus would never be able to prove his suspicion.

Dismissing the incident from his mind, Pelayo stripped to the waist and headed down to the river. It had been raining for the last few days and the Rio Ter was engorged with brownish water. Stepping gingerly over the sharp stones, he waded thigh deep into the river, then began scooping water over his head. When he felt clean again, he made his way back up the bank to where he had left his pack and his clothing. He wiped himself down with his tunic, then sat down and watched the reddening sky, letting the evening breeze dry him off.

He was slipping his tunic back on when he noticed some commotion taking place at the river's edge. At first he couldn't quite make out what was happening, then everything fell into place. Quintus' friends Habel and Morrisco were holding the struggling figure of Ramundo between them. Habel had Ramundo's neck in the crook of his arm and was forcing the boy's head down into the water. Morrisco was laughing as Ramundo thrashed about, trying to come up for air.

Pelayo rose to his feet, swearing under his breath, as he watched Ramundo wriggle free from Habel's grasp.

Anxious to escape his tormentors, Ramundo splashed through the water toward the bank. The two men launched themselves after him. Just before they closed in, Ramundo ducked under their arms and darted away in the opposite direction, back toward the middle of the river.

Pelayo saw at once that Ramundo had made a grave mistake. Although the river was shallow near the banks, its depth increased rapidly as one moved toward the center. There, the current was flowing swiftly, posing a threat to anyone foolish enough to wander into its watery embrace.

Concerned only with getting away from his two tormentors, Ramundo did not realize the danger he was getting into until the river was lapping at his chest. Finally becoming aware of his predicament, he turned and tried to head back toward the shallow end. Fighting the current, he managed a few steps, but then lost his balance. At once the turbulent waters swept him off his feet and began carrying him downstream.

Pelayo set off at a splashing run along the shallow end of the river, his gaze locked on Ramundo, now fighting desperately to keep his head above water.

"Don't panic!" Pelayo hollered at the top of his lungs. "Try to swim for shore!"

Pelayo ran on, his gaze sweeping the river ahead of him, searching for a stretch of calmer waters so he could wade in and pull Ramundo out.

His frustration grew with each passing moment. He ignored the needles of pain from stepping over the jagged-edged stones lining the shallows. Twice he attempted to veer in deeper, but each time he was forced to draw back when he felt himself being sucked in by the current.

Ramundo, obviously tired from the day's march and no great swimmer to begin with, began to disappear beneath the surface of the water for longer and longer periods. Finally, on a particularly turbulent stretch of the river, Ramundo sank from sight and never resurfaced again.

Pelayo kept running until his breath began burning in his lungs. When at last he gave up hope, he found himself more than half a league away from where he had left the squad. Feeling drained, he stood on the bank, his chest heaving, unable to wrench his gaze away from the rushing water. He stood there for a long time, feeling as if a giant hand was squeezing his chest, making breathing painful.

Ramundo's gone, Pelayo thought in shock. He was aghast that their regular stop at the river's edge had ended in such a tragic manner. Ramundo had been a good lad, big hearted and courageous, absorbing the endless attacks leveled at him without a word of complaint or a sign of bitterness. A sense of deep sadness and loss took hold of Pelayo.

The passing of someone one cared about was always difficult, more so when it was sudden and unexpected, such as that resulting from an accident. But Ramundo's drowning had been no mere twist of fate; he had been hounded to death.

Night was falling as Pelayo began the long trek back along the riverbank to where he and his squad had stopped to wash up. When he reached the area, he found it deserted and his belongings gone. Quintus hadn't even had the decency to wait for his return.

The sky was full of stars by the time Pelayo reached the campgrounds. The guards at the gate knew him by sight and let him through without questioning him. There was a knot of anger seething in his belly and despite his weariness, his gait was quick and determined. The glow of the campfires lit his way as he stalked down the paths between the tents, searching for Quintus.

Habel watched Quintus sop up the last of the gravy in his dish with a piece of bread, popped it into his mouth, then wiped his greasy fingers on his tunic. The light of the campfire played over his face as he fixed Habel with a baleful look.

"Are you going to keep yapping about this all night?" Quintus asked.

Habel was not used to being addressed so disrespectfully and he stared back at Quintus, weighing his response. He was no coward, but he had long admitted to himself that Quintus intimidated him. Hell, the bastard intimidated everybody. At first glance, the broken nose, the scarred face and heavy brow marked Quintus as just another run-of-the mill brawler, a mean drunk who enjoyed picking fights and was good with his fists. But Quintus was more than that; he was cunning and smart. That combination made him a dangerous man to cross and Habel knew it.

When Habel said nothing, Quintus snorted. "You worry too much. It was just an accident. That's what I reported and that's what everyone is going to think in the morning. So forget about it, all right?"

Habel nodded uneasily. Since the incident at the river, every man in his squad was avoiding him. Although no one had said anything to him, he could feel their eyes on him, blaming him for the farm boy having been swept away.

Morrisco came over to join them, a dish of food in one hand, a cup of watered wine in the other.

"Where have you been?" Quintus asked, stifling a yawn. "We're just about finished eating."

Morrisco sat down cross-legged on the ground, then cradled his plate between his knees. "I had to take my turn at the back of the line," he said in an aggrieved tone. "Nobody would let me cut in."

"They wouldn't, eh?" Quintus said, looking unconcerned. He pulled out a knife from his belt and began honing the blade on a whetstone. "We'll have to take care of that tomorrow,"

Habel was the first to catch sight of Pelayo striding down one of the paths between the rows of tents. Habel couldn't say what it was that made him think there was going to be trouble, but he knew it just the same. Perhaps it was the way the arrogant son of a bitch was walking, neither hurrying nor casual, his eyes fixed on them, like he was a goddammed arrow and they were the target. He looked across the campfire at Quintus and Morrisco, suddenly glad of their company. The three of them were more than a match for anyone. If the bastard stepped a hair out of line, they would have all the excuse they needed to pound him into a bloody pulp.

Pelayo felt Quintus tracking him with his eyes as he approached the campfire.

"What the hell do you want?" Quintus asked, an undercurrent of menace in his voice.

"Did you send those two lice of yours to harass Ramundo at the river?" Pelayo said.

"No, it was their own idea. Isn't that right boys?"

Habel glanced at Morrisco, who answered for both of them, "Yeah, sure."

Ignoring the two men, Pelayo's gaze remained locked on

Quintus. "You're a pox-ridden liar. I know they were following your orders."

Quintus' eyes narrowed. "I'd watch my tongue if I were you. Habel and Morrisco were just having a little fun with the boy. If the fool drowned, it was his own damned fault."

"It wasn't," Pelayo said. "You bullied him for months, then hounded him to his death. Now you're going to answer to me for that."

"Is that so?" Quintus drawled. Unfolding his legs, he rose slowly to his feet. "I thought you were smart. Turns out you're just another dumb bastard who doesn't know when to walk away from trouble."

"You don't scare me, Quintus. I've run across blowhards like you my whole life."

"All right, have it your way," Quintus said with a sigh, nodding to Habel and Morrisco.

The two men got to their feet, then came to stand at Quintus' side.

"Come on," Pelayo said. "What are you waiting for? There's three of you against me."

What the men didn't know, however, was that Pelayo had come prepared for those odds. The knife tucked into his belt, in the small of his back, he'd use on Quintus in the first moments of the fight. He'd either slash open Quintus' throat or plunge the blade into his heart, depending on which target presented itself first. He would then face off with Habel and Morrisco. Armed with his knife, and with the element of surprise on his side, he though he'd have a decent chance of taking the two men down. When and if he prevailed, he would leave the scene before the ruckus attracted the attention of one of the officers, who in the evenings normally kept to their barracks. With a bit of luck, he'd be able to reach his horse, now tethered outside the camp, saddled and ready to beat a hasty retreat out of the city. Whatever the outcome, his time here had come to an end. He could no longer serve under Quintus' command. And he owed it to Ramundo to exact a measure of justice.

"You think I need help fighting you?" Quintus asked Pelayo.

"Of course. You're too dumb and slow to take me on your own."

"Is that what you think?"

"Prove me wrong."

Quintus turned toward Habel and Morrisco, who had begun circling around Pelayo, trying to outflank him. "Why don't you boys sit this one out. Let me show you how it's done."

Habel and Morrisco paused in their stride. After looking at Quintus for confirmation, they backed away.

Quintus bunched his hands into fists, drew his elbows close to his chest, then tucked in his chin and advanced.

Pelayo reconsidered his idea of using his knife on Quintus. It just didn't seem honorable to him anymore, as Quintus had chosen to fight him alone. Instead, he raised his fists and took a swing at Quintus as the man closed in.

Quick as a hunting spider, Quintus danced to the side, avoiding Pelayo's fist, the blow barely ruffling the thick, black curls of his head.

The strike left Pelayo open.

Quintus shifted his weight, then thumped his fist into Pelayo's midriff, just below the ribcage.

The blow drove Pelayo's breath from his lungs and sent him staggering back. He was surprised by Quintus' speed and agility. He had never in his life seen a muscle-bound man move so quickly. In dismay, he realized that what he had counted on as his one advantage over Quintus had just been so much wishful thinking. Gulping down air, trying to shake off the effects of the blow, he raised his fists and circled around Quintus.

Quintus looked surprise to see Pelayo coming toward him again.

The men in the surrounding area began hollering and egging on Pelayo and Quintus. Fighting was strictly forbidden in the camp, so the sight was a rare occurrence. Making the spectacle even more irresistible was the fact that the fight involved Quintus, a figure most of the men there hated.

Stepping in nimbly, Quintus unleashed a combination of quick, hard jabs at Pelayo's head and torso.

Pelayo deflected or dodged most of the blows, but a few landed on target. One opened a gash over his brow. Blood began dripping into his right eye. Only moments into the fight, Pelayo's midriff was aching from the pounding he was taking.

A rare opening came and Pelayo smashed his fist into Quintus's chin, snapping his head back. Keeping the pressure on, he hammered three quick blows in succession to Quintus' stomach, giving him a taste of his own medicine.

Quintus grunted and backed away, but Pelayo followed him, pummeling his head and face with short, hard jabs.

Quintus brought up his arms and fists around his head, absorbing Pelayo's blows. He feinted to the right, then threw a punch that caught Pelayo in the mouth.

Pelayo tasted blood. Another blow smashed him on the side of the head, making his ears ring.

Quintus stepped up the pace of his attack, raining blows on Pelayo's head and stomach.

Pelayo's left eye swelled shut. Seemingly smelling victory, Quintus pummeled him even harder, driving him back, toward the ring of soldiers around them. Someone pushed Pelayo from behind, making him stumble forward. From the corner of his half-closed left eye he caught a glimpse of Habel grinning.

Pelayo knew that he was losing the fight. Quintus was stalking him around the campfire like a predator smelling blood.

It suddenly dawned on Pelayo that fighting with bare fists was Quintus' game. The longer the fight went on, the higher the chances that he was going to end up senseless on the ground. It was time to change tactics.

Ignoring the pounding he was taking, Pelayo let his arms drop a little, as if too weak to fight on. Actually, it wasn't too far from the truth.

"Not feeling so cocky anymore, are you, whoreson?" Quintus said with a sneer as he moved in for the kill.

Pelayo waited until the last moment, then turned and stepped back into Quintus. As soon as he felt contact, he drove his elbow into Quintus' stomach. Hearing a grunt near his ear, he whipped his head back and heard the crunching sound of Quintus' nose breaking.

Knowing he had bought himself a moment's grace, Pelayo turned and hammered his fist into Quintus' stomach, just below his ribcage.

The wind knocked out of him, Quintus went slack jawed.

Pelayo kicked Quintus' legs from under him, sending him crashing to the ground, landing a few feet away from the campfire.

Pelayo pounced on top of him, pinning him down. Knowing he had but a moment before Quintus bucked him off, Pelayo drew back his right arm, then struck him in the face with every ounce of muscle he had.

Quintus let out a howl as Pelayo's fist crushed into his already damaged nose.

Pelayo hit him again, on the mouth this time and felt the

crack teeth breaking. He was raising his fist to strike again when he heard someone bellow, "Stop that!"

Pelayo glanced up and saw Commander Pio pushing his way through the ring of spectators. Striding at the camp commander's side was his personal aide.

"On your feet!" Commander Pio barked at Pelayo.

Pelayo rose up, leaving Quintus senseless on the ground, blood pouring from his mouth and nose.

"What's your name, soldier?" Commander Pio asked through gritted teeth, his fury palpable.

Pelayo wiped the blood dripping down from his split lip with the back of his arm. "Pelayo, sire."

"Are you aware that striking a superior is a serious offense?"

For a moment Pelayo weighed the idea of trying to explain his actions, but then he thought better of it. He knew Quintus would argue persuasively that the drowning of Ramundo had been nothing but an unfortunate accident. The truth was that he had broken a cardinal rule of military life and no matter how justified he felt, no commanding officer could afford to overlook the disruptive example of a soldier striking his squad leader.

"Well?" Commander Pio said.

"I'm aware of the regulation," Pelayo answered.

Commander Pio waited a moment to see if Pelayo would add something in his defense. When it became evident that Pelayo was not going to say anything more, Commander Pio scowled darkly at him. "You're going to regret your actions today, soldier, I promise you that."

Pelayo stared back at Commander Pio, feeling a reckless abandon. *Might as well be truthful; what else can they do to me?* "With all due respect, sire, I doubt that."

The corners of Commander Pio's lips curled up in a tight,

hard smile. "Trust me, you'll sing a different tune when the lash bites into you tomorrow."

When Pelayo said nothing, Commander Pio turned and addressed a group of soldiers standing nearby. "You three, take this man to the stockade."

Pelayo spent the night stretched out on the ground in a small cell. His sleep had been fitful and his dreams troubled. He had presided over several floggings and he knew exactly what to expect. The lash would be the regulatory eighteen strips of rawhide braided together to form nine, thin cords, just over four feet in length. The handle would be of carved oak, probably shiny from years of being gripped. After each use, the rawhide strands would have been washed free of blood and then carefully oiled to keep them supple for the next flogging.

The lash could strip the skin off a man's back in as few as six or seven strokes. If too many lashes were meted out or too much force applied, a man would go into a faint from which he would never recover. In the hands of an expert, however, the lash would dole out unimaginable pain without killing or permanently maiming the offender.

At dawn, a detail of six soldiers marched Pelayo out to a field where the entire garrison had been assembled to witness his punishment. The men led him to an eight-foot post planted in the ground. After stripping him of his tunic, they tied his wrists around the post, exposing his naked back, then marched away.

Pelayo didn't know whether it was dread or the pounding he had received the day before from Quintus that was making him feel light-headed. It could also be that he had not eaten since noon the previous day. His left eye had swollen shut and his body was aching from a dozen bruises. *All I need now is a good whipping to round things out.*

After what seemed like an interminable wait, Pelayo caught sight of Commander Pio and a staff officer marching his way. The camp commander came to a stop a few paces away from Pelayo. His hands on his hips, he stood in silence, surveying the ranks of the assembled soldiers before him.

"Before you stands one of your comrades," Commander Pio called out in a loud voice that carried to the furthest man. "He has been found guilty of striking his squad leader." He paused for a moment, to let his words sink in before continuing. "The offence would normally call for a sentence of death. However, as he is a new recruit, I have chosen to grant him clemency. I have therefore reduced his punishment to thirty lashes. Be warned that I may not be so lenient the next time one of you is charged with a similar offense."

In the silence that followed, Commander Pio turned and nodded to the soldier assigned to carry out the flogging.

Pelayo tensed involuntarily, fear curdling in his belly. At long last came an ominous, hissing sound. A bolt of red-hot pain exploded across his back, forcing a moan out of his lips. Cold sweat erupted from his forehead as the agony blossomed, spreading throughout his body, from his head down to his toes.

Caught in the throes of torment, Pelayo saw the soldier drawing back his arm again. He clenched his teeth and prepared himself. *Twenty-nine more to go. Oh God, give me strength.*

The sound of galloping in the distance cut through the silence that had fallen over the field.

"Wait," Commander Pio said, holding his hand up to the soldier wielding the lash.

Pelayo turned his head and through his one good eye,

followed the approach of a horseman galloping in his direction. The rider, an officer, brought his horse to a halt several paces away.

Commander Pio shot the officer a stern look. "You'd better have a good reason for interrupting these proceedings."

"I do, Commander Pio. The man you are about to lash has been requested to attend a meeting of the Baron's council."

Commander Pio looked quizzically at the mounted officer. "Are you certain you have the right man?"

The officer glanced briefly in Pelayo's direction and nodded. "Yes, sire. He's the one. I met him several months ago."

Pelayo studied the mounted man, dredging his memory. After a moment it came to him. The officer was the commander who had been in charge of the guards at the gate when he had first arrived in the city.

Commander Pio looked up at the mounted officer. "What does the council want with him, Lugo?"

"I don't really know," Commander Lugo replied.

In truth, Lugo knew full well the reason, but under the circumstances, he thought it best not to voice it out loud. When he had first reported for duty that morning, the captain of the house guards had told him to expect visitors as the Baron was going to be holding a council meeting to discuss the ultimatum delivered by the Moorish delegation the previous day.

He had mentioned to the captain that he had run across a field commander who had fought with King Roderic in the battle at Guadalete and he thought that perhaps the council might find the man's advice useful.

Surprised to hear that there was an officer of such rank and experience in the city, the captain of the guard had ordered him to fetch the man immediately. Luckily for Lugo, the unusual name of the King's commander had stuck in his head and he had been able to find out from the officer of the watch that the man he was seeking was about to be flogged.

"It's a bad precedent to be setting," Commander Pio told Lugo, a frown of disapproval on his face.

"I can mention your objection to the Captain if you wish, sire."

"No, don't bother; I shall take it up with him myself."

CHAPTER 33

THE MANSERVANT SLIPPED the moss green tunic over Baron Ernesto's head, then smoothed the creases of the garment around the baron's shoulders. "Would you like a hat today, Don Ernesto, the red one with the feather perhaps?" he murmured.

Lost in thought, Baron Ernesto stared sightlessly across the bedchamber into the distance, forcing the manservant to repeat his question.

"I think not," Baron Ernesto finally answered, "It's too warm for a hat today."

There was a discreet knock on the door and the manservant went off to see who it was. At the sight of the commander of the guard, the manservant opened the door wide and ushered him in.

"Good morning, Don Ernesto," Captain Diego called out, striding into the bedchamber.

"Ah, Diego…" Baron Ernesto broke into a smile. "It's good to see you on your feet again. I trust you're feeling better."

"I am, thanks to your physician. The man's a wonder."

"He's from Alexandria. They train physicians the proper way there," Baron Ernesto said. Despite Diego's reassuring words, he could see that the captain looked pale and gaunt. The last time he had seen Diego looking so enfeebled was after he had been wounded by the Saracens while escorting Valentina home eight years earlier.

After making small talk for a moment, the two men left the bedchamber and strode down the hallway toward the staircase.

"So, what have I missed these last few weeks?" Diego asked. "How are the fortifications coming along?"

"They're just about finished," Baron Ernesto replied. "I wish we had built them up another ten feet when we had the chance, though."

"We didn't know how much time we'd have, Don Ernesto."

"True," Baron Ernesto said, as they reached the bottom landing.

"What about our supplies?" Diego asked. "Where do we stand on that?"

"We have enough food to sustain us for about six months," Baron Ernesto said, walking down the great hall. "A little more if we begin rationing at some point."

"Maybe there's still time to buy some grain from Saragossa, assuming they have any to spare, of course."

"That won't be possible, I'm afraid."

"Is our treasury running low?" Diego asked.

"It's not that. Saragossa has fallen to the Moors."

Diego's step faltered. "Good Lord."

The two men continued walking in silence, a sense of gloom overtaking them.

As they descended a flight of stairs, Baron Ernesto said to Diego, "Are you aware that Bishop Oppas is going to join us this morning?"

Diego's brow furrowed. "That's rather unusual, isn't it?"

"He asked if he could come. I couldn't think of a reason to say no to him."

"Well, I can think of one," Diego said, an edge in his voice.

"Really? What would that be?"

"There's a rumor that Oppas and his brother Siberto deserted the King at the battle of Guadalete."

"Rumors are as plentiful as fleas on a dog these days Diego, you know that."

"Some rumors have a nugget of truth to them, Don Ernesto."

"I doubt this one does. Oppas and Siberto never struck me as cowards."

"Maybe it wasn't cowardice that drove them to desert the King," Diego said. "Perhaps they had other reasons."

"Before you start letting your imagination run free, you should remember that we know precious little about what actually happened in Guadalete."

"That could be easily remedied, Don Ernesto."

"What do you mean?"

"We have someone here in the city who fought at the King's side in Guadalete."

Baron Ernesto frowned. "Why am I only hearing about this now, Diego?"

"I only learned of it this morning myself, Don Ernesto."

Bishop Oppas was speaking to one of the council members when Baron Ernesto and Captain Diego entered the audience chamber. Without stopping to speak to anyone, Baron Ernesto made his way toward the raised platform at the front of the chamber, then sat down on the ornate chair. "Good morning, gentlemen," he said. "We have a lot to discuss today. Shall we get down to business?"

As the room fell silent, Baron Ernesto studied the somber

looking faces turned toward him. "First of all, thank you for coming here on such short notice."

There were nods and murmurs from the council members.

"As you all can see," Baron Ernesto continued. "Bishop Oppas has joined us this morning. Perhaps we can start by having him tell us his reasons for wanting to attend what is after all a council of war. I would have thought that such matters would be of little interest to a man of the cloth."

"Under normal circumstances you would be correct, Baron Ernesto," Bishop Oppas said. "But these are perilous times, and in all humility, I am the Lord's shepherd. I would be remiss in my duties if I failed to provide advice to the council at this most critical time."

"How fortunate for us then that you happen to be in Girona this morning," Baron Ernesto said dryly.

"It is not by chance that I am here, Baron Ernesto," Bishop Oppas said piously. "It is God's hand at work."

"Yes, of course," Baron Ernesto murmured,

Captain Diego stirred. "May I be permitted to say a few words to Bishop Oppas, Don Ernesto?"

"By all means, Diego."

Diego turned to address Bishop Oppas. "I must admit I am mystified by your offer, your worship. I'm certain your intentions are honourable, but I have to wonder about the usefulness of the counsel you intend to give us. Perhaps you could tell us what experience you have in preparing a city for a siege, or repelling an attack, or shoring up the walls to withstand an assault, and so forth."

A look of irritation flitted across Bishop Oppas' face. "I have followed soldiers into battle many times, captain. As a matter of fact, I'm sure I can wield a sword as well as any man here. But the advice I was referring to is general in nature. One need not be a cobbler to offer an opinion as to whether or not one should wear shoes when walking over sharp stones."

Baron Ernesto nodded. "Point taken, Bishop Oppas. Please proceed."

"Thank you. I promise not to waste the council's time." Bishop Oppas said. "Let me begin by saying that I understand that every instinct you possess must be urging you to reject the Moors' terms of surrender. You are all brave men, it is only natural that you would want to fight for your independence."

Bishop Oppas paused for a moment, then continued, "And yet, I urge you to resist that impulse. The Moors have overcome every force that has stood up to them. Defy them now and you will bring down ruin on everyone and everything you hold dear."

Baron Ernesto raised an eyebrow. "That's a rather bleak assessment of our chances, isn't it?"

Lord Montañez, one of the council members spoke up, "The bishop is merely stating the obvious, Don Ernesto."

Baron Ernesto turned his gaze toward the gray-haired patriarch of Girona's leading family. "Perhaps I lack your clarity, Don Montañez, but I do not see how Bishop Oppas can state that opinion with such conviction without having any knowledge of our military strength or our readiness for war."

"He can say it because none of that matters a whit, Don Ernesto," Lord Montañez said. "Bishop Oppas is making the observation that no one has yet been able to withstand an onslaught from the Moors. Not the king's legions, nor the fortified cities in the south, nor the garrison towns along our coasts. I think any reasonable person would conclude that we probably won't be able to do so either."

"Respectfully, Don Montañez," Captain Diego called out. "I disagree with your assessment. While it is true that the Moors have been successful thus far, they're in a different situation now. They've been forced to establish garrisons in the cities they have seized in order to control the populace. Considering all the territory they've swallowed up in the last six months, it is reasonable to assume that their forces must be stretched thin. I wager that they are less interested in sweeping up the few remaining cities still in Iberian hands than they are in consolidating whatever lands they have already acquired."

General Forlan, frequently at odds with Captain Diego at council meetings, joined the discussion. "What are you saying, Captain Diego? The Moors won't attack us if we reject their demands?"

"No, they will come for us, I'm certain of that," Captain Diego answered. "But I think the force they'll field against us will be small in number. We would probably have a good chance of beating them back."

"Probably?" General Forlan said. "And what the devil happens if you're wrong?"

Lord Castellanus, an elderly noble with a blunt manner, spoke out, "General Forlan, we must have the courage of our conviction. Nothing less than our freedom is at stake here. The moment we open our gates, we will become a conquered people, slaves to our new masters for the rest of our lives."

"You paint too gloomy a picture, Don Castellanus," Bishop Oppas said. "I grant you there will be some changes, but I doubt they will be as drastic as you fear. By all accounts, the Moors are benign overlords who rule their subjects with a fair hand."

Lord Castellanus snorted. "Oh yes, we've heard all about their benevolence."

"Scoff all you want," Bishop Oppas said. "But negotiating peace with the Moors is the only chance you have of saving Girona from destruction."

"Bishop Oppas," Captain Diego's voice rang out across the chamber. "Did you have the same low regard for King Roderic's chances of victory at Guadalete as you do now for ours?"

Bishop Oppas stiffened. "I do not appreciate your tone, Captain. The situation here has nothing to do with what happened in Guadalete."

"On the contrary," Captain Diego answered, ignoring Baron Ernesto's warning glance. "I think it has plenty to do with it. There is talk that you and your brother deserted the King in the thick of the battle."

Bishop Oppas' face flushed an angry red. "How dare you repeat such slander to my face!"

"That's enough, Diego," Baron Ernesto said sternly. "Bishop Oppas is our guest. You should know better than to level unsubstantiated accusations against him."

Bishop Oppas lost some of his stiffness. "Thank you, Baron Ernesto. I have suffered greatly from these malicious rumors that have been circulating lately."

"It must be a difficult ordeal for you," Baron Ernesto said solicitously.

Bishop Oppas let out a long-suffering sigh. "It is the unfairness of it all that hurts the most."

Baron Ernesto nodded, his expression sympathetic. "Perhaps there is a way we can put these stories to rest."

Bishop Oppas' brow furrowed. "How so?"

"As luck would have it, we have a soldier in our garrison who we're told fought with the King at Guadalete. I have taken the liberty to summon him to our council."

"That is most considerate of you, Don Ernesto, but that is not necessary. I realize your time as well as that of the council is limited."

Baron Ernesto waved his hand in the air. "This will take no

time at all, I assure you. Captain Diego arranged to have the man brought here. Unless I am mistaken, he awaits our pleasure outside that door behind you."

Bishop Oppas' eyes darted to the far side of the audience chamber, where two soldiers were standing guard by the door. Catching himself, he turned back to the baron. "I am certain your effort is well meant, Don Ernesto, but I doubt the testimony of a common soldier is going to sway anyone's opinion."

"The man I'm referring to is no common soldier, Bishop Oppas. He is the son of a man I once considered my dearest friend. He's also related to my daughter's husband... and to you as well."

With that Baron Ernesto motioned to the two guards stationed at the door.

The eyes of every council member turned toward the chamber's entrance.

A moment later, a bedraggled-looking soldier came walking in through the open doorway. He was tall, sturdily built, and appeared unfazed by the illustrious company staring at him with open curiosity. In a steady gait, he marched across the chamber, the sound of his hobnailed sandals clicking on the flagstone floor. The council members parted, creating a space for him to approach the baron.

Mystified as to why he had been brought to a council meeting, Pelayo made his way toward Don Ernesto, whom he knew well from the baron's many visits to his father's castle. His stride suddenly faltered as he caught sight of Bishop Oppas, standing alongside the other council members. The fingers of his hands curled involuntarily into balled fists as a surge of anger swept through him. It took all his willpower not to leap at the bloated, treacherous figure and grab him by the throat.

Baron Ernesto rose up from his chair and clasped Pelayo by the shoulders. "It's a pleasure to see you again after so many years, my boy," he said, smiling broadly.

The warmth of the baron's greeting went a long way to quelling the emotions roiling inside Pelayo. "It's good to see you too, Don Ernesto. You're looking as fit and hale as ever."

"I wish I could say the same about you," Baron Ernesto said, shaking his head. "What on earth happened to your face?"

"An encounter with a rather unpleasant brute, Don Ernesto."

Baron Ernesto raised an eyebrow but chose not to pursue the matter further. "I only heard this morning that you were in Girona. Why have you not come to pay us a visit?"

"I didn't want to impose, I thought you'd be busy with matters of state," Pelayo said, his answer ready. It was a poor excuse, he knew, but it was the only one he'd been able to come up with. The truth was he knew that a visit to the baron would have led to conversations on many subjects, including that of Valentina, and he hadn't wanted to stir up memories that were best left forgotten.

"You should know better than that," Baron Ernesto said. "My door will always be open to you."

"It's kind of you to say so, Don Ernesto," Pelayo replied. "How is Doña Katerina? I trust she is well?"

"A few minor aches and pains, but otherwise she's fine."

"I'm glad to hear it." Pelayo hesitated. "And how is Valentina?"

"She's well. Did you know that she and Julian are back in Gijón?"

"No, I hadn't heard. I thought they were still in Ceuta."

"Oh no. They've been back for months now. After the King's death, Julian's exile was effectively over."

"You must be happy to have your daughter back."

"And granddaughter," Don Ernesto smiled. "She's so much like Valentina."

"I can imagine," Pelayo said. As he had foreseen, speaking about Valentina had released a host of unwelcomed emotions in him, mostly of loss and resentment. "And how is the captain of the guard?" he asked, wanting to change the subject. "The one who was wounded in the Saracen attack. I'm afraid I've forgotten his name."

"You mean Diego?"

"Yes. Would you convey my regards to him when you next see him?"

"Why don't you tell him yourself? He's standing right behind you."

Smiling broadly, Captain Diego stepped up to Pelayo and extended his hand. "It's a pleasure to see you again, Commander Pelayo."

"Likewise, Captain," Pelayo said, clasping Diego's wrist. "You can forego the 'commander' part, by the way; I'm just a regular man-at-arms now."

"Yes, so I was told. You'll have to explain that to me sometime."

Baron Ernesto said, "I suppose we should get back to the matter at hand."

"Yes, of course, Don Ernesto," Captain Diego answered.

Silence settled over the assembly as Baron Ernesto sat down again. Resting his elbows on the arms of the chair, he singled out Pelayo with his gaze. "You must be wondering what you're doing here?"

"I have to admit I'm a little curious."

"The Moors have sent a delegation demanding we surrender the city. We are trying to decide on our response."

Pelayo felt a chill running down his spine. *So, they're finally at our doorstep.*

"The reason I've brought you here this morning is to ask you a question: is it true that you fought with the king at Guadalete?"

"Yes, I had that honor," Pelayo said. "I was one of his field commanders."

"You're young to have been given that responsibility. The King must have thought highly of you."

"I like to think he did," Pelayo answered

"Your position must have given you a unique understanding of how the battle played out. Could you tell us about it?"

Pelayo was taken aback by the request. He couldn't see how what had happened that day in Guadalete could possibly play a part now in the council's decision. But he trusted Baron Ernesto's judgment and he would do his best to give as factual an account of the battle as possible. He collected his thoughts for a moment, then began to speak.

He started off well enough, but as his story unfolded, he found it increasingly difficult to keep his emotions in check. When he recounted the part where the northern barons' men had fled the field, leaving the King's right flank exposed, his voice faltered.

"I realized then that Bishop Oppas, Lord Siberto and the other northern barons hadn't come to help us. They were there to execute a well-thought-out plan to betray the King."

"That's a damn lie!" Bishop Oppas exclaimed. "Our men simply panicked when the Moors charged us. We couldn't stop them from—"

"Bishop Oppas," Baron Ernesto cut in. "If you don't mind, I'd like to hear the rest of Pelayo's account. You will have a chance to speak when he's done."

Bishop Oppas nodded, visibly agitated.

"Please go on," Baron Ernesto said to Pelayo.

Pelayo told everyone how the Moors had split their forces; how they had encircled the King's legions, entrapping them in a vice, denying them any chance of escape. He told them of his anguish when he had realized that the royal standard had fallen. As he described the latter stages of the battle, his gaze turned inward, and the cries of his men echoed in his head. By the time he finished his story, his voice had turned into a hoarse whisper.

A hush fell over the chamber as every member of the council turned toward Bishop Oppas, now standing in the center of a space that had cleared around him.

"That's quite a story my nephew has spun for you," Bishop Oppas said, shaking his head from side to side. "And the strange part is that he probably believes every word of it. Nonetheless, he's completely mistaken. By his own account, he was positioned at the other end of the battlefield, much too far to see clearly what was happening on the King's right flank, which is where we were positioned. That was over half a league away, and through pouring rain, mind you. The truth is that our men broke and ran when the Moors charged us. Our commanders did their best to stop the rout, but they couldn't get the men to turn back. This talk of betrayal is complete nonsense."

"Bishop Oppas," General Fernan, in charge of Girona's forces, called out. "How do you explain your men breaking like that?"

"There's no mystery to it, general," Bishop Oppas answered. "It is the same human frailty that has driven soldiers throughout history to desert their position in the heat of a battle. Cowardice, plain and simple."

Baron Ernesto turned toward Pelayo. "Is it possible that you could have been mistaken in your judgement of the situation?"

"I'd be a damn poor commander if I couldn't tell the difference between men fleeing in panic and an organized withdrawal from the battlefield," Pelayo answered.

Bishop Oppas erupted again. "The notion is absurd! Why would we side with the Moors against our own people?"

Before Pelayo could reply, Captain Diego cut in, "It is impossible for us to know what arrangement the Moors may have made with Bishop Oppas and the northern barons, if indeed any was made. But the bishop's presence here today, trying to convince us to surrender, may suggest that he is still doing the enemy's bidding."

Bishop Oppas' face once more reddened with anger. "How dare you impugn my integrity? My presence here is proof of my good will, nothing more."

"Baron Ernesto," Lord Castellanus called out. "I for one think Captain Diego's point is well taken."

Suddenly every council member began voicing his opinion, shouting over each other to be heard.

Bishop Oppas' voice cut through the din. "Don Ernesto, I demand you put an end to this farce and allow us to get back to our discussion."

"You're quite right, Bishop," Baron Ernesto said. "We should get back to the matter at hand. But I think we shall do so without your presence."

"Without my presence?" Bishop Oppas asked, looking dumbfounded. "Are you going to take the word of this mongrel over mine?"

"Yes, that's exactly what I intend to do," Baron Ernesto said. He beckoned to the two guards standing by the door, then turned back to Oppas. "Pelayo's account confirms the rumours we've been hearing about you for months. I, for one, have no doubt you betrayed the King. If there is a god in heaven, you shall pay for that one day, if not in this world, then surely in the next."

Before Bishop Oppas could utter a word in his defense, Baron Ernesto turned and addressed the guards, "Take the bishop to one of the chambers in the tower. Keep him there under lock and key until I decide what to do with him."

Bishop Oppas' eyes bulged in outrage. "You have no authority over me! I am a bishop of the Holy Roman Church!"

Baron Ernesto shook his head in disgust. "You may hold that title, but what you really are is an abomination to your holy office and a disgrace to your country."

The guards seized Bishop Oppas and though he protested loudly and indignantly, marched him unceremoniously away.

When the sound of the bishop's voice had faded, Baron Ernesto turned back to the council members. "All right, we've wasted enough time on this, and God knows we have little of it to spare."

There were somber nods all around.

"With your permission, Don Ernesto," Lord Castellanus said. "I would like to ask Commander Pelayo a question."

"We can dispense with formalities today," Baron Ernesto said. "Just speak your mind freely. That goes for all of you as well."

Lord Castellanus turned toward Pelayo. "Commander, given your experience fighting the Moors, what do you reckon our chances are of withstanding a siege?"

It was an astute question, and one that Pelayo had been asking himself ever since he had arrived in Girona. "To give you an accurate assessment, I would need to know more about the city's defenses, its stores of grain, salt, water, weapons and such."

"Just give me your best estimate, commander."

"I can offer you an opinion, if you wish, as long as you understand that's all it is," Pelayo said.

"That will do splendidly," Lord Castellanus said.

Pelayo thought for a moment. "If the rumors are true that the Moors have taken Saragossa, they'll have no problem breaching our walls as well."

Lord Castellanus nodded glumly. "That's not too encouraging, is it?"

"Well, then...." Baron Ernesto said, surveying the long faces around him. "It seems that any resistance we put up is pointless. Bishop Oppas was right after all."

An oppressive silence settled over the chamber.

"Don Ernesto," Pelayo ventured quietly. "There is another option that you and the council may wish to consider."

Baron Ernesto looked at Pelayo. "Go on."

"Instead of surrendering or waiting for the Moors to lay siege to the city, we could take the war to them."

General Fernan made a scoffing sound. "The reports we're getting put the size of the Moorish force marching against us at between two and a half and three thousand men. That's roughly three times our number. They will crush us if we face them on the battlefield."

"Which is why we won't do that," Pelayo said.

General Fernan's brow furrowed. "You just said—"

"What I'm suggesting is that we launch a pre-emptive strike on the Moors," Pelayo said. "We can choose the time and place, thus neutralizing to some degree their numerical advantage."

Baron Ernesto mulled over the idea for a moment then said, "Let's assume for the sake of argument that you're right and that we manage to defeat the Moors. Surely, they'll just field a larger force against us. What do we do then?"

"We shall not win a second encounter, Don Ernesto, not on our own," Pelayo answered. "But it will buy us time to seek out alliances. Winning the initial battle will make that task a lot easier to achieve."

Lord Castellanus spoke up, "Commander Pelayo, are you just giving us false hope, or do you really believe we can defeat the Moors?"

Pelayo considered the question, knowing there was no simple answer to it. *How do I explain to civilians that war is a contest involving probabilities, not certainties? That the difference between victory and defeat is often due to some act of fate that could not have been foreseen?*

In the end, he realized that most of the men in the chamber were not seeking complex answers. They just wanted blind assurances. But he could not in good conscience give them that. All he could do was offer them hope. "My instincts tell me we can win against them," he said finally.

"And mine tell me we can't," General Fernan retorted "The idea of surrender is as distasteful to me as it is to anyone here. But should we gamble the lives of everyone in the city on the chance that we can defeat a war-hardened force that greatly outnumbers us? I think if we are honest with ourselves, the answer to that question is obvious."

"General," Pelayo said. "There have been many times in history when brave men in defense of their homeland have prevailed against overwhelming odds. If we have the courage and the will to fight, I believe we can win."

Pelayo's words sparked a fierce debate that went on for some time. Finally, Baron Ernesto held up his hand and called for silence.

"All right, we've gone over this long enough," Baron Ernesto said. "It's time for each of you to declare where you stand. Let's start with you, Diego."

Squaring his shoulders, Diego drew himself up to his full height. "I say we tell the Moors to go to the devil."

Baron Ernesto smiled. "Yes, I thought that would be your answer."

One by one, every man there announced where he stood. By a margin of two votes, the council rejected the Moor's demand to surrender.

Baron Ernesto, who had not yet voiced his own view, surveyed the faces before him, seemingly aware of the momentous decision he was about to make. Leaning back in his chair, he spoke out quietly, "I too think that our freedom is worth fighting for. Let us prepare for war."

There was no outward reaction from the council members. Even those who had voted to accede to the Moors demand accepted the decision with quiet resignation.

"Baron Ernesto," Captain Diego said, his tone uncharacteristically tentative. "May I offer up a suggestion to you and the council?"

"Of course."

"I'm afraid it's rather contentious."

"Just get on with it, Diego," Baron Ernesto said.

Captain Diego nodded. "I do not mean to cast doubt on General Fernan's abilities, which we all know are formidable. But with the daunting challenge facing us, it might be wise to have a field commander who has firsthand experience in battling the Moors."

There was a chorus of murmurs from the council members. General Fernan stood stiffly, his expression inscrutable.

Baron Ernesto frowned at Captain Diego. "General Fernan

is more than capable of leading our forces. We'll have no more talk of replacing him."

General Fernan stirred, then cleared his throat. "I appreciate your confidence in me, Don Ernesto, but Captain Diego's suggestion is not without merit. If Commander Pelayo was able to earn the King's trust, perhaps we should give him ours."

Lord Castellanus smiled in approval. "Well said, general."

Pelayo did not like the turn the discussion had taken. "Gentlemen, I'm more than willing to stand shoulder to shoulder with you and do my share of the fighting. But I'm afraid you'll have to look elsewhere for a commander to lead you."

"It is not your sword arm we need, Pelayo," Baron Ernesto said. "It's your knowledge of war, your judgment, your experience."

"I'm afraid that's not worth very much, Don Ernesto. The last time I led men into battle, they didn't fare so well."

"Nonsense." Baron Ernesto said. "Their blood isn't on your hands. You said it yourself: it was the northern barons' treachery that brought about the defeat."

"Still, I should have done better," Pelayo said.

"Then consider this your chance to redeem yourself."

Pelayo opened his mouth to argue but Baron Ernesto cut him off, "Your father always put the good of his people ahead of his own needs. Are you willing to do any less when your country is fighting for its very life?"

Pelayo had no answer for that, at least not one he liked.

Six days after the council meeting, Captain Diego looked out over the battlements and gazed moodily at the distant mountains, now turning purplish gray beneath the darkening sky.

"I'm sorry, I just don't believe your plan is going to work," Diego said.

"Why, what's wrong with it?" Pelayo asked his newly appointed second-in-command.

"It's too damned complicated. If any part of it goes wrong, and something usually does in the heat of battle, all the other pieces will fall apart."

"We can't meet the Moors in the standard formation, Diego. They'll crush us if we do."

"I'm not disagreeing with you on that. All I'm saying is that we need to come up with tactics that are simpler, more straightforward."

"The plan will work, Diego. Just have a little faith."

"You keep saying that. How do you know the plan will work?"

"Because it's already been used once before to great success," Pelayo said.

"Is that so?" Diego looked suspiciously at Pelayo. "By whom?"

"Hannibal."

Diego's brow furrowed. "Hannibal? Never heard of him. What kind of name is that, anyway?"

"He was a Carthaginian general who lived eight hundred years ago."

"Eight hundred years ago..." Diego groaned. "God help us."

Three days later, after snatching a few hours of sleep, Pelayo put on the armor that he had laid out the night before, then strode out of the officers' barracks. Breathing in the cool, morning air, he made his way through the row of tents as the sun began rising over the horizon. In the distance, the sun's rays washed over the walls and turrets of Baron Ernesto's castle. The sight reminded him that Valentina had grown up there, exploring its nooks and crannies. He wondered where she was now at this very moment. Was she happy or at least content with the life she had chosen for herself? Did she ever think of him, perhaps even miss him a little?

Catching himself, Pelayo shook his head ruefully at the pointlessness of his thoughts. He found it strange and more than a little pitiful that after all these years, memories of Valentina still had the power to evoke in him a sense of loss and regret. It was probably a normal reaction given the solitary life he had chosen for himself. He really should have made more of an effort to find a wife when he had had the chance. Perhaps some comely girl with a pleasant disposition. Maybe then there would have been at least one person on God's earth who would have mourned his passing if he fell in battle that day.

Every able-bodied soldier in the city had gathered by the staging area around the southern gates, filling up the nearby plaza and spilling over into the branching streets. Except for the odd snuffling of a horse or the dull clink of metal, it was eerily quiet, with hardly any sound to betray the presence of the force that was amassing.

When every company was in position, Pelayo gave the order to open the gates, then led the column of horsemen under his command out of the city. He had gambled everything on the fact that the Moors, encamped some distance away, would feel no great sense of urgency to engage them. The next few moments would reveal whether or not he had been right in his judgment.

Pelayo reined in his horse, bringing his column to a halt. Following behind, a cohort of infantrymen under Diego's command came marching out through the gates. Once outside, Diego began deploying his men alongside the city walls.

Reacting to their maneuvers, the Moors began assembling

on the ridge near where they were camped. It was the only high ground in the area and the exact location that Pelayo had predicted they would choose.

Behind Diego's foot soldiers, Commander Pio led two cavalry squadrons, each consisting of one hundred and ten horsemen, through the gates. Once outside, the two squadrons rode away in opposite directions, eventually taking position on both flanks of the foot soldiers lined up along the walls.

Across from them in the distance, the entire ridge was now covered with thousands of Moorish horsemen.

So far so good, Pelayo thought to himself, breathing a little easier.

When all Pelayo's forces were in position outside the city, he turned to address his squadron of one hundred and seventy horsemen, all armed with shields and lances.

"You must be wondering why you are riding with me this morning instead of with your regular units," he called out from his horse. "You can blame your commanding officers for that. They have singled you out as the bravest men in their squads. Soon, each of you will be tested as never before. I ask that you put your trust in me and that you follow my orders without question or hesitation."

Pelayo paused and let his gaze wander over the helmeted faces before him. "Are you with me?"

There was a momentary pause, then a roar of assent went up from the men.

When they quieted, Pelayo shared with his men his strategy for the battle and what he expected of them. When he finished, he saluted them with a raised sword.

"For God and country!" he cried, digging his heels into his horse's flanks and setting off across the plain.

As had happened every time Pelayo had ridden into battle,

all his senses sharpened. The sky seemed bluer than it had any right to be. The drumming of the horses behind him sounded louder than thunder. The earthy scent of the plains smelled headier than a field of wildflowers.

The Moors, assembled on the far-off rise, held their ground and watched Pelayo and his troops advance.

As the distance to the enemy narrowed, Pelayo was suddenly beset with doubt. All his carefully crafted plans hinged on one central premise: that their charge would provoke the enemy to abandon their position on the ridge and engage them. But so far, they were standing firm. *Come on, you pox-ridden bastards, what are you waiting for? Get off the damned hill and charge us!*

Some three hundred paces away from the ridge, Pelayo urged his horse into a full gallop. Riding to engage a vastly superior force entrenched on the high ground felt a little like running at full speed toward the edge of a cliff. All his instincts were urging him to stop and turn around before it was too late. Ignoring his mounting dread, he forced himself to continue his run until he closed in to within one hundred paces from the enemy horsemen arrayed on the ridge.

Pelayo reined in his horse, then held his arm up high, the agreed-upon signal to his men to cast their javelins. Dozens of missiles flew across the sky, then rained down on the enemy. Adding to the Moors' chagrin, Pelayo and his men started waving their swords, jeering and hurling insults at them.

This proved to be too much for the Moors. Their discipline crumbling, they began swarming down the slope of the ridge.

Pelayo and his men wheeled about. With the enemy closing in fast, their ululating cries ringing behind them, they gave their horses their heads and raced back to the city.

From the distance came the wail of a trumpet blast.

Captain Diego's foot soldiers, arrayed in front of the city

walls, started to march forward. The men at both ends of the line began rotating, like two arms of a body swinging inward to meet each other. The unbroken line split at the center, forming two distinct sides that continued to pivot inward. Slowly a V-shaped formation, a sort of a funnel, began to take shape, the broad end facing the field, the narrow mouth pointing toward the city walls.

With his men spread out behind him, Pelayo galloped back toward the city walls. The success or failure of his plan now lay balanced on a knife's edge. If Diego's foot soldiers re-formed too early, the Moors would see the trap for what it was and would have time to evade it. But if Diego's men reassembled too late, they would not be able to contain the enemy streaming toward them and the battle would be lost.

With the Moors lapping at their heels, Pelayo and his men fled down the broad mouth of the nascent V-shape formation. As he raced through the ever-narrowing channel, he caught glimpses of the faces of Diego's men whipping by him.

At last the wall of the city rose up before him, presenting him and his men with an impregnable barrier that signalled the end of their run. With nowhere else to go, they wheeled about sharply and braced themselves to bear the full brunt of the charging horde.

An instant later the leading edge of the Moorish wave smashed into Pelayo and his men, instantly overwhelming them.

Over the din of the battle, two shrill trumpet blasts tore through the air.

The archers that Pelayo had deployed atop the walls released their first salvo on the packed enemy horsemen below them. Piercing through the screams of agony and the sound of clashing metal came a second trumpet blast.

Commander Pio's two mounted squadrons came charging in from opposite sides of the field. They circled behind the Moorish horsemen streaming down the broad, funnel-like formation of soldiers, then stopped, blocking the enemy's only way out.

The two sides of Captain Diego's V-shaped formation gathered speed and began swinging inward, like the jaws of a trap closing. Unable to stop their momentum, the Moors continued their run down the wall of bristling spears toward a swath of ground that Pelayo and his men had carefully avoided. As the enemy rode over the area, the thin wooden framework that had been covered with dirt gave way, plunging both horses and riders into the deep trench that had been studded with sharpened stakes.

Chaos erupted and panic began to set in amongst the charging Moorish horsemen as they caught sight of what awaited them. But there was no escape now as Captain Diego's foot soldiers prodded them onward with their spears.

Sensing that the tide of the battle was turning, Pelayo and his men began pressing forward, squeezing the Moors into an ever-shrinking space that made it impossible for them to fight effectively. Except for those on the outer perimeter, all the enemy could do now was hold their shields over their heads to ward off the hail of arrows that kept raining down on them from the archers perched along the walls.

As the morning wore on, the battle turned into a slaughter. The Moors had shown them no mercy at Guadalete. Now that the tables were turned, Pelayo and his men were paying them back in kind.

Finally, in the waning light of dusk, the fighting came to an end.

His face etched with exhaustion and his armor splattered

with blood, Pelayo stilled his horse and dismounted. In the eerie stillness, he gazed at the carnage around him, sickened by the butchery he had overseen. His men seemed similarly affected as they shuffled listlessly about, gazing with hollow eyes at the bodies of the dead Moors piled around them.

Up on the battlements, above Pelayo and his soldiers, the mood was quite different. There, the archers were breaking out in ragged cheers, adding to the celebratory chorus of pealing church bells coming from the city.

Later that evening, Pelayo learned that his forces had lost one hundred and eighty-five soldiers. Another two hundred and ninety-two men had suffered wounds of varying degrees of severity. Those unable to walk were being transported in wagons to a designated area where physicians were waiting to tend to them. He planned to use those same wagons later to cart away the dead and bring them to consecrated grounds. When time permitted, they would be given a proper Christian burial. The bodies of the enemy would be hauled away and dumped unceremoniously into a mass grave, hopefully before the stench of the rotting corpses began to waft over the city.

Pelayo was speaking to a wounded soldier when he caught sight of a group of horsemen heading in his direction. As the riders drew closer, he spotted the gray-haired figure of Baron Ernesto riding in the lead. Following him were several men, a few of which he recognized as members of the Council.

"Well done, Pelayo!" Baron Ernesto called out from atop his horse, his face wreathed in a smile. "I have to confess I had some doubts about your plan, but I was wrong. What you've accomplished today is nothing short of a miracle!"

"Thank you, Don Ernesto," Pelayo answered. "Luck was on our side today."

"It was more than luck. You had God's grace."

Not wanting to believe that God had played any part in the day's butchery, Pelayo made no comment.

"So, what are you still doing out here?" Baron Ernesto asked. "You should be in the city. The people are clamoring to see their savior."

Pelayo would have preferred to share a jug of wine with Diego and some of the other officers, but duty had to come before indulgence, as his father often said. "I suppose the people deserve something to cheer about after what they've gone through."

"My thoughts exactly," Baron Ernesto answered. "Come, we'll ride together."

As the two men made their way back to the city, Baron Ernesto glanced toward Pelayo. "How much time do you think we have before the Moors send out another force against us?"

"We've just handed them their first defeat since they landed on our shores. I would think that would give them pause before launching another attack against us."

"Let's hope you're right; we need time to prepare. The Moors will not be offering us peaceful terms when they come our way again. They'll be thirsting for blood; nothing else will satisfy them."

"I agree," Pelayo said. "We should try to find others who are willing to fight at our side as quickly as possible."

"I'll draw up a list of possible allies in the morning. Not many will have the stomach for war, of course. I suppose I'm going to need suitable emissaries as well. Can I count on you for that?"

"I'll do anything you ask, Don Ernesto, but I'm a soldier, not a courtier."

"The mission I have in mind for you is a simple one. It involves asking a favor of a brother."

"Do you mean Julian?" Pelayo asked.

Baron Ernesto nodded. "I'd like you to go to Gijón and enlist him as an ally."

"I'm the wrong man for the mission, Don Ernesto. You should send someone else."

"I'm aware of the bad blood that exists between the two of you," Baron Ernesto said. "Your father once confided in me how troubled he was that you were always at each other's throats. But Julian is still family to you, and I have faith that you'll be able to convince him to join our cause."

"You place too much trust in my abilities, Don Ernesto."

"On the contrary. You've proven today that my faith in you is well-founded."

"Not when it comes to dealing with Julian."

"Look, if you don't get anywhere with him, seek out Valentina and ask her to intercede with him on your behalf. One way or another, the two of you must find a way to bring Julian to our side."

Pelayo mulled over the baron's request. Perhaps Julian could be swayed by reason. After all this was a matter that concerned the survival of Gijon as well. With an inward sigh, he gave the baron a nod of consent. "Very well, Don Ernesto, I shall do as you ask."

"Thank you," Baron Ernesto said.

"I'll leave tomorrow. I'll travel alone; it'll be safer that way."

CHAPTER 34

JULIAN STUDIED THE ruined buildings around him as he rode through the once proud capital of the Iberian realm. "Where are all the people?" he asked the turbaned man on his left, the only one of the four Moors riding alongside him who spoke his tongue.

"They are like bats," the Moorish horseman replied with a contemptuous smile. "They only come out at night."

Julian turned his gaze back to the road. It had been over two weeks since the Moorish horsemen had shown up at the castle in Gijón and told him that General Tariq had requested his presence in Toledo. He had welcomed the summons, as he had been trying to arrange a meeting with the general for several months.

During most of the ensuing journey, the four men had kept to themselves. With the table manners of dogs and stinking of the pungent spices they put into their food, Julian had been glad the men had kept their distance from him.

It was late afternoon when Julian and his party reached the citadel in Toledo. The sprawling complex of grim, stone buildings seemed to have escaped the conflagration that had swept through the rest of the city. His relief that the journey was at its end gave way to a gnawing anxiety as he entered through a door into one of the buildings. This would be his first face-to-face encounter with General Tariq since before the invasion, and all his hopes were riding on reaching an accommodation with the Berber warlord.

For close to a year now, Julian had been plagued with remorse over what he and his great-uncles had unleashed upon the land. When they had first conceived of their plan to ask Governor Musa for help in putting King Witiza's son on the throne, they had not really expected that the Saracens would keep their end of the bargain and meekly go home afterward. But no one had foreseen that the Saracens and their Moorish allies would be so spectacularly successful in their war against King Roderic.

Siberto and his allies had done their best to ensure that King Roderic lost the battle at Guadalete. However they had believed that the King and his legions would exact a heavy toll on the Moorish invaders, rendering them a spent force. As it turned out, the Berbers had survived the battle with surprisingly few casualties, leaving them with a standing army that dwarfed that of Siberto's northern alliance.

Julian and his great-uncles had also expected that a sizeable number of the King's soldiers would survive the battle and later flock to their standard. The addition of the King's men would have boosted their numbers enough to confront what they thought would be a weakened Moorish army and force them into collecting their payment and returning home. The plan had seemed perfectly sound when they had first conceived of it. Instead, the unthinkable had occurred. The horde of desert dwellers had wiped out the King's legions.

In the months following the battle, all the barons of their

northern alliance had concluded that they could profit from their favored status amongst the new overlords, and they had continued cooperating with the Moors.

When it became clear that the Moors had no intention of leaving anytime soon, Julian had sent General Tariq a string of letters protesting the violation of their agreement. At first, the dispatches he had received back from the general had been full of appeasing promises. But as the Moors' grip on the country had tightened, the responses to his increasingly frantic letters became less and less frequent, until at last, after months of silence, he had received Tarik's summons to come to Toledo.

"This way," Julian's escort said, leading him through one of the dimly lit passageways of the citadel. After several turns, they reached a chamber that looked vaguely familiar, but the tapestries that he remembered hanging on the walls were gone, as was the heavy oaken furniture. In their place stood a low, square table in the center of a large red and blue carpet.

Two men were sitting on plush cushions by the table. One was an elderly Saracen man with a long, gray beard. The other was a heavyset man clad in a black leather jerkin. There was no mistaking the second man for anyone other than General Tariq.

Julian dredged up a smile as he strode toward the two men. "Greetings, general," he called out. "It's a pleasure to see you again."

There was no returning smile on the lean, hard face of the man addressed, just a brisk nod. Tariq rattled off something to the elderly man at his side. The translation came an instant later.

"Lord Tariq extends his welcome to you," the elderly man said in passable Iberian. "Please sit."

Julian eased himself down on a cushion and tried to imitate the cross-legged posture adopted by the two men before him. There were several turbaned officials walking through the chamber, but no one so much as glanced in his direction. *Why would they bother with me? In their eyes, I'm just another infidel who's come to plead for a favor.*

"General Tariq says he hopes you've had an uneventful journey," the interpreter said.

"I did, thank you," Julian said. "Would you tell the general that I am pleased to be here; I have much to discuss with him."

The bearded Saracen translated Julian's words, then after a short exchange, answered back, "Unfortunately, General Tariq does not have as much time to spend with you as he would like. I'm afraid your discussion with him will have to be brief."

Julian kept his expression neutral. "Of course, I understand. I'll get right to the point then. Would you ask General Tariq when he plans to honor our agreement and place King Witiza's son on the throne."

The interpreter translated Julian's words, waited for the reply, then said, "General Tariq has decided to remain in Hispania for a longer period than what was originally agreed upon. As a result, placing the young prince on the throne will have to wait for now."

"How much longer a wait?" Julian asked, his throat tightening.

The interpreter translated Julian's question, eliciting a fleeting smile from Tariq.

"Who can say?" the interpreter answered.

Julian saw the thinly veiled contempt in the general's eyes as he stared back.

The truth was now in the open and Julian could no longer lie to himself. He and his uncles had handed Hispania to the Saracens on a silver platter. In their blind ambition, they had played with fire and now they were going to have to watch the flames burn down everything they held dear. A sort of paralysis gripped him, destroying his will to plead or to argue.

"General Tariq says you need not have any concern about your personal fortunes," the interpreter said. "He plans to appoint you the governor of your province."

Julian could not dredge up the energy to answer, so he simply nodded.

"General Tariq wishes you a safe journey back to Asturias."

Understanding that he'd been dismissed, Julian rose to his feet, muttered something that passed as a farewell, then walked away.

General Tariq gazed at Julian as he slunk out of the chamber. He had seen the defeat in the infidel's eyes, and he felt confident that the Asturian lord would continue to serve him, thus sparing him the effort of having to take the city of Gijón by force. The reinforcements that Governor Musa had promised him had not yet arrived and he could not afford to wage any more battles. But the day would soon come when he'd be able to cast off all the infidels he'd been forced to appoint as governors. Eventually, no position of power would be held by anyone other than those born to the true faith.

CHAPTER 35

STANDING UNDER THE overhanging roof, eying the pouring rain that had turned the inn's courtyard into a muddy pond, Pelayo decided to keep his room for another day. Aside from sparing himself the misery of riding through the rain, an extra day's rest would give his Arabian steed more time to recover from the limp it had recently developed. But time was passing, and rain or shine, he would have to leave the following day. If his horse hadn't recovered by then, he would have to walk to Gijón, a day's journey on foot, and purchase another mount.

After informing the innkeeper of his decision to stay another night, Pelayo took the clay pot containing the poultice of mud and oats that he had prepared, then headed off to the stable to check on his horse. He slathered the poultice around the Arabian's right fetlock joint, then wrapped a strip of cloth around it and hoped for the best.

He returned to the inn and sat down at one of the tables in the common room. When he grew bored, he went up to his room, stretched out on the thin, straw mattress of his bed, and listened to the sound of the wind whistling through the shutters.

Once darkness fell, he roused himself, then went downstairs to the common room. He had no trouble finding a vacant table. At this hour of the evening, the inn should have been filled with travelers, but there were only seven or eight tired-looking men scattered about, each one nursing a flagon of ale.

The windows had been shuttered due to the rainstorm, and the smell of cooking was thick in the air. Other less welcome scents competed for his attention: stale ale, wet woolen clothing and the acrid tang of smoke rising from the hearth. However, those were minor complaints. What mattered most was that the room was warm and dry.

As he waited to be served, he glanced idly around the inn. Near the entrance door, a serving girl was setting down a bowl of broth on the table before a portly, middle-aged man who had the look of a tradesman about him. After serving the man, the girl walked toward his table. She was young, fresh-faced and pretty, with a faded red apron tied around her waist. Brushing a stray wisp of black hair from her face, she smiled down at him.

"What would you like tonight, sir?"

"I'll have an ale," Pelayo replied.

"Anything else? Some broth and bread, perhaps?"

"Not for now."

The serving girl walked off into the kitchen area, then reappeared with a flagon of ale in her hand. She was setting it down in front of Pelayo when a draft of cold air blew into the room, causing the candles to flicker. A tall man, his face hidden by the hood of his cloak, ducked under the lintel over the door and entered the inn. He stood for a moment, water dripping from his clothing, then pulled back the hood of his riding cloak. Dark eyes in a bearded face, topped by a steel helmet, surveyed the room. Through the open doorway, other cloaked and hooded figures filed in behind him.

Pelayo froze, part of him struck by how calm everyone around him appeared to be. The sight of Moorish soldiers entering an Asturian inn should have sent everyone scrambling either for their weapons or for the door.

After shaking off the rain from their cloaks, the Moorish soldiers took one of the empty tables at the back of the room. The inn's patrons seemed to lose interest in the newcomers and the quiet hum of conversation resumed.

The serving maid waited a moment for the Moors to settle in, then hurried to their table. Pointing and gesturing, the men gave her their orders. The girl nodded her understanding, then made her way to the kitchen.

As she passed his table, Pelayo grabbed her arm and stopped her. "What the devil is going on here?"

The serving girl stared blankly at him. "What do you mean?"

"No one so much as batted an eye when the Moors entered."

"They just want something to eat."

"We're at war with them. They're the enemy."

Her face cleared. "Oh, I see… You're a stranger to these parts, aren't you?"

"What does that have to do with anything?"

"Lord Julian signed a pact with the Moors two weeks ago," the girl replied. "We have nothing to fear from them now."

Pelayo stared at her in consternation, feeling the blood rush to his face. *Damn your craven soul to hell, Julian! How could you bend your knee to the Moors so quickly?*

The girl's expression softened. "It's all right; the Moors aren't so bad really," she said. "There are only a handful of them around here anyway. Those over there are probably just passing through; I'm sure they'll be gone by morning."

After the girl walked away, Pelayo stared sightlessly at the flagon in his hands. *What am I supposed to do now? Is there any point in my going to Gijón now?*

Doing his best to ignore the Moorish soldiers, Pelayo finished his ale, then ordered a bowl of bean stew, the staple food at every inn in Asturias. While he ate, he mulled over the question of whether to proceed as planned or to turn back. There was a chance, he supposed, that he could talk Julian into dissolving the pact he had made with the Moors and forming an alliance with Baron Ernesto instead. But everything he knew about Julian told him that the attempt would turn out to be a colossal waste of time. All Julian cared about was advancing his own interests. And yet, perhaps there was some dormant sense of decency in him, a love of country maybe, that could be reawakened with the right sort of appeal or inducement.

In the end, despite his near certainty that his effort was doomed to failure, he concluded that there was too much at stake and he couldn't leave any stone unturned.

CHAPTER 36

THE TOWNSFOLK HAD been gathering by the eastern gate since before dawn. They stood by their handcarts, shuffling anxiously as they waited for the guards to open the gates. The thought that at this very moment the farmers from the outlying areas were on their way to the fairground to stake out the best locations for themselves stirred up their resentment.

Ignoring the crowd's entreaties, the stone-faced guards waited for the sun to clear the distant mountain tops before unbolting the gates.

Amongst the thirty or so feast days celebrated in Gijón, the Festival of Spring was the most popular of all. The reason was simple, it required no fasting, no churchgoing, and no listening to long-winded sermons. It was simply a day of unfettered festivities to celebrate the coming of the planting season.

By midmorning, every hectare of the field normally used as common grazing land was thronging with people. Dressed in their Sunday best, most of the city's inhabitants were in attendance that morning, strolling along the grounds, enjoying the sights, smells and sounds of the fair.

There was much there to tempt them. Both sides of the

paths were lined with trestle tables stacked with all manner of goods and produce. Anything could be had there that day. Beaded jewelry, smoke-cured sausages, Egyptian imported linen, rounds of assorted cheeses and wine that could be bought in jugs or by the cup.

Behind the stalls, some of the farmers had erected temporary pens to house a favorite bull or pig that they were planning to enter in one of the contests in the hope of winning a prize. The town's tradesmen and merchants were well-represented there as well and could be seen hawking their wares from blankets spread on the ground. Tumblers and roving musicians added to the excitement, playing tunes and passing the hat for a coin or two. Doing brisk business also were the fortune tellers and barbers, tale spinners and hucksters enticing the innocent with their games of chance.

There was a cheerful atmosphere in the air and Valentina was glad that Carmela had talked her into coming. Julian had gone hunting that morning, and in his absence, she had planned to keep an eye on the stonemasons that were rebuilding the chapel roof that had collapsed that winter. But the warm weather and the lure of spending the day with Ermesinda and Carmela had, in the end, proven impossible for her to resist.

The three of them were strolling down one of the main paths when Valentina saw a squad of mounted soldiers trotting toward her. Riding in the lead was Commander Yxtaverra. Upon seeing her, he reined in his horse and touched the side of his helmet in greeting.

"Good day to you, my ladies," Yxtaverra called out.

"Good morning," Valentina answered with a smile. The handsome commander in charge of the guards was one of the few people in the castle she genuinely liked, perhaps because he reminded her of Captain Diego. But unlike the crochety captain of her youth, Yxtaverra was young and affable, and speaking with him was always pleasant. "What are you and your men doing here at the fair?" she said.

"Your husband asked us to keep an eye on things here today, Doña Valentina. If you recall, we had problems with cutpurses last year."

"We can't have that again, can we, commander?"

"Indeed not; they're a slippery bunch that lot. Make sure you ladies keep an eye on your purses."

"We shall," Valentina answered. "Good day, commander."

After the soldiers rode away, Ermesinda tugged at Valentina's hand. "Could we go over there, Mama?" she asked, pointing toward a large bonfire in the distance, her eyes round with excitement. Strains of panpipes, flutes and cymbals drifted in over the chatter and laughter of the crowd.

"Of course, dear," Valentina answered.

As they walked toward the bonfire, Valentina recalled a conversation she had once had with Theodosius about the origins of the fair. He had told her that hundreds of years before it came to be known as the Festival of Spring, the fair had been called by another name: Quinquatrus, the fifth day after the Ides of March. The festival had been a religious holiday to honor Mars, the Roman god of war. Some of the ancient rituals, such as the sacrificial slaughter of animals to appease the pantheon of Roman gods, were no longer practiced. But others had, over the years, been absorbed and transformed into their current traditions. Bulls brought to the fair were still crowned with garlands of white carnations. Sheep pens were festooned with evergreen boughs to ensure the fertility of the flock. And the sprinkling of sulfur over bonfires produced the same yellow, choking smoke that the Romans had used in their purification rites.

Valentina wondered what had happened to Theodosius,

who had vanished without saying goodbye to anyone some five years earlier. Despite the possibility that something dire could have happened to him, she chose to believe that he was still alive and that he had had a good reason to have left is such a hurry.

At her side, Ermesinda and Carmela stopped to watch a group of shepherds jumping over a bonfire, whooping loudly as the flames licked at their heels. A ragtag group of children, playing catch-me-if-you-can, ran by them.

Ermesinda steered Valentina and Carmela toward some stands by the side of the path. One of the tables had an assortment of felt footwear, another a selection of cloth and spools of colored yarn. They walked on and passed by a display of belt buckles, clasps, combs and pins. Unable to resist the glittering objects, Ermesinda stopped to examine them.

Valentina let her gaze wander over the people streaming down the path some thirty paces away. Walking behind a young couple who were shepherding their children along, she caught a glimpse of a man wearing a brown cowl over his head. Something about the man made her follow him with her eyes.

Her heart suddenly skipped a beat.

"Do you like this one, Mama?" Ermesinda asked, looking up at her.

Valentina tore her gaze away and looked at the clasp Ermesinda was holding out to her. "Yes, dear, it's very nice." She turned back and searched for the man with the brown cowl, but he had disappeared into the crowd.

"Could you buy it for me, Mama?" Ermesinda asked.

Valentina turned toward the stand's owner, a gray-haired, middle-aged woman. "How much for the clasp?"

"Half a real, señora."

Without bothering to bargain, Valentina reached for her purse and pulled out a coin. "Here you are."

As soon as the woman took the coin, Valentina turned and searched for the man with the brown cowl. *You're just being silly,* she admonished herself, trying to quell a mad impulse to dash off and chase after the man.

"Look, Mama, a storyteller," Ermesinda said, pointing to where a dozen people were sitting on the grass around an elderly man wearing harlequin colors. "Can we sit and listen to him for a while?"

Valentina hesitated for a moment, then decided to give in to her impulse. "Do you mind taking Ermesinda, Carmela? I'd like to go off on my own for a while."

Carmela gave Valentina a quizzical look, then after a moment, she nodded. "Of course. Ermesinda and I will have fun on our own, won't we dear?" she said, taking the child by the hand.

"I'll look for you both around this area later," Valentina said. "If you wander off, be sure to stay on the main path so I can find you."

"See you later, Mama," Ermesinda called out over her shoulder as she pulled Carmela away.

Valentina set off in the direction that the man with the cowl had taken. The path, one of the fairground's main thorough-fares, was lined with stands and swarming with people, making her progress maddeningly slow. Her patience ran out almost at once and she began pushing her way through the crowd. Just past a major crossway, the throng thinned a little, allowing her to catch another glimpse of the man she was following. He was walking with long, confident strides some fifty paces ahead of her. She craned her neck to get a better a look, but he melted into the crowd again.

Quickening her pace, Valentina threaded her way through the people. Faces flowed by her in a blur. She began to think that perhaps the man had turned down a different path, but a moment later, she caught sight of a broad-shouldered figure walking a dozen paces ahead of her. Her heart began to pound as she closed in behind him. Her hand shook a little as she reached out and touched him on the shoulder.

The man stopped and turned. He was in his thirties, with a skewed nose, bushy eyebrows, and a short, black beard. Seeing Valentina, his stern expression thawed immediately. "Is there something I can do for you, señorita?"

Valentina's face fell. "Pardon me, I thought you were someone else."

The man smiled. "I wish I was."

Valentina turned and walked away in the opposite direction. The man called out to her, but she ignored him and kept on walking. The excitement that she had felt moments earlier drained out of her, leaving her feeling empty inside. *What on earth are you doing?* she scolded herself, allowing the stream of fairgoers to sweep her along. *You're acting like a silly girl.*

After wandering aimlessly for a while, Valentina slowly made her way back to where she had left Carmela and Ermesinda. As the knoll where the storyteller had been plying his trade came into view, she heard a snatch of conversation coming from somewhere to her right.

"You have a good eye, young man. This is a damn fine horse, best I got," a man's voice said.

"How much?"

"Twenty silver reales."

"Twenty? Why you're no better than a horse thief." Despite the man's accusatory words, there was light-hearted humor in his voice.

Valentina turned and fixed her gaze on the two men standing inside a paddock filled with horses. The buyer, the man who'd spoken last, had his back to her. A brown cowl covered his head and shoulders. Before him stood a portly man with an impressive-looking belly, holding a rope tied around the neck of a black stallion.

"I'll give you fifteen," the man with the cowl said. "And you throw in the harness and the saddle."

A tremor of excitement rippled through Valentina. *There's no doubt about it. It's him.*

"I'll let you have everything for eighteen," said the horse trader. "Trust me, that's a bargain for a fine animal like this."

"All right, you have a deal."

Valentina's heart was pounding in her chest as she squeezed through the two horizontal spars of the wooden fence and stepped inside the enclosure.

Noticing Valentina, the horse trader shot her an inquiring glance. "Good morning, señorita. Is there something I can do for you?"

The man in the brown cowl turned and Valentina suddenly found herself looking into the cool, gray eyes that she remembered so well.

"Is it really you?" Valentina said, her voice little more than a whisper.

Pelayo appeared startled to see her, but his expression quickly smoothed out. "I thought I might bump into you here today," he said, smiling faintly.

"You did?" Valentina said, still in the grip of shock at seeing Pelayo alive.

"Of course, everyone comes to the fair," Pelayo said, surprised at how calm he sounded to his ears. He was anything but that inside. He had thought it likely that he might run across Valentina at the fair and he had prepared himself for that eventuality. He knew that the girl of his memories was gone forever, and that the person he'd encounter might look like her, but she would in fact be someone else. She would be the wife of his half-brother and the mother to his child. The truth was that he still resented her for having chosen to marry Julian and the pain of that betrayal had never faded away. But his mission demanded total dedication, and he had told himself that he would be civil to her, if and when he came face to face with her. He needed her as an ally for a common cause and that goal was all that mattered. "You're looking well."

"We…we thought you were dead… Where have you been all these years?"

"Here and there. North Afriqiyah, Toledo, Leon."

"How long have you been in Gijón?"

"Only since yesterday," Pelayo said. He turned to face the horse trader who was standing a few feet away gazing at them with open curiosity.

The man cleared his throat. "I'll go find a saddle for you."

"Yes, why don't you do that," Pelayo said.

A moment later, Pelayo and Valentina found themselves alone. There was an awkward silence as they gazed at each other.

"So, what's brought you here?" Valentina asked, saddened by the gulf that seemed to have opened up between them.

"My horse went lame. I figured I'd be able to buy another one here at the fair."

"I mean here in Gijón. Why have you come back after all these years?"

"You can blame your father for that," Pelayo said with a faint smile. "He's sent me as his emissary to form an alliance with Julian."

"What sort of alliance?"

"To fight the Moors."

"I thought the war with the Moors was over."

"Not in our part of the world. We just fought a major battle with them two weeks ago."

"I've not heard a whisper of it. Where did the battle take place?"

"Just outside Girona."

Valentina gave a start. "Are my father and mother all right?"

"They're fine; so is the city. We won the battle."

"Oh, thank God," Valentina said with feeling.

"Yes, God was on our side, this time anyway. But the Moors will be back, thirsting for revenge and wanting to make an example of Girona. That's why your father is looking for allies."

"I am not sure Julian is going to be interested," Valentina said. "The Moors just appointed him governor. He seems content with the arrangement."

"I know, I've heard of Julian's pact with the Moors," Pelayo said. "I realize my coming here will probably turn out to be a waste of time."

"Not for me. It's been wonderful seeing you again."

Pelayo stared at her, wondering what was the point of her saying that. "Yes, of course."

Valentina felt hurt by the perfunctory way in which Pelayo had tossed back his reply. *What do you expect?* a voice said inside her head. *He's no doubt made a new life for himself. Did you really think the two of you could just resume where you left off nine years ago?*

"So, what will you do now?" she asked him.

"I figure since I've come this far, I might as well go ahead and try to talk to Julian. Then I'll head back to Girona with his answer, whatever that turns out to be."

"I'll help you in any way I can, but I'm afraid I don't have much influence over Julian."

Pelayo nodded. "I understand."

An awkward silence settled between them again.

"What are you doing now?" Valentina asked. "Are you in a trade?"

Pelayo gave her a puzzled look, then his face cleared as he realized that his shabby tunic and cowl had led Valentina to make that assumption. "I'm one of your father's commanders."

"Oh, I thought—"

"It's not healthy to travel in a military uniform these days."

"Yes, of course," Valentina said.

A sudden gust of wind carried the smells of manure and freshly cut hay as they both gazed at each other in silence.

It wasn't that Valentina didn't have a dozen questions to ask him, but she sensed that he found talking to her burdensome and that he was anxious to leave. *He seems so distant*, she thought, *so different from the way I remember him*. She wondered if he too felt that she had changed. Sadness welled up inside her as she realized that they had become strangers.

"I heard you have a daughter," Pelayo ventured.

"Yes, her name is Ermesinda," Valentina said, brushing a strand of hair off her eyes. "She's here somewhere. Would you like to meet her?"

Pelayo hesitated. "Perhaps some other time."

"Of course. What about you? Do you have a family?"

"I'm not married. I suppose I found it harder than you to move on."

Valentina stared at Pelayo, thinking about everything she had sacrificed for him, the long and empty years of living with a man she loathed. "I didn't find it all that easy," she said quietly.

Pelayo had seen the way Valentina had flinched at his words and he instantly regretted voicing them. It was a churlish thing to say to her after so many years. "I'm sorry I said that. There's no point in bringing up the past, is there?"

"No," Valentina said sadly. "I suppose there isn't."

A child's voice piped up behind them, "Mama, we've been looking everywhere for you."

Pelayo turned and saw a pretty, red-headed girl in a blue tunic. The sights and sounds of the fairgrounds faded away from his consciousness. He stood there, rooted to the spot, unable to tear his eyes away from the child. There was very little he remembered about his mother after so many years, but one memory of her stood out clearly: her red hair, the same russet shade as that of the little girl standing before him.

"What are you doing here alone, Ermesinda?" Valentina asked. "Where's Carmela?"

"She's coming," the child said. "Who are you talking to, Mama?"

Valentina hesitated then said, "This is your uncle, dearest. His name is Pelayo."

Ermesinda stared curiously at the man standing in front of her. "I didn't know I had an uncle."

Pelayo walked toward the young girl, then crouched down, so that he was at eye level with her. "I'm pleased to make your acquaintance," he said, noticing her eyes were gray. Aside from her hair and her eyes, the child had clearly taken after Valentina. She had her mother's heart-shaped face, finely sculpted nose and bow-shaped lips. "How old are you, Ermesinda?"

"I'm eight," she answered shyly.

The sound of pounding hooves arose in the distance.

Valentina turned and spotted three horsemen riding down one of the paths in her direction, scattering fairgoers before them. It was Julian and his companions returning from their morning hunt. At first it seemed they were going to ride past her, but then at the last moment, Julian caught sight of her and with a tug of his reins, brought his horse to a halt.

Julian's companions slowed down, then circled back toward him.

"I nearly rode by you," Julian called out to Valentina from atop his horse. His gaze strayed a little further and fell upon Pelayo, standing a dozen paces away. "Who's that with Ermesinda?"

Before Valentina could reply Pelayo rose to his feet and pulled back his cowl. "It's me Julian, the prodigal son has returned to the fold."

Julian gave a start, then his face hardened. "What are you doing here?"

Pelayo arched an eyebrow. "What kind of a welcome is that to give your long-lost brother?"

"The kind you bloody well deserve." Julian turned toward Valentina. "Did you know he was going to be here?"

"How could I? I thought he was dead," Valentina said coldly. "That's what you told me was in your great-uncle's letter."

Julian's expression turned guarded. "It seems he got it wrong, doesn't it? I'm as surprised as you are to see Pelayo here."

"You didn't look very surprised to me," Valentina said.

Julian turned his gaze from Valentina toward Pelayo again, "You didn't answer my question. What are you doing here?"

"Baron Ernesto sent me to seek you out," Pelayo said.

"Why?"

"He's looking for allies to fight the Moors."

Julian snorted. "Looks like the old man's gone senile."

Valentina's eyes flashed with anger. "I don't appreciate you speaking that way about my father."

Julian shrugged. "Anyone who believes that we can fight off the Moors has lost his senses."

"I disagree," Pelayo said. "If we all join forces, we can beat them back."

"For how long? A month? Maybe two?"

"For as long as we have the will to resist."

"Spare me the stirring words. In case it's escaped your notice, the war is over, and the Moors have won. If you don't understand that, then you're as big a fool as the man who sent you."

Pelayo realized that it was pointless to try to appeal to Julian's better nature. "I'd rather be a fool than a coward."

Julian's eyes narrowed. "I would choose my words carefully if I were you. You don't have Father to hide behind anymore."

"I'm actually glad he's not here to witness what you've become."

"What do you mean by that?" Julian said, his voice low and menacing.

"Were you part of the plot to betray the King at Guadalete? At the time, I couldn't bring myself to believe that you were capable of such treachery, but now I realize that nothing is beneath you."

"You don't have the sense to hold your tongue, do you?" Julian said.

"Julian!" Valentina cried out. "Just go about your business, please."

"It's too late for that, my dear," Julian said. "My bastard brother has insulted me for the last time."

Hearing the words, Julian's two companions unsheathed their swords.

"Take him," Julian told his men. "But I want him alive."

Julian's command unleashed Joaquin and Casimiro into action. Urging their horses forward, they rode around the fence toward the gate located at the far side of the paddock.

"Julian!" Valentina cried out, her voice strained. "Call your men back, I beg you."

"Stay out of this!" Julian shouted back.

"What's happening, Mama?" Ermesinda asked, gazing up at Valentina.

Valentina saw the fear in her daughter's eyes. Wanting to get Ermesinda out of harm's way before the fighting broke out, she grasped her child's hand and hurried toward the gate, giving wide berth to Julian's men who were just riding into the paddock.

Pelayo saw the horsemen spread out across the enclosure, then circle around to come at him from both sides. Before the two men could converge on him, he sprinted toward the fence separating him from Julian. Scrambling up the rails, he launched himself through the air an instant before the timbers began collapsing under his weight.

Julian raised his arm up instinctively, an instant before Pelayo slammed into him, knocking him off his horse. In a tangle of arms and legs, they both went tumbling to the ground, Pelayo landing on top of Julian.

Stunned, Julian lay flat on his back, the wind knocked out of him.

Before he could recover, Pelayo struck him on the jaw. Julian's head snapped to the side, then he went limp.

Across from the now collapsed fence, Julian's men slid off their horses. With murder in their eyes, they scrambled over the jumble of timber railings toward Pelayo.

Pelayo scrambled to his feet, grabbed the mane of Julian's warhorse, then swung himself up onto the saddle. After taking the reins, he brought the steed around to face the men, then dug his heels into the animal's flanks.

Trained for war, Julian's horse shot forward, ramming the

closest of the two men, hurling him toward an undamaged section of the fence.

Pelayo turned the horse toward the second man, then pulled up sharply on the reins. Responding to his command, the animal reared up on its hind legs, front hooves pummeling the man before him.

Julian's companion tried to protect his head with his arms, but it was a poor defense against the hooves of a warhorse. A heartbeat later, he crumpled to the ground senseless, blood trickling down from his hairline.

Pelayo stilled his horse and looked around him. In the distance, beyond the crowd that was gathering around the paddock, he caught sight of horsemen heading his way. The commotion must have attracted the attention of Julian's soldiers.

Valentina called out to him, "There's a patrol coming. You need to get away now!"

Pelayo knew she was right; there was no time to spare, not even to ask her the question now burning inside him. Pulling on the reins, he dug his heels into his horse's flanks and shot off at a gallop.

The stands along the path flew by him as he raced off, threading his way through the fairgoers. When the way cleared a little, he chanced a quick look over his shoulder. The patrol was definitely in pursuit.

He kept going at full gallop. When he reached the edge of the fairgrounds, he steered a course westward toward the mountains in the distance. If he could make it to the foothills before the soldiers caught up with him, he thought he might just be able to escape their grasp.

He was beginning to feel optimistic about his chances, when he noticed his horse seemed to be laboring. With a sinking feeling in the pit of his stomach, he figured that Julian must have ridden the steed hard all morning, and now, with the all-out run, the poor animal must be just about spent.

The terrain Pelayo was riding through was flat and treeless. If he was going to evade capture, he had to get out of the open before his horse collapsed under him. The only area, however, that seemed to offer him any possibility of cover was a swath of forest between some cultivated fields lying half a league away. It was far from the perfect sanctuary that he would have wished for, but there seemed to be little else in sight.

He coaxed his tired mount toward the trees. Some three quarters of the way there, the warhorse came to a stop and refused to take another step forward.

Well, that's that, Pelayo thought. He turned in the saddle and saw a plume of dust rising in the distance. Spurred on by the sight, he slid off his horse and set off at a run toward the tree line.

Ignoring the urge to turn and look back, he kept his eyes straight ahead and concentrated on not losing his footing. Only when he was surrounded by trees did he allow himself to stop and look behind him. As expected, Julian's soldiers had drawn considerably closer.

Despite his burning lungs, he set off again, trying to put as much distance as he could between himself and the oncoming horsemen. Aware that he needed to husband his strength, he kept his pace at a slow run as he plunged deeper into the woods.

He was coming down the side of a hillock, trying to keep his feet from sliding under him, when he heard what sounded like distant voices. The thought of being captured and cast into the dungeon again sent him hurtling recklessly down the slope. When he reached level ground, he continued running, sweat pouring out of him, his lungs on fire.

For a time, the only sounds were the rasp of his panting

breath and the crackling of twigs and leaves beneath his sandaled feet. Then from somewhere behind him he heard the
sound of horses tramping through the underbrush.

His first impulse was to run faster still, but a cooler part
of his mind told him that trying to outrun men on horseback
was a fool's errand. Casting a glance around him, he spotted a
fallen tree some twenty paces away. Though near exhaustion,
he ran toward it.

Once he reached the rotting tree trunk, he sank to his
knees, then used his knife and hands to dig out a narrow trench
alongside it. The soil was moist and crumbly, and the work
proceeded quickly. When he finished, he eased himself down in
the shallow depression, then began piling leaves and dirt over
himself, hoping the thin cover would render him invisible, at
least to a casual eye. Once he was done, he lay on his side, his
body nestled in the trench, his face pressed against the moss-
covered tree trunk. Under a blanket of twigs, leaves and dirt,
he willed himself to remain as still as a rock.

Time passed slowly as he waited for either the soldiers to
ride by him or else to hear their cry of alarm. In his mind's
eye, he imagined a line of mounted soldiers, fanned out in
formation, searching every foot of the woodlands as they
moved systematically through the area. His heart suddenly
began to pound when he again heard horses treading through
the underbrush.

From somewhere in the distance, a man's voice called out,
"Why are you stopping, Tomas? Did you find something?"

There was no reply.

Unable to resist his impulse to look, Pelayo inched his head
up so he could peer over the rotting tree trunk. Some twenty
paces away, a stocky, helmeted soldier was sitting atop his horse,
staring in his direction.

Before Pelayo could duck down, their eyes met.

"You deaf, Tomas?" the voice in the distance called out again, impatiently. "Did you spot something?"

Pelayo thought he recognized the horseman who was staring back at him. He was one of the old guards at the castle. He had known the man since he was a child of ten, though they had hardly exchanged more than a few dozen words over the years.

"It's nothing," Tomas cried out, his gaze still fixed on Pelayo. "Just a hare." Without acknowledging Pelayo in any way, he turned his horse and rode away.

Pelayo let out his breath, scarcely believing what had just happened. There was no other conclusion to reach other than some of the old guard must remember him with some fondness.

After the sound of the horses faded away, he rose to his feet, then ran as noiselessly as he could in the opposite direction.

He was loping down the side of a hillock, when he saw a flash of red through the trees. It could only be an officer's cloak, he thought. The idea had barely formed in his mind when he caught sight of three uniformed horsemen riding through the woods in his direction.

Before he could hide, one of the riders spotted him.

"There he is!" the man cried out excitedly.

Pelayo broke into a run, away from the horsemen. Part of him knew that it was a pointless now as he had been spotted. But the thought of falling into Julian's hands drove him to desperation.

He was running through a clearing when horsemen began emerging from the fringe of trees on the far side.

His luck had finally run out.

The officer that Pelayo had spotted through the trees steered his horse toward him, then stopped at a distance of some five or six paces away. Seemingly in no hurry now, the man sat on his horse for a moment, gazing at Pelayo with a bemused look on his face.

Panting from his run, Pelayo stared stonily back at him. "Yxtaverra," he said with a curt nod. The last time he had seen the man, he had been Julian's adjutant years ago at the mock battle between the Eagles and the Principes. "Still doing Julian's bidding, I see."

"I'm commander of the house guards now. It's my duty to keep an eye out for troublemakers."

"Is that what you think I am?" Pelayo asked. "Some drunken lout stirring up trouble?"

"Whatever you've done, your half-brother wants your hide."

"All I did was relay a message to him," Pelayo said.

Yxtaverra's lips curled up in a cynical smile. "Was that before or after you stole his horse?"

"It was a trade. I was in a bit of a hurry and his horse was in closer reach."

"Then there's no problem, is there?" Yxtaverra said. "I'm sure Julian will let you go once you explain that little misunderstanding to him."

Pelayo said nothing.

Yxtaverra motioned to one of his soldiers, "Tie him up."

The soldier singled out dismounted, then pulled out a length of rope from his saddlebag.

Yxtaverra turned and addressed the rest of his men who were grouped around him.

"Flavio and Tomas will stay behind to help me escort the prisoner back to Gijón. Thiago, you will take command and lead the men back to the fairgrounds. Keep an eye on things there until nightfall."

"Yes, commander."

"All right, get going," Yxtaverra said.

There was a smattering of banter amongst the men before they rode off, leaving Flavio and Tomas behind.

Yxtaverra prodded his horse toward Pelayo, whose hands were now securely tied behind his back, and said, "It must be what, eight or nine years since I last saw you?"

Pelayo shrugged, not in the mood for small talk.

Yxtaverra threw a leg over the back of his horse and slid to the ground. "I heard you had served as field commander in King Roderic's legions."

Pelayo strained against the rope binding his wrists. He felt a little slack. Given enough time, he thought he might be able to wriggle free. "Where did you hear that?"

"From my youngest brother. He was a lancer in the Fourth."

Pelayo raised his head and met Yxtaverra's eyes. "Was?"

"He was killed at Guadalete."

"Oh, I'm sorry."

Yxtaverra nodded.

"What cohort was he in?" Pelayo asked after a while.

"The Black Wolves."

Pelayo stared into the distance, remembering. "They were a good bunch; they died bravely."

A shadow seemed to flit across Yxtaverra's face. "How do you know they died bravely?"

"I was there."

Yxtaverra walked closer. "You're the first person I've met who's claimed to have fought in the battle."

"I'm not surprised. Not many of us survived," Pelayo said.

There was a moment of silence as Yxtaverra studied him. "They say the Moors outnumbered the King's forces ten to one."

"Not true. We were evenly matched, at least until the northern barons' men deserted the field."

The two mounted soldiers behind Yxtaverra exchanged glances.

Yxtaverra looked as if he didn't know what to make of Pelayo's statement. "This is the first I hear about anyone panicking and running away."

"They didn't."

"You just said—"

"It wasn't a rout. Their retreat was orderly. They left our right flank defenseless, allowing the Moors to circle behind us."

Yxtaverra stared at him skeptically. "Are you saying the northern barons intentionally deserted the field?"

"That's exactly what I'm saying."

"Why would they do that?"

"I don't know what bargain they struck with the Moors."

"That's quite a charge you're making," Yxtaverra said.

"I can make another," Pelayo said. "I believe Julian was part of the conspiracy as well."

Yxtaverra frowned. "Do you have proof of that?"

"No."

"Then you shouldn't be making those sorts of accusations. What are you doing back in Gijón anyway?"

"Baron Ernesto sent me here as his emissary."

"For what purpose?"

"To petition Julian for an alliance."

Yxtaverra seemed to lose some of his hostility. "A merchant at the fair told me that there was a major battle in Girona a few weeks ago."

"The story is true."

Yxtaverra's eyes narrowed as he studied Pelayo. "The merchant also mentioned that Girona's forces were led to victory by a brilliant, young general who apparently once served in the King's legions."

"True as well. Except perhaps for the brilliant part."

The sounds of the birds in the forest filled the silence as Yxtaverra held Pelayo's gaze. "It's the first victory we've had against the Moors since they landed on our shores."

"All we managed to do is give them a bloody nose."

"You expect they'll be back?"

"Yes. And in greater numbers. That's why Baron Ernesto was hoping to form an alliance with Julian."

"How did that work out?"

"What do you think?"

Yxtaverra said nothing.

Pelayo smiled mirthlessly. "I believe Julian made up his mind a long time ago which side of the bed he wants to lie on."

"Not all of us were pleased when Julian made his pact with the Moors," Yxtaverra said quietly.

"Yes, well, it's all in the past now, isn't it?" Pelayo said, growing tired of talking. "So, are you going to let me ride with one of your men or are you going to make me walk all the way back to Gijon?"

CHAPTER 37

JULIAN DODGED A manservant tottering under the weight of a tray stacked with loaves of bread, then made his way to the head table. Most of the members of his retinue were already seated and the great hall was abuzz with the hum of voices. Father Antonius was rambling on to the new quaestor whose eyes were glazed over with boredom. Across from them, the chamberlain was listening attentively to the young, pretty wife of one of the town's wealthiest merchants. Morisco, Usebius and Joaquin were sitting next to the woman's husband, arguing over something or other. Sitting at a table apart from the other guests, the two Saracen envoys were observing with watchful eyes the activity around them.

The two men had arrived a few days earlier, ostensibly on a courtesy visit. But judging by the information they'd been asking for, Julian had figured out that their real purpose was to take inventory of his holdings, so they could siphon off his wealth as quickly as possible.

Valentina, Ermesinda and Carmela were sitting in their usual places. Next to them, the chair reserved for his mother lay vacant. It had been at least a fortnight since she had last joined them for supper. She now took all her meals in her bedchamber. Covered in boils, she had become so hideously disfigured that he hardly recognized her anymore.

She had been struck down by a mysterious illness shortly after a visit to her Uncle Siberto. It had begun with general aches and pains, then her body had erupted in boils. Fearing she had contracted something serious, he had had the foresight to immediately isolate her in her bedchamber. Over the following days, a string of physicians had been summoned to examine her. The men had administered a variety of remedies, some of which had turned his stomach. But none had brought her any relief, much less a cure.

When his mother became bedridden, he had ordered a servant girl to stay with her in her room and tend to her needs. When the girl began displaying the same symptoms as his mother, he had ordered a slot cut in the bottom of the door, just large enough to slip in food and water, then had locked the two of them inside the chamber. The measure had staved off further contagion and no one else in the castle had fallen ill.

Every few days or so, though terrified of catching the disease, Julian had dutifully paid his mother a visit. He always kept a safe distance from her bed, as well as from the servant girl, and made sure his face was covered with a cloth sprinkled with holy water. Though outwardly solicitous, he secretly wished that the illness would run its course quickly and claim his mother once and for all. Then he would only have the servant girl to worry about.

Now Julian sat down in the chair next to Valentina, who continued speaking with Carmela without so much as a glance in his direction. Ignoring her as well, he eyed the platters of food arrayed in front of him. Deciding he'd start off with some roast chicken, he reached across the table and tore off a leg.

As he took his first bite, he heard the sound of approaching footsteps.

Julian turned and saw several helmeted soldiers marching into the great hall. In their midst was a cloaked and hooded figure. As the group emerged into the torch-lit area of the hall, Julian recognized Yxtaverra and guessed at once the identity of the mysterious figure at his side.

Julian put down the chicken leg and leaned back in his chair. "I expected you back yesterday, Yxtaverra," he called out, his voice cutting through the hall, now grown quiet. "Did you have trouble tracking him down?"

"More than we anticipated, sire," Yxtaverra answered.

Julian glanced at Valentina and noticed her face had gone pale. He smiled with satisfaction as he turned back toward Yxtaverra. "Did you bring back my horse?"

"It's in the stable, safe and sound."

"Good, well done."

Julian rose from his chair and walked around the table until he was facing Pelayo. "I would have stretched your neck like a common thief if anything had happened to my horse."

"It's my lucky day then," Pelayo answered. "I suppose you're going to let me go now that you've got it back."

"And deprive myself of your company? Oh no, I don't think I could bear that."

"What are you planning to accuse me of now?"

Julian leaned over close and said quietly into Pelayo's ear, "Whatever it is, I promise it'll be enough to keep you in a deep, dark hole until you rot."

"What, again?" Pelayo said. "That's the problem with you, you lack imagination."

"You think so? Maybe I'll come up with something new for you."

"No, not this time, Julian. It's my turn to surprise you."

Julian stared quizzically at Pelayo, then with a shrug, addressed Yxtaverra, "Take him away before he spoils my appetite."

Yxtaverra remained motionless, as did the other guards.

Julian looked in annoyance at Yxtaverra. "Did you not hear what I said? Take him away."

Pelayo pulled back his cloak, revealing his chainmail shirt and a sword strapped to his belt. "Did I forget to mention that Yxtaverra and his men no longer take their orders from you?"

A collective gasp erupted from the people sitting around the tables.

Julian's eyes darted around the hall, clearly noticing for the first time the dozen or so guards standing at the far wall. The sight made the blood rush to his face. He whirled around toward Yxtaverra, his eyes wide with incredulity. "You're turning against me, after everything I've done for you?"

Yxtaverra held Julian's gaze. "I'm afraid there's more at stake here than personal considerations."

Julian's face contorted with fury. "Why you treacherous snake; I hope you burn in hell!"

Yxtaverra bore Julian's anger without flinching.

Julian turned to face the men and women sitting around the tables. "Are you all going to just sit there and do nothing?"

The guards along the wall leveled their spears, a blunt warning to everyone that they were prepared to use force at the first sign of trouble.

Everyone sitting at the tables, even those upon whom Julian had lavished favors for years, avoided his eyes. The sole exception was Ermesinda, who appeared to be on the verge of tears.

"Looks like no one's coming to your aid," Pelayo said.

Julian glared at Pelayo. "You've finally gotten what you've always wanted, haven't you?" he said, his voice dripping with venom.

"If by that you mean justice, then yes," Pelayo said. "It's what I told your mother I'd be back for one day."

"Justice?" Julian's lips curled up in a sneer. "Is that what you call this? I should have done away with you when I had the chance."

"So, what stopped you? Brotherly love?"

"You're not my brother," Julian said through clenched teeth. "You're just a mongrel father spawned in some hovel somewhere."

Pelayo's face hardened. "Take him away and lock him up in the dungeon," he told the guards. "He can have the Saracens and those three over there for company," he said pointing toward Julian's friends.

Julian shook off the soldiers' hands, his eyes locked on Pelayo. "Savor your victory while you can, you bastard. I'll see you dangling from the gallows before the year is out."

"Farewell, Julian. Enjoy your new quarters."

Julian gave Pelayo a murderous look as he was dragged away by the soldiers.

It's over, Pelayo thought. They had taken control of the castle without spilling a drop of blood, something that just twenty-four hours earlier had seemed unimaginable.

The previous day in the clearing, after he had resigned himself to his fate, he had noticed that Yxtaverra seemed to be in no particular hurry to head back to Gijon. Looking as if something was troubling him, Yxtaverra mentioned that he and his men had been appalled by how quickly Julian had sided with the Moors. It hadn't seemed right to them when so many northern cities were still at war with the invaders. However, being soldiers, he and his men had continued to serve Julian, doing their best to ignore this latest contemptible act amongst the many others undertaken by a lord they had come to thoroughly despise.

Pelayo had told Yxtaverra that it wasn't too late, that there was still a way the situation could be reversed. To his surprise, Yxtaverra had not dismissed his claim out of hand. On the contrary, his words seemed to have landed on fertile ground.

Later, under the cover of darkness, wearing a military cloak and riding Julian's horse, Pelayo had followed Yxtaverra and his men past the guards at the gate and into the castle. Once inside, Yxtaverra had secreted Pelayo into his private quarters. There, he had met with groups of guards that Yxtaverra thought might be sympathetic to their cause.

Pelayo had told them about the battle against the Moors two weeks earlier, then had gone on to explain his mission to seek an alliance with Julian in order to bolster Girona's forces when the Moors returned to exact their revenge. After adding that Julian had spurned Baron Ernesto's request, he had told the men that they represented their country's last hope for freedom and that he was asking them to join him in the effort to drive the Moors off their land. By the secrecy surrounding their meetings, it must have been evident to every man there that he was asking them to betray their oath to Julian. Despite knowing that they were risking their lives in an undertaking that could get them hung, all the men brought before him had sworn their allegiance to him.

Pelayo realized that Yxtaverra had correctly judged the character of his men. Their love of country and sense of honor had in the end outweighed any loyalty they may have felt for Julian. It probably also helped that he was Fáfila's son, and therefore had some small claim to lead them. But the strongest argument in his favour, though it had never been stated explicitly, was that he had defeated the Moors once and with their help, he would do so again.

It had taken all the previous night and most of the morning to gain the support of eighteen of the thirty-one house guards. For various reasons, Yxtaverra had decided that it would be unwise to let the other thirteen men into their confidence. At sunrise, Yxtaverra had sent all thirteen to patrol the southern border, a task designed to keep them away from the castle until well into the night.

Now Pelayo's gaze swept over the faces of the men and women sitting around the tables. Some were staring back at him with wariness, others with veiled hostility. The majority, however, just seemed uncertain as to how to react to the unexpected turn of events.

"I'm afraid no one will be allowed to leave the castle for a few days," Pelayo told them. The news that he had forcibly overthrown Julian had to be suppressed until he could secure the allegiance of the soldiers stationed at the garrison.

Upon hearing Pelayo's pronouncement, the dozen or so guests who lived in town let out groans and voiced their protests.

Ignoring their objections, Pelayo raised a hand for silence. "The servants will help you find places to sleep."

This time Pelayo's words were met with a resigned silence.

Yxtaverra approached Pelayo and said quietly, "The castle is secure. No one can get in or out. All we have to do now is wait for the men I sent out this morning."

"Are you prepared for them?"

"I'll go and take care of that now."

Once Yxtaverra had left, Pelayo walked toward the head

table, and ignoring everyone else, nodded in greeting to Valentina, Ermesinda and Carmela.

Valentina stared back at him. Clad in a blue satin tunic, her hair drawn back from her face and secured with a pearl-encrusted headdress, Pelayo thought she outshone every other woman in the hall.

"Could I speak to you in private, Valentina?" Pelayo called out to her.

No doubt aware that everyone was staring at her, Valentina kept her face expressionless. "I'd like to go to my chamber to fetch some spare cloaks and blankets for the guests. You can accompany me there if you wish."

Pelayo nodded, then gestured for her to lead the way.

Valentina rose from her chair to came around the table. Pelayo fell in step beside her and together they made their way out of the hall.

They were climbing the staircase to the upper floor of the castle when Pelayo broke the silence. "You must be surprised by what just happened."

"To say the least," Valentina said, staring straight ahead of her.

Aware that their voices carried over great lengths within the stone walls of the corridors, they did not speak again until they had entered her bedchamber.

Pelayo trailed behind Valentina as she picked up a lit taper and began lighting the oil lamps scattered around the chamber.

"You seem remarkably calm, considering I've just thrown your husband into the dungeons," Pelayo said.

The glow from a flickering oil lamp lit up Valentina's face. "Julian can rot in hell for all I care."

Pelayo stared at her in silence.

"Surprised?" Valentina asked.

"I probably shouldn't be. I heard the way you spoke to him at the fair."

Valentina went to light another oil lamp. "The last time I saw you, you were running for your life. How did you manage to get the guards to turn on Julian?"

"It wasn't all that difficult, once I got Yxtaverra on my side. For some reason he seems to think that I'm the only one who can unify the northern cities and keep the Moors at bay."

"Is there a realistic chance of that happening?"

"Not the way things stand. Even if every city in the north empties out its garrisons, all we can do is field enough men to put up a good fight."

"So, it's hopeless then," Valentina said.

"We still have a chance. If we can get the Basques to join us."

"The Basques have been our enemy for centuries. What makes you think they'll want to help us?"

"Because the Moors pose a greater threat to them than we do."

"They're barbarians; they don't think logically like us."

"I hope you're wrong. Without the Basques at our side, the Moors are going to crush us."

Valentina nodded, her expression somber. "When are you planning to head north?"

"Within the week. I don't know how much time we have before the Moors come hunting for us."

They both fell silent, contemplating the harrowing prospect.

"I have something for you," Valentina said.

Pelayo looked at her in surprise. "What is it?"

Valentina went to her clothes chest and returned with a small pouch. She untied the drawstring and spilled its contents into the palm of her hand. "Julian's great-uncle Siberto said his soldiers had found this around the neck of a dead man he claimed was you."

Pelayo gazed down at his mother's medallion. "I thought I'd never see that again," he said, breaking out in a smile.

"I've kept it all these years, knowing how much it meant to you."

Pelayo took the medallion, then ran his fingertip over the script incised into its surface. "Thank you," he said, slipping the gold chain over his head.

"You're welcome," Valentina said. "So, what is it you wanted to talk to me about?"

"I'd like to ask you a question about Ermesinda," Pelayo said.

Valentina's brow furrowed. "What do you want to know?"

Pelayo hesitated. "She doesn't look anything like Julian."

Valentina did not answer for a moment. "I suppose she's taken after my side of the family."

"Does any one of them have red hair?"

Valentina's puzzlement cleared with sudden understanding. "No, not that I know of," she said quietly.

Pelayo's eyes locked on hers. "My mother did; the same shade as Ermesinda's."

When she didn't respond, Pelayo pressed her. "Is Ermesinda my daughter?"

Valentina let out her breath. "From what you've just told me, I think she could well be."

"Could well be? What kind of an answer is that?"

Valentina realized the time had come to share the secret that she had kept to herself all these years for Ermesinda's sake. "Do you remember the day we arrived in Gijón, when the guards took you prisoner?"

"I do."

"That night, while I was sleeping, Julian broke into my room and forced himself upon me."

Pelayo stared at her aghast.

"Because of the timing of Ermesinda's birth," she continued. "I was never quite certain which of you was her father."

Pelayo stared at her in shock, then his eyes filled with sympathy. "I'm so sorry Valentina, I can't imagine what you must have gone through."

"It was difficult. I found it very hard to go on."

"I don't understand. How could you bring yourself to marry him after what he did to you?"

Valentina held his gaze. "That was the price he exacted from me for your freedom."

Pelayo looked as if he'd been struck by a mailed fist. "You sacrificed yourself for me?"

"I couldn't bear the thought of you locked up in the dungeon like an animal."

Valentina noticed some emotion flicker behind Pelayo's eyes. "What is it?"

Pelayo took a moment, as if reluctant to answer. "Julian lied to you when he said he was going to set me free. He only pretended to let me go."

"But I was up on the battlements that night; I saw you walk out of the castle a free man."

"I barely got half a league away before Julian's men sprung up from the darkness and took me captive again."

A wave of anguish swept over Valentina. "No, it can't be…"

"I spent the next three years in Siberto's dungeon. I'd still be there had it not been for Theodosius helping me to escape."

Something gave way inside her and she began to cry. "I can't believe it… All those wasted years, living with a man I loathed."

Pelayo put his arms around her and held her against his

chest. "I'm sorry, I knew it was going to upset you, but I had to tell you the truth. Only the truth now can set us free from the web of lies in which Julian has ensnared us both."

Valentina looked up at him, her face glistening with tears. "Why did Julian go through all that trouble to force me to marry him? He doesn't love me; he never did."

"He must have figured out that you cared for me. He could not have stomached the idea of losing you to me."

"If his intention was to keep us apart, he certainly accomplished his goal." she said sadly.

"Well, we're together now, Valentina. And I still want you."

"But you were so cold and distant with me at the fair," she said.

"I was angry with you."

"Why?"

"I resented you for marrying Julian. I thought you had forgotten about me."

"How could you think that? There's not been a day since we parted that you haven't been foremost in my thoughts."

Pelayo drew her into his arms and kissed her.

"I love you, Valentina," he whispered, his face close to hers.

The feel of his body pressing against hers, the scent of his skin, it was all that she remembered, and more.

She could have stayed in his arms all night, but after some time, he drew away from her.

"I have to go check on my men," he said. "I'll come back to your chamber when I'm done."

Valentina hesitated, then said, "As much as I would like that, I don't think it's wise. All eyes are going to be on you. The last thing you need is for people to whisper that the reason you threw your half-brother into the dungeons was to steal his wife."

"I don't care, let them whisper what they want," Pelayo said. "I've put up with rumors all my life."

"This time is different. You've never had to raise an army or persuade men to follow you into battle before."

"We can be careful. No one needs to find out about us."

"You know as well as I do that there are no secrets in a castle," Valentina said. "A guard might see you coming out of my room, or a servant girl could find something you've left behind in my chamber. The moment there's even a whiff of a scandal, it'll spread like fire."

Pelayo stared at her in silence, then nodded. "You're right. There's too much at stake here. It seems fate is always conspiring against us, doesn't it?"

"It'll just be for a few weeks," Valentina said. "Until you gain the trust of the guards here, and of the soldiers in the garrison."

When the thirteen men that had been sent away returned from their patrol, Pelayo, Yxtaverra and the rest of the house guards met them in the courtyard. Standing in the torchlight, Pelayo informed the returning horsemen that he had overthrown Julian, then explained his reasons for doing so.

The men sat unmoving on their horses, looking unsure as to how to respond.

The tension mounted, until Yxtaverra called out, "What is it to be, gentlemen? Will you join us and do the right thing for your country?"

Though Yxtaverra had not threatened them in any way, the men could not have helped but notice that their comrades facing them were all wearing full battle gear. Understanding the consequences of rejecting the offer, every man dismounted, then, kneeling on one knee, swore an oath of fealty to Pelayo.

Neither Yxtaverra nor Pelayo harbored any illusion that

pressuring the guards to swear an oath of fealty was anything but a short-term remedy to what was in fact a thorny problem. The truth was that these thirteen men could not be trusted. For that reason, Yxtaverra had planned that, at the first opportunity, he would deploy them to various outposts across the province.

At dawn, Pelayo made his way up the castle staircase that led to Julian's bedchamber. He unlocked the door with one of the keys the chamberlain had given him, then made his way to a large chest lying at the foot of the bed. After rifling through its contents, he found what he had been searching for, a military tunic and a commander's red cloak.

After changing into the clothing, he found a saddlebag and stuffed some other items into it: an oiled travel cloak for rainy weather, a pair of clean leggings, a woolen shirt and a light blanket. When he was done, he headed back down the stairs. Taking a torch from a sconce in the corridor, he unlocked an iron-studded door with another key from the chamberlain's ring and stepped into the darkened chamber.

The armory looked neglected and the racks of armor and weapons lay under a layer of dust. Lifting the torch over his head, he made his way down a narrow aisle toward the back of the chamber where his father's personal armor and his weapons were stored. He was relieved to see they were all still there in their stands.

Carefully propping up his torch against a wall, he removed his cloak, then put on his father's chainmail shirt, helmet and greaves. To his surprise, they all fit him perfectly. As he strapped on his father's sword belt around his waist, he caught his reflection on the polished metal of a nearby shield. A grim-looking, helmeted stranger gazed back at him.

After relocking the armory, he returned the keys to the chamberlain, then made his way outside to the courtyard. The sky was overcast and the air heavy with the threat of rain. He slung his saddlebag over his shoulder and walked toward the stable where Yxtaverra stood waiting for him with two horses.

After greeting Yxtaverra, who like him had stayed up most of the night, he threw his saddlebag over the back of his horse. He was just about to mount when he heard Valentina call out to him.

"Leaving so soon?"

Pelayo was surprised to see Valentina up so early. "We're heading out to the garrison. I'm going to break the news to the soldiers there that I've placed Julian in the dungeon and taken his place. If they don't hang me as a traitor, I'll be back before nightfall."

"Perhaps I should come with you," Valentina said. "Having me at your side will lend you legitimacy."

"Are you certain you want to get involved in this? It could turn out badly."

"I'd like to do my part," Valentina answered.

Pelayo thought about it for a moment, then nodded. "Very well, let's get your horse saddled."

After the sentries let them onto the grounds of the garrison, Pelayo, Valentina and Yxtaverra steered their horses toward a fenced-in enclosure. They left their horses in the care of a groom, then headed out on foot toward a large wooden building which Yxtaverra identified as the command center.

Entering through the door, Pelayo found himself inside a large, nearly deserted hall. At the far end, by a window, a group of officers stood hunched over a wooden table, gazing down at what appeared to be a map. The man who Pelayo assumed was the garrison commander turned toward him and his companions, eying them with surprise.

The garrison commander was a small, wiry man with close-cropped, gray hair, and a dour look on his beardless face. His proud, erect stance and puffed out chest, reminded Pelayo of a fighting cock.

As they approached, the commander dismissed his officers, then turned to Valentina and gave her a quick, precise bow. "Good morning, Doña Valentina. It's a pleasure to see you again."

"Good morning, Commander Cordario," Valentina replied. "May I present to you Lord Pelayo, my husband's half-brother?"

Commander Cordario studied Pelayo with open curiosity. "It's an honor to make your acquaintance, Lord Pelayo," he said, with a bow. "You don't look anything like I imagined you to be."

"I hope you're not disappointed, commander," Pelayo answered, knowing Cordario was probably alluding to the stories of his youthful indiscretions.

"Not at all," Commander Cordario said easily. He nodded to Yxtaverra in greeting, then said, "Would any of you like something to drink or to eat?"

Pelayo, Valentina and Yxtaverra all declined the offer.

"Well then," Commander Cordario said briskly. "May I ask what brings you all here?"

"I'd like to address your men," Pelayo said. "Would you mind assembling them for me?"

Commander Cordario seemed taken aback. "May I ask why, sire?"

"You'll find out soon enough, commander," Pelayo answered. "Yes, of course."

Standing alongside Commander Cordario, Valentina watched as the garrison's soldiers gathered on the parade ground. With impressive precision, they lined up in formation, the squad leaders standing before their units. Once everyone had settled and grown quiet, Pelayo marched across the field toward the viewing stand, then climbed up the steps to the top of the wooden platform.

Misgivings about their undertaking suddenly began assailing Valentina. These men were Julian's troops; how were they going to react to a stranger telling them that he had wrested power from the very man whom they had sworn an oath to follow?

Pelayo gazed out at the two hundred and fifty or so soldiers lined up before him. The silence stretched on, broken only by the cawing of gulls as they swooped overhead. He had gone over in his head the core of what he wanted to say, but he had learned over the years that it was best to speak spontaneously and from the heart, when addressing large groups of men. Relying on his instincts once again to guide him, he cleared his mind of distractions and began to speak in a strong, loud voice.

"There are some who say that the war with the Moors is over, that they've beaten us into submission, that they've broken our spirit. They say that there is no one left in the country with the stomach to oppose them."

Pelayo fell into the familiar cadence that he used when addressing troops, allowing the silence to settle before speaking again.

"These people will tell you that the Moors are too numerous, their armies too powerful, their grip on our land too firmly entrenched. They say we should accept our defeat with grace."

Pelayo paused as a gust of wind sent his cloak billowing behind him. "I'm here to tell you that they are wrong, that all is not lost, that we can fight back against the scourge that has befallen our country."

He paused, longer this time, before continuing. "I know some of you must be thinking, who is this stranger who stands before us and makes these claims? What does he offer us besides empty words of hope?"

"But I am no stranger; I'm an Asturian, just like you. The blood of your forefathers runs through my veins as well. The songs and stories of our land are just as much a part of me as they are of you. I have trained with you in this very field, broken bread with you, shared your campfires. I have fought at your side, seen our comrades fall in battle, watched them die."

"I have also dealt out death to the invaders. Two fortnights ago, I led an army of brave men to victory against the Moors in Girona. We cut them down to a man, without mercy, as they did to us when I fought with the King in Guadalete."

Someone in the ranks cried out, "It's Lord Pelayo! Duke Fáfila's son!"

A buzz-like murmur rippled through the lines.

"Yes, I am Pelayo. And I've returned to finish the task my father once asked of me, to cast the invaders off our land."

Some of the men broke into cheers.

Pelayo waited for the cheers to die down, the said: "In order to fulfill my father's wish, I've had to first wrest power from a man who was unworthy of wielding it. A man who betrayed our king and his own people: my half-brother, Julian."

Another murmur rippled like a wave through the ranks. Pelayo saw the garrison commander stiffen, then exchange glances with the officers at his side. Putting them out of his mind for the time being, he continued his address.

"I did not act against my half-brother to satisfy a lust for power. I did so for the sake of our country, for our people, and for your children. And for the generations that will come after us."

He paused to let his words sink in. "I have come to you this morning because I have need of brave men willing to follow me to war. I shall not lie to you. I cannot assure you that we will be victorious. It may come to pass that fortune will not smile upon us and that we may fail in our endeavour. And even if we prevail, some of you standing before me this morning will fall under the sword. And more of you will bear scars for the rest of your lives. How then can I ask this sacrifice of you?"

Pelayo's gaze swept over the faces before him. "I ask because you are our people's last hope. I ask because you are all that stands between their freedom and their enslavement. I ask because it is your duty as soldiers to fight for your country, and yes, if necessary, to lay down your life in its defense."

Pelayo stopped to let his words sink in. No one so much as stirred.

"Well, what say you?" Pelayo cried out, his voice ringing across the field. "Will you fight at my side? Will you join me to cast off the invaders from our land?"

There was a momentary silence, then the men erupted in a collective roar.

Pelayo's voice cut through the din, "May God watch over us and lead us to victory!"

The cries of the men gathered momentum, building to a crescendo of voices that washed in waves over Valentina.

CHAPTER 38

"HOW COULD PELAYO have seized power without laying siege to the castle?" Olmund asked.

Riding at his nephew's side, Siberto shrugged. "I don't know," he admitted. The message the informant had given him had been scant in details.

"Do you really believe he's overthrown Julian?" Olmund asked.

Siberto pointed a thumb at the six men riding behind him along the dirt road. "I wouldn't have brought them with me if I didn't, now would I?"

Olmund made a scoffing sound. "I'm sure we'll get to Gijón and find Julian sitting at the table, stuffing his face. How he's going to laugh at us!"

Siberto gazed balefully at his nephew. It was hard to believe the cretin was Witiza's son. With a bitter shake of his head, he dismissed the boy from his thoughts and studied the position of the sun. It was mid-afternoon. There was plenty of daylight left. A good thing too, as they still had a considerable distance to go.

Siberto and his party finally reached the city of Gijón in the evening. Before approaching the main gates, they split into three groups, hoping to avoid undue attention from the guards. Once inside, they regrouped in the main square. Knowing they had some time on their hands, they found an inn and ordered some food. Afterward they nursed a flagon or two of ale until the inn closed.

It was well past midnight when they took to the road again. Siberto had timed the journey to take advantage of the full moon, but the cloudless sky was an added boon.

After riding in silence for a time, Siberto turned in the saddle and called out quietly to Olmund, "I'll do all the talking with the guards. So shut your mouth and answer only if you're spoken to directly, understand?"

Olmund nodded.

"Afterwards, you'll stay behind with the horses."

Olmund shot him a sullen look. "If I'm to play no part in this, why did you ask me to come with you?"

"Because I wanted the pleasure of your company, that's why," Siberto said, his voice dripping with sarcasm. Truth was he had neither planned nor wanted to bring Olmund along, but he had been asked to do so by the boy's mother.

"I want you to take Olmund with you," she had told him.

"It'll be dangerous for the boy, Eldora" he had warned her.

"He's not a boy; he's eighteen. It's time for him to prove he has the mettle to sit on the throne."

It was then that Siberto had realized that Eldora had not given up the dream that her son would one day be crowned king. That had about as much chance of happening now as pigs learning to fly. After going back and forth on the issue for a while, in the end he had ceded to her request, feeling that he owed it to his dead brother.

After cutting across the city, Siberto and his party followed a dirt road that led them up the side of a hill. Some time later, the ghostly outline of a castle materialized in the darkness ahead of them.

"Remember," Siberto whispered to Olmund. "Act naturally; don't fidget." He was not reassured when Olmund nodded to him nervously.

With his men trailing behind him, Siberto rode up to the barred gates of the castle, then halted his horse. Two torches perched in iron brackets on both sides of the massive doors flickered in the night breeze.

"Who goes there?" a guard called out from the watchtower, clearly unsettled by the sight of eight riders emerging from the darkness.

"It is I, Baron Siberto."

"Oh, good evening, sire. I didn't recognize you in the dark."

"That's all right. Can you open the gates and let us in? We've come a long ways to pay Lord Pelayo a visit."

"I'm sorry, sire, Lord Pelayo is away."

Siberto feigned surprise. "Really? Well, no matter. We can visit with Lady Izaskun until he gets back."

"I'm afraid that won't be possible either, Don Siberto. We have orders not to let anyone in."

"Surely those orders do not apply to your lord's family?" Siberto said, allowing an edge of impatience to creep into his voice.

The guard looked down from the watchtower, clearly at a loss as to what to do or say next.

"Come now, take pity on us," Siberto said. "We've been on the road for days. Be a good man and let us in."

"I...uh...Perhaps I could ask my commanding officer."

"Why disturb him?" Siberto said recovering his amiable tone. "We're not exactly strangers, are we?"

His words were met with silence. *Easy now*, Siberto warned

himself. *Don't arouse his suspicions.* "But if you feel you must, then by all means, go check with him."

"It won't take long, Don Siberto."

After the guard disappeared, Siberto and his men dismounted.

A short time later, one of the two wooden gates swung open and a helmeted officer in the company of three guards, including the first one from the tower, came striding forth.

"Good evening, Baron Siberto," the officer called out. "My name is Marcus. I am the officer in charge of the night watch."

"Well met, Commander Marcus," Siberto said. "May I present my nephew, Olmund, son of our late king, Witiza."

Commander Marcus appeared impressed. Siberto knew that it wasn't every day that one got to meet the son of a king.

"It is an honor to make your acquaintance, sire," Commander Marcus said with a respectful bow to Olmund.

Olmund mumbled a reply.

Commander Marcus turned back to Siberto. "I'm told you've come for a visit?"

"In truth it's more than a visit, commander," Siberto said. "As you probably know, my niece, Lady Izaskun, is gravely ill. This could very well be the last time my nephew and I get to pay our respects to her."

The young officer nodded understandingly. "I would like nothing better than to grant your request, Don Siberto, but unfortunately I have been instructed not to let anyone inside until Lord Pelayo's return."

"As I told your sentry, I am quite certain that my nephew could not have intended those orders to apply to his own family."

"I do not know what he intended, my lord, only what he said," Commander Marcus said more firmly.

Siberto's smile became a little forced. "Commander Marcus,

you're not seriously suggesting turning us away after we've come all this way, are you?"

"I'm sorry Don Siberto, I'm afraid my hands are tied."

"I have a letter in my saddlebag from Lord Pelayo," Siberto said. "It is an invitation to come at any time, whether he's here or not. I think it will satisfy you. May I show it to you?" he asked, swinging his leg over his horse and dismounting. Without waiting for an answer, he took his saddlebag from the back of his horse and brought it over to Commander Marcus.

Unfastening the flap, Siberto reached inside the bag, shielding his actions with a slight turn of his body. Behind him, his men began as unobtrusively as possible to outflank the castle's soldiers.

Without warning, Siberto drew a dagger from his saddlebag, then rammed it into the chest of Commander Marcus, aiming for the heart. As if a signal had been given, Siberto's men sprang into action, swarming over the three castle guards who, in the relative darkness, took a fraction too long to comprehend what had just occurred. Siberto covered the commander's mouth with his hand and held on until he felt the man go limp.

In a moment, it was over, with wall three guards lying on the ground, their throats slit.

Siberto stood frozen in a half-crouch, his heart pounding, all his senses on alert. But there was only the sound of leaves rustling in the night breeze. He motioned to his men to proceed. They dragged away the guards' bodies and disposed of them down a ravine.

Siberto turned his gaze toward Olmund, who was standing by his horse, looking shaken. His decision to leave him behind in charge of the horses had been the right one. That was all the weak-kneed fool could handle, Siberto thought with contempt.

With a gesture to his men to follow him, Siberto entered

the short passageway under the gatehouse that led into the courtyard. Before stepping out into the open, he stuck his head around the corner of the wall and scanned the moonlit grounds. Assured there was no one in sight, he led his men at a run toward one of the stone buildings on the other side of the courtyard. He was panting lightly by the time he reached a small, side door in the building. As expected, it was unlocked, and he and his men scurried inside.

Though Siberto kept the door open behind him, it took time for his eyes to adjust to the even dimmer light of the small, suffocating space which served as the top landing of a staircase. Arms spread out, he felt his way down the steps. Slowly, he descended into the bowels of the castle, his men treading quietly behind him. When he reached the bottom landing, he fumbled around in the darkness until he located a door. Finding it locked, he thumped on the thick, wooden planks with his gloved fist and waited.

"Who's there?" came a muffled voice from the other side of the door.

Siberto covered his mouth with his hand. "It's Commander Marcus! Open up."

There came the sound of a bolt being withdrawn, then the door swung open. A bearded face peered back at Siberto.

The man's bored expression turned to one of surprise. "Who the devil are you? How did you —"

Siberto kicked the door open, sending it crashing against the guard. From behind him, his men stormed into the room. One of them dispatched the guard with a thrust of his sword.

Sitting at a table in the middle of the chamber, the second guard scrambled to his feet, his arms raised in the air in a gesture of surrender. The terrified expression on his face revealed his desire to escape the fate of his comrade.

One of Siberto's men leapt at the guard, then cut his throat with a knife. The stricken guard went down without a sound. *So far, so good*, Siberto thought to himself, his chest tight with tension. A quick search of the guardroom revealed a ring of keys hanging on a wooden peg. Siberto took the keys and one of the torches, then led his men down a dimly lit passageway flanked with doors that, like in his own dungeon, small viewing slits cut into them at eye level.

After looking inside each cell, one of his men found Julian halfway down the passageway.

Julian lay unshackled on the ground, and though filthy and wild-haired, he appeared to be fairing well, considering the circumstances.

"Is that you Uncle?" Julian called out in a raspy voice, shielding his eyes from the torchlight with his hand.

"Of course it's me. Who else would have the balls to free you from this stinking hole?"

"I knew you wouldn't forget me," Julian said, as he rose to his feet, his voice thick with emotion.

When Siberto had first heard of Julian's predicament, he had concluded that it would be too dangerous a venture to come to his great-nephew's rescue. As time had gone by however, he had reconsidered his decision. He had been a party to Pelayo's imprisonment years earlier, and the fact that the bastard was now more or less living at his backdoor, probably plotting revenge on him, was deeply unsettling. What had finally driven him to act however, was the realization that the loss of Gijón would cause the Moors to question whether any of their Christian administrators, and that included himself, could be counted on to maintain control over the territories that had been entrusted to them. After weighing the issue carefully, he had concluded that his own fortunes were inexorably tied to those of Julian. There were limits though to the risks he was prepared take.

"I swear I'll never forget this, Uncle," Julian said with heartfelt sincerity.

"That's all right. Let's get out of here."

"There are three of my companions down here somewhere," Julian said. "We have to free them too."

"Forget it. We didn't bring enough horses for them."

"Are you just going to ride out of here?"

"Of course; what do you think?"

"You could have taken back the castle with a few dozen men-at-arms."

"No, I couldn't. It's one thing to steal into the castle in the middle of the night, and quite another to get into a pitched battle with thirty or forty house guards. Besides, even if we had done that, your garrison would have sent out troops and retaken the castle in short order."

Julian stared at Siberto. "So, the bastard's turned the garrison against me."

"To a man."

Julian clenched his jaw, hatred glittering in his eyes. "Well, six is more than enough to kill the treacherous bastard while he's sleeping in his bed."

"Pelayo's not here," Siberto said. "He left the castle weeks ago. Come on, let's get the hell out of here. We'll talk later."

Julian grabbed his uncle's arm. "I'm not leaving without my friends. They can ride double with your men."

Siberto hesitated, then reluctantly nodded. "All right; let's go find them."

A quick search revealed Julian's companions in a cell near the end of the corridor. After unlocking their cell door, everyone headed back toward the guardroom. Julian and one of his companions helped themselves to the dead guards' weapons, then followed Siberto up the staircase to the courtyard.

Siberto stuck his head out to make sure there was no one in sight, then broke into a run. Again, fortune smiled upon him and he and his men managed to slip out of the castle unseen.

In the light of the false dawn, Siberto spotted Olmund standing by the horses, looking around nervously. *We're bloody lucky he didn't bolt on us,* he thought, breathing a sigh of relief. As he was walking toward his horse, Julian grabbed him by the arm.

"I'm going back to get my wife and daughter," Julian said, pitching his voice low.

"Have you lost your senses?" Siberto said in a hoarse whisper. "You want to end up in the dungeon again?"

During these last few weeks, imprisoned in the bowels of the castle, all Julian had thought about was the way Valentina had looked at Pelayo at the fair and the way she had tried to protect him. It was clear that she still had feelings for him. He was damned if he was going to leave her to the bastard. And Ermesinda was the sun and moon of his world. He could not imagine his life without her. "Everyone's asleep. My men and I can get to Valentina's and Ermesinda's chambers without being seen."

"You're tempting fate. You're going to get us all killed."

"Just wait here with your men. If we're not back in short order, you can ride off and leave us behind."

"You're damn right I will," Siberto said. "At the first cry of alarm, you're on your own. And this time I am not coming back for you, understand?"

"Fair enough," Julian answered. Turning away, he gestured to his men and led them back into the gatehouse.

Siberto mounted his horse, noticing how quickly the sky was brightening. The thought of losing the cover of darkness brought butterflies to his stomach. The one consoling thought was that dawn also meant that the city gates would soon be opened. If the alarm was sounded, he and his men would probably have time to ride out of the city before word reached the guards to bar the gates.

Time trickled by slowly for Siberto as he did his best to keep his horse quiet. After what seemed like an eternity, he heard the soft patter of running feet. His heart began to pound in his chest as he drew out his sword and stared intently at the dark passageway.

Ghost-like figures emerged from the interior. Julian was carrying a young girl in his arms. Two of his companions were holding Valentina, who was clad in her nightclothes. A third man was holding a knife to her throat.

Damn me to hell, Siberto thought with grudging admiration. *The fool's gone and done it.*

CHAPTER 39

A BITING WIND blew in from the snow-capped peaks encircling the valley. It was early morning and so quiet that Pelayo could hear the bleating of sheep grazing on a slope half a league away. It had taken the better part of three weeks for his Basque guide, Eguzki, to lead him there and he felt relieved at the thought that his search might finally be coming to an end.

The town in the distance, the supposed lair of the Basque warlord he was seeking, sat perched halfway up the mountainside. With a long and unpronounceable name that he couldn't wrap his tongue around, the town seemed surprisingly large, with hundreds of stone houses that looked as if they could withstand the fiercest of gales or the harshest of winter storms. He was surprised that the people he had always thought of as savages possessed such accomplished building skills. He wondered what other of his assumptions about them might be wrong. Who were these strangers who had been their hostile neighbors for centuries? All he really knew about them was that they were an ancient people with a strange language, and customs that were so different from their Iberian culture.

It took Pelayo and his guide most of the morning to reach

the town on the mountainside. Eguzki had been there twice before and was able to guide them down one of the narrow streets toward the town center.

They passed by a smattering of shops and soon began encountering some of the townspeople walking about. The women were garbed in colorful bodices, shawls and long skirts, while the men wore white shirts, lambswool vests, and pale-colored leggings.

They rode by an ironsmith's shop, whose doors were open wide. The heat of the forge wafted out to the street. Inside the shop, two men wearing sweat-stained leather aprons were hammering away at a chunk of red-hot iron. Another man stood idly by, seemingly waiting for some item to be made for him.

Pelayo and Eguzki reined in their horses, drawing the attention of the three men inside. Eguzki greeted them in their tongue, then spoke with them at length. Though his guide's words were incomprehensible to him, Pelayo knew that Eguzki was telling the men that they were seeking Bortaroitz.

The three men inside stared back at them, giving no indication of having understood a word of what Eguzki had said.

His guide took out a silver coin from this purse, held it aloft, then addressed the three men again. Once more he was met with blanks stares.

Pelayo looked at Eguzki, "Tell them the offer is only good until sunset and that we'll be at the alehouse in the town center, the one you told me about."

As they rode away, Eguzki told Pelayo, "We're wasting our time, my friend. No one is going to tell us anything, not with an outsider like you at my side. You should go on ahead and let me see what I can find out on my own."

Pelayo knew that Eguzki was just trying to be helpful and earn the bonus that he had been promised, if and when they found the Basque chieftain. His advice in other circumstances would have made perfect sense, but not today. "I'd like to do it my way, Eguzki."

His Basque guide shrugged. "Suit yourself."

Pelayo and Eguzki made three more stops along the way to the town center. Each time Eguzki repeated the offer to pay for information on Bortaroitz' whereabouts. As was the case at the ironsmith's shop, he might as well have been talking to statues for all the response he got from anyone.

The road eventually led them to the main square. It was small by Asturian standards, barely four or five times the width of a house and encircled by two-story buildings with iron bars on the windows of the lower floors.

Pelayo and Eguzki came to a stop in front of one of the buildings that had a weather-beaten sign hanging over its door. After tying their horses to the hitching rings imbedded in a wall, they both went inside.

The inn's common area was a medium-sized room with a low ceiling, exposed rafters and stale air that smelled of ale and smoke. There were six tables, all vacant except for one occupied by a man eating from a bowl. Pelayo and Eguzki took a table at the back of the inn.

"Might as well order us something to drink," Pelayo told Eguzki. "We could be here for a while."

The wait turned out to be far shorter than Pelayo had anticipated. They had barely downed their first cup of ale, when the door to the inn swung open and four men filed inside. There was little to distinguish one from the other: barrel-chested, broad-faced, with thick dark beards.

The four made their way toward Pelayo and Eguzki. Coming to a stop at their table, one of the men rattled off something in Basque.

Pelayo had no idea what the man had said, but the brusque manner of his delivery made it clear that it hadn't been a friendly greeting.

Eguzki turned toward Pelayo. "He wants to know what we're doing here and what we want from Bortaroitz."

"Tell him that what I have to say is for the warlord's ears only," Pelayo answered.

A look of concern flitted across Eguzki's face, but he followed Pelayo's instructions.

The man spoke again, this time with an edge of anger in his voice.

Eguzki translated his words for Pelayo, "He wants to know who you are...or words to that effect."

"Tell him I am a chieftain in my own land, like Bortaroitz."

Eguzki did as he was told.

The hulking figure above them, clearly the leader of the group, stared insolently at Pelayo, then said something.

Eguzki translated again. "He says you do not look like a chieftain to him."

Pelayo rose slowly to his feet, his right hand on the pommel of his sword. He stared into the eyes of the Basque man, who like his companions, was armed only with a knife. "Tell him I consider his words an insult."

Eguzki's eyes widened in alarm.

"Go on, tell him," Pelayo snapped, his expression grim. If his youth had taught him anything, it was that showing weakness to an oaf was a bad idea that would only lead to the idiot feeling emboldened.

The innkeeper rushed to their table and spoke rapidly to the four Basque men. Eguzki joined in. Whatever was said, it seemed to ease the tension. The bearded Basque leader mumbled something.

Looking relieved, Eguzki told Pelayo, "He says he regrets not choosing his words with more care."

Pelayo's gaze remained locked on the bearded face before him. "Tell him that the message I carry for Bortaroitz is of grave importance and that his lord will thank him for taking me to him."

After Eguzki translated Pelayo's words, the bearded leader mulled over the question for a moment, then nodded his assent.

The Basque men had their horses waiting outside. After mounting, they led Pelayo and Eguzki out of town, then took them up a mountain road that spiraled upward for several leagues.

It was late afternoon when they reached a fortress of rough-hewn timber perched on a cliffside overlooking the valley. The front gates were open, and they rode into a courtyard filled with running children, servants, and dogs that immediately burst into a cacophony of barking.

One of the Basque men called out to a kerchiefed woman who was on her knees, washing clothes in a stone basin. The woman pointed toward a side structure with two large doors of weathered wooden planks. The bearded Basque leader dismounted, then beckoned to Pelayo and Eguzki to follow him.

The whicker of a horse and the smell of manure and freshly cut hay greeted Pelayo as he stepped inside the building. When his eyes adjusted to the dim light, he spotted three men in one of the stalls at the far end of the barn. The three were on their knees, tending to what appeared to be a sick horse lying on its side. Two of the men looked like stable hands; the third was a thickset, gray-haired man with a fur cape draped around his shoulders.

It seemed that his search for the warlord Bortaroitz had come to an end.

The gray-haired man looked across at Pelayo and Eguzki as they approached. After peppering their bearded escort with what sounded like a string of questions, the man turned toward Pelayo and studied him with open curiosity.

"I'm Bortaroitz," the man said in deep voice. "Why are you looking for me?"

Pelayo was caught off guard at being addressed in Iberian.

"Surprised a barbarian can speak your tongue?" Bortaroitz asked with an amused smile.

"You must admit that ability is rather rare in these parts," Pelayo answered. "How is it you speak Iberian so well?"

"You can blame my father for that. He wanted all his children to be able to speak your tongue. He thought it would prove useful when the day came to establish trade between our people and yours."

"I commend your father on his foresight."

"Do you? I think it was nothing but a foolish dream."

"Perhaps the world has need of more dreamers like him."

"What my people need are leaders who can see the world for what it is."

Pelayo had no answer for that.

Bortaroitz rose to his feet. "Who's the man with you?"

"He's my guide."

"He can wait outside."

Before Pelayo could say anything, Eguzki turned and walked away.

Bortaroitz fixed his gaze on Pelayo again. "So, why are you here? My man thinks you're a spy."

"I haven't spent three weeks searching for you to count how many cows and sheep you have. There are more pressing issues facing my people at the moment."

"I've heard of your war with the Moors, if that's what you're referring to," Bortaroitz said.

Pelayo nodded. "We are in a desperate situation. The Moors are going to overrun us unless we can find allies to fight on our side."

Bortaroitz looked amused. "Do you really expect my people to come to the aid of their sworn enemies? You must be addled to think we'd lift a finger to help you."

"The Moors pose as much of a threat to you as they do to us. It would serve both our interests to join forces in a common cause."

"Have you heard the old saying: the enemy of my enemy is my friend?"

"The enemy of your enemy will seize your land after they've stolen ours."

"Let them try," Bortaroitz said. "They'll discover that we are not an easy people to conquer."

"Your mountains will not protect you forever," Pelayo said. "If the Moors defeat us, it'll just be a matter of time before they come marching into your valleys."

Pelayo's words seemed to have an impact on Bortaroitz and he remained silent for a moment.

"Even if I found your argument persuasive," Bortaroitz said. "there are limits to what I can accomplish. We Basques are an independent lot; we don't have a common ruler. That means that I have neither the power nor the right to speak for any warlord other than myself."

"You never had any trouble banding together to make war upon us," Pelayo remarked dryly.

"That is true, but fighting Iberians is a time-honored tradition," Bortaroitz said with a sardonic smile.

The horse lying at Bortaroitz' feet snorted, then raised

its head feebly. The Basque warlord bent from the waist and stroked its neck for a moment before straightening again. "I heard that your King was killed in battle. On whose authority do you act?"

"My own," Pelayo answered. "I am the lord of a province called Asturias. My land lies to the west of—"

Bortaroitz cut him off brusquely, "I know where it is. My people and I are well acquainted with Asturians, much to our great misfortune."

"As are my people with the Basques."

Bortaroitz acknowledged Pelayo's point with a nod. "So, you are Julian, Fáfila's whelp."

"No. I am his second son, Pelayo. Julian is my half-brother."

Bortaroitz' expression underwent a remarkable change. "You're Ermasinda's son?"

Pelayo's brow furrowed. "How do you know my mother's name? No one knows that."

"No one except her family, you mean," Bortaroitz said. "Ermasinda is my sister."

It took a moment for Pelayo to absorb the warlord's remarkable claim. "You may have a sister named Ermasinda, but I assure you she is not my mother."

"Why do you doubt it?"

"Because the notion is absurd."

"Is it?" Bortaroitz reached under the neckline of his tunic then pulled out a medallion dangling from a gold chain around his neck. "I'm going to wager that you've seen something like this around your mother's neck."

Pelayo froze, staring at the gold medallion.

"Well? Does it bring up any memories?"

Pelayo pulled out his own medallion from under the collar of his tunic.

"Ah." Bortaroitz broke into a smile. "So, you have it now."

Pelayo nodded, staring wordless at the man before him.

"My father had three of those made," Bortaroitz said, pointing to the medallion in Pelayo's hand. "He gave one to me and one to my sister. The third, which he kept for himself, was buried with him."

Pelayo thought back to the day when his father had recounted meeting his mother in the mountains of what his father had called the 'north'. As he went over his father's story in his head, at least those parts that he could remember, he realized that nothing his father had said contradicted Bortaroitz' claim.

"Has your mother not spoken to you about us, her family?" Bortaroitz said.

Pelayo's head was still reeling from shock, but he tried to gather himself. "My mother didn't have much of a chance to speak to me about anything. She died when I was very young."

Bortaroitz' face fell. "Oh," he said quietly, his expression turning somber. "So, Ermasinda is dead?"

Pelayo nodded. "She died seventeen years ago, when I was eight."

Bortaroitz let out a long breath, his grief apparent. "I always hoped I would see her again one day. He was silent for a moment, then asked, "How did she die?"

"From a long illness. She was bedridden for months."

"Did she suffer much?"

An image of his mother's pain ravaged face formed in Pelayo's mind. "It was not an easy passing."

"Poor Ermasinda," Bortaroitz murmured. "I can't begin to tell you how much we all missed her after she was sent away. My father came to regret his actions, you know. It tormented him for the rest of his life."

A silence settled between them.

"Can you tell me what is written on the medallion?" Pelayo asked.

"The words are in Basque. It's our family motto: 'Courage conquers all'.

"I always wondered what it meant," Pelayo said.

"It means you are one of us. How does it feel to know you have barbarian blood coursing through your veins?"

Pelayo knew the question was meant in jest, but as he looked into his uncle's eyes, the words came out of his mouth unbidden, "It makes me feel proud."

Bortaroitz smiled and clasped Pelayo by the shoulders. "Well said. I suppose this changes things between us now, doesn't it?"

CHAPTER 40

GOVERNOR MUSA IBN Nusayr made his way down a long corridor, certain that he had made a wrong turn somewhere and that he was no longer heading in the right direction. Though he had called Toledo home for about a month now, he had still not mastered the maze of passageways linking the buildings that made up the core of the former Christian citadel.

At the end of the hallway, Musa stepped through a door and walked out into a large courtyard thronging with soldiers. Somehow he had gotten to his intended destination. His gaze swept over the men unloading crates from a wagon, then fixed on a tall, mail-clad figure overseeing the work.

The officer caught sight of Musa and immediately hurried toward him.

"Greetings, your excellency," the officer called out.

"How did it go with General Tariq this morning?" Musa asked him.

The officer's swarthy face creased in a smile. "He swore to bring down the wrath of Allah on us."

"Yes, I can imagine. What did you do with him?"

"I confined him up in one of the chambers in the west

tower. I've tripled the guards outside and restricted access to the area."

"Well done. Make sure you keep an eye on him. I'll hold you responsible if he escapes."

"You need not worry, your excellency; he will not get out."

Musa retraced his steps back to his quarters. He was pleased with how well his plans had worked out. For over a year and a half he had bided his time in Carthage, waiting for the Berber invasion to reach its conclusion, whether it was to be in success or in failure. When he had finally gotten word that the conquest of the Iberian Peninsula was nearing its end, he had sailed off to Damascus to surprise Caliph Al-Walid with news of the victory. To his chagrin, he had discovered that a delegation from General Tariq had beaten him to the Caliph.

Caliph Al-Walid, however, no doubt realizing he had his governor to thank for conceiving and planning the invasion, had placed an army of fourteen thousand Saracen soldiers under Musa's command. The Caliph's instruction to him had been unambiguous: wrest control of the new territories from the Berbers, set up an administrative system of governance, then take charge until further advised.

Upon his return to Carthage, he had begun the arduous task of commandeering the ships needed to transport his new army to what many were now calling Al-Andalus, the land of light. A few months afterwards, upon receiving word that the fighting was nearing its end, he had set sail with a flotilla of one hundred and sixty-eight ships, each one filled with soldiers and supplies.

It had taken them four and half weeks to sail from Carthage to Valentia, a port city on the eastern coast of Al-Andalus. Save for a vicious storm that had battered them for days, swamping three ships, including one carrying his prized horse, the voyage had been otherwise uneventful. After landing in Valentia, he had led his army west to Toledo, the Berbers' newly founded center of command.

Musa's arrival in the city had caught Tariq by surprise. Though the Berber general had tried to be civil, his eyes had smoldered with outrage at what he correctly assumed was Musa's grab for power. But with his Berber warriors spread out in garrisons across the land, Tariq had had no choice but to accept the fact that the authority which he had wielded over Al-Andalus was about to slip away from his grasp.

Over the following weeks, Musa had made several attempts to buy off the Berber chieftain with gold in an attempt to have him go home. But the stubborn fool had refused to return to obscurity, making the situation untenable. Musa knew that he could not allow Tarik to lay about idle and embittered, not with an army of Berber warriors at his command. And so, he had acted.

As Musa walked into his audience chamber, his three advisors rose from their cushions and bowed in his direction. Musa waved them back down and joined them around a low-slung table of inlaid wood.

Abdul-Azim, his senior advisor, a tall man with stooped shoulders and a neatly kept beard, gave Musa a summary of the morning's events, the most interesting being a visit by Lord Julian, the infidel who had made the conquest of Al-Andalus possible.

"What did he want?" Musa asked, his curiosity piqued.

Abdul-Azim gave Musa a full account of the meeting.

Musa frowned in annoyance. "It seems the fool has been rather careless with the lands we entrusted to his care."

"Indeed so, your excellency."

Musa grunted. "Get rid of him. I don't care how you do it."

"With all due respect," Abdul-Azim said. "the infidel could still be useful to us."

"How?"

"He claims he has a spy on his half-brother' s war council. Apparently, the man could pass on to us all sorts of valuable information that we can use to take the Asturians by surprise and quash the rebellion before it has a chance to flourish."

The second advisor, Wahid, a slight man with sharp features spoke out, "I think it would be unwise to trust the infidel, your excellency. He may have been helpful to us once, but who knows what is in his heart now? What assurances do we have that he won't feed us lies? Imagine the harm such misinformation could cause us."

Musa sighed inwardly. He could always count on Wahid to give him the negative view. Still, all points needed to be considered. Indeed, it was because all three of his advisors usually offered him such contrasting advice that he was able to weigh every consequence when deciding on a complex issue.

The advisors continued to argue amongst themselves about Julian's proposal; when they began repeating their views, Musa held up his hand. "All right, that's enough."

Everyone quieted at once.

Musa turned toward Abdul-Azim. "Tell the infidel that if his efforts to aid us are fruitful, I shall restore his lands to him. To ensure he does not betray us, his wife and daughter, as well as the young heir, Olmund, shall remain here with us."

"Lord Julian might object to leaving all three of his family members behind, your excellency," Abdul-Azim said.

"Then it will be up to you to convince him otherwise."

"Yes, of course," Abdul-Azim murmured.

Musa turned to his third advisor, an elderly man with a long, gray beard and a habitual, mournful expression. "Khurram, you will be responsible for looking after our new guests."

Khurram nodded. "Yes, your excellency."

"The young man, Olmund will need your personal attention, of course."

Khurram's expression clouded. "Your excellency?"

Musa held Khurram's gaze without speaking, then said with exaggerated patience, "Think Khurram, what sort of attention should we lavish on the last remaining heir to the Iberian throne?"

The other two advisors looked away, seemingly finding the view through the window fascinating.

"Of course, your excellency," Khurram said. "I shall ensure that the young man's stay with us will be... permanent."

Musa nodded without comment.

"The fates have been kind to deliver the young heir into our hands," Abdul-Azim, the senior advisor, said.

Musa grunted in agreement. He could not fathom why Tariq had not bothered to eliminate the Iberian heir from the very beginning. How could the fool not see that King Witiza's son posed a long-term threat to the caliphate? This lapse of judgment was the clearest indication that, though Tariq appeared to be a fine general, the man was out of his depth when it came to governing the new province of Al-Andalus.

However that would not be the reason Musa would claim for ousting Tariq. Instead he would point to the humiliating defeat the Moors had suffered at the hands of the Christians in Girona the previous year. Though Tariq had not personally taken part in the battle, as supreme commander, he was ultimately responsible for the loss, at least that was the case that Musa would make publicly.

Of course, he would have preferred to have Tariq quietly

eliminated in the middle of the night. But killing the general who had won such a great victory for them might not sit well with either his Berber army or with the caliph. So in the end Musa had chosen to place Tariq under confinement. And unless unforeseen circumstances decreed otherwise, he was quite content to let the Berber chieftain languish in a cell under lock and key forever.

A week after discussing Lord Julian's proposal with his advisors, a servant entered Governor Musa's audience chamber and announced, "General Al Qama is here to see you, your excellency."

Musa looked up from the letter he was writing. "He's in Toledo already?"

"I'm told he arrived this morning."

"He must have made good time. Show him in."

A moment later, a stocky, helmeted figure came marching through the door. Everything about him spoke of military precision. Even the bronze roundels studded on his black leather tunic had been polished to a gleam. Though he had to be in his early fifties, there was no sign of gray in his coarse black beard.

"Welcome to Al-Andalus, general," Musa said with a smile.

General Al Qama gave Musa a quick bow that conveyed an awareness of the near equality of their positions. "Thank you, your excellency."

"How was your voyage from New Carthage?"

Al Qama's toad-like face wrinkled in disgust. "Ach, it was cursed from the start. Nothing but gales and storms, everyone vomiting their guts out over the sides. I'll take a horse over a ship any day."

"At least you arrived safe and sound," Musa said politely, studying the olive-skinned figure standing in front of him. It was said that Al Qama's father had been a common soldier and his mother a Galatian slave. Certainly his appearance attested to the fact that the story was more than just hearsay. His short, stocky build, as well as his blunt features, were common attributes of the Galatian people.

Remarkably, despite his humble origins, Al Qama had risen to the pinnacle of the military hierarchy, and at a relatively young age at that. Such success could not be attributed simply to talent on the battlefield. A rise such as Al Qama's indicated a high degree of shrewdness in navigating the political waters of the caliphate court and Musa told himself that he'd be wise to remember that.

Al Qama's reputation had been growing steadily over the years and it was now widely believed that there was no one better at stamping out the uprisings that kept erupting in the far-flung regions of the land. There were some, however, who thought the general's methods were overly harsh. They pointed out the wanton slaughter that followed him wherever he went, leaving entire regions depopulated.

But Musa was not one of Al Qama's detractors. These were dangerous times for the new caliphate. With so much territory to consolidate, creative methods to maintain law and order had to be found. And if that included a certain heaviness of hand, in Musa's opinion, it was more than warranted.

Musa recalled a story he had heard about one of General Al Qama's campaigns in a far-flung region of the caliphate called Quárqam. After months of trying to chase down a group of agitators across the desert-like plains that made up most of that country's inhospitable terrain, Al Qama had hit upon the idea of raiding the villages and seizing the native women. Every evening his soldiers would march a dozen or so of the females into the desert, tie them to posts, slather them with grease, then set them on fire.

In the darkness of night, the orange glow of the flames had reportedly been seen from a dozen leagues away. And in the desert air, the women's blood-curdling screams had carried nearly as far. Word of the nightly ritual had spread and after only a few weeks, the rebel force —husbands, brothers, sons and fathers of the captive women — had surrendered to the general.

Everyone had expected that the remaining women would be freed. However, Al Qama had ordered them all killed as a reminder to the populace that there was a price to pay for insurrection.

After exchanging polite conversation with Al Qama for a suitable amount of time, Musa broached the subject of General Tariq, recounting how he had relieved the Berber chieftain of his command.

Al Qama, used to the machinations of power, must have understood the forces at play, for he made no comment about Musa's actions. Eventually the conversation turned toward the uprising that had flared up in the north of the country.

"I want the rebellion contained as quickly as possible, general," Musa told him. "We must not give it a chance to spread to other regions."

"Don't worry, governor," Al Qama said with a smile. "I shall take care of the problem for you."

Musa hid his irritation at Al Qama's condescending tone. "What do you know about our situation?"

"Not much." Al Qama said with a shrug. "A local warlord stirring up trouble."

Both men turned as a servant entered the chamber carrying a tray of refreshments.

Al Qama took a goblet of sweetened lime water from the servant. "So how large is the rebel force?"

Musa took the other goblet from the tray. Subtly asserting his authority, he sipped his drink before answering, "It's difficult to say. Two or three thousand, perhaps."

"That's about what I expected," Al Qama said, seeming not to be too concerned about the number. "We should have this business finished by springtime."

Musa raised an eyebrow. "Are you planning a winter campaign?"

"You said you wanted the uprising contained as quickly as possible."

"Do you have any idea what the north of this country is like in winter, general? There's likely to be snow in the mountain passes."

"I've led our armies to the four corners of the caliphate, Governor Musa; I am well acquainted with warfare under winter conditions."

"I just think it would be wise if you waited for spring."

"The best time to catch an enemy unawares is when he's least expecting you to come."

"That make sense, general. I should know better than to question your judgment."

Al Qama drank from his goblet. "So, where exactly is this rebel force of yours hiding?"

"We have a spy in their camp. I expect to know the answer to that question soon."

"Good; it would be nice if we didn't have to scour the countryside looking for them."

The door of the chamber swung open and Musa's son, Ali, sauntered in. His face lit up with surprise as he recognized his father's visitor. "General Al Qama! I didn't know you had arrived."

"Greetings, young Ali." Al Qama said with a smile. "How you've grown since I last saw you! How old are you now?"

"Seventeen."

"Ahh, how time flies."

Ali and Al Qama made small talk while Musa waited patiently, his gaze flicking between his slim, fashionably garbed son and Al Qama, who with his armor-wrapped, bulky frame looked like a hippopotamus standing alongside a plumed crane.

Ali was Musa's second-born son. Fine featured, with long, almost feminine eyelashes, Ali took after his mother, the youngest of Musa's three wives. Though he wasn't the strongest or the most clever of his eight sons, Ali was his favorite, perhaps because the boy was so unlike him, guileless and indifferent to the allure of power and wealth.

When the conversation between Al Qama and his son began dying down, Musa cut in smoothly, "General, I have a favor to ask of you."

"Of course; name it."

"I want you to take Ali with you."

Al Qama gave the request a moment's consideration then nodded. "Of course, Governor Musa. It would be a pleasure to have him."

"And in your future reports to the caliph," Musa added with a bland expression. "Perhaps you could make mention of how useful the boy has been to you."

General Al Qama's eyes were shrewd as he studied Musa. "You have plans for the boy, I see."

"I'm not going to live forever. This land will need a new governor when I'm gone."

"And it might as well be Ali." General Al Qama said, with

only a trace of irony in his voice. He drained his goblet, then wiped his mouth with the back of his hand. "I suppose we can come to some arrangement."

Used to the subtle language of negotiations, Musa found the general's words crude. *But then again*, he thought to himself, *what else can one expect from a low-born peasant?*

CHAPTER 41

IT HAD BEEN over a month now since a band of Saracen soldiers had escorted Valentina and Ermesinda to their new quarters on the ground floor of the citadel in Toledo. Valentina remembered her dismay as the soldiers had locked the only exit door behind them when they had left. Until then, she and Ermesinda had been given free rein to wander around the grounds of the citadel, so it had been a shock to discover that their world had further shrunk to a windowless chamber with an adjoining courtyard. As the weeks had gone by, she had consoled herself with the thought that their fate could have been worse. She and Ermesinda could have been confined to a chamber in one of the towers. Here at least they had access to a courtyard that offered them a view of the sky.

The courtyard was ten paces long by ten paces wide and was enclosed by the walls of the adjoining buildings. In the middle sat a fountain with a marble bench encircling the basin. It was there now that Valentina and Ermesinda spent most of their waking hours, sitting and talking under a patch of open sky, soothed by the sound of the gurgling waters.

"Shall we start our lesson, dear?" Valentina asked her daughter, sitting on the bench beside her.

Ermesinda eyed the wax tablet in her mother's hand, then reached for it with a marked lack of enthusiasm.

"Let's see if you remember what I taught you yesterday," Valentina said. "Can you write down the days of the week for me?"

Ermesinda picked up a sharpened stick from a small wooden box, then, with a frown of concentration, began scratching out letters on the wax tablet.

Valentina was watching Ermesinda work when she caught sight of someone coming through the door into the courtyard.

Following her mother's gaze, Ermesinda's expression brightened as she spied the bearded figure walking in. Jumping to her feet, she ran over to greet him. "Good Morning, Khurram."

"How are you today, my little one?" the Saracen counselor said, patting Ermesinda on the top of her head.

"Are those for us?" Ermesinda asked, pointing to the items of clothing tucked under his arm.

Khurram's usually solemn face creased with a smile. "They are indeed."

Valentina came to join them. "Good morning, Khurram."

"Greetings, my lady. I brought you both some new cloaks," Khurram said, handing one to Valentina and another to Ermesinda. "With winter coming, I thought you might have need of something a little warmer than the ones you have."

"How thoughtful of you," Valentina said. "Thank you."

Khurram turned toward Ermesinda. "I see you're putting the writing implements I brought you to good use. One day you will find it a blessing to be able to read and write."

"I suppose so," Ermesinda said, clearly not convinced.

Valentina noticed Khurram's gentle smile. "You have such a kind way about you, Khurram. You must be a comfort to your wife and children."

"I'm not married, my lady."

"Oh," Valentina said, surprised. "If it's not too bold of me to ask, how is it a man as kind and thoughtful as you never married?"

"It was not my destiny my lady. I am a eunuch."

Valentina's face fell. For a moment, she couldn't think of a single thing to say.

"What's a eunuch, Mama?" Ermesinda asked.

"I'll tell you later, dear."

Khurram seemed amused by Valentina's reaction. "It is common practice where I come from, my lady. It's done when a boy is very young. There's very little pain."

"That may be so…It's just that…I suppose I find it difficult to understand how a father or a mother could allow such a thing to be done to their son."

"It was not my parents' decision to make. They were both slaves themselves."

"Oh, I didn't know that. I'm sorry, Khurram."

"You needn't be, my lady. My path has brought me other rewards, though perhaps not as fulfilling as the love that comes from a wife. Or from a child," he said, looking down at Ermesinda with a smile.

An awkward silence settled over them.

"Well," Khurram said. "I suppose I should attend to my other duties. Is there anything I can do for you before I take my leave?"

"You could leave our door unlocked," Valentina said with a wry smile.

Khurram's expression turned serious. "I'm afraid there's no

escaping from here, my lady. There are guards posted at every exit point. Even if I were to leave your door unlocked, you and Ermesinda would not get very far."

"I just said that in jest, Khurram."

"Yes, of course."

Valentina hesitated then turned toward Ermesinda. "Could you to take the cloaks inside for me, dear?"

"All right, Mama."

When Ermesinda was out of earshot, Valentina turned to Khurram. "Do you have any idea how much longer we're going to be kept locked up in here?"

"That depends on circumstances," Khurram said vaguely.

"Such as?"

"I'm sorry, I'm not free to discuss that with you, my lady. I am Governor Musa's counselor. I cannot betray his confidence."

"I'm not asking you to reveal state secrets, Khurram, I just want to know what Governor Musa has in store for us."

"That may seem like a simple question to you, but I assure you it is not."

"Could I ask you something else then, something that will not compromise your governor's trust?"

"Yes."

"Could you ask Governor Musa to allow us the run of the citadel again? It would mean the world of difference to Ermesinda. We won't try to escape, you have my word on it."

"I can speak to him on your behalf if you wish, but I'm afraid my standing with Lord Musa is rather precarious at the moment. As a result, my influence with him is rather limited."

"You're his counselor, how can that be?"

"It's a long story, but the short of it is that he has lost his trust in me. You should not be surprised if one of these days I cease coming to see you."

"I hope you'll not leave before saying goodbye to us, Khurram. Ermesinda and I have grown very fond of you."

"And I of you both, my lady. But I doubt I shall have the chance to say farewell to anyone. As keepers of state secrets, advisors who outlive their usefulness tend to vanish in the middle of the night."

Valentina was horrified. "Surely, you don't mean—"

"That's just the way things are done in my world," Khurram said.

"Why don't you get away from here then, while you still have the chance?"

"Where would I go? I'm an old man. The Governor's soldiers would have little trouble tracking me down. Then, I suspect my death would be a very unpleasant affair."

Valentina did not press Khurram any further, figuring that he had probably assessed his chances accurately. "It must be difficult to live with that threat hanging over your head."

"One has to accept the will of Allah," Khurram said serenely.

"I wish I had your strength," Valentina said, tears welling up in her eyes.

Khurram's expression softened. He studied her for a moment then said tentatively, "Do you really want to know your situation, my lady? Think carefully, sometimes it is better to remain ignorant of one's fate."

"You're wrong. There's nothing worse than uncertainty, Khurram, especially when your life is in someone else's hands."

Khurram looked at her for a long moment, then nodded, as if coming to a decision. "Your husband has made a pact with Governor Musa. You and your daughter are being kept here to ensure that Julian delivers on his promise."

Understanding dawned on Valentina. Suddenly her

situation made sense. "Do you think my husband will deliver on that promise?"

"It appears likely," Khurram said.

Valentina felt relief wash over her. "Then it's just a matter of time before Governor Musa releases us."

Khurram did not answer.

Doubt began to dampen Valentina's rush of optimism. "What is it you're not telling me?"

Khurram spoke slowly, as if picking his words carefully, "There are some among us who say that Asturian lands could be better utilized by parceling them off to our Moorish allies."

"What would that mean, for Ermesinda and I?"

Khurram looked uncomfortable. "It is difficult to say."

"I think you know. Tell me."

Khurram's eyes were full of sympathy as he gazed back at her. "It would be a needless risk to let you and your daughter go free, my lady."

"Why?" The word was wrenched out of her. "What possible danger could we pose to the Governor Musa?"

"It's not so much you as Ermesinda. She's the daughter of the former Duke of Asturias, as well as the granddaughter of the Baron of Catalonia."

"Why does that matter?"

"If you want to rid yourself of an unwanted plant, you don't leave any of its seeds behind," Khurram said.

The blood drained from Valentina's face. It took a moment before she could speak. "If Governor Musa never intended to release us, why did he not simply order us killed instead of keeping us imprisoned like this?"

"He needs you alive, at least until your husband carries out his task."

"And then?"

"Governor Musa may be a hard man, but he is not cruel by nature. There is no benefit to be gained by killing either one of you. My guess is he'll probably just leave you here. After all, it's little enough bother to him."

Valentina had an image of Ermesinda, sitting by herself in the courtyard, growing old and gray as the years went by. A dark despair washed over her. "What did Julian offer to do for Governor Musa?"

"He's going to help us put down the rebellion led by his half-brother, Pelayo."

"Julian has no men-at-arms. He's lost the garrison'"

"We know that, my lady."

"Then how can he be useful to you?"

Khurram hesitated, but then seemed to think he had revealed too much to stop now. "Your husband has a spy in his half-brother's war council. Through the spy, we've been able to learn all sorts of information, including the location of the rebel camp."

"Is that important, the location of the camp?"

"Very much so, my lady. Governor Musa now knows where to catch Pelayo and his men by surprise."

Valentina felt overwhelmed by what she was learning. "I can't believe Julian is helping Governor Musa attack Asturian soldiers."

"He's done something similar before, my lady. Ambition is a powerful hunger in a man."

Valentina took a deep breath to steady her nerves. "Has Governor Musa already sent his soldiers against Pelayo and his men?"

"Not yet. It takes weeks to gather supplies for a winter campaign."

"There is time then," Valentina said, a note of relief in her voice.

Khurram looked at her, clearly puzzled. "Time? For what?"

"To warn Pelayo that there's an army marching against him."

"How are you going to warn him, my lady? I told you there is no escape from here."

"I wasn't speaking about myself, Khurram. I meant you."

"Me?" Khurram's eyebrows arched in alarm. "No, no. I'm sorry, what you are asking is impossible."

"Think of it as a way to save yourself, Khurram. If you leave at night, on a fast horse, you could be twenty leagues away before anyone discovers that you've gone. Even if Governor Musa sends out men to search for you, they'll probably go eastward, thinking you've headed for the coast in order to take a ship home. But you could ride north instead, to Asturias, and find Pelayo's camp. I'm sure he'll grant you sanctuary as a reward for your warning."

"There is a certain logic to what you are suggesting, my lady. But casting your lot with a rebel warlord who has an army of fifteen thousand men marching against him is hardly the advice I would give anyone."

"You'd change your mind if you knew Pelayo, Khurram. He's not like anyone you've met before. He's capable of achieving victory, no matter what the odds are against him."

"You seem to hold him in high regard."

"I do," Valentina said. "He's the only man I've ever loved. And he is Ermesinda's father."

Khurram let out a tired breath. "I am sorry, my lady, but I'm too old to undertake such an arduous venture for you."

Valentina clutched his arm, her face etched with desperation. "You're the only hope we have to escape, Khurram. Please help us."

Khurram gave her a puzzled look. "How can my warning Pelayo affect your fate, my lady?"

"If he learns where we are, I know he'll move heaven and earth to set us free."

Khurram stood there unmoving, staring at Valentina, torn by indecision.

CHAPTER 42

IT WAS A cold December morning and the sun in the sky did little to warm Pelayo and Yxtaverra as they waited outside the gates of the spiked-timber palisade. Wrapped in their fur-lined cloaks, they watched the convoy of horsemen, pack animals and wagons plodding down the road toward them. When the convoy drew a little closer, Pelayo hailed the uniformed officer riding in the lead, "Welcome to Cangas de Onis, Diego."

"Thank you!" Captain Diego hollered back. "Good thing you sent a man to guide us here. Without him, we'd still be riding in circles through these cursed mountain passes."

"That's why we chose this place, Diego, to stay hidden from the Moors," Pelayo said.

"Well, they won't stumble upon you here, that's for sure," Diego said. "Do you have room for us in town or should we pitch our tents here outside the walls?"

"It might be a little tight inside," Pelayo said.

"Not a problem," Diego replied. He turned to an officer at his side, gave the man instructions, then dismounted.

When Diego approached, Pelayo introduced him to Yxtaverra.

"Please to meet you, Commander Diego." Yxtaverra said. "I've heard a lot about you from Pelayo. How was your journey from Girona?"

"Long and trying. I'm not used to sleeping on hard ground anymore. I must be getting old."

"Well, you'll be able to enjoy a warm bed tonight," Yxtaverra said. "We've made room for you in the officers' quarters."

"Won't say no to that," Diego said.

"Come on then," Pelayo said. "I'll show you around Cangas de Onis."

Diego handed the reins of his horse to one of his men, then turned back to Pelayo. "All right, I'm anxious to see what you've been up to all these months."

Pelayo led the way through the gates and into a square thronging with people. Though Cangas de Onis had been founded in Roman times, the new construction he had ordered had given it the appearance of a raw and bustling garrison town. Half the people striding about were soldiers, the other half were tradesmen, shopkeepers and common laborers who had been drawn to the town by its sudden spurt of growth.

"So, how goes the situation in Girona these days?" Pelayo asked Diego as they turned down one of the narrow streets toward the town's ancient core.

"There's a cloud of fear hanging over the city," Diego answered. "Everyone is expecting the Moors to appear over the horizon at any moment, just like they did the last time."

"How many soldiers are left to guard the city?" Pelayo asked.

"Forty or fifty, just enough to keep the peace. Baron Ernesto thought you should have every soldier we could muster."

"He's not wrong about that," Pelayo said.

As they walked on, Diego glanced at Pelayo and said, "I

heard from your messenger that you'd been gone on some mysterious errand. What was that all about?"

"I went north to ask the Basques to join us in our war against the Moors," Pelayo answered.

"Good Lord. How did that turn out?"

"Unexpectedly well, actually," Pelayo answered.

Diego stopped dead in his tracks. "Wait. Are you saying they've agreed to an alliance with us?"

Pelayo smiled. "As of this moment, they're our brothers in arms."

"Well I'll be damned. How the devil did you manage to talk them into it?"

As they strode down the streets, Pelayo gave Diego an account of his meeting with Bortaroitz.

"That's some story," Diego said in response, shaking his head. "Talk about the hand of providence."

"Unfortunately, they can only come once their planting season is over."

"That's understandable," Diego said. "It' s difficult for a people without a standing army to mobilize for war."

Pelayo pointed to the single storey building they were approaching. "That's our command post."

Diego followed Pelayo and Yxtaverra through a door and into a dimly lit hall filled with long tables and benches. It was early and except for two servants, the hall was deserted.

Pelayo chose a table by one of the windows.

"So, what do we do if the Moors descend upon us earlier than expected, say late spring?" Diego asked Pelayo.

"If that happens, I'll send word to Bortaroitz. He's promised to drop everything and come to our aid as quickly as possible."

"Did he say how many men he thinks he can muster?"

Diego asked, easing himself down on the bench across the table from Pelayo.

"A thousand, maybe fifteen hundred," Pelayo answered.

Diego made a face. "I was hoping for twice that number."

"We'll just have to make do with that," Pelayo said.

Diego nodded. "With the soldiers I've brought from Girona and your Asturians, we'll have what, some three thousand men?"

"More or less," Yxtaverra said.

One of the cook's assistants came over to their table.

"Is there any fresh bread?" Pelayo asked the man.

"Just out of the oven, Commander Pelayo."

"Bring us a loaf and some cheese and olives," Pelayo said.

When the servant walked away, Diego looked across the table at Pelayo. "So, any news of Julian, or of Lady Valentina?"

"No, nothing," Pelayo answered.

"Did you ever find out who helped Julian escape?" Diego asked.

Pelayo shook his head. "There were no witnesses; every man on duty that night was killed." He told Diego about the bodies of the guards that had been found dumped into the ravine outside the walls. He also shared his suspicion that Baron Siberto was behind the affair, though he could not rule out the possibility that it could have been someone else.

Pelayo, Yxtaverra and Diego spent a good part of the morning discussing military matters.

Pelayo was telling Diego about his efforts to increase their production of weapons when a soldier marched up to their table.

"Your pardon, sire," the soldier said to Pelayo. "There's an old Saracen man at the gate who wishes to speak to you."

Pelayo was taken aback. "Did he mentioned me specifically?"

"Yes, sire. He said he wanted to speak to Lord Pelayo. Those were his exact words."

Pelayo, Diego and Yxtaverra exchanged glances. Except for Baron Ernesto, no one outside Cangas de Onis was supposed to know Pelayo's whereabouts. It would be a devastating blow if the enemy had learned the location of their new base.

"Bring the man here," Pelayo told the soldier, feeling a knot of tension in his belly.

After a short time, a dark-skinned, turbaned man escorted by two soldiers came walking through the door. He seemed to be in his late sixties, with a white beard and deep-set eyes that gave him a melancholic air. Coming to a stop by the table, he bowed politely, his travel-stained white robes swirling around his ankles.

"Greetings, my lords," the Saracen said in stilted, yet understandable Iberian.

"Who are you?" Pelayo asked.

"My name is Khurram. Until recently, I was one of Governor Musa bin Nusayr's counselors. Do I have the honor of addressing Lord Pelayo?"

Pelayo nodded curtly. "How did you know where to find me?"

"There are many things we know about you, Lord Pelayo. Your taking refuge here is but one of them."

"Would you care to enlighten me as to how you know that?"

"Certainly," Khurram answered pleasantly, as if Pelayo had asked him about the weather. "You have a spy in your camp. He's been passing information to my master for close to two months now."

Pelayo saw Yxtaverra and Diego stiffen with shock. "Why are you telling me this?" he asked.

"For two reasons. The first being I'm hoping that you will grant me sanctuary."

"Sanctuary from whom?"

"My master, Governor Musa," Khurram said. "He has a well-known penchant for garroting counselors who have outlived their usefulness, a category in which alas I now find myself."

"And your second reason?"

The old man stared blankly at Pelayo. "I beg your pardon?"

"You said you had two reasons for coming here. What is the other?"

The vagueness in the old man's eyes disappeared. "Ah yes, I came to warn you that there is an army marching against you."

Pelayo erupted to his feet. "I don't know what game you and your master are playing, but I'm not going to fall for it."

"It is not a trick, Lord Pelayo, I assure you."

"No commander in his right mind would lead an army through these mountains in the winter." Pelayo turned toward the guards standing by the advisor. "Take him out and put him in chains."

"Wait!" Khurram cried out as the two guards seized him by the arms. "What are you doing?"

"I'm going to find out what you're really up to. One way or another you're going to tell me, I can promise you that," Pelayo said.

"I'm speaking the truth," Khurram said quickly. "I have a letter for you from Lady Valentina. It's in my purse."

Pelayo lifted a hand, motioning to the guards to stop. "All right, show me," he told Khurram.

The old man took out a small, folded parchment from the purse on his belt, then handed it to Pelayo.

Pelayo unfolded the parchment and scanned the contents. It contained a single paragraph written in a graceful script.

"My dearest Pelayo. Ermesinda and I are being held captive in Toledo by Governor Musa. During this difficult time, Khurram has been a true friend to me and to our daughter. He is risking his life to bring you warning of a planned attack against you. Give him your trust, I beg you. Valentina."

Pelayo reread the message, then turned his gaze on the old Saracen. "Why is your governor holding Valentina and Ermesinda?"

"They are there to ensure that Julian delivers your head to him on a platter."

"How can he—?" Pelayo stopped, suddenly figuring it all out. "The spy in our camp is Julian's man."

Khurram nodded. "Yes."

"Who is the spy?"

"I'm sorry, I was not told his identity."

"What about Julian, what did your master promise him?" Pelayo asked, unable to mask the bitterness in his voice.

"Once the rebellion is crushed, he will be given back his lands."

Pelayo studied the turbaned figure before him. He figured the Saracens could have forced Valentina to write the letter. If that was the case, believing anything coming out of the mouth of Musa's advisor could lead him and his men to their destruction. But Valentina had mentioned that Ermesinda was his daughter, a detail she had not needed to reveal, if she had been coerced to write the letter. The burning question was whether or not he was reading too much into those few words.

Some three weeks after Khurram's appearance, Pelayo led a squad of six soldiers up the steps of Cangas de Onis' old cathedral. After slipping inside through the front doors, he and his men made their way down the nave toward the altar. It was past midnight and the rows of stone columns were barely discernible in the gloom.

On the right-hand side, halfway down the nave, the alcove normally used for baptisms was aglow in candlelight. There were two men there, holding a whispered conversation. They had not seen Pelayo and his soldiers entering the cathedral, but the draft that sent the candle flames dancing must have alerted them that the front door had been opened.

"Cordario!" Pelayo's booming voice echoed through the cathedral. "I know you're in here. Show yourself."

Silence stretched for a moment, then from around one of the pillars, two men, one of them wearing a priest's cassock, stepped into view.

"Is that you, sire?" Commander Cordario called out, peering through the darkness. "Are you looking for me?"

Pelayo did not answer until he was standing a few feet away from the two men. "What are you doing here at this hour?"

"I couldn't sleep," Cordario answered. Though it was a cool night, there was a faint sheen of sweat on his brow. "I thought I'd try to find a priest to hear my confession, in case things don't turn out well for us the day after tomorrow, pardon my saying so, sire."

Ignoring Cordario, Pelayo studied the priest, who was clutching his hands, his eyes darting about. The face beneath the cowl looked vaguely familiar and Pelayo searched his memory, trying to place the man. Suddenly it came to him: the priest was Bishop Oppas' young acolyte whom he had shoved into the fountain years ago.

"Search them," Pelayo told his soldiers.

Three of his soldiers stepped forward and set to the task. One of them pulled out a rolled parchment from the pocket of the priest's cassock, then handed it to Pelayo.

Commander Cordario suddenly broke free and shot off at a run down the nave toward the entrance. Several soldiers gave chase and caught up with him as he was fumbling with the door latch. After a brief struggle, Cordario was hauled back, one arm pinned behind his back

Pelayo went to stand by the light of one of the candles in the sconces. He unrolled the parchment his men had taken from the priest and began to read. As he expected, the letter contained a detailed account of the latest developments of military significance that had occurred in Cangas de Onis. It included the most recent event: the arrival of the Basque contingent a few days earlier.

After rolling up the parchment, Pelayo stared sightlessly into the darkness, realizing the cleverness of Julian's plan. A priest could travel anywhere, at any time of day or night, without drawing suspicion to himself. Had it not been for Khurram's warning, he would never have suspected anything was amiss.

Though he had not fully believed Khurram's story, he had had every member of the military council secretly watched. Every time one of them stepped out of his tent during the night to relieve himself, or if one wandered off into a tavern, or took a whore to a room, there were always two men nearby, watching for signs of suspicious activity.

Tonight, that effort had paid off.

Pelayo gazed at Cordario, now firmly in the grip of his soldiers. "So, what did Julian promise you? What was so tempting that you were willing to betray your own men?"

Cordario stared brazenly back at Pelayo. "You're a great one to talk about betrayal; you who threw your own half-brother into the dungeon so you could take his place."

"Was it gold? How much did he offer you?"

"I received no payment. I did it because I swore an oath to serve Lord Julian."

"Your loyalty is touching. Pity it is so misplaced," Pelayo said. "I put my trust in you and you reward me by running to the Moors with our secrets."

"Spare me the sermon," Cordario cut in curtly. "Get on with what you have to do."

"Very well, so be it." Pelayo turned and addressed the commander of the squad who was standing at his side. "Take them back and put them in chains. We'll hang them in the morning."

The priest let out a moan. "Please, sire, have mercy on me. I beg you—"

"Quit your blubbering," Cordario said gruffly. "Accept your fate like a man. He can't let us go; he has to make an example of us."

Pelayo shook his head in regret. "You are a good officer, Cordario. God knows we could have used your courage and experience when we face our real enemy in two days' time. Instead you will swing from a rope and your death will serve no purpose. Sadly, you will be remembered as a poor misguided fool who sided with the Moors against his own people."

Cordario stuck his chin out defiantly. "Go to hell."

Pelayo gestured to his soldiers to take the two men away. The cries of the priest begging for mercy echoed down the nave until he was dragged out the door.

CHAPTER 43

WITH A PULL on the reins, General Al Qama brought his white Arabian steed to a stop. Behind him, the column of horsemen, marching soldiers and supply wagons ground to a halt. Despite the rugged terrain they'd been travelling through all morning, every unit had remained in tight formation, a testament to the strict discipline he had drilled into his men over the years.

Al Qama sat unmoving, studying the valley into which they were heading. There was another route he could have taken to reach the rebel camp in Cangas de Onis, and that was to come at it from the southwest. That route would have allowed him to skirt most of the mountainous terrain. He would have chosen it had it not been for a report that the only bridge spanning a major river had recently collapsed. Luckily, this region of the country was experiencing warmer than average temperatures and the mountain passes were still free of snow.

Bundled in a fur-lined cloak, Governor Musa's son spurred his horse and rode up beside Al Qama. "Is there something troubling you, general?"

"Heading into narrow valleys always makes me nervous, Ali. You never know what trouble awaits you there."

"I don't see that we have much choice at this point," Ali answered. "Unless you want us to double back all the way to Leon."

Al Qama let out a grunt that could have meant anything, then turned and singled out one of his officers. "Saif! Take some men and ride through the valley. Keep an eye out for anything that looks out of place."

After Saif acknowledged the command and rode away, Al Qama ordered a short rest. As the command was relayed down the length of the column, he dismounted and stretched the cramped muscles of his back. He was reaching for the water-skin looped around the pommel of his saddle, when he caught sight of the Asturian lord and his minder steering their horses toward him.

"Your pardon, general," the minder called out. "Lord Julian wishes to know why we've stopped."

"Tell him we're scouting the valley ahead to make sure we're not riding into an ambush." Al Qama pulled off the cork of his waterskin and poured a stream of water into his mouth.

"Lord Julian says that the winter sun goes down early in these mountains," the minder told Al Qama. "He advises you to resume the march if you want to reach Cangas de Onis before dark."

Al Qama wiped a dribble of water from his chin with the back of his hand. "Tell the infidel that when I want his advice, I shall ask him for it."

After his words were translated, Al Qama saw Julian stiffen, then give a reply.

"Your pardon, general," the minder said, looking

uncomfortable. "Lord Julian says that he was sent to assist you and that is what he is attempting to do."

"I heard what he has to say; now get him out of my sight."

"At once, general," the minder said quickly. "I'm sorry to have disturbed you."

Some time later, Saif and his men returned from their scouting sortie and reported to Al Qama. "There's nothing out there general. The way is clear."

"Did you ride all the way through?"

"Every foot of it. All we saw were a few wagons in the distance."

Al Qama fixed Saif with an unblinking stare. "Tell me you weren't seen."

"No one saw us, general, I assure you. They were far away, and we kept to the shadows."

After dismissing Saif, Al Qama looked up and studied the position of the sun, trying to gauge the time of day. According to their Asturian spy, the rebel base was a small town fortified with a narrow trench and a wall of sharpened wooden timbers. Such puny defenses would not keep back his fifteen thousand-strong army for long. However, as the Asturian lord had correctly pointed out to him, there might not be enough daylight hours left to carry out their attack. If night fell before his men could encircle the enemy stronghold, some of the rebels could slip away under the cover of darkness. A more advisable course of action might be to surround the rebel base and prepare for an all-out assault the following morning. A third possibility was to set up camp right where they were standing and postpone any action until the next day. This last option, however, left them open to the risk of being spotted by one of the enemy's scouting parties. Which was it to be, he wondered, weighing his choices.

A hawk circling in the cloudless sky caught Al Qama's eye. As he followed its flight through the air, the hawk suddenly tucked in its wings and shot downward with the speed of a dropped stone. To the left and below, a flock of geese was flying placidly along in an arrowhead formation. The hawk streaked downward at an angle, then struck one of the geese, sending the other birds scattering in panic.

A shiver of awe ran down Al Qama's spine. He believed with absolute certainty that what he had just witnessed was an omen. The portents were easy to decipher. He was the hawk, and the Christian rebels were the hapless geese. A sense of confidence surged through him, sweeping away his lingering doubts. The stars were aligned in his favor. All that was needed now was for him to do his part and set in motion his preordained destiny.

Feeling the pressure of time to move on quickly, he turned to address his officers who had been waiting for his orders. "Mount up!" he called out to them. "We ride for the rebel camp. We shall strike before the sun sets."

As the order was relayed down the line of men, Al Qama mounted his horse and nudged it forward with his knees. Like the uncoiling of a great snake, the vast column began moving forward again.

By the time Al Qama reached the mouth of the narrow valley, the slanting angle of the sun had cloaked much of its left side in shadow. As he led his men ever deeper into the valley, the shrub covered slopes on both sides of the road grew steadily closer, funneling the cold wind blowing from the snow-capped mountain peaks.

About a third of the way into the valley, Al Qama began noticing that there were caves dotting the mountainsides. Some were at ground level, others higher up. The dark openings seemed to stare out like eye sockets in a skull and for an eerie moment, he felt as if he was being watched.

From his vantage point several hundred feet up the mountain slope, Pelayo had an unobstructed view of the Saracen column winding its way through the valley below. Behind him, inside the cave, two-hundred and forty-eight Asturian soldiers huddled in the semi-darkness, armed and ready for battle. Their cave was the largest of the half-dozen or so pitting the mountainside and every one of them was similarly filled with Iberian soldiers lying in wait.

Above Pelayo' cave, spread out across a flat-topped ridge, seventeen hundred Basque warriors under the command of Bortaroitz sat on the ground, trying to be as still and silent as possible. Nearby along the edge of the ridge, lay hundreds of large rocks that he and his men had labored for days to move into position. Situated just far enough away from the edge so they couldn't be spotted from the road below, the rocks just needed a final push to send them tumbling down the slope.

Al Qama had ridden through almost the entire length of the valley, when a deep rumbling sound intruded into his consciousness. Turning in the saddle, he scanned the area behind him. Some sort of commotion had erupted amongst a group of horsemen down the line, but he couldn't figure out what was causing it. Then his gaze shifted toward the mountain slope on his left. The sight that met his eyes chilled him to the marrow.

Large rocks, with dirt and pebbles cascading behind them, were hurtling down the mountainside toward the trunk of his column. Those in its path were struggling to control their terrified horses. Before they had a chance to flee, the first wave of rocks smashed into them.

Al Qama's eyes widened in consternation as he watched half his column disappear under a curtain of thick dust. After what seemed like an eternity, the rockslide slowed to a trickle, then stopped, leaving behind a cloudy haze drifting across the basin of the valley.

An eerie silence followed.

Untouched by the devastation that had struck the men behind him, Ali lifted his arm and, with a trembling finger, pointed upward. "General, look!" he cried. "Up there!"

Al Qama craned his neck and looked up. The ridge above them was lined with hundreds of men. The still, menacing figures sent a shiver down his spine. His worst nightmare had come to pass. He had led his men straight into an ambush.

Inside their cave, Pelayo called out to the soldiers under his command, "It's time! May God grant us victory!"

Shouting at the top of their lungs, Pelayo and his men rushed out from the cave. Half- running, half-sliding down the mountain slope, they began converging with the other soldiers spilling out from the other caves. Above them on the ridge, the Basque slingers launched their first volley of stones at the Saracen foot soldiers positioned at the rear of the column.

On reaching level ground, Pelayo's men charged the line of Saracen horsemen who had survived the rockslide. With the momentum of a crashing wave, they hurled themselves at the invaders, pulling them down off their horses. The air rang with the clash of steel and the cries of pain.

Pelayo and two of his aides made their way toward a ledge on the slope that offered a commanding view of the valley. Slipping once again into his role as field commander, he surveyed the fighting before him.

Nearly two-thirds of a league away, Yxtaverra and the two

hundred horsemen under his command launched an attack on the Saracen wagons bringing up the rear of the column. His objective was to overturn the wagons across the entrance of valley and block the enemy's ability to retreat.

At the opposite end of the valley, Captain Diego had the identical task, but with some wagons they themselves had brought from Cangas de Onis. Soon, the Saracens would find themselves trapped inside the valley, with both exits blocked by a barrier of well-defended, overturned wagons.

Pelayo knew they were reaching a critical point in the battle. He and his men had to continue to press the Saracens and keep them unbalanced in order to prevent them from regrouping. As he had foreseen, the steep slopes and the narrow width of the valley was restricting the enemy horsemen's range of movement. Unable to spread out, their panicked horses was adding to the chaos.

So far his plan centered on breaking down the enemy's cohesion seemed to be working. As he watched his men attack the Saracen column at different points, trying to shred their lines even further, he wondered if he had done enough to achieve that goal.

Al Qama was struggling to supress his instincts to strike out blindly and impulsively. But it was difficult to watch his disciplined army dissolve into a confused rabble. If he didn't find a way soon to extricate his men from the ambush, his force would suffer catastrophic losses.

He considered rallying his men to launch a counter offensive, but the narrowness of the valley would make that difficult, if not downright impossible. If they couldn't make a stand, then that left them with only one option: to fight their way out.

He was about to relay an order to his officers, when he

caught sight of movement in the distance. Squinting his eyes, he saw oxen-pulled wagons rolling across the mouth of the valley. The Asturians were attempting to block their way out. For the first time since the enemy had sprung their ambush, he began to feel real dread.

No matter, we'll just go back the way we came, Al Qama told himself. But before he could act on his decision, a premonition made him stand up in his stirrups and look behind him. At the other end of the valley, a line of wagons was strung out across the entrance. The infidels had commandeered his supply wagons and were now using them to block their escape from that end of the valley as well.

Al Qama's face darkened with fury as it dawned on him how cleverly the Christians had ensnared him in their trap. It was a novel experience for him. He had always been the hunter, never the prey. He had been prepared to mete out a quick death to the Asturian rebels, but all that had changed now. The infidels would pay dearly for what they had done. He would gut them open, cut off their testicles and stuff them into their mouths. Then he'd leave them for the birds to feast on. Oh, how he would revel in their screams as they begged for an end to their agony.

"We need to take action, general," one of his officers shouted over the clamor of the battle.

Snapping out of his revenge-filled fantasy, Al Qama focused his attention on the challenges facing him. Though his force still outnumbered the Iberians, the punishing losses they were incurring meant they would soon lose their numerical advantage. The fact that he had faced other near hopeless situations in the past settled his nerves, and he began to draw up in his mind a list of possible countermeasures that he could take.

After settling on one that he thought had the likeliest chance of success, he began issuing orders to his officers.

He tasked his second-in-command to round up some of their horsemen and clear the wagons from the eastern entrance of the valley. He called upon another officer to gather some foot soldiers and provide support for the horsemen. Once the officers had ridden away, he turned and addressed what was left of his men, "We'll wait here until the passage is clear, then we'll fight our way out of this accursed valley!"

As Al Qama waited for his men to carry out his orders, he caught a glimpse of Julian sitting on his horse a short distance away. It suddenly struck him that the infidel must have played a part in luring them into this trap. How else could the Asturians have known they were coming? Finding a target upon which he could vent his pent-up anger, he turned toward the two officers at his side and pointed at Julian. "Kill the Asturian dog," he said with a snarl.

Julian saw the two Saracen horsemen coming for him with drawn swords. Reacting instinctively, he dug his heels into his horse's flanks and bounded away. Unfortunately, the two Saracen riders had built up speed and quickly narrowed the distance to him.

From the corner of his eye, Julian saw one of the horsemen raise his arm, readying to strike. He tried to twist out of the way, but he couldn't move fast enough to evade the Saracen's sword as it cleaved into his shoulder.

He let out a strangled cry as a bolt of pain radiated down his left arm. Engulfed in agony, he saw the Saracen horseman preparing to strike him again. Once more his effort to twist out of the way proved ineffectual and the blade struck him on his helmet. A loud clang reverberated through his head, followed by a flash of light that mushroomed behind his eyes. Like sand trickling out of an hourglass, his strength ebbed out of him. Desperately, he tried to cling on to consciousness as he slumped over the back of his horse. Soon the world receded into darkness, and he felt himself falling as if from a great height.

Standing on a rise, in the company of his two officers, Pelayo peered across the distance to the entrance of the valley. He could just make out Yxtaverra and his men positioned behind a barricade of overturned wagons. Up to now the Saracens had made no attempt to retreat in Yxtaverra's direction, but he knew that could change at any moment.

When he next turned his attention back to the battle raging in the valley below, he caught sight of a soldier running toward him, waving his arms.

"Commander!" the man called out from afar. "Captain Diego's line has been breached."

Pelayo's heart sank as he turned and scanned the western end of the valley. The entire area was crawling with Saracens, both on horseback and on foot. He couldn't quite make out what they were up to, but he knew they had to be trying to drag the wagons away. Once their effort proved successful, they would be able to ride out of the valley, find somewhere to lick their wounds, then come after him and his men again in a few days time.

The opportunity for a surprise attack such as the one they had just launched today would never present itself again. The next time they faced each other, the Saracens' superior numbers would undoubtedly give them the upper hand.

Pelayo balled his fists in frustration as he realized that victory was slipping away from his grasp. *There must be something we can do*, he told himself. As he cast about desperately for a solution, he caught sight of a party of Asturian horsemen threading their way through the fighting in his direction. A moment later, Yxtaverra drew his horse to a stop some half-dozen paces away from him.

"Why have you left your post?" he called out, fearing that Yxtaverra's position had also been overrun.

Yxtaverra's voice cut through the din of the battle. "I got tired of waiting for something to happen! I left a hundred soldiers under the command of my second and brought the rest here. I thought you might be able to use a company of mounted soldiers."

"Indeed I can," Pelayo shouted back. "The Saracens have overrun Diego's position."

"That's a serious setback! What are we going to do?"

The answer to Yxtaverra's question came to him suddenly. "We go after the Saracen command staff."

"Cut off the head off the snake?"

"We've got to do more than that. We have to crush it under our heel and stomp it to death," Pelayo shouted. "See you if you can find me a horse."

As darkness receded and consciousness returned, Julian found himself lying flat on his back, gazing up at a patch of blue sky. The sounds of battle swelled in his ears, reminding him of where he was. A floodgate inside him seemed to open and waves of pain began pulsing with torturous regularity from his left shoulder. As if that wasn't bad enough, his head felt as if he'd been kicked by a mule. Fighting through the pain, he rolled over on his stomach, then struggled to his knees. He was gathering his courage to stand up when he heard a voice penetrate through the fog in his head: "Seize the youth! Careful not to hurt him!"

The familiar voice sent a jolt through him. Gritting his teeth, he managed to get to his feet, his useless left arm dangling at his side. There were fighting men everywhere, Iberians, Saracens, on horseback and on foot, pummeling and hacking at each other with every weapon imaginable. A wave of dizziness overtook him, and he closed his eyes, trying to keep himself from falling flat on his face. *The blow has scrambled my brains*, he thought dully.

The familiar voice he'd heard before rang out again: "Yxtaverra! Watch your left! There are horsemen heading your way!"

Julian searched for the source of the voice and caught sight of a horseman who was under attack by two mounted Saracens. It was the man's distinct armor that drew his attention. He had seen the breastplate and helmet countless times before, hanging in the castle armory or worn on ceremonial occasions by his father.

The armor-clad figure turned Julian's way, allowing him to catch a glimpse of the man's face.

Instead of the loathing that the sight of Pelayo had always evoked in him, this time Julian felt something different, a sense of concern. Even more surprising was the urge he felt to come to his half-brother's aid. Perhaps it was the sight of Pelayo wearing their father's armor and beset by enemies that had sparked a newfound awareness of the bond of blood that bound them both immutably to each other.

In a flash of insight, Julian understood that it was this bond that had kept him from crossing a certain line in the past and ordering Pelayo's death.

Using his one good arm, he unsheathed his sword, then, trying to shake off the strange lethargy stealing over him, he staggered forward. "Hold on, I'm coming," he called out.

In shock, Julian realized that his intended shout had been no louder than a hoarse whisper. Dragging his sword along the ground, he came up behind the two Saracen horsemen trading blows with Pelayo. Ignoring his pain, he lifted his sword and swung at the broad back of one of the horsemen, the ugly, toad-like Saracen general.

The blow, though weakly delivered, had had enough bite in it to make Al Qama flinch in pain. Turning in the saddle, his deep-set eyes blazed with fury as he looked down upon Julian. Mouthing a curse, he raised a muscular arm and swung down hard with his sword.

Julian lifted his blade in an attempt to ward off the descending blow. Al Qama's sword knocked his blade aside, then continued its downward trajectory, the sword tip gouging a bloody furrow across his chest.

Pelayo couldn't believe his good fortune, when a soldier had appeared out of nowhere and attacked one of the two Saracen horsemen assailing him. The distraction bought him the time to deal with the second man, whom he drove back with several blows. When his opponent's horse skittered away, Pelayo turned his attention to his other adversary, a squat Saracen officer who had his back to him. When the officer turned toward him a moment later, Pelayo rammed his sword into the man's chainmail-shirted belly.

The officer's bullfrog-like face took on a look of surprise as he stared down at the blade protruding from his stomach.

Pelayo drew out his sword and turned in the saddle to face the remaining horseman, expecting to have a fight on his hands. But the warrior sat frozen on his horse, staring wide-eyed at the squat Saracen officer who had slumped over in the saddle, his hands clutching his stomach.

A clatter of horses sounded in the distance. A moment later Yxtaverra and a company of soldiers came galloping toward him. Seeing them coming, the remaining Saracen horseman bolted away.

"We captured the boy!" Yxtaverra hollered, pointing to a slim Saracen youth at his side. "You all right?"

"Yes, I'm fine," Pelayo answered.

When Yxtaverra and his men drew their horses to a stop, Pelayo pointed with his sword at the body of the squat officer lying on the ground. "I think I just killed their general."

"Well done," Yxtaverra answered. "Let's hope it does the trick."

Pelayo jumped down off his horse.

"Hey!" Yxtaverra called out. "Where do you think you're going?"

"I'm just going to check on a soldier who came to my aid."

"Better make it quick; we don't have much time."

Pelayo knelt at the side of the stricken soldier, then carefully turned him over on his back. His breath caught in his throat when he caught sight of the man's face. "Good Lord."

Julian gazed up through half-lidded eyes at him. "You're wearing Father's armor," he whispered.

Pelayo turned toward Yxtaverra who, with his squad of horsemen, had formed a protective circle around him. "It's Julian," he called out. "Help me get him up on my horse."

"There's no point. Look at him, he's lost too much blood."

Pelayo gazed at Julian's deathly-white pallor, then noticed the scarlet pool spreading around him. *Yxtaverra's right. Julian doesn't have long for this world.*

"I never realized how much you look like Father," Julian whispered to him.

"Do I?" Pelayo murmured, doing his best to ignore the battle raging around him.

"You set a clever trap," Julian whispered. "How did you know the Saracens would be coming this way?"

"One of Musa's advisors came to warn me."

"You always had the luck of the devil. Another reason why I hated you," Julian said, the faintest of smiles taking the sting out of his words.

"Why did you do it, Julian, why did you side with the Saracens against your own people?"

"We thought they'd help us put Olmund on the throne. I wish I could go back and undo it all," Julian's voice trailed into silence.

"And Father? Was ordering his death a mistake too?"

"I had nothing to do with that," Julian said, becoming agitated. "It was all mother's doing. I would have stopped her if I'd known what she was planning."

"All right, rest easy, I believe you," Pelayo said.

Julian closed his eyes.

Pelayo waited in silence. He had seen men die before. Julian's time was nearing.

"Pelayo..." came a faint whisper.

"I'm here, Julian," Pelayo said, placing a hand on his shoulder.

"If you see Ermesinda again ...tell her..." Julian couldn't get the words out.

"That your last thoughts were of her?" Pelayo said quietly.

Julian murmured something.

Pelayo leaned down and put his ear close to Julian's lips.

"I'm sorry..." Julian whispered. A tremor went through him, then he became still, his half-open eyes staring out into space.

Pelayo looked down upon the still face of the person he had hated most of his life, trying to sort out his emotions.

Yxtaverra called out from atop his horse, "Come on, we have to go! We've got a battle to win!"

Pelayo took one last look at Julian's lifeless body, then rose wearily to his feet. He felt a strange emptiness inside him as he mounted his horse. Despite Julian having come to his rescue, he couldn't quite bring himself to mourn his half-brother's death. Julian had done too many hateful things to him over the years for him to feel anything but a sense of regret at what might have been.

The elimination of the Saracens' command staff proved to be the turning point in the battle. Unable to mount a counter-offensive, the Saracen forces remained pinned down by Pelayo's men. Squeezed on all sides, they fell by the hundreds, then by the thousands.

By nightfall, the shouting and the clash of steel gave way to silence.

As the last of the evening light faded from the sky, Pelayo guided his weary horse down the corpse-strewn grounds of the valley. His eyes were gritty with exhaustion, as he watched his men scour the battlefield, dispatching the last of the Saracen wounded. It wasn't easy killing someone who was begging for mercy, even though that man was speaking in a different tongue. But the message they needed to convey to the enemy had to be brutally clear: venture onto our land again and you will forfeit your life.

After having ridden through the length of the valley, Pelayo reached the line of overturned wagons. He thought he had come to terms with Diego's death, but the sight of the captain's body slumped on the ground tore painfully at his heart. It took him a moment before he could bring himself to lift Diego's body onto the back of his horse.

It was dark by the time Pelayo made his way toward the temporary camp his men had just erected. Built some distance away from where the fighting had taken place, the air beneath the starry sky was free from the stench of death. Two exhausted-looking sentries barely glanced in his direction as he guided his horse through the gate of the defensive perimeter.

Inside the camp, some two thousand men, about half the number that had set out that morning from Cangas de Onis, were sitting around the bonfires, huddling in blankets against the cold night air.

Pelayo left his horse in a roped-off area, then slung his travel bag and blanket over his shoulder and set off in search of Yxtaverra. As he wandered through the camp, he could see the terrible price they had paid for the day's victory. There were injured men everywhere, some sitting, others stretched on the ground. The surgeons and their aides were doing their best to tend to their wounds, but it was clear from their frantic pace that they were overwhelmed by the high number of casualties they were facing.

Though the general mood in the camp was subdued, there were pockets of soldiers here and there that seemed to be in more ebullient spirits. Pelayo knew these men weren't so much celebrating a victory as they were relieved that they had survived the battle.

As he walked by a seated group, one of the men rose to his feet and called out, "Care for some warmed wine, commander?" he asked, holding out a tin cup. "It'll ward off the chill."

"Sure, why not?" Pelayo said, reaching for the cup.

The soldier smiled. "We showed those bastards a thing or two today, didn't we?"

"That we did," Pelayo replied, handing back the cup.

"It's been a day I'll never forget. It was an honor following you into battle, commander."

Another soldier rose to his feet. "He speaks for me as well, sire."

The rest of the men around the fire rose to their feet, echoing similar sentiments.

"The victory belongs to all of you," Pelayo told them. "You should all feel proud."

After wandering through the camp, Pelayo found himself in a section the Basques had claimed as their own. Threading his way through their tents, he spotted Bortaroitz sitting with several of his men around a fire.

"Ah, there you are, nephew," Bortaroitz called out, rising to his feet. Despite his battered-looking appearance, his uncle seemed to be in good spirits. "Looks like we both cheated death today."

"Yes we did, by the grace of God. Any of that blood on your tunic yours?"

"Might be," Bortaroitz admitted. "I'm afraid to look."

Pelayo smiled for the first time that day.

"What about you?" Bortaroitz asked. "Are you all right?"

"A scratch or two, nothing serious."

"Glad to hear it," Bortaroitz said. "Not a bad outcome for the first alliance ever between our peoples, is it?"

"I agree. We should do it again some time."

"As long as it's not too soon," Bortaroitz said, "Another victory like this one and we'll have nothing but widows and orphans to till our fields."

"We certainly paid a heavy price for today's victory, didn't we?" Pelayo said.

"I'll not begrudge it if it keeps the Saracens at bay."

"It should," Pelayo said. "At least for the time being."

"For the time being? I was hoping for an outcome a little more permanent than that."

"If the situation was reversed, would you leave an enemy at your back door to plot your demise?"

His uncle arched his eyebrows. "Are you saying all this was for nothing?"

"Not at all. Today marks an important turning point in the war. We now have a real chance, where before we had none."

"How do you figure that?"

"The Saracens have a vast empire, but they are going to feel the sting of losing fifteen thousand men. It might just spoil their appetite to take us on again, at least for a few years. And we are going use that time wisely. We'll build fortresses along our borders, then train a new army to man them. When the Saracens come for us again, we'll be ready to take them on."

"Well, when that day comes, you can count on us to stand by your side again," Bortaroitz said. "The Saracens have become our enemies too now."

After speaking a while longer with his uncle, Pelayo bade him goodnight, then headed off toward the area where his men had set up their tents. Halfway there, he ran across Yxtaverra.

"I heard about Captain Diego," Yxtaverra said as he approached. "I'm sorry."

Pelayo nodded. "We lost a lot of good men today,"

"I know; too damn many."

"I noticed you're limping," Pelayo said. "What happened to your leg?"

"My horse got a spear through its chest and fell on me," Yxtaverra said.

"Bad luck."

Yxtaverra nodded glumly. "I know, I loved that horse. I'm going to miss him."

Pelayo pointed to a pen in the distance that was filled with the Saracen horses they had rounded up after the battle. "Getting you a new mount isn't going to be much of a problem, though,"

Yxtaverra's doleful expression remained in place. "I suppose I could get used to one of those runty Arabians."

"There are a lot of things we're going to have to get used to from now on," Pelayo said.

"Like sharing our country with the Saracens?"

Pelayo nodded. "For the time being."

"Let's not lie to ourselves," Yxtaverra said. "The Saracens are here to stay. All we've done is carve out a sanctuary for ourselves."

"We've done more than that. We've given our people hope. We may have a long and difficult struggle ahead of us, but today's victory is a good beginning. Who knows, one day we may be able to cast the Saracens completely off our lands."

CHAPTER 44

RIDING ALONGSIDE ERMESINDA near the center of the Saracen convoy, Valentina idly glanced around the barren landscape that they'd been travelling through for days. They had been heading north ever since leaving Toledo, and now, after two and a half weeks on the road, she figured they had to be nearing Asturian territory. Certainly the snow-capped peaks looming over the horizon had to be the Picos de Europa, the mountain range marking the Asturian southern border.

Valentina tried to work out how long it had been since Julian had spirited her and Ermesinda away from Gijon. It was now early summer, so she figured it had to be over a year and a half. She found it impossible to narrow it down any further. After Khurram's departure, time had crawled by with seamless monotony, the days blending one into another. Except for the guards who had brought them food in the mornings and evenings, she and Ermesinda had had no contact with anyone from the outside world.

Their confinement had come to an end two weeks earlier when a handful of Saracen soldiers had unlocked the door to their quarters and gestured for them to follow. The summons had sent her heart racing. She had not known whether she and Ermesinda were going to be set free, transferred to a new quarters, or taken somewhere to be killed. All three outcomes had seemed equally plausible to her at the time.

The Saracen soldiers had led them to a courtyard filled with horsemen and pack animals. There, a turbaned man astride a white Arabian stallion had caught her eye. Judging by the finery of his clothing, she had correctly guessed that he had to be the Saracen governor whom Khurram had spoken to her about.

She and Ermesinda had been led toward two saddled horses. It was then she had realized that Julian must have successfully concluded his mission for the Saracens, and that in return, she and Ermesinda were going to be handed over to him. She remembered thinking that she was about to trade one form of captivity for another, since once reunited with Julian, he would undoubtedly have her watched day and night. But at least Ermesinda would be free to resume a normal life and that was something for which Valentina would have sacrificed anything.

Now, after only a few weeks on the open road, exposed to fresh air and sunshine, Ermesinda seemed as revived as a wilting flower after a summer rain. There was a sparkle in her eyes again and her cheeks were aglow in a rosy hue. Her demeanor was different too. She was more expressive, less prone to the long stretches of silence into which she had been increasingly retreating. As she eyed her daughter sitting atop her horse, her back straight, her manner composed, there was something about Ermesinda that reminded Valentina of Pelayo.

"Why are you looking at me like that, Mama?" Ermesinda asked, noticing her mother's gaze upon her.

"I was just thinking."

"About what?"

"You're looking different these days. You seem happy."

"I am; I can't wait to go home and see Father again."

"Yes, of course," Valentina said. She had never told Ermesinda the truth about who her real father was, as the time had never seemed right. She hoped that the day would come when she would feel that her daughter was ready to hear truth.

Morning turned into afternoon, and the distant mountains grew noticeably closer. After crossing a sun-scorched plain, the convoy finally came to a stop some distance away from what appeared to be either a narrow canyon or the entrance to a mountain pass.

Two Saracen horsemen came for Valentina and Ermesinda and brought them to the front of the column. There, four other horsemen took positions around them.

After glancing about him briefly, Governor Musa heeled his horse and cantered away. The six Saracen horsemen peeled away from the rest of the convoy and set off after the governor, shepherding Valentina and Ermesinda along with them.

When the riding party had halved the distance to the canyon, Governor Musa slowed his horse and came to stop. Time passed by, with no one making any attempt to dismount.

Valentina wondered what they were waiting for. As her eyes swept the barren terrain around her, she caught sight of movement in the recesses of the narrow canyon. A moment later several horsemen burst out of the shadows at full gallop into the sunlight.

Valentina tracked the horsemen with her eyes as they beat a path toward her, a plume of dust trailing in their wake.

Governor Musa and his men watched unmoving until the horsemen came to a stop a half-dozen paces away from them.

At first, Valentina had thought that all the horsemen were Asturian soldiers, but up close, she saw that one of them was an Arab youth, his hands tied in front of him. The other five riders were men-at-arms, all wearing coats of chainmail and helmets with downward-extending nose guards. At first glance there was little to distinguish one man from another, but the bearing of one of them drew her eyes to him.

Sparing only a quick glance at Valentina and Ermesinda, Pelayo drew out his knife and began sawing away at the rope binding the wrists of the Saracen youth. When the rope fell away, he slapped the rump of the youth's horse, sending it scampering forward.

The youth pulled up beside a robed figure who Pelayo guessed was Governor Musa and the two exchanged quiet words. Afterwards, the governor turned toward Valentina and Ermesinda, and with a flick of his hand, gestured they were free to go. When they rode away, he turned his attention toward Pelayo and his men.

"Do any of you speak Greek?" the governor asked.

"*Malista*," Pelayo answered. *I do.*

Musa studied Pelayo closely for a moment. "It is refreshing to meet an educated Christian for a change. Are you in command of these men?"

"I have that honor," Pelayo said in Greek.

"I'll direct my questions to you then. Are you holding any more of our men captive? If so, I have brought gold to ransom them."

"We have no prisoners of yours. Every man you sent against us was killed on the day of the battle."

Governor Musa appeared stunned. "Out of fifteen thousand men, no one survived?"

"That's what I said."

The governor took a moment to absorb the news. "At least they had the courage to fight to the end."

"They didn't," Pelayo replied.

Governor Musa's eyes narrowed as the meaning of his words sank in. "What is your name?"

"Pelayo."

Recognition flickered in the governor's eyes. "So, you're the rabble-rouser who's been stirring up trouble for us."

"I've only just begun being a thorn in your side, Saracen. The day will come when we'll take back all the land you've stolen from us."

Governor Musa let out a taunting laugh. "Every miserable barbarian tribe we've ever conquered has uttered the same empty threat to us at one time or another."

"And how many of them have wiped out your army?"

Governor Musa's sneer faded from his face. "We underestimated you. We shall not make that mistake again."

"See those mountains behind me, Saracen? You shall have to cross them to find us. There are a hundred places in there where your superior numbers will count for nothing."

Governor Musa saw the implacable hatred burning in the Christian's eyes. *This one is going to be trouble for us.* "I'm glad to have met you, Infidel. I'll be able to ensure it is really you, when they bring me your head in a sack."

"Are we done?" Pelayo asked, impatient for the Saracens to ride away so he could greet Valentina and Ermesinda.

"For now."

"Till we meet again then, Saracen."

Governor Musa held Pelayo's eyes for a moment, then he wheeled his horse around and led his men away.

"They're leaving, Mama!" Ermesinda cried out excitedly.

Valentina had watched the conversation between Pelayo

and the governor, unconsciously holding her breath, afraid that even the slightest movement on her part would affect the outcome of their exchange. Only after the Saracens had ridden away did she trust what her eyes were telling her, that she and Ermesinda were being released to Pelayo instead of to Julian.

Pelayo dismounted and walked towards her. "Your ordeal is over, Valentina," he said offering her his hand to dismount. "You're free."

The world took on an air of unreality, as if she was in the grip of a dream. "What has just happened?" she asked, taking his hand and sliding down to the ground.

Ermesinda dismounted as well and came to stand at her mother's side.

"I made a trade with the Saracen governor," Pelayo said, his gaze encompassing Ermesinda. "His son in exchange for you both."

"I knew you'd find a way to free us," Valentina said, her voice thick with emotion.

Pelayo smiled. "I can't take credit for it. It was Khurram's idea."

"I spent a year wondering whether he had reached you," Valentina said. "It was torture not knowing if you were alive or dead."

Pelayo turned toward his men. "Why don't you all head back? We'll catch up to you later."

"I wouldn't tarry here too long, sire, if you don't mind my saying so," one of the horsemen said. "The Saracens may decide to come back in numbers."

"I'll keep an eye out for them."

The soldier nodded, then touched the side of his helmet. "See you back in town then, sire."

When the horsemen rode away, Pelayo turned back toward Valentina and gazed at her in silence.

Though it had only been two years since she had last seen Pelayo, time had left its mark on him. She noticed faint frown lines on his brow, and the small scar on his cheek had not been there before. Something stirred inside her and she suddenly felt an overwhelming desire to throw herself into his arms and tell him that he was never ever to leave her side again.

"I've missed you," Pelayo told her. "I was afraid I'd never have the chance to tell you that."

"I've missed you too," she said, feeling constrained by Ermesinda's presence, knowing her daughter would not understand any display of physical affection between herself and Pelayo.

Pelayo seemed to be aware of that situation as well, and they both stood there for a moment, letting their eyes convey their feelings.

"So where do we go from here?" Valentina finally asked.

"Cangas de Onis."

"Where is that?"

"It's some twenty leagues east of here. I'm planning to make it our capital."

"You're abandoning Gijón?" Valentina asked, surprised.

"It's not safe for us there anymore. We need a stronghold in the mountains, a place hard to find and easy to defend. Cangas de Onis meets those needs."

"I don't want to go there," Ermesinda suddenly interjected.

Pelayo and Valentina both stared at her in surprise.

"I want to go to Gijón and live with father," Ermesinda said, her tone resolute.

Pelayo looked at Ermesinda, his expression turning solemn.

"I wanted to wait until later to tell you both, but I'm afraid I have some sad news to tell you both."

"What is it?" Valentina asked.

"Julian fell in battle against the Saracens six months ago."

Ermesinda's eyes widened, then her face crumpled with anguish. "No," the cry ripped out of her.

Valentina stood there, feeling neither pity nor sorrow. There was only a sense of relief in her, as if a heavy weight had been lifted from her shoulders.

"He died saving my life, Ermesinda," Pelayo told her gently. "I was surrounded by enemy horsemen who were trying to kill me."

Tears began flowing down Ermesinda's cheeks.

"His last thoughts were of you," Pelayo told her. "He said he loved you very much."

Ermesinda began to sob, no longer holding back her grief.

Pelayo reached out for Ermesinda and held her in his arms.

Valentina took in the sight of the tough, battle-hardened soldier, holding Ermesinda with such a tender look on his face that she knew she would never forget this moment. A sense of family and belonging filled the void that had existed inside her for so many years. From this moment on, she knew that no matter what challenges the future held, she would stand by Pelayo's side and they would face them together. Never again would she allow anyone or anything to come between them.

EPILOGUE

IT IS SAID that a year after the Battle of Covadonga, the Umayyad caliph, Umar II, recalled Musa ibn Nusayr to Damascus. Displeased by Musa's treatment of General Tariq, the caliph presented the governor with a covered silver platter. Inside lay the severed head of the governor's favorite son, Ali.

Very little is known about the fate of General Tariq. However, it can be assumed that after his eventual return to Damascus, he lived a long life and savored his success. Gibraltar, a corruption of 'Jebal-Tariq", will forever be known as 'Tariq's Mountain'.

In the Chronicles of Albedense, written circa 883 A.C.E., we are told that Pelayo spent the rest of his life defending his mountain kingdom from the Saracens. He died some 19 years after the Battle of Covadonga.

Pelayo's son, Favila, inherited his kingdom. After his untimely death from a bear attack, he was succeeded by Alfonso, the son of the Duke of Viscaya, who married Pelayo's daughter. Alfonso became known as King Alfonso I, the first in a long line of Spanish monarchs.

Pelayo was buried with his wife (called Valentina in this

story) in Covadonga, inside the same cave in which he and his men had once hidden to ambush the Moors.

Translated from Spanish, the epitaph on his tomb reads:

"Here lies the Holy King Don Pelayo, elected in the year 716, who in this miraculous cave began the reconquest of Spain."

On January 2, 1492, after some eight hundred years of nearly constant war, King Ferdinand II of Aragon and Queen Isabella of Castile expelled the last of the Saracen invaders from Spanish soil.

Made in the USA
Coppell, TX
20 June 2020

28598233R00298